Nichole Severn writes explos strong heroines, heroes who dare challenge them and a hell of a lot of guns. She resides with her very supportive and patient husband, as well as her demon spawn, in Utah. When she's not writing, she's constantly injuring herself running, rock climbing, practising yoga and snowboarding. She loves hearing from readers through her website, nicholesevern.com, and on Facebook at nicholesevern

Juno Rushdan is a veteran US Air Force intelligence officer and award-winning author. Her books are action-packed and fast-paced. Critics from *Kirkus Reviews* and *Library Journal* have called her work 'heart-pounding James Bond–ian adventure' that 'will captivate lovers of romantic thrillers.' For a free book, visit her website: junorushdan.com

Also by Nichole Severn

New Mexico Guard Dogs
K-9 Security
K-9 Detection
K-9 Shield
K-9 Guardians

Defenders of Battle Mountain
Dead on Arrival
Presumed Dead
Over Her Dead Body
Dead Again

Also by Juno Rushdan

Cowboy State Lawmen: Duty and Honor
Wyoming Ranch Justice
Wyoming Undercover Escape
Wyoming Christmas Conspiracy
Wyoming Double Jeopardy

Cowboy State Lawmen
Wyoming Mountain Hostage
Wyoming Mountain Murder
Wyoming Cowboy Undercover
Wyoming Mountain Cold Case

Discover more at millsandboon.co.uk

K-9 CONFIDENTIAL

NICHOLE SEVERN

CORRALLED IN CUTTHROAT CREEK

JUNO RUSHDAN

MILLS & BOON

All rights reserved including the right of reproduction in whole or in part in any form. This edition is published by arrangement with Harlequin Enterprises ULC.

This is a work of fiction. Names, characters, places, locations and incidents are purely fictional and bear no relationship to any real life individuals, living or dead, or to any actual places, business establishments, locations, events or incidents. Any resemblance is entirely coincidental.

This book is sold subject to the condition that it shall not, by way of trade or otherwise, be lent, resold, hired out or otherwise circulated without the prior consent of the publisher in any form of binding or cover other than that in which it is published and without a similar condition including this condition being imposed on the subsequent purchaser.

® and ™ are trademarks owned and used by the trademark owner and/or its licensee. Trademarks marked with ® are registered with the United Kingdom Patent Office and/or the Office for Harmonisation in the Internal Market and in other countries.

First Published in Great Britain 2025
by Mills & Boon, an imprint of HarperCollins*Publishers* Ltd
1 London Bridge Street, London, SE1 9GF

www.harpercollins.co.uk

HarperCollins*Publishers*
Macken House, 39/40 Mayor Street Upper,
Dublin 1, D01 C9W8, Ireland

K-9 Confidential © 2025 Natascha Jaffa
Corralled in Cutthroat Creek © 2025 Juno Rushdan

ISBN: 978-0-263-39707-9

0425

This book contains FSC™ certified paper and other controlled sources to ensure responsible forest management.

For more information visit: www.harpercollins.co.uk/green

Printed and Bound in the UK using 100% Renewable Electricity at CPI Group (UK) Ltd, Croydon, CR0 4YY

K-9 CONFIDENTIAL

NICHOLE SEVERN

To the men and women who've committed their lives
to fighting the drug crisis taking over our country.

Chapter One

There had to be something here.

Charlie Acker shoved a stack of folded clothes to the other side of the dresser. The flashlight shook with the tremors in her hand. Unstable. "Come on. Come on."

Her fingernails scraped against cheap wood. Nothing in this drawer. She moved on to the next and the one after that. Coming up empty. Facing the rest of the bedroom, she took in the four-poster bed neatly made up with handmade quilts and crocheted throws. The bed itself had been carved by hand when her sister was old enough to sleep on her own. Charlie's heart squeezed too tight in her chest at the thought of her father giving it away to someone else. But that was how it worked in Vaughn, New Mexico. Nothing really belonged to the individuals living in this town. Everything was done for the benefit of the family.

"Talk to me, Erin." Charlie lowered the flashlight to keep from attracting outside attention. No matter how much she wanted answers, she couldn't risk exposing herself to the people of this town. Bad blood tended to stain more than anything else.

Her little sister had been dead for two days. Already buried in the family cemetery, but there were still pieces of her here. In the knickknacks Erin had collected as a kid sitting on the bookshelf, even that gross old snail shell she'd picked up while weeding rows of corn when she'd been around five years old.

Charlie closed the distance between her and the nearest nightstand. In truth, she and Erin hadn't talked in years, but she'd known her sister suffered as much as she had after what they'd done.

After what they'd helped their father do.

There was no reason for her sister to start talking now, but that didn't mean Erin hadn't left something behind for Charlie to find. Because no matter how many years they'd gone without staying in touch, Erin had never given up on her. And no matter what anyone said, Charlie knew the truth. Erin hadn't died in a hunting accident, as she'd read in the papers.

Her sister had been murdered.

And she was going to find out why.

She slid onto the edge of the bed, careful not to let the box spring protest from her added weight. The nightstand drawer stuck on one side as she tried to slide it free. Her heart rocketed into her throat as she stilled. Listening. She wasn't supposed to be here. If the family—if her father—caught her within town limits, he'd make sure she never walked out again. Though her final resting place wouldn't be in the family cemetery. Not unless he'd reconsidered labeling her a traitor. Henry Acker: judge, jury and executioner. Had he been the last person Erin had seen before she died?

She couldn't think about that right now. Charlie pulled a handmade bound journal from the depths of the nightstand. Loved, worn, soft with oils from her sister's hands. A ribbon marked her sister's last entry, and she set the flashlight on the nightstand at the perfect angle to wash across the pages. Thick, uneven pages pried away from each other as Charlie opened the journal and read the perfect cursive inside. It was all too easy to imagine Erin sitting right here, penning her final entry. Her sister would've taken her time. She would've made sure to document everything about her day to give an accurate picture of life in Vaughn at this very moment. Acting as historian had been Erin's job. Just as stocking and inventorying food and supplies and taking care of the house had been Charlie's growing up. And their eldest sister... She didn't want to think about that right now.

Tears burned in Charlie's eyes as a lavender flower—compressed between the pages—slipped free. Erin's favorite. There had to be a dozen in this journal alone.

She swiped a hand down her face. She was wasting time. Her father could realize she'd broken in any second. Shoving off the bed, Charlie knocked into the nightstand.

The flashlight hit the hardwood floor with a heavy thud.

A creak registered from somewhere else in the house. "Who's there? You're trespassing."

Heavy footsteps charged down the hallway. Growing louder with every step. Erin's bedroom door rattled. At least she'd thought enough ahead to lock it, just in case. But now she was out of time.

"Damn it." Charlie backed toward the window she'd come through. She'd broken her only rule for coming back into this house. She'd let emotion distract her.

"You have three seconds to identify yourself." Her father's voice drove through her in a mixed battle of love and fear. "One. Two."

She clutched Erin's journal as she threaded a leg through

the window. The flashlight rolled out of reach. She'd have to leave it.

The door crashed open.

It slammed against the wall.

A massive outline filled the doorframe, rifle aimed at her. "You've got a lot of nerve breaking into my house—" His booming voice caught. The gun wavered for just a moment as cold gray eyes narrowed on her through the darkness. "Charlie?"

Her fight-or-flight response pulled her through the frame in a panic. Gravity dragged her down, and Charlie hit the ground. Hard. Air knocked from her chest as she lost her hold on Erin's journal.

Those same heavy footsteps echoed from inside the house.

She had to get up. She had to run. Oxygen suctioned down into her lungs as she heard the front screen door scream on its old hinges. She clawed into the frozen ground to get her bearings and pushed to her feet. Stumbling forward, she scooped up the journal and pumped her legs as fast as she could.

A gunshot exploded overhead.

A warning shot.

It singed her nerves to the point her skin felt as though it were on fire. Spotlights flared to life as she ran down the dirt driveway. Wire fencing corralled her on either side to the end, and she cut to her left at the end. Her feet failed to absorb the impact of her boots against asphalt as she raced toward the neighboring farm where she'd left her car.

Another shot filled the night. Closer than before.

"Charlie! Stop where you are!" Henry Acker's voice cut

through the night as clearly as one of the air raid sirens he'd had installed throughout town.

She wouldn't. She couldn't. Because no matter how much her body wanted to, the moment she surrendered, she'd lose any chance of proving her father and this town had a hand in the terrorist attack that'd left four people dead. *Ten years.* She'd been an outcast for every single one, had left her sister to die here alone. No. She wasn't going to stop. She was the only one who could fix this. Who could prove Erin had been murdered.

Charlie dared a glance over her shoulder to gauge the distance between them. Too close. Even in his late fifties, her father had kept himself ready for a war he'd prepared them to fight. The road inclined up, and the toe of her boot caught. She fell forward, hands out to catch herself.

Gravel cut into her palms and knees. The journal protected most of one hand, but the pain was still a shock to her system. She ordered her legs to take her weight.

A strong grip fisted the collar of her jacket and spun her around. She slipped the journal into her waistband a split second before she slammed into a wall of muscle. Forced to look up at the man she'd always feared. Feared to disrespect. To oppose. To disobey. Henry Acker had always been bigger than her. Harder. With no patience for the three girls he'd had to raise on his own. He pulled at her collar with one hand, leveling the rifle in the other straight toward the sky. "I told you what would happen if you came back here."

"I was never good at following orders, was I, Dad?" She tried to wrench out of his hold. Only she wasn't strong enough. She never had been. Not against him. "Never a good enough soldier for you."

The dark brown hair that'd once matched hers had whitened to the point he could've subbed for Santa at the mall. Heavy bags took up position under his eyes, as though he hadn't slept—not just in days, but weeks, months. Years. And she hoped like hell he'd suffered from whatever kept him up at night. "Hand it over. Whatever you took. I want it back."

"I don't know what you're talking about." Charlie rocketed her arm into his and thrust out of his hold. And he let her. She added a few feet of distance between them, but it wouldn't do a damn bit of good. Vaughn, New Mexico, wasn't some small town dying off from lack of tourism. It was a safehold. The birthplace of Acker's Army, where outsiders weren't allowed. This place? This was Henry Acker's kingdom, and she was nothing compared to the resources he held.

"You didn't break into your sister's room for nothing." Movement registered from her right as her father leveled the gun back on her. A shadow broke away from the tree line protecting her father's property. Then another from the left. He was having her surrounded. Cutting off her escape. "The journal. Hand it over or these two will take it from you by force."

Charlie took another step back. She could run, but there was no place in this world she could hide. Not anymore. "Why? Is it because you're afraid of what Erin wrote about you? About this place? Are you afraid she might expose you for what you really are?"

"And what is that, Charlie?" He countered her pitiful attempt to add distance between them.

She couldn't say the words. Couldn't accuse him, no matter how many times she'd thought of his dark deeds. Of what he'd made her and her sisters do. Her voice shook. "I know Erin didn't die in a hunting accident."

"Enough! I've given you a chance to cooperate, but as always, I'm going to have to force my hand with you." Her father's jaw flexed under the pressure of his back teeth, a habit he'd always had when she'd dared to defy his command. "Get the journal and bring her to my house. We have a lot to talk about."

The men waiting for her father's orders, like the good soldiers they were, moved in. She was out of time, out of patience waiting for Henry Acker to do the right thing. To prove he cared about her.

"I'm not going anywhere with you." Unholstering the small pistol stuffed on the front of her right hip, she took aim. At her father. Both men pulled their own weapons. "And I'm going to prove you had something to do with Erin's death. No matter how long it takes, Dad. Because she deserved better than you. Better than this place."

"You're making a mistake, Charlie." Seconds ticked by, each one longer than the last, as he leveled that bright blue gaze on her. "As always, you're only thinking of yourself instead of your family."

She took a step back, closer to the vehicle she'd stashed off the side of the road. Far enough away not to garner attention. One wrong move. That was all it would take, and she'd lose this game they'd been playing for so long. "Someone has to."

Charlie moved slower than she wanted to go, prying the driver's side door open. She lowered her weapon and collapsed into the seat as both gunmen ran to catch up. She started the engine as the first bullet punctured through the windshield. Low in her seat, she shoved the vehicle into Reverse and hit the accelerator, heart in her throat.

And knew Henry Acker was going to tear this world apart to find her.

"YOU'VE GOT TO be kidding me." Former counterterrorism agent, Granger Morais, memorized the surveillance photos sprawled in a haphazard pile on the desk. It didn't take long. He'd been studying this subject for nearly a decade. The chestnut bangs that framed an oval face, dark eyes the color of coal, a sharp jawline that always seemed to be set in defiance. Granger checked the date on the surveillance. Yesterday. He rifled through the rest of the stack. "Where did you get these?"

Ivy Bardot—Socorro Security's founder and CEO herself—refused to give any hint as to how they were going to proceed with this new intel. This wasn't Socorro's case. His former life was coming back to haunt him, and she knew it. "Our source inside *Sangre por Sangre* sent them over an hour ago."

Sangre por Sangre. A bloodthirsty cartel hobbling on its last legs thanks to the men and women of Socorro who'd put their lives at risk to stop the infection spreading through New Mexico. Bombings, executions, drug smuggling, human trafficking, abductions, torture—there were no limits to the kind of pain the cartel could inflict, and they'd done so freely up until a year ago. Before the Pentagon had realized the threat and sent Socorro in to neutralize it. Now the cartel lieutenants were running with their tails between their legs. Hiding.

Granger reached out to test the glossy surface of the photos—to make sure this wasn't some kind of nightmare he'd gotten caught in for the thousandth time. Hesitation kept him from making contact. Ivy wasn't FBI anymore, but there was a reason she'd risen to the top of the Bureau's investigators in under a decade. She saw everything. He tensed the muscles in his right shoulder. "She wasn't at her sister's funeral three days ago. These were taken somewhere else. Who else knows?"

"You, me, our source." The weight of Ivy's gaze refused to let up. She was studying him, trying to break through his armor and get something that would tell her he was too invested in this, and hell, she was right. But he wasn't going to give her anything to use against him. "And we picked up radio chatter from Henry Acker."

The name sucker punched him harder than he expected. Henry Acker had a tendency to do that in the counterterrorism world. The unspoken decision-maker of a small angry militant group out of Vaughn, New Mexico was a man with his fingers in a lot of pies, but not a whole lot of evidence to prove it. Someone who prided himself on getting away with murder by having others do his dirty work. Including his three daughters, two of whom had paid for his sins with their lives. And now Charlie was back. After ten years of hiding. Why? "You said these came from inside *Sangre por Sangre*. What would they want with a woman who blew up a pipeline ten years ago?"

"I don't know, but they're not wasting time trying to find her." Ivy shifted in her seat, the first real sign of life from Socorro's founder. "I've got a report that says they want to use her for something big. Something that may tip power back into *Sangre por Sangre*'s hands. Though my source couldn't tell me what, exactly."

"You want me to find her." It made sense. Granger was

the only one on this team who had experience with homegrown terrorism and the painful aftermath people like Charlie Acker inflicted on bystanders who got in the way.

"There's a reason Charlie has chosen to show her face after all this time. If she's working for Daddy again, I want to know what Henry Acker is up to. Before we have another national incident on our hands," she said. "You've studied her behavior. You know what kind of resources she has at her disposal. Where would she go?"

Charlie Acker had managed to stay off his radar for a decade. There was no telling how many skills she'd picked up in that time or how many favors she'd called in, knowing she had to come back here. "Back in the day, I learned Charlie had a safe house outside of Vaughn. From what I could tell, nobody in Acker's army knew about it. There was a code members had to stick to, especially the general's daughters. Loyalty is prized above all else. You stick with your kind, stay in the confines of town, but she managed to slide one by them. Bought it under an alias. She was careful whenever she went out there. Only reason I discovered the place was by accident. It's been abandoned since the bombing."

"You think she'd chance going back there?" Ivy asked.

"If she was desperate." He collected the photo from the top of the pile. A side-angle shot of Charlie Acker. "And something tells me if she's back, she's desperate."

"Take Zeus. Check it out." Ivy Bardot rose to her feet with a grace that shouldn't have been possible for a woman of her skill set and gathered the surveillance photos. "If Charlie's there, bring her in for questioning. I want to know what the hell *Sangre por Sangre* is up to before it's too late."

"You got it." Granger tossed the photo back on the top of the pile and headed for the door.

"And, Granger," Ivy said from behind. "Be careful."

He didn't have a response for that. The work he and his team did didn't come with kid gloves. More like as many blades as they could carry. They wedged themselves into unwanted dark places and pried secrets from shadows that never wanted to be exposed. They took down cartel lieutenants, demolished hideouts and drove evil back to where it came from—all to protect the innocent lives caught up in the violence.

He let the office door swing closed behind him and carved a path through the building's rebuilt maze of hallways and corridors. White cracks still stretched down blackpainted walls as contractors worked to systematically patch the damage done by *Sangre por Sangre*'s attack three weeks ago. Though Granger suspected it would take more than drywall and mud to erase the past.

He rolled his aching shoulder back as he shoved into his private room. Dr. Piel—Socorro's resident physician—had gotten most of the bullet he'd taken during the attack, but not even she'd been able to get the last piece of shrapnel out without disabling his arm for good. He made his way to his private quarters and kicked the door with the toe of his boot. Quiet. Too quiet.

Scanning his room, he stilled. Waiting. "I know you're in here, and the fact you're being quiet makes me think you got into something you shouldn't have."

A low groan registered from the other side of the bed.

Granger took his time as he rounded the built-in desk and cabinets and the end of the messy bed he never bothered making anymore. He sat, noting a single camel-colored leg sticking out from beneath the bed frame. "Zeus."

The four-year-old bull terrier pulled his leg out of sight.

"I can see you." Keeping his weight off his right shoulder, Granger slid to the floor to get an idea of what his K9 had gotten into. "You ate the entire pack of beef jerky, didn't you?"

Another moan and the scent of teriyaki confirmed his suspicions.

Of all the K9 companions, he'd been the one to end up with a bull terrier suffering from a binge eating disorder. Granger dragged a handful of wrappers from under the bed. Bitten through. Not a single piece of meat left. "The only way you could've gotten to these is if you somehow learned how to fly, man. I'm going to have to install a camera in here."

He grabbed onto Zeus's back legs and pulled all eighty pounds of dog from underneath the bed. Granger scrubbed a hand along the K9's side. Yep. Twelve full beef jerky sticks. "We had a deal. One a day if you follow your diet."

A bright pink tongue darted out as though to communicate the dog wasn't the least bit sorry about anything other than the upset stomach that was coming his way.

"Come on. We've got an assignment." Granger shoved to stand and collected his gear. Within minutes, he and Zeus were descending to the garage. The K9 sniffed at the duffel bag with oversized black eyes. "No. These are my snacks. You already ate yours for the entire week."

The elevator pinged, and the shiny silver doors deposited them into Socorro's underground garage. Pain flared in Granger's shoulder as he left the confines of the elevator car. The bloodstains had been scrubbed out of the cement, but his memories of facing off against a dozen cartel soldiers alone would stay with him forever.

Zeus hopped into the rear of the SUV as Granger tossed

his gear into the back. In seconds, noonday sun cut across the hood of the vehicle, and he directed them northeast. Toward Moriarty, a town with at least fifty miles distance between it and Vaughn. Granger had driven this route four times since the Alamo pipeline bombing, each time knowing he wasn't going to find what he was looking for. Each time not wanting to believe Charlie Acker had died along with her oldest sister in the terrorist attack that'd killed four others.

Except now they had proof she was still alive. That she was here in New Mexico. Granger's hands seemed to flex around the steering wheel of their own accord as the miles passed, Zeus's stomach growling the entire trip.

Breaking the borders of a town no one but two thousand people knew existed, he followed Route 66 to the opposite edge. Just far enough out of reach of nosy neighbors or unwanted guests. Scrub brush, cacti and dried grass swayed with the breeze, cutting across twenty-two acres purchased under a dead-end alias. In cash. Property taxes had been paid up front with a ten-year old money order sent directly to the city from a bank that no longer existed.

No way to trace it.

The house itself wasn't much. A single-level rambler that looked more like a double-wide trailer than a home. Bright teal wooden handrails stood out against the white siding and led up to a too-small covered porch. Bars on the windows. Oversized boulders funneling visitors in front of the largest window out front. Charlie Acker might've bought this place to escape Vaughn and her father's prepper army, but old habits died hard.

Granger threw the SUV into Park and loaded a bullet into the barrel of his sidearm before pushing out of the vehicle. Zeus huffed in annoyance as he hit the gravel driveway.

Nothing but the sound of the wind reached his ears, but he was experienced enough to know silence hid all kinds of things from human perception. He took his time, moving slow to the north side of the house. The breaker box opened easily. All switches were active. The place had power.

No point in going for the front door. That was where she would've put most of her security measures. Granger and Zeus rounded to the back. He tested the laundry room door and twisted the knob. The door fell inward. No explosives. Nothing poised to spring out of the dark.

A low growl rumbled in Zeus's chest.

Granger ventured a single step inside, weapon raised.

The barrel of a gun pressed against his temple from the left. "Toss your weapons. Now."

Chapter Two

Her hand shook as she tried to keep the gun pressed against his head.

Charlie's nerves hiked into overdrive as the intruder's gun hit the dingy carpet with a hard thud. Seconds ticked off in her head. A minute. She wasn't sure how long she stood there or what she was going to do next. This wasn't part of the plan.

"I knew you were still alive. Even after all this time." His voice worked to counter the uneasiness clawing through her, but she wouldn't let it. Not this time. "This is usually the point where you close the door so no one sees you're holding a gun to my head and order me into the other room."

"This house is in the middle of twenty-two acres of land." She kicked the door closed, because that seemed to be the logical thing to do, all the while trying to keep both hands tight around the gun. The dog at his feet stared up at her as though expecting some kind of treat for parking his butt in her laundry room. "No one is going to see you coming and going."

"Does that mean I'm walking out of here alive?" he asked.

How could he ask that? After everything that'd happened, how could he still believe she'd been responsible for the deaths of those four people, of her *sister*, in that bombing? That she was a terrorist? Charlie forced herself to take a deep breath as next steps formed in her mind. "Into the living room. Straight ahead. You and your little dog, too."

"Might be hard to believe, but I'm familiar with the layout of this place." He followed her orders, moving forward through the tight hallway leading back into the laundry room from the main part of the house. "I've been here a few times."

She knew that. Security cameras had picked up his incessant search for clues each time he'd visited and relayed the live video to her phone. Despite her being thousands of miles away. After a few months, she'd come to crave that notification. To know that he was still thinking about her, that she hadn't been forgotten by the man tasked with bringing her in. Which didn't make a lick of sense.

She hadn't gotten those notifications in a long time.

Charlie maneuvered behind him, the gun now aimed at his spine. A thousand fantasies of this moment had kept her from going insane all these years. How she would approach him, what she would say. None of them seemed to fit the moment though. "What are you doing here, Agent Morais?"

"It's just Granger now." He pulled up short in the middle of the living room, turning as though to study his surroundings, but she was familiar with his way of working. How he liked to keep the threat in view. His sidekick didn't seem to care she was holding a gun to its owner though. Some guard dog. Afternoon sunlight highlighted all the little details of his face. The shaggy hair that always seemed to stay in place without effort, the divots between his brows that'd creviced deeper over the years, that long perfectly straight nose she'd come to love. His eyes though. They'd somehow gotten darker. Heavier. As though he'd lived two lifetimes in the span of ten years. "Dropped the agent part soon after you went off the radar."

He'd quit Homeland Security? It didn't matter. Charlie kept herself from shifting her weight, from giving him any idea that her nerves were getting the best of her. "That doesn't answer my question."

"I came here because I got a stack of surveillance photos this morning. Of you." He said it so matter-of-factly, without emotion, that the lack of inflection threatened to carve through her. "I don't know why you came back. Frankly, I couldn't care less about what you're doing here. I imagine the only reason your father hasn't killed you is because he doesn't know about this place. But considering how we got our intel, my boss seems to think you might be a target of the local drug cartel, and she wants to know why before a bunch of people die."

Her brain struggled to keep up with all the bits and pieces of that statement. Charlie gave in to the need to shift her weight onto her other leg. "Your boss? You said you quit Homeland."

"I'm with Socorro Security," he said.

"Socorro." The word took some of the strength she'd managed to summon over the past few seconds. Her arm ached with the weight of the pistol in her hand. People like him trained for things like this, and while she'd been raised around guns and how to use them to defend what was hers, she wasn't like him. "You work for the private military contractor that declared war against the *Sangre por Sangre* cartel. You're one of their operatives."

"Despite what you might've thought when you disappeared, Charlie, the world moved on without you. *I* moved on. Only now, here you are, dragging me back into a life I fought to give up." Granger took his time facing her. Stepped into her, pressing his chest against the gun. "So we can do this one of two ways. You can come back to Socorro with me willingly to answer a few questions about your connection to *Sangre por Sangre* and what they want from you, or I can drag you out of here kicking and screaming. Either way, you're coming with me and Zeus."

The dog cocked his head to one side at the sound of his name.

"I didn't kill those people." Did he even care? Her mouth dried as memories she'd forced herself to relive every single day played at the back of her mind. "We were told there wouldn't be any civilians around. Sage set the explosives on the lower section of pipe while Erin worked ahead, but then we heard a vehicle approaching. It was dark. We couldn't see who it was, but it didn't matter. I told her to stop the countdown. She wouldn't listen. We argued. I had to knock her out, but when I ran to stop the explosives from going off, it was too late."

She could still feel the blistering fire and searing heat flash across her skin, driving beneath her clothing and burning her from the outside in. His gaze lowered to the lines of scarred, folded skin wrapping both forearms from beneath her jacket cuffs. "I tried to stop it."

"And yet you're the only one alive who can corroborate your version of events, Charlie." The hardness in his voice severed the final string of hope in her chest. This Granger Morais wasn't the man she'd studied—who she'd gotten to know, who she'd trusted—before the bombing.

He was right. Her oldest sister's body had been recovered at the scene, along with four other sets of remains. Erin had managed to escape, but she'd ended up six feet under back in Vaughn all these years later. Charlie had no proof of her story. Her father certainly wasn't going to step forward and incriminate himself. She had no home. She had no family. She had…nothing. Nothing except this moment with a man she never thought she'd see again. "It's the truth. I need you to believe that."

"The truth?" The deadpan tone in his voice suffocated the last of her optimism that they could work this out. "You're holding a gun to my chest, Charlie. You lied to everyone in your life, trying to convince them you were dead, including me. You had the chance to make this right since the moment that bomb went off, but you chose to run. You made the choice every single day to hide. What part of that is the truth?"

The survivor in her, the one who'd managed to keep herself off the radar, kicked her back into the present. She wasn't going anywhere with him. Not until she kept her promise to her sisters. "That was always your problem, Granger. Everything is so black-and-white for you, but that's not how the world works. You've been trained to think your assignments are the right thing to do, the right choice. But you don't know me anymore. And you have no idea what I'm willing to do to survive."

"Don't run, Charlie. You're only going to make matters worse," he said.

"I don't have a choice." She slammed her heel into the floor. The board she'd pried loose to once hide cash, a new identity and anything else she'd had to keep from her family collapsed under the weight. The other end shot up behind Granger. Charlie twisted away from him at the sound of impact and lunged for the front door. This wasn't a safe house anymore. She had to go.

Her hand met the doorknob. She wrenched the reinforced steel open and dashed into the New Mexico desert. Despite clear skies and a blazing sun, cold flooded through her from the change in temperature.

Heavy footsteps pounded through the house. Closer than she expected. But Charlie only had attention for the rental car stashed in the garage at the back of the house. The keys were already in the ignition in case she had to run. She could make it. She *had* to make it.

She pumped her legs harder, out of breath, as she turned the last corner. She didn't dare glance back to gauge the distance between her and Granger. It didn't matter. Exposing Henry Acker for the monster he was? That was all that mattered.

A low huff reached her ears.

Just before an impossible weight landed on her back.

The world tipped off balance as she collapsed forward. Her palms took most of the impact with bits of dirt embedded in the skin. Air exploded from her chest. Ten more feet. That was all that was left between her and the car. Charlie threw her elbow back to dislodge the weight on her back but met nothing but rolls of fat and fur. She tried to roll free. Only the mass of bull terrier refused to budge. She dug her toes into the ground and got a mouthful of dirt for her effort. It was no use. "For crying out loud, what does Granger feed you? I can't breathe."

"I warned you not to run. Zeus's favorite game is jump-on-the-bad-guy."

Is that what he really thought of her? That she was a bad guy?

"Get this thing off of me." Her ribs protested every inhale. This wasn't how she was supposed to die. She'd always imagined her final moments entailed facing off with her father and his army for not only ruining her life but her sisters'. Not suffocating beneath an overweight K9.

"Off." There was a bit of life in that single word, a kind of affection he'd once used when talking to her. "Now, are you coming back with me to Socorro willingly, or will Zeus have to sit on you again?"

She gasped for breath, rolling onto her back. "Please. I can't take anymore dog butt."

Granger centered in her vision. Nothing like the man she remembered all those years ago, and yet at the same time, everything she'd missed about this place.

Zeus penetrated her vision with a near smile as his tongue lolled to one side. And drooled down the side of her face.

A WAR HAD started behind his sternum. One between his personal life and the job he was supposed to do as a counterterrorism operative. Charlie Acker hadn't just betrayed her family when she'd dropped off the grid. She'd betrayed him and everything they'd done together.

Their secret plan to erode Henry Acker's immunity, to get her sisters as far from their father as possible, to free the people of Vaughn—it'd all gone up in flames with the pipeline she'd destroyed. He'd put his entire career on the line for her. And she'd merely used him to fake her death. All these years, the evidence hadn't lined up, but there was nowhere else for her to run now. If Charlie wanted to keep the new life she'd built, she'd have to rely on him.

"You found her." Ivy Bardot folded her arms over her chest, emerald green eyes dead set on the woman pacing the interrogation room.

It was an observational tactic. Leave a suspect or witness alone and study their behavior. Right now, the amount of tension in Charlie's shoulders told him she didn't like being kept in one place. Which meant she most likely hadn't let herself settle down in one location for long. Maybe a few weeks at a time. Never more than a couple months. Even after convincing everyone she'd died in that pipeline explosion, there was still a part of her that believed she could be found at any moment. And with good reason.

"Scarlett and Jones are searching the safe house as we speak." Socorro's security and combat experts wouldn't let anything slide by them. If Charlie was hiding something in that place, they were going to find it. "She would've had to go by an alias all this time. I instructed them to start there. Give us a chance to see what she's been up to the past ten years. Maybe build a map of her activities."

"Why do I get the feeling you don't believe they're going to find anything?" Ivy's insight almost seemed supernatural, as though Socorro's founder could read the minds of her team. No matter what each of them were feeling or denying, Ivy saw right through every single one of them. She was a force to be reckoned with against congress, in the boardroom and her personal life. If that last one even existed.

"Henry Acker raised Charlie and her sisters to clean up after themselves. It's one of the reasons it's been impossible for us to pin any of these attacks on him or his army." Granger took in every movement, every shift from the interrogation room. The longer they left her inside, the higher chance she'd shut down. He had to time this right. Like a countdown on one of the bombs she used to handle, there was always a point of no return. "Based on what I saw of the safe house, she wasn't planning on staying there for long. No supplies, no more than a couple days of food. I've searched that property a dozen times. She wouldn't have left anything behind that could expose her. Like father, like daughter. She tried to wash it off, but there was dirt under her fingernails and smeared on her face."

"She dug something up. A new alias? Cash?" Ivy unwound her arms, turning toward him. "You're thinking she might still be in contact with Acker and his army?"

"I'm not sure." It would be easy to assume the connection, but he didn't have any proof. "Charlie has always resented her father's political leanings. Called him the homegrown terrorist nobody suspected. She faked her death after the pipeline explosion to get away from him. I can't imagine her willingly participating in his organization again."

"And how would you know that?" Ivy's attention attempted to dig deep past his armor. "From what I understood of your time with Homeland Security, you and Charlie Acker were never in contact. You were investigating Acker's Army from the outside. Or was there something missing from the reports you submitted?"

"No. Just a hunch." As Socorro's counterterrorism operative, Granger had spent the past four years helping Ivy build her own personal army to counter *Sangre por Sangre*. He'd risked his life, his morals and his trust in the people he served with, and he didn't owe her a damn thing. Certainly not an explanation into how little he'd included in his final report concerning the investigation into Charlie and her family.

He shoved through the interrogation room door with Ivy on his heels.

Charlie turned in expectation, instantly neutralizing any hint of the tension she'd let build over the past thirty minutes of isolation at the sight of Ivy at his back. Like the good terrorist she was supposed to be. "Who's this?"

"Ivy Bardot, Charlie Acker." He motioned between both women. One a monument of his past, the other his future. Granger slapped a file folder onto the table, and the surveillance photos Ivy had shown him this morning spilled out. "Ivy is the founder and CEO of Socorro. You're here because we got these from an inside source of the *Sangre por Sangre* cartel."

Charlie moved—far too gracefully—to pick up the top photo of the file. No sign of distress. Nothing to suggest she was taking this as seriously as they were, apart from the loss of color in her cheeks. Good. She needed to know what kind of mess she'd left behind and just how far the cartel would go to survive. "Who's your source?"

"That's none of your concern, Ms. Acker," Ivy said. "Now I've been patient, but I'm afraid we don't have much time before *Sangre por Sangre* traces you back to Socorro, and I can't risk a head-on attack at the moment. So let's just get everything out in the open, shall we? You were responsible for the destruction of the Alamo pipeline ten years ago."

Charlie's gaze cut to Granger, but he wasn't going to help her out of this one. Despite her claims of innocence, of arguing with her sister and trying to stop those explosives from going off, evidence never lied. It'd been her blood investigators had collected from the scene. Preserved with that of five others. She refocused on Ivy, pulling her shoulders back. "Yes."

Surprise pricked at the back of Granger's neck. Then turned ice-cold in his veins. No matter what the evidence said, he'd wanted to believe her. To believe that she wouldn't have gone along with Henry Acker's plan to sabotage the government and everyone he considered a threat. Then again, he hadn't really known her, had he? She'd been a suspect, then a source. Then something far more. All in the span of weeks.

"I designed the mission. My sisters and I were instructed to set charges at two intervals along the southwest curve of the pipeline outside the town of Bennett." Slow breathing exaggerated the rise and fall of Charlie's shoulders, to the point Granger was convinced she was forcing herself to keep her inhales and exhales at an even pace. To prove she was in control. "My younger sister, Erin, took care of the first one. Sage was in charge of setting the second. I was assigned to be the lookout."

"At Henry Acker's instruction," Ivy said.

Charlie notched her chin higher. A visible struggle twitched the corner of one side of her mouth. A fight between defending herself or defending the man who raised her. Henry Acker was responsible for three separate attacks aimed at government property, like the one carried out at the Alamo pipeline. That they knew of. Dozens of innocent lives taken. Massive amounts of financial damage, not to mention the installation of fear across the state, but in the end, he would always be Charlie's father. She tented her fingers over the top surveillance photo. "That was a long time ago. What does any of this have to do with a drug cartel?"

"That's what we're trying to find out," Granger said. "*Sangre por Sangre* isn't in a position to waste resources at the moment. What's left of the cartel is scattered and in hiding after they attacked Socorro head on three weeks ago, but this surveillance tells us they've got their sights on you. Why?"

Charlie folded her arms across her chest. Not in defense.

He knew as well as anyone the kind of rigorous combat training she'd been put through as a kid. No. She was hiding something. Trying to keep him at a distance. "How should I know?"

"Because you're the only Acker daughter still alive." Ivy leveled the statement almost like an accusation. The last connection to the inside of Acker's Army. "*Sangre por Sangre* might be on its last legs, but they still have resources we can't even begin to imagine. It's possible whoever is targeting you knows you and your sisters were involved in the Alamo pipeline attack and want something specific from you." Ivy slid her hands into her blazer pockets. "Or this could have nothing to do with you and everything to do with getting to your father. Through you."

"What do you mean?" Charlie asked.

"Henry Acker has continued his mission since you've been gone, including two other attacks in the state." Granger leveraged his weight against the oversized conference room table. "Both were aimed at undermining the government, and by doing so, Acker's Army has proven themselves a real threat. *Sangre por Sangre* may be taking notice. Might even use his daughters to get to manipulate or influence him."

"Wait." Charlie released her hold on herself. A physical calm washed over her features, a stillness that could only be achieved through years of training. "You think this cartel could be involved in my sister's murder?"

"Murder?" Granger stood a bit taller as he cut his attention to Ivy and back. "As far as Vaughn PD and the media are concerned, Erin died in a hunting accident."

Charlie's mouth parted on a shaky inhale. The first real sign that something was very wrong.

"That's why you came back." Granger should've seen it

before now. There was no plausible situation he'd been able to think of that would explain her return to New Mexico, and yet here she was, after all this time. The muscles down his back pulled tight as a chain reaction of sympathy and anger and grief charged through him. Erin Acker didn't have the same views of her father and his anti-government protests as her sister, but Charlie had loved her sister all the same. Even tried to get her out of Acker's Army before the attack on the pipeline. Only she hadn't been fast enough. "You don't believe your sister's death was an accident."

"No. I don't." Charlie locked away the vulnerability that'd taken over for a brief moment. "And I'm not going anywhere until I find who killed her."

Chapter Three

This place was so cold.

Not in the sense she expected. Just...empty. Lonely. Though she should've been used to that by now. North Dakota, Montana, Utah, parts of Colorado. She hadn't let herself stay in any of them long or get to know anyone. She couldn't take the risk with her father and his army on the hunt, but Socorro's headquarters felt even more isolating. Like a prison.

Charlie lowered herself onto the edge of the mattress. The bedroom Ivy Bardot and Granger had stuck her in looked comfortable enough, but there was a reason she'd survived this long. She never took anything at face value. What was this place? A private military contractor and bed-and-breakfast? Her stomach growled at the thought. She hadn't stopped moving since she'd crossed state lines.

Pulling Erin's journal from the back of her waistband, she flipped to the first page. She could still recall the expression on her father's face as she'd sped away last night, but disappointment came with the job of being that man's daughter. And Henry Acker was the kind of person to never forget a grudge.

He would punish her if he got the chance. Just as he had

when she'd been a kid. Whine about how much her body hurt after training all day? Run ten laps around the farm. Fail to clean her rifle that week? Stand outside in below freezing temperatures until her fingers no longer worked.

At the time, she hadn't considered how wrong those punishments had been. How…traumatic. She'd simply seen them as a way to become a better daughter, facing them head-on and believing her father was only doing it because he loved her. In reality, all he'd wanted was another soldier to add to his ranks.

Tears prickled at her eyes as she traced the well-loved leather of her sister's journal. Erin and she used to write notes to each other in a journal exactly like this. They'd designed a secret code only they knew. If their father ever found it, he wouldn't know what to make of it, because they'd been the only ones who'd had the key to decipher the message. She missed that. The cover wasn't new. It'd once belonged to their mother. Erin had reused it a hundred times as she recorded events throughout their childhood, a much-needed habit the Acker matriarch had instilled in only her youngest child. Charlie had always claimed to have better things to do. Learning the latest war-game strategy, checking the perimeter of the farm for the dozenth time, running inventory on emergency supplies. Though there were times she wished she'd journaled. For evidence. But maybe there was something in these pages that could help. Could point her in the right direction.

She flipped through the notebook. The contents were routinely swapped out for new pages whenever Erin filled the latest journal up. This one was half-full of coded handwriting, with the final entry dated four days ago. The day of Erin's death. Only this code wasn't the one they'd created as kids. This was something more...complicated.

"Thought you could use something to eat," that deep voice said.

She hadn't heard him come in, too distracted by Erin's final words. Rookie mistake. If Henry Acker had witnessed her slip, she'd have to dig ditches until her hands bled. "How long have you been standing there?"

He moved slowly, as though approaching a wild animal, and, in a sense, that was exactly what she was. Feral, without a home, alone. Granger maneuvered to her side and set a tray of what looked like sweet-and-sour chicken and white rice on the bed. The scent alone was enough to remind her she hadn't been taking care of herself the past few days. Hell, he could probably smell the three days' worth of sweat and tears on her. "Not long."

She wouldn't get anything else out of him. Not unless it was on his terms. That was one of the things she'd liked about him the most when they first met, one thing that they'd had in common. It wasn't much, but it'd been more than she'd had with anyone else. "Thank you."

He added a good amount of distance between them. At least as much as the room would give him. "Is that Erin's?"

"I took it from her room last night." Her attention was split between her need for answers in the journal and her need for calories. Her father would be so disappointed to learn her stomach was winning the fight.

"You went back to Vaughn." A concern she recognized from the old days tinted his words and set her nerves on red alert. They weren't friends. They weren't even acquaintances at this point. "And you lived to tell the tale."

"I saw him. My father." Charlie held herself back from

shoving in more food than her mouth could take, simply pulling the tray onto her lap. She stabbed at a hefty piece of chicken covered in sauce and sticky rice, and her mouth watered. Chinese food had always been her favorite. It'd been such a delicacy compared to the canned and dehydrated foods she'd grown up on. Had Granger remembered that? "He caught me, tried to drag me back. Even had a couple of his lieutenants try to bring me in."

"But you escaped." Was that a hint of respect she sensed in his tone?

"I didn't have a choice." The bite of sweet-and-sour chicken coated her tongue and sent the first real glimpse of relief through her. One bite. That was all it took to lose herself in the experience, to the point this place, the cartel, her father—none of it existed. All that was left was this sweet-and-sour chicken and Granger. A laugh rushed up her throat. "Thank you for this. I haven't had something this good in a long time. Not a whole lot of options while you're in hiding. Going to restaurants or anyplace with security cameras was too big a risk"

"And yet the cartel got you on surveillance," he said.

"I was careful." She was getting full, but she didn't dare stop eating for fear she'd never have this small joy again. "Those photos you have of me must be from street cameras, because I sure as hell didn't put myself at risk. Not after everything I worked to keep."

He didn't seem to have an answer for that. Or he'd decided she wasn't the person to trust with one, and that...hurt.

Deep. Where she thought she'd buried everything about the past and him. It hadn't been easy. Granger Morais had been a big part of her life there for a while. In more ways than one. But she couldn't think about that right now. Erin was dead. She needed to know why. Charlie stared down at the mix of vegetables, sauce and chicken, no longer captive to her appetite. This thing that'd brought them together was more important than either of them. "My goals haven't changed, Granger. I still believe my father and his army are a massive threat. I want to tear them apart."

"Then why did you leave?" That last word seemed to catch in his throat. "We had a plan. You signed an agreement with the US government, Charlie, and you backed out by running. The feds have your name and picture at the top of their terrorism list, and there isn't anything I can do about that. If Homeland realizes you're alive, they'll do whatever it takes to put you behind bars and keep you there for a very long time."

"I know." She'd lived with the reality of what she'd done every day since crawling away from that explosion. And not without scars. "You trusted me, and I… I got scared."

"Scared." Granger turned away from her. "From what I remember, there isn't a damn thing in this world that scares you, Charlie. You were willing to give us intel on your father and the people who raised you, knowing exactly what they would do to you if they found out. Hell, you weren't even supposed to be there the night of the attack."

"I thought…" An uncomfortable pit weighed heavy in her stomach, and suddenly Charlie wished she hadn't eaten before having this conversation. There were still pieces of the past that could get to her. No matter how far she tried to run. Tossing the meal he'd brought her back onto the tray, she slid her clammy palms down her jeans and shoved to stand. Her sister's journal bounced with the absence of her weight on the mattress. "You know what? It doesn't matter what I thought. The only reason I'm here is because Erin is dead,

Granger. And you're right. We had a deal. I gave you everything you needed to take down my father a decade ago and get her away from him, but it seems you didn't hold up your end of the deal either. So here we are. You said this cartel you've been fighting might have something to do with her death, to get to my father, and now they're gunning for me. I want to know everything you know, and I want to know now. Who killed my sister?"

Mountainous shoulders pulled tight and accentuated his chest. Granger didn't look strong in the sense of the other male operatives she'd clocked in the building. He didn't need hours in the gym or gallons of protein powder to incapacitate a threat, though she knew he took care of himself. No. He had something far more dangerous packed into his lean six-foot-two frame. Something far more valuable: hard-to-come-by skills the US government wouldn't have wanted to lose. Strategy, foresight, high deductive reasoning. Not to mention extensive training in surveillance and combat. Everything a counterterrorism agent would need to save the world. In truth, he'd intimidated her the first time they'd met. Though she could argue they were evenly matched in many respects, Granger Morais always seemed to surprise her in the best of ways.

"What makes you think Erin didn't die in a hunting accident as the coroner reported?" His voice had slipped back into that near-whisper—too calm, too distant.

"Because Erin was the best damn hunter our father has ever trained. She knew her way around a rifle better than any of us. It was one of the reasons Sage and I always felt she was the favorite." Which left the question of whether her father had anything to do with his third daughter's death. Had he grown so callous, so vengeful, that he'd sacrifice one daughter to get to the other? Had he known Charlie had survived the explosion before she'd broken into the house last night? He'd seemed genuinely surprised to see her, but Henry Acker was a strategist. Never one to show his hand until the perfect moment. "Erin could hit a buck from five-hundred yards dead between the eyes. There's no way she made a mistake and got herself killed. Something else is going on here."

"Could someone have killed her to draw you out of hiding?" he said.

Charlie kept herself from folding her arms, from giving any kind of clue as to what was going on in her mind. She'd already come to a conclusion. The answer to that could be all right there in Erin's journal. She just needed to decode Erin's final days. Find the decipher key that would unlock the whole entry. "It crossed my mind."

"All right." Granger crossed the room to the built-in bureau taking up one side of the room. He popped the cabinet open and hit a series of numbers on the gun safe inside. The door swung open, and he pulled a sidearm from inside. "Let's go test that theory."

THIS WAS THE stupidest idea he'd ever considered.

Setting foot in Vaughn, New Mexico, could only end in a death sentence now that he wasn't employed by the federal government. Henry Acker had all the rights and reasons to shoot him on sight. And all the answers as to why the *Sangre por Sangre* cartel had targeted Charlie.

She hadn't said a word from the passenger seat. Though Granger could argue she wasn't really taking in the sights out the window either. Her hands were too tense, fingernails digging into her knees with every mile gained on Vaughn.

He checked on Zeus through the rearview mirror. The overstuffed K9 was asleep across the back seat after having gorged himself on the leftovers of Granger's lunch.

"You don't have to go in with me." It wasn't the first time he'd made the offer. "I've done this a few times. I'm kind of good at gathering intel and working my way into places I'm not supposed to be."

"You think my father is going to just let you walk up to his front porch?" Charlie graced him with one of those rare smiles, as though the thought of him taking a bullet center mass entertained her, before she turned back to the window. "You'll be dead the second you cross the town border unless I'm with you."

"And if he's not in the welcoming mood?" Granger tried not to let his hands tighten around the steering wheel at the thought. Not of him being taken down in action. He'd signed on with Socorro knowing exactly what he was getting himself into and was carrying a piece of a bullet around to prove it. But Charlie was a civilian despite her militaristic upbringing, and there was a difference between thinking she'd been dead all this time and watching her take her last breath beside him.

"We always knew there was a chance he'd kill us for working against him." Her inhale shook more than he imagined she'd intended. Fear did that to a person. Took everything they believed in and turned it against them. Charlie might believe some part of her father still loved her enough not to shoot her on sight, but there was still a high chance neither of them would walk out of Vaughn alive. "I guess now we'll find out if that's true."

"He didn't shoot you when you broke into the house last night," he said. "I'd take that as a good sign."

"I didn't really give him the chance." She pressed her shoulders back into the seat, tense. "I might hate everything he stands for and the way he brainwashes people into following his beliefs, but the only reason I was able to disappear was because of the things he taught me. How to live off the grid, which high calorie foods would serve me better in the long run, how to recognize if I'm being followed. In some weird way, I owe my life to him."

Granger didn't know what to say to that, what to think. Trials had a way of preparing the sufferer. Some better than others. "Where have you been living?"

"Here and there. Nowhere longer than a couple weeks at a time. I took odd jobs for cash and stayed in hotels. I couldn't take the risk of…wanting more," she said. "North Dakota, Montana. Visited Washington state for a while. They were nothing like this place. Everything here is so… harsh. And up there, I felt like myself. Surrounded by trees and the smell of dampness from the rain. It was like I'd become someone else. Almost enough to convince me I could escape what I'd done."

"Yeah. I bet it was easy to pretend after convincing everyone who cared about you that you were dead." Granger regretted the words the moment they escaped his mouth. This wasn't about him. This wasn't about them and what they'd lost that night. The cartel had plans for Charlie, and it was his job to figure out what they were. Nothing else mattered. He was here to do a job. Nothing more.

Charlie swung her gaze toward him. "I'm sorry. For everything, Granger. If I'd stuck to the plan, maybe none of this would've happened. Maybe Sage and Erin would still be alive."

"So why didn't you?" Dirt kicked up alongside the SUV

as he maneuvered onto a one-way unpaved road that would take them straight into the heart of Vaughn. He had to tell himself to press against the accelerator to keep himself from letting the vehicle roll to a stop. To give them more time. "Why didn't you stick to the plan?"

"Because I was afraid." She hadn't shied away from him this time, the weight of her attention solid and vulnerable. "We started out needing something from each other. You needed me to help you take down my father, and I needed you to get me and my sisters out of Vaughn safely, but then it became something more than that. We became something more. I was in love with you, Granger."

That final statement gutted him more efficiently than a blade.

"I was willing to give up everything we were working for if you had just asked. To the point I actually hoped you would, but those words never came. You wanted me to go through with my end of the deal, and I needed you to hold up yours," she said. "The night of the pipeline attack, Sage confronted me. She knew about us. I don't know how, but she was ready to expose me to our father. Tell him everything I'd done. That was what we were arguing about before the charges went off. She accused me of destroying our family, when all I'd wanted to do was save it. And she told me you were just using me to get to Dad. That the moment I was done being useful, you would throw me behind bars with the rest of Acker's Army."

Hell. An ache swelled along his jaw from the pressure on his back teeth. Granger kept his attention forward, but his entire nervous system had honed on Charlie. On the pain in her voice, in her words. "You believed her."

"Yeah, Granger. I believed her." She settled back into

staring out the passenger side window. "So I did what I thought I had to do to protect myself, and I never looked back."

Silence cut through the SUV, apart from the crunch of dirt and rock beneath the vehicle's tires. A barbed wire fence came into view along the right side of the road, signaling Vaughn's western border. Granger took his foot off the accelerator, and the SUV slid to a stop mere feet from crossing that sacred, invisible line.

Charlie moved to get out of the vehicle.

"I was in love with you too." Granger needed to make that clear. That what'd happened between them hadn't been part of some grand scheme to get inside Acker's Army and her pants. There were rules against relationships between agents and their confidential informants, but he hadn't been able to keep himself in check. Not when it came to her. In a sense, the forbidden nature of their relationship had made it all the more exciting, but those initial feelings of lust had quickly dissolved and left something more real behind. "Your sister was wrong. Whatever she convinced you of was a lie, Charlie, and when I got word you were involved in the attack, I wasn't angry you hadn't held up your end of the deal. I was worried I'd lost you."

Zeus's stomach growled in the silence and seemed to knock Charlie back into the present.

Her attention cut out the windshield, and the tension she'd managed to lose over the past few minutes returned. "They're here."

Granger diverted his senses to the threat coming down the road. Dirt puffed around three trucks charging straight for them. For a militaristic operation, Henry Acker could use some new wheels. His training took over then, and Granger whistled low to wake Zeus. The bull terrier launched himself out of the vehicle and followed on Granger's heels.

He and Charlie moved as one toward the SUV's front bumper. Ready for anything. They met as a team for the first time in over a decade. "You armed?"

"Don't worry about me." Long brown hair blew back over her shoulders as she faced the oncoming storm. Just as he remembered. "My father isn't going to let anyone but himself kill me, if that's how he chooses to end this. He'd consider it the coward's way out, and Henry Acker is no coward."

Granger fought the urge to unholster his weapon. Acker owned the entire town, the land, the buildings, the people who resided here. This was all private property that'd been incorporated through political pressure and a whole lot of personal funds. One wrong move and he'd lose any chance of figuring out *Sangre por Sangre*'s intentions for Charlie.

Zeus's growl vibrated into Granger's leg.

"Steady. You won't be flattening anyone today, mutt," he said.

"You really need to put that dog on a diet." Charlie took a clear step forward, crossing the demarcation line, raising her hands in surrender as the lead truck skidded to a stop. The two vehicles behind it each veered off to both sides, one right, the other left. Driver's side doors fell open, and a handful of pretend soldiers splayed into formation, taking aim.

"Hold it right there! You're trespassing on private property."

"Get down on your knees and put your hands behind your heads."

Charlie cut her gaze back over her shoulder, locking Granger in her sights. A single nod preceded her agreement. She'd warned him of the ways in which Henry Acker would exert his dominance over them. This was just the beginning. She dropped onto one knee, then the other, and interlaced her hands behind her head.

One of the soldiers centered his weapon on Granger. "I said on your knees! Or can't you hear?"

Granger had faced all kinds of danger in his pursuit of terrorists like these men. The ones who followed orders blindly for a cause that had nothing to do with them. The masterminds who disregarded the lives devoted to them as nothing more than ants under their boots. Like the *Sangre por Sangre* lieutenants he and his team had taken on. These men weren't more than thirty, some even younger. They had their entire lives ahead of them, and yet Henry Acker had somehow convinced them to fight against the very country that'd been born into.

"Granger. It's the only way to get to my father." Charlie's voice carried to him. They had one shot at this. They had to play their cards right.

He lowered to his knees.

The soldier who'd ordered Granger down rushed forward.

Charlie reached for him with one hand. "No!"

The butt of the soldier's rifle connected with Granger's temple.

And the world went black.

Chapter Four

Pricks of sunlight pierced through the bag over her head, but not enough to gauge where they were taking her.

Charlie stumbled forward at a push from behind, only managing to catch herself by taking small steps. They'd secured her wrists behind her back with zip ties. Didn't they realize she'd been brought up just like them? It would take more than zip ties to hold her back. Small rocks worked into her boots as they walked. "You didn't have to knock him out."

"Mouth closed. Keep moving." It was the same soldier, the one who'd taken charge and clocked Granger with the butt of his rifle. The distinct sound of dragging punctured through the pound of her heart. They had to carry Granger now that he was unconscious. And where was Zeus?

A whine pierced her ears. The bull terrier was struggling without orders it seemed.

Charlie tried to distract herself from the sick feeling that'd taken hold as Granger had hit the ground. Her fists tugged against the zip ties, and she couldn't contain the laugh sticking in her chest. Men like this particular soldier didn't get to take charge. Not as long as her father was alive, and Daddy didn't like to share the glory. She turned her head where she thought the soldier might be standing. "I'm going to remember you long after Henry Acker uses you up and discards you like the ones who've come before you."

Pain speared across her back, and she launched forward. The ground rushed to meet her faster than she expected. Her shoulder caught the brunt. It was a miracle she managed not to hit her head. Something heavy lodged into her ribs and rolled her onto her back. A foot.

"I told you to keep your mouth shut." Rough hands wrenched her to her feet and guided her a few more steps.

They were coming up on her father's barn. Because it didn't matter that they'd put a bag over her head to keep whatever secrets they had safe. She'd been born here, learned to walk here, ran laps around this property a thousand times. Every inch of Vaughn had been carved into her brain a long time ago. She knew exactly where they were headed.

The crunch of gravel beneath boots slowed. A heavy thud registered from her left as the soldier at her back pulled her to a stop. Despite the full-blown sun overhead, a chill took hold along her spine. November in the desert had always been magical to her. When nature seemed to freeze for a time, when she got a break from working the land and the livestock didn't need her as much. It was a time of gratitude in her house. For what they'd accomplished and what they'd been blessed with throughout the season. When Henry Acker seemed more like the father she remembered than the hardened extremist he'd become after her mother's death.

"Looks like we got visitors." The gravelly voice accompanied a series of footsteps. Close but with enough distance to counter an attack. Just like he'd taught her.

"Trespassers, sir."

"Caught them at the edge of town, the end of Magnolia."

"Take the hoods off," her father said.

Stinging pain ripped across her skull as the soldier who'd shoved her fisted the bag over her head and pulled. She automatically winced against the onslaught of blinding sun and didn't see the next strike coming. The soldier launched his rifle into the back of her knee, and she collapsed.

"Don't touch her!" The words were more predatorial than human. Shuffling kicked up dirt onto her hands and forearms as she caught sight of Granger fighting for release between two other soldiers. A fist rocketed into his gut and took him down to his knees. "I'm going to make you pay for that, you son of a bitch."

Henry Acker didn't need to see her face to recognize her, but Charlie got to her feet to face him all the same. To prove she could. The soldier at her back moved to subdue her again. Her father raised a hand to warn him off.

She breathed in the scent of dried-out hay, the odor from the chickens and the cooling scent of dropping temperatures as the sun reached the second half of the sky. So many memories battled for dominance here. Some good, some bad. But all of them hers. All of them combining to make her into the woman she was today. "Hi, Daddy."

A wall of nervous energy hit her from behind. The soldier who'd brought her in hadn't recognized her. She wasn't surprised, given the ten or more years between them.

"The prodigal daughter returns." Henry Acker let a half smile of amusement crease one side of his mouth as he wiped his hands clean with a work towel. Black smudges spread across the strong hands she'd once trusted to protect her. Never one to shy away from the work that needed to be done. One of the tractors must be out of commission. He motioned to Granger. "Who's your friend?"

"Nobody you need to concern yourself with." Charlie managed a glance at Granger. A dark bruise had already started forming alongside his face, but she couldn't see any swelling. A concussion? "But I'd watch out for the dog, if I were you. He likes to sit on people."

Zeus cocked his head to one side and parked his butt on the ground. Ever the loyal companion.

"Granger Morais." Her partner wrenched out of the hold of both soldiers working to contain him.

"Morais. I remember the name. Homeland Security, right? You investigated the death of my firstborn after that attack on the Alamo pipeline. Sage." Henry absently nodded. "You brought a federal agent into my town?"

Her father closed the distance between him and Charlie. He stuffed the rag in the back pocket of his worn jeans. That all-too-familiar shiver of his authority raced through her as he reached for her. Charlie tried to dodge his attempt at contact, but there was nowhere for her to run this time. He gripped her chin, giving her a full view of his aging face. "You're bleeding."

Acid charged into her throat at his touch.

"I fell." Half-truths. That was how she'd managed to survive in Vaughn for so long while she and Granger strategized on how to dismantle Acker's Army. The more honest she could be when talking to her father, the higher chance he'd continue to trust her. Charlie maneuvered out of his hold.

"I see." Her father unholstered the gun at his right side, letting it dangle in his hand for a moment. "Do I have you to thank for that, Johnny?"

"I asked her to keep her mouth shut, sir." Johnny. The soldier who'd bagged her and knocked Granger unconscious shifted his feet. He held onto the strap of his rifle as though to prove he belonged. "She refused."

A low laugh rumbled through Henry Acker as he circled behind her. Charlie knew what was coming next, and she didn't have the stomach to watch despite Johnny's treatment of her. "Nobody lays a hand on my daughter."

The first strike was the loudest, and a cringe cut through Charlie. Johnny's cry didn't come close to the sound of the butt of her father's weapon against his skull. She tried to focus on Granger, on the rise and fall of his chest, of the pattern of the bruise on his face, but it didn't help. The second strike accompanied a thud of the soldier's body hitting the ground. No cry this time. Granger turned away from the attack. The third strike to Johnny's head sounded more wet than any preceding it.

Zeus set his head against his master's leg.

Then silence.

Heavy breathing reached her ears as her father handed off his weapon to one of the other men. He wiped his head and hands with the same work towel he'd used while fixing his tractor. As though it'd never happened.

"Was that really necessary?" Granger didn't understand the rules here, that he didn't have any authority or rights. Vaughn police were controlled by Henry Acker. The mayor was controlled by Henry Acker. Anything and everything that happened in this town went through him, and there was nothing anyone could say or do to change that.

"He's alive, which is more than he deserves." Henry motioned for two of the other soldiers to clean up the mess he'd made, and they collected Johnny's body and hauled him out of sight. "Now, Charlie, considering you brought Agent Morais onto my property, I'm starting to think you're not here to apologize for making me think I lost two daughters in that pipeline explosion. When you broke into my house last night, you accused me of having something to do with Erin's death. Is that what this is, Charlie Grace?" He motioned to Granger. "You here to have Agent Morais bring me in?"

First and middle-named. It'd always been a warning for when she'd crossed a line as a kid. Only now it seemed to have a much stronger effect, despite her years of emotional and physical distance. "Erin wanted out, Dad. She'd been trying to leave for years, but you just wouldn't let her. You wouldn't let any of us. Sage had to die to get away, I had to fake my death and run, and Erin—"

"Erin died in a hunting accident. Just like the coroner said." A slip of her father's eyes gave her the answer she craved, and her heart squeezed too tight in her chest. He scrubbed at the same spot on his hands, a little too hard.

"A coroner who would write whatever you told him to write in his report." The zip ties were cutting deeper due to the tension in her hands and arms. "Because that's how it works around here, doesn't it? Everyone here worships you. Every word out of your mouth is gospel. No matter how many lives have to be sacrificed, nobody is allowed to question you for the good of the cause."

"I keep them safe. They know that, and they reward me with their service." Her father shoved the towel back into his jeans and headed for the barn, leaving her and Granger zip-tied in the middle of the most dangerous place on earth. "Let them go. See if they can make it to the town border alive."

Bastard.

But she wasn't finished. After all these years, she finally

had the courage to stand up for herself, for her sisters. "You brainwash them, just like you brainwashed your own daughters, and look what happened. Two of them are dead, and the other is the target of a drug cartel. Because of you and your extremist bullshit."

"Drug cartel?" Henry Acker turned to face her, years of age, any hint of grief he'd shown and some color melting away. In front of her was the man she'd wanted to love her more than anything—to choose her over his cause—who had come up short every chance he got. "Don't come back, Charlie. There's nothing left here for you."

"I'm not leaving until I find out what happened to my sister." She squared her shoulders, feeling stronger than ever. Maybe it had everything to do with Granger at her side or the fact she really had nothing left to lose, but she would take it. All of it. "You don't scare me anymore, Dad. I'm going to find out the truth. In the end, you're going to pay for everything you did to us."

"You've been warned, Charlie," Henry said. "Get them out of my town."

HIS HEAD POUNDED harder than it should.

Sundown was in less than twenty minutes.

Henry Acker walked into his barn without another glance in their direction. The Acker patriarch had set the rules. Breaking them would bring a rain of hell on earth. Granger had witnessed it firsthand. But he'd gotten what they'd come for. Confirmation. Henry Acker had paused at the mention of *Sangre por Sangre*. Might as well told them right then and there he knew exactly what the cartel wanted with Charlie.

"Let's go, princess." Another one of Acker's soldiers

shoved Charlie forward, but she managed to stay on her own two feet.

"I told you. I'm not going anywhere." Charlie broke out of the zip ties as if the plastic was mere sewing thread. And hell if that wasn't one of the sexiest things he'd ever seen. She turned on the soldier at her back and rammed her fist into his face. No, wait. That was the sexiest thing he'd ever seen.

The man hit the ground. Out cold.

Granger wrenched his wrists down as hard as he could and snapped the zip ties loose. He turned on the escort behind him and knocked the soldier out cold. Rubbing at his wrists, he stared into the barn. Hell, they were in the middle of enemy territory. "An abduction, a beating and a death threat all in one day. You sure know how to show a fellow a good time. Hadn't expected to meet the parents so soon though."

"It could've been a lot worse." Johnny obviously hadn't known who he was dealing with when he'd dragged Charlie into town. She turned that dark gaze on him. "He could've strip-searched you like the first boy who dared ask me on a date. Get their feet."

They dragged each soldier away from the front of the barn and behind a wall of bailed hay. Not ideal but the best option they had.

"Guess I should be grateful." His laugh took him by surprise. "All right. So we're in the middle of a hostile town with twenty minutes until the sun goes down. What now?"

"We make those twenty minutes count." Charlie charged for the side of the barn, leading him straight past the structure and toward a house an eighth of a mile up the drive.

The Acker family home was everything he'd imagined,

but nothing like he'd expected. Vaughn, New Mexico, wasn't exactly the type of place people from renovation shows visited. Not when a single man controlled the import and export of every grain of rice, wheat and piece of fruit. Jobs here consisted of farming the land, livestock raising and the occasional trade. The nearest dentist or physicians were in the next town over. Henry Acker and the townspeople didn't trust anyone outside these borders. More likely to take care of any ailments themselves and utilize natural remedies they'd made or stockpiled over the years. But the Acker home itself could've starred in one of those design shows.

Clean white horizontal siding gave the impression of a large home, but the structure couldn't have been more than two-thousand square feet. Dark shutters highlighted large windows from the covered porch. Old brick steps—hand-laid from the looks of it—were still in perfect condition. As though the place had been built yesterday. An equally well-built redbrick chimney stretched up along one side of the house. Despite the constant threat the people of this town believed was coming, Henry Acker had done a fine job taking care of his home.

Understanding hit as Charlie hiked up the steps.

"You're not serious about going in there." Granger pulled up short. Zeus ran into his leg, unable to stop his mass quick enough. Happened more often than not. "Your father ordered us to leave. Not to mention anyone could be inside."

Charlie swung the screen door open. Old hinges screamed in protest, but it didn't stop her from shouldering inside the house. "If I followed every order my father gave me, Granger, I'd be buried next to my sisters' headstones in the backyard."

She didn't wait for his response, letting the house consume her.

Wind shifted through the trees protecting the property from the rest of the town with a false sense of privacy. Large thin trees that had no business growing here in the middle of the desert. Granger stared past the house, through the trees as an uncomfortable weight of being watched hitched his pulse higher. He didn't have a choice. Because a stranger standing outside Henry Acker's house was sure to attract attention. And not the good kind.

"Come on, Zeus." He and the bull terrier followed after Charlie up onto the porch, though Zeus had far more trouble than usual. Damn dog had probably gotten into something else he shouldn't have. Old boards creaked with his additional weight as a pair of rocking chairs—most likely hand hewn—shifted back and forth from the breeze. He had a perfect view of the driveway and the barn from this angle. Less chance of an ambush. Granger worked his way inside, instantly confronted with wood paneling, orange drapes and a wood-trimmed bay window looking out into the side yard. A thin layer of dust coated decades-old family photos, and cracked leather couches hinted at the stark difference between the outside of the home compared to the inside. Strong and pulled together on the exterior. Suffering on the inside. Granger catalogued everything within sight as he moved through the squared-off wood-trim arch into the kitchen. "Charlie?"

Old cabinetry stuck out. Old appliances. Wood countertops. A table with six chairs stood alone in the oversized space of the kitchen. The dining room looked as though it hadn't gotten any use in years. No new scratches against the linoleum. What the hell were they doing here? What was Charlie hoping to find? A stack of boxes stuffed behind the dining table threatened to tip over at any second. Overpacked. Granger rounded the end of the table and pried the lid of the top box open as Zeus sniffed his way around the kitchen. Most likely looking for crumbs off the floor.

"It's meticulously inventoried." Charlie's voice had lost some of the power it'd had as they'd witnessed a man beaten to near death, and Granger couldn't help but take it in. The vulnerability, the pain that came with coming back here. She crossed the kitchen from the family room and pried the other lid open, pointing out the handwritten numbers on the underside of the cardboard. "Every week for the past twenty years. See these?"

She slid her finger closer to the beginning of the numbers where the handwriting had changed.

Granger pulled himself up taller, having not really come to terms that this place was where Charlie and her sisters had been raised. Until now. "Is that your handwriting?"

"One of my weekly jobs. I was in charge of inventorying all of our supplies. Here in the house and out back in the bunker. I had to make sure nothing was unaccounted for. Doesn't look like much has changed in that regard." She studied the kitchen as though seeing it for the first time.

"And if the numbers didn't match up?" He wasn't sure he wanted to know the answer, but these were the kinds of things he and Charlie had kept out of their short relationship. The stuff she hadn't wanted to give up to the man looking for a way to arrest her father. Not out of any kind of loyalty to Henry Acker but as a way to move on. To distance herself from the life she would be leaving behind.

"Then I would have to replace it with my own wages. If it happened enough times, I paid for it in other ways, but when you're trying to escape an extremist group, you make sure that never happens." She folded the lids back into place, sealing the inventory inside. "You know, I was here last night, but it was so hard to see. In the daylight, it's almost like…"

Granger couldn't look away from the familiarity softening her face. It was nothing like that invisible armor she insisted on presenting to the world. Here, in her childhood home, she reminded him of the woman he'd known ten years ago. "Like what?"

"Like I'm home. I haven't felt that way in a long time." She shook her head, snapping herself back into the moment. "If my father catches us in here, his warning won't matter. He's very protective of his property. No one outside the family is allowed to even know this stuff exists."

She was right. They were running out of time. Acker's supplies, the house, her childhood—none of it had anything to do with her sister's death. "Did you find anything during your search?"

"I went through Erin's room again, but it's the same as last night." Charlie threaded her dark hair out of her face, highlighting the terra-cotta coloring of her skin. Henry Acker was the epitome of an angry white man determined to protect his constitutional rights in the extreme, but somewhere along the way he'd fallen for a woman of Cameroon heritage. Charlie had never told him about her mother. Another one of those pieces of her childhood she wanted to forget. "My father has an office at the end of the hall. He always kept it locked, even when I was a kid. Going in there was forbidden, and I wasn't masochist enough to break that rule. If there's something tying him to Erin's death or any of the attacks you suspect him of being involved in, it would be in there."

Granger crossed the kitchen to the window above the sink. Only this window didn't give him a visual on the barn or the front of the house. A cement bunker took up most of the view. It wouldn't take long before someone found the men they'd knocked unconscious. "We better move fast. The sun is behind the trees now. It'll be ten times harder to get out of town if we can't see where we're going."

"I've got that covered." Charlie didn't wait for him to catch up as she vanished back into the family room. Zeus took it upon himself to follow her. Traitor.

Granger tracked her past worn couches, an old box TV and a crocheted rug that'd seen better days. The house wasn't large, making it easy to navigate down the hallway where Charlie crouched in front of the last door in the hall. "Any idea where we're supposed to get a key?"

"I don't need one." The door fell open. Only as she stood did he recognize the miniature lockpick set she was sliding back into her jacket. Shoving to her feet, she smiled, with victory etched into her face.

"Another one of your weekly tasks when you were a kid?" he asked.

"No. That one I picked up on my own." She grabbed the doorknob and pushed inside the too-small office taken over by the massive desk in the center of the room. Charlie didn't wait for permission, rounding the other side of the desk. She tested drawers and went through papers as Granger surveyed the rest of the room.

A closet stood off to his right, pulling him toward it as effectively as gravity held him to the earth. He dragged the door open. And stepped back. Guns. Lots of guns. Granger lost count after he hit twenty, and that was just the rifles. Reaching for one dead center of the lineup, he tested the modifications. High-powered and definitely not used for hunting. At least not the legal kind. Boxes of ammunition stacked along the overhead shelf nearly reached the ceiling. "He's got enough guns here for an entire army."

Though he guessed that was the point.

"Granger." Charlie's voice had taken on that wispy quality again. "I found something."

He replaced the weapon on its mount and shut the closet door behind him. "What is it?"

She flattened what looked like a blueprint across the desk with both hands. "Plans."

"These are dated two weeks ago." Granger took out his phone and took a photo. Handwritten notes took up the margins, with lines cutting across the page. He sent the photo to Scarlett Beam, Socorro's security specialist. If anyone could get them an answer, it was her. "Looks like the layout of a building, but I won't know from where until I get one of my teammates to look at them."

"You don't need to. I already know where these blueprints are from, and I know what my father is up to." She took a step back, though she didn't take her attention off the blueprints in front of her. "He's planning to attack the state capital."

Chapter Five

This couldn't be right.

Her father and his homegrown army had never plotted something this big before. Age was supposed to come with wisdom. Where the hell was Henry Acker's common sense? Attacking a state capital building would put him behind bars for the rest of his life. However long he had left anyway.

Charlie grabbed for the blueprints, crumpling the thin paper between both hands. No. She wasn't going to let this happen. She'd find a way to stop him, even if it meant taking the few notes he'd made in the margins. Heavy footsteps echoed through the house from the porch. "We need to go."

"Leave the blueprints. I've got photos." Granger grabbed her arm and tried to maneuver her toward the door.

She tugged herself free, looking for anything else that might slow Acker's Army down. They were already responsible for so many lives. She couldn't let them do this. "We can't leave these here."

The front door screen protested, just as it had when she'd pulled it open to come inside.

Granger got close—too close—pressing his chest against her arm. His mouth dropped to her ear. "If you take them, he'll know we've been in here. He'll know we found them, and he might change his plans. Right now, we have a way to stop him, Charlie. Do you really want to risk that?"

He was right. Of course, he was right. But the thought of allowing her father to do what he did best knotted panic deep in her gut. The front door creaked open with two even thuds. Only her father wasn't coming inside the house. At least not completely.

Charlie nodded, forcing herself to release her hold on the blueprints. "There's a hatch that leads under the house on the left side of the closet."

Granger didn't hesitate. He released her, leaving a cold trail of sensation around her arm. Swinging the closet door open, he shoved her father's hunting camo hanging across the metal bar out of the way and exposed their only escape.

Sundown had passed.

They were out of time.

Charlie quieted her breathing to listen for signs of movement as Granger worked to clear the hatch. There was nothing to suggest her father suspected she hadn't left town as ordered, but the one mistake she'd made growing up was underestimating the monster he kept inside. The one he only let out when he was in the middle of one of his operations.

Her gaze cut back to the blueprints, then to Granger. She already lived with the guilt of four innocent lives taken that night at the Alamo pipeline, not including her oldest sister. She couldn't handle the weight of any more. She couldn't give Henry Acker the chance to even try. Charlie closed the distance between her and the desk for a second time and folded the main blueprint as quickly as possible. She shoved the plans down the back waistband of her jeans.

Granger hauled the hatch open and reached back for her. "You first."

Old wood whined from the hallway. Just outside the office door.

Air caught in her throat as she watched a shadow shift beneath the crack between the floor and the bottom of the door. Fear and a thousand questions bubbled up her throat. She needed to know why. Why her father had become an enemy of his own government. Why he'd decided the lives of the people of this town were worth sacrificing in a losing battle. Because no matter how many attacks Acker's Army carried out, they were going to lose. *He* was going to lose, and when that happened, everyone she'd ever loved would be gone.

"Charlie, we've got to go." Granger latched onto her hand and pulled her into the closet. He shoved her into the square opening and pressed her head down.

Cold air whipped her hair into her face. She kept low and moved fast as she headed for the back of the house. Zeus dropped out of the opening behind her with a huff.

A gunshot ripped through the wood flooring.

"Go!" Granger was out of the opening and shoving her forward.

Her nerves shot into overdrive. Charlie clawed out from underneath the house.

Another bullet exploded from behind them. "Charlie!" Her father's bellow seemed to shake the house right off its minimal foundation. "Get back here, girl!"

Granger's hand found hers as they ran for the trees. They kept pace with each other as though they'd been together this entire time. Like they'd never lost touch.

Twigs and pine needles scratched at her hair and face as they broke the line of trees that'd stood guard over her family's property her entire childhood. Once upon a time, she'd known these trees as well as she'd known the back of her own hand. Dozens of summers of her and her sisters playing hide-and-seek struggled to fit into the overgrowth and darkness. Despite the encroaching desert and miserable temperatures throughout most the year, this patch of paradise went on for miles. Her family had relied on it more than once for wood in the winter, for mushrooms in the spring and growing produce not meant to survive in this part of the world in the summer.

They'd made a mistake coming here.

Henry Acker never gave up, and he never surrendered. Even when faced with the exposed involvement and potential arrest of his daughters for his dirty deeds, he hadn't admitted anything that could implicate him in his attacks. And he wouldn't stop looking for her. Not after knowing she was the one to take his blueprints. There was a chance she and Granger would never make it out of Vaughn, and she'd lose the one tie to that old life she'd never wanted to let go of. Him.

Her breathing overwhelmed the pounding of her footsteps until it was all she could hear. She'd been running for so long she wasn't sure she could stop. Her body wouldn't let her. Not until she got them as far from this place as possible. It was the only way to survive what was coming for them.

"Charlie." Granger grabbed for her, but she wouldn't slow down. She couldn't. "He's not following us. You can stop." His hand latched around hers, and he seemed to anchor her to the spot. Her momentum swung her into that comforting wall of muscle, but the need to keep fighting was too strong. Arms of steel secured her against his frame. "Charlie, stop."

She couldn't contain the sobs. They cut through her like thousands of shards of glass. "He's coming for us. He's never going to let me go. No matter how hard I fight or how long I hide, I'll never escape this place. I'll never escape him."

"I've got you." His hand threaded through her hair as something warm and slobbery collapsed against her leg. The dog. "I gave you my word when you agreed to be my CI. I'm not going to let him touch you. Ever. Understand?"

She latched onto that promise with everything she had as the adrenaline rush of escape ran out. Because it was the only thing that made sense in this world. The internal battle between loving the man who'd raised her and the man who'd carelessly sacrificed innocent lives for his cause—including her sisters'—was tearing her apart, piece by piece. But Granger was holding her together right now. And that was enough.

Charlie brought her arms around him, taking in everything she could about these few seconds. They'd had moments like this that'd sustained her before her disappearance, but this…this felt different. Stronger and more fragile at the same time. It was familiar and terrifying and absolutely needed in the middle of a fight for their lives. "My father will already have someone raiding your vehicle for supplies. We're stuck out here without flashlights or a compass or a plan. Sooner or later, he's going to send someone in to flush us out. For this."

She pulled the blueprints from the back of her waistband. Sweat permeated the paper. There was a chance she'd screwed this up. But letting Henry Acker go through with his plans and potentially being too late to stop him wasn't a risk she'd been willing to take.

"You took the blueprints." No hint of disappointment. Nothing to suggest anger or any other emotion got the better of him. And hell, she wished Granger would show her something. That she could read him as well as she used to. "No wonder your father's pissed."

"I just wanted…" The pain of that night, of watching people die because she'd been too weak to stand up to her father, clawed through her. "I wanted to do something good for once. Something that might make up for my mistakes. I can't let him hurt anyone else, Granger."

"It's going to be okay. We'll figure this out. Together." Granger secured her against him. Right where she needed to be. "Not sure if you know this, but I have a little experience with getting out of tough situations."

The rumble of his voice soothed her cracked nerves, and Charlie wanted nothing more than to stay in this moment for a little longer. To pretend her father wasn't about to attack the state's most protected landmark. That ten years of silence hadn't changed things between her and Granger.

But they had.

She pulled out of his arms. Because no matter how much she wanted to believe they were the same people they'd been back then, it just wasn't true. Her fingers grazed the left side of his rib cage. Wetness spread across her fingertips. Concern hijacked her central nervous system. "You're hit."

"It's nothing." Granger clamped a hand over the wound, coming away with blood in the last blur of sundown. He cut his attention down to hide the flash of pain in his expression. "Just a graze. It'll stop bleeding as long as I keep pressure on it."

"You were shot. That's not nothing." Charlie shoved the blueprints back into her waistband and ripped her jacket from her shoulders in a flurry of needing to do something. "Take off your shirt. I need to see the wound."

"It's fine. I've survived worse. We need to get moving

if we want to stay ahead of your dad's underlings." He attempted a step forward, but Charlie wouldn't let him budge.

She planted a hand on his chest, directly over that heart she'd once believed belonged to her. That was the thing about fairy tales. They'd always been too good to be true. Including the one she'd created between them. "Unless you're trained in field medicine like I am, you're going to do exactly as I tell you. Now sit down and lift up your shirt."

SHE WAS GOING to be the death of him.

And not in any kind of physical way.

Granger braced against the boulder jutting out from a grouping a trees. A place like these woods shouldn't exist in the middle of the New Mexico desert, but the people of Vaughn had taken advantage of the protection they offered between them and the outside world.

He took out his phone, raising it up to search for those out-of-reach bars. No service. No way to get ahold of Socorro out here. The photo he'd sent to Scarlett with those blueprints hadn't gone through. Hell, Henry Acker and his army were probably dismantling his satellite phone from the SUV at this very moment. Preppers didn't like to rely on government-monitored technology. Too many chances they'd attract attention or tip their hands. In fact, he knew firsthand that Henry Acker forbid the use of any kind of cell phone within Vaughn. They mostly worked with private radio channels if they had to communicate. Wouldn't do Granger or Charlie a bit of good out here though.

Zeus stared at him from a few feet away with those marble-like black eyes, ready to pounce on Granger's command. But despite the image of Charlie struggling to get out from under the bull terrier again, his wound was still bleeding.

Adding pressure hadn't done a damn thing the past few minutes. Which meant the graze was worse than he'd originally estimated. She was right. They were stuck out here in the middle of a hostile town without supplies, first aid or an idea of where to run.

"Hold still. I need to get a look at the wound." The sound of something tearing reached his ears. The skin across his stomach tightened in response to the outside elements filtering through the lost fabric of his shirt. Every muscle in his torso tensed at her touch, and Granger couldn't help but flinch at the contact. "Sorry. Cold hands."

"Don't apologize. Just do what you have to do." Every second they wasted trying to get his wound taken care of was another second Henry Acker had to find them. Oxygen sucked through his teeth as he tried to relax against her probing. Pain spiked through him and bucked his shoulders against the boulder. "Except that. Don't do that again."

"You're right. It's a graze, but it's pretty deep." She sat back on her heels, searching for something around them. Hauling herself upright, she collected something out of sight. "This might sting at first, but the longer we leave it pressed against the wound, the faster it'll stop bleeding."

Hell, he'd taken a bullet through his shoulder less than three weeks ago. A graze should be nothing. But it was as though his senses and pain receptors had gone into overdrive with Charlie so close. Enough for him to recognize the plant in her hand. "Is that a cactus?"

"Prickly pear. The pads contain astringent and antiseptic qualities. I've had to use them a couple times growing up around here. Lucky for you, we're surrounded by them. And if this doesn't work, we can use pine sap. Same antiseptic properties, just harder to get to." Unholstering a small blade from an ankle holster he hadn't spotted until now, she set to work stripping the cactus of its thick skin as easily as an apple. "Figured you Socorro types would be required to carry your own first-aid kits with the kind of work you do."

"We are." He watched her hands move as though she'd done this a thousand times before. Which she most likely had, growing up in a place that put so much value on independence and using what one had to survive. "Mine is in the SUV."

Her laugh rolled between them. She flipped the blade of her knife closed and holstered the small weapon, shuffling forward on her knees to get closer. Charlie had removed the hot pink bulbs on the edges of the cactus and stripped the skin down until nothing but a shiny surface remained. Maneuvering what was left of his shirt out of the way, she pressed the cool flesh of the plant against his rib cage. Instant relief melted across his skin and took the pain of the wound. "Well, thank goodness I'm here. Otherwise you might have to use that dog to get you out of this mess, and we all know he's going to get distracted by whatever food he comes across."

"Hey. Zeus is perfectly capable of staying on task when ordered," he said. "It's all the other times I have to make sure he doesn't accidentally eat my mattress or shoes."

"Here. Hold this in place while I make some bandages." She grabbed for his hand and used it to secure the cactus to his side. Charlie collected her knife once again and set about cutting through the jacket she'd been wearing, shaping them into long strips. "How long have you been together? You and Zeus?"

"Going on nine years." Granger mentally double-checked his math as Zeus pushed his front paws into the dirt and settled down. Apparently, the bull terrier had realized Charlie wasn't going anywhere. "Came into my life right when I needed him and hasn't left since. Though I'm not sure he could at this point. Any other K9 unit would've shipped him off to the shelter for his binge-eating."

"I've never met a dog with an eating disorder." Charlie measured out the longest stretch of denim from her jacket and wound it around his rib cage. Her mouth came into contact with his ear, and a shiver of warmth exploded through him. Too soon, she pulled back to secure the cactus in place. "And wow. Nine years? And all that time was with Socorro?"

Granger forced himself to take a breath that wasn't coated in Charlie's scent. Soap with a bite of citrus. "Ivy recruited me after I left Homeland. Every operative is assigned a dog when we sign on with Socorro, but we all know the K9s are the real heroes. They detect explosives, identify remains, protect our handlers against threats. They have our backs when we're in danger of taking our eyes off the mission. Loyal to the end."

"And what does Zeus do other than suffocate people with his enormous weight?" Her fingers worked to straighten the bandages, though they didn't need to be straight to do their job, and a piece of him realized it'd been years since Charlie had let herself connect with someone else like this. It was human nature to want affection and to give that attention to someone else. And she'd denied herself since the moment she'd run.

Zeus snapped his head to attention at the mention of his name, then slowly army-crawled closer until he was able to set his chin over Granger's leg.

"This chunk is the best tracker the Pentagon has. Once he

picks up a scent, he doesn't let it go until he finds its location." Granger scrubbed his hand between the K9's ears. "I think that's one of the reasons he's been able to get into my stash of treats at the top of my closet. He never gives up."

"You two seem close." Charlie let her hands fall back into her lap. She'd taken care of his wound and ensured he wouldn't bleed out before they came up with a plan to get the hell out of here. He owed her for that. "You're different now. The counterterrorism agent I knew would've spent the rest of his life hunting down terrorists for Homeland Security. Not playing house with an overweight dog."

Granger pressed back into the boulder to get his legs underneath him. A deep ache wrapped around his rib cage, but it was nothing compared to the initial pain. The cactus was doing its job. He just hoped it'd keep him on his feet.

"Yeah, well, I didn't exactly have a choice." He inventoried the supplies and weapons on his person. Not much. And not nearly enough if they ran into trouble. The sun had disappeared completely behind the mountains. His vision would adjust to the darkness, but they still had to figure a way out of Vaughn without coming across Acker's path. "After that night at the Alamo pipeline, I had to come clean about my source. My superiors weren't too thrilled I'd taken on a member of Acker's Army as my CI. Not to mention the fact that I'd gotten her killed. Every piece of intel I'd gathered on your father and his army was questioned and discarded, especially since I had no way of proving any of it was real. Seems the United States government wasn't willing to risk keeping me around."

Charlie got to her feet. "You were fired? Because of me? Even though you knew I hadn't died in that explosion."

"Yeah. I knew." He took another step. To add some distance between them. To make sense of what they'd gotten themselves into. Charlie had taken her father's blueprints, and right now, they had no way of getting that information to his team without cell service. But the part of him that had believed she'd died in the attack on the pipeline that night didn't want the distance. It wanted nothing more than to protect her like he should have that night. "Didn't make a damn bit of difference though. You'd gone off the grid. And I realized after a few months you weren't coming back. In the end, it was for the best. I moved on, landed this job with Socorro. With Homeland, I was always too late. Always at the scene of an attack after it'd already happened, but now I have a chance to stop attacks before they happen. I can save lives before they're ruined."

"Granger, I—"

Static cut through the trees.

Granger rounded on her and slid his hand over her mouth. Her exhale warmed his hand as they waited for a sign they weren't alone.

There. North of their position. The static was louder now. Getting closer. He removed his hand, angling down for his sidearm. He whispered in Charlie's ear. "Behind me. Move."

She did as he asked.

But her impulsive move to redistribute her weight snapped a dry twig—too loud in the silence.

"Over here!" An explosion of brightness overwhelmed Granger's senses as a flare shot straight into the air.

They'd been found.

"Run. Now!" He shoved Charlie ahead of him as multiple shouts followed them through the pines. The enemy would cut them off if Granger gave them the chance. He wasn't going to let that happen. Zeus's growl registered as the K9 struggled to keep up. Granger dropped back and hauled the dog over his shoulder. Pain ripped through his side from the bullet graze, but he'd have to rely on adrenaline to get him through. "Keep going."

A second flare lit up their position. Only this one had been shot horizontally. It hit a tree ten feet in front of them and exploded on impact.

Granger grabbed for her. "Charlie!"

She protected her face as the tree burst into flames, falling back to counter her momentum. Granger rushed to keep her from losing her balance, but it was too late. He, Zeus and Charlie all hit the ground as one.

The flames jumped from the originating tree to the next and the next.

Blistering heat cut them off from escape as a wall of darkness and flames moved in.

Chapter Six

Pain seared up her back and into the base of her skull.

"Get her to the truck. He'll want to deal with her himself," a voice said. "Leave the agent and the dog. Let the flames have the bodies."

A glow penetrated the seam of her eyelids. Too bright. Too hot. Charlie fought to shake off the haze clouding her head. She was moving. Not being carried. Dragged. Gravel and rock cut through her thin T-shirt, her arms stretched above her head. The voice was too low to put a face to. Him. Who was *him*? Her father?

She wasn't going back to her father. She wouldn't help him in another attack. No matter what he threatened her with this time.

Movement registered in her mind, growing more distant.

Charlie forced herself to come around, struggling to escape that addictive pull of unconsciousness. Heat burned along one side of her body. Blistering enough to kick her brain into gear. *Kill the agent.*

Panic swelled in her throat as her mind processed the meaning of each of those words. They'd escaped her father's house. Granger had been grazed by a bullet. She'd treated the wound as best she could and secured it with her jacket.

And then…they were running. A flash of red shot across her mind. The flare gun. Someone had shot at them with a flare gun. "Granger."

"Tranquila," that voice said. Quiet.

Grabbing for a half-buried rock, she tried to wrench herself out of the man's hold, but it was no use. He was too strong and had too much leverage. She secured her hand around the base of the next tree and kicked with everything she had.

Her boot slipped free in her abductor's hand. He turned on her, his features aglow in the flames spreading fast through the woods. Charlie rolled out of reach and dodged his attempt. She grabbed for her ankle holster, coming up empty.

"Looking for this?" The clarity of her attacker's features diminished with the appearance of her knife in his hand. He tossed her boot out of sight. "There's nowhere for you to run, *chica*. No one escapes *Sangre por Sangre*."

Sangre por Sangre? The cartel? Understanding hit. These men didn't work for her father. The cartel Granger and Socorro had warned her about had finally found her. How?

Smoke burned down the back of her throat. The heat intensified, beading sweat along her hairline. The fire was consuming everything in its path. And sooner or later, it would consume her and everyone left in these trees. Charlie turned her attention on a way out, but the man holding her at knifepoint was blocking the only escape. She would have to go through him. "What the hell do you people want from me?"

"To restore *Sangre por Sangre* to its original glory," he said.

Charlie dared a step back. Her heel landed on a smoldering branch. The wood cracked and sent embers around her legs. "I'm not doing anything for you or the people you work for. Understand?"

A low laugh crackled over the flames. "Not even when your father's life depends on it?"

"What are you talking about?" A thread of cold worked through her. "How do you know my father? And where is Granger?"

"We know everything about you, Charlie Acker." The man with her knife stepped to his left, forcing her to counter as he attempted to circle behind her. He was giving her an opportunity to run. Almost as though he was daring her to take the risk, to give him the chance to hunt her down. The steel of her blade glimmered in the reflection of flames. He was all that was standing between her and freedom from this place. "The work you did for your father. Where you've been hiding all these years. Did you really think my superiors fell for your ruse?"

He tsked, shaking his head. "You planned the attack on the Alamo pipeline. It was you who put Acker's Army on the map. Not your father. And now, you're going to do the same for us."

The need for answers battled with her survival instincts until paralysis held her in place. The fire would be seen for miles. Vaughn didn't have a large fire department, but the people of this town were prepared for any disaster, natural or not. Someone was coming. Charlie spotted a downed, rotted-out branch between her and the only escape. "Did your cartel kill my sister?"

"You're wasting time," he asked. "Pretty soon neither of us will be able to walk out of here alive."

"Then I suggest you answer the question." The sweat was almost suffocating now, prickling along both sides of her face, but the worst was at her back, where the blueprints poked into her skin. "Did the cartel have her killed? When *Sangre por Sangre* couldn't get to me, did they kill her and leave her to rot in these woods to draw me out?"

"Come with me without a fight, and I'll tell you everything you want to know about your sister's death." The promise hung between them for two seconds. Three. Her attacker closed the blade in his hand, offering it to her. It would be so tempting to believe she could just reach out and take it. That she could escape, but Charlie had learned to recognize false promises long before the cartel had come into her life. He was trying to establish a rapport, trying to take the fight out of her. He wasn't going to give her any information. Instead, he and the people he worked for would dangle that carrot and the lives of everyone she cared about in front of her until they forced her to do what they wanted. Because that was how power worked. "Or…start running. It's been a long time since I've had a challenge, but I can't promise how our game will end."

Charlie had been controlled enough in her life.

"That's it? I come with you willingly, you leave my family alone and you tell me what happened to my sister?" She took a step forward as though to accept his offer, one hand stretched out.

"That's it." That voice eased through her. Trusting, confident.

"Why don't I believe you?" Charlie lunged for the downed branch at her feet and swung as hard as she could. The tip of the rotted wood slammed against her abductor's head, and he shot off to one side. Her blade hit the ground in a burst of embers. She grabbed for it, burning her hand on the growing flames, and ran.

His scream bellowed behind her as she raced for the only clearing of trees not on fire.

"Get her!" Anger replaced the trust and confidence in her attacker's words, and Charlie pumped her legs faster.

Her pulse skyrocketed with the added pressure on her lungs to keep up, but she couldn't stop. Not until she found Granger and Zeus. Shouts bled through the trees around her. There were four of them. Maybe five. All closing in on her position.

Shadows shifted up ahead, and Charlie darted to the left to avoid contact. She had no idea where she was. No idea where the cartel would take Granger and Zeus. A tremor vibrated through her legs the harder she pushed. She was running on empty and most likely suffering from a concussion, but experience told her all those punishing laps she'd run around the farm would keep her on her feet for hours if necessary.

Charlie heard the snap of wood behind her.

A force she'd only ever encountered in the aftermath of the Alamo pipeline explosion slammed into her. She hit the ground face first. Air crushed from her chest as the weight on her back increased.

"I told you. No one escapes *Sangre por Sangre*." Her attacker dug his knee into her back to make a point.

Flashes of memory—of being pinned beneath a man twice her size and struggling to breathe—forced their way to the front of her mind. A training exercise. One in which she'd lost consciousness as rain pounded on her back. Her father's face in the center of her vision. Only she wasn't twelve years old anymore.

The glow of flames grew brighter. Ash collected around

her face. Sweat collected on her upper lip. She could hear the roar of the fire drawing near. This was her last chance.

Charlie threw her elbow back as hard as she could. Bone connected with her attacker's shin, taking away his leverage as his knee flared in the same direction as her momentum. She rolled hard and fast. One kick to his groin. That was all it took to bring him down. He landed face-first as she crawled to her feet. Her lungs had yet to get the message to inhale, but she couldn't wait.

She darted for a tree big enough to hide her.

Just as a bullet punctured the bark.

"You won't make it, Charlie!" The cartel soldier had lost that smooth manipulation in his voice. Instead, a demon seemed to be trying to tear free from his chest. "You're in too deep now."

Pressing her skull into the bark, Charlie finally caught her breath. He was right. She wouldn't make it as long as she'd brought a knife to a gunfight. She closed her eyes to calm her fight-or-flight instincts. She had to think. She'd grown up on this land. Knew more about it than anyone else. There had to be something here…

The shed. The one she would run to when training, or dealing with two sisters, or losing her father's approval hit a little too hard. It was nothing compared to what she kept on hand in the safe houses she'd built over the years, but there were supplies. Weapons. She just had to remember where it was. And hope her father hadn't demolished and raided it.

Footsteps cut through the chaos in her head.

Charlie scanned the trees up ahead. They were thinner. If she ran, she'd lose her cover. But it was worth it.

"There's nowhere to run." His voice had regained some of that control she'd noted earlier. "Whether you like it or not, you belong to *Sangre por Sangre* now, Charlie. You are going to change everything for us."

She picked a spot through two pine trees ahead. And ran.

The second bullet whizzed past her by a couple of feet.

But the third hit its mark.

Zeus's bark punctured through the haze of unconsciousness.

Granger tried to get past the roll of nausea in his gut, but he lost the battle. Turning onto his side, he emptied his stomach as the bull terrier tugged on the cuff of his pants. The K9's whine was nothing compared to the heat blistering along Granger's back. "I'm up. I'm up."

He planted both hands on the ground and shoved to stand. Facing off with a ring of fire closing in. "Oh, hell."

Zeus backed into Granger's leg.

There was no escape. Every tree around them had caught fire, and they had nowhere to go. The flames inched forward every second Granger tried to come up with a plan, but they were out of options. Acid lingered in his throat. The wind kicked up, aggravating the wall of heat. Tendrils danced and flickered toward them. He collected Zeus from the ground as embers flared at their feet. The K9's added weight pulled on the wound along his ribs. "It's going to be okay, buddy. We've been through worse."

A crack of wood pierced through the raging fire growing louder. A tree off to their right groaned a split second before Granger caught sight of the top tipping toward them. "Hang on, Zeus!"

He lunged out of the way. They hit the ground with a hard thud. Granger's shoulder screamed as the shard of bullet left inside took the impact. Rolling onto his back, he could barely make out the stars through the thickness of the smoke. An ember burned through the sleeve of his shirt and down to skin. Searing pain kept him in the moment when all his brain wanted to do was give up. Granger swatted at the ember as Zeus climbed to his feet. "We got to get out of here."

Reaching for Zeus, he hit the emergency tracking built into the K9's collar. He didn't know if the signal would go through without cell service, but he had to try. It would take the Socorro team at least an hour to arrive on site. Granger just hoped to hell and back there was something left here for them to save. Sweat dripped into his eyes as he maneuvered onto all fours. The ring of flames was closing in fast, giving them less than eight feet in circumference to work with. And they were the only ones inside. "Charlie."

Granger scoured the base of the flames around them. Looking for a sign of something that would tell him she'd gotten out of this alive, but it was too hard to determine with the wind aggravating the fire. No. She had to be alive. Nothing else mattered. "Charlie!"

Zeus called after her with a low howl.

No answer.

"We can do this, boy." Tearing through the knotted denim Charlie had tied around his ribs to hold the raw cactus against his wound, Granger secured the denim over his mouth and nose and tied another knot at the back of his head. A single layer wouldn't do much, but it was better than nothing, as the oxygen decreased this close to the ground.

Granger searched his holster. Empty. The men who'd attacked them with the flare gun must've taken his firearm. Damn it. They were going to pay for that. If they ever got out of this alive. He searched for something—anything—

that could be used as a weapon. Every second he wasted wondering if Charlie was alive was another second he was stealing from himself and Zeus. If he didn't get out of here, there wasn't anything he could do to keep her out of the wrong hands. He'd already failed her once. He wasn't going to lose her again.

Another gust of wind drove the fire into the protective circle around them.

Whatever he was going to do, he had to do it now.

"Where is she, Zeus?" Granger ripped the denim off his face and positioned it under the K9's nose. The dog buried his dry nose in the fabric as his tail went wild. He had the scent. A low gruff said Zeus knew exactly where Charlie had gone. Or where she'd been taken. The bull terrier lunged across the circle, kept inside by a wall of fire. "Good boy."

Granger kicked a four-inch dead pine branch free of its trunk. It wasn't much, but it could get the job done as long as he used it well. Closing the distance between him and the spot Zeus had alerted to, he faced off with the flames. He pushed the K9 behind him in case a rogue flame lashed out. Zeus was the only one who could find Charlie. Granger was going to do whatever it took to make that happen. Firemen trained for moments like this in full gear and armed with containers of oxygen. He didn't even have gloves. Still, this had to work. "This is going to hurt, but we've got no other choice."

He hauled the makeshift weapon overhead. Then slammed it down on the tree slowly burning to ashes. The branch he hit fell to the ground, taking the flames consuming it with it. He did it again, then again, breaking the tree to pieces. Embers lit up with each strike and attached to his skin and clothing, but he couldn't stop. He was almost through. He just needed another foot to get through the wall of heat.

A whisper of warning sizzled up his spine.

Granger turned just in time to watch as the ground he'd once stood on caught fire. Grabbing for Zeus, he pulled the K9 through the too-small opening he'd made by taking down one of the burning trees.

Just as the circle closed.

The dog was shaking in his arms, and Granger had no assurances he'd done anything to extend their lives. Because the fight wasn't over. They'd made it out of a small section of woods, but this entire place was on fire. Granger set his forehead against the dog's shoulder. "Take me to Charlie, Zeus, and let's get the hell out of here."

The bull terrier locked onto the same direction he'd indicated a few minutes ago and bolted ahead as far as the next obstacle in their way. A headache pulsed at the back of Granger's head with every swing of the branch to clear their path. Pain radiated up his arms. Dehydration was setting in. Not to mention the blow to the head he'd taken earlier. But he couldn't stop. Not yet. Not until they located Charlie.

Granger pushed through pain and exhaustion, and memories of that night at the Alamo pipeline refused to let go. He'd tried to get to Charlie then too. Studying every body the coroner had bagged before he'd gotten onto the scene. Searching for some clue that his grief was lying to him. The fires had raged much like this one with the combination of pure oil and explosives. Even from beyond the perimeter the fire department had set, it'd been so hot; he could still feel the warmth on his face.

She'd lost faith in him. He knew that now. Despite everything they'd been through and the intel she'd stolen from inside Acker's Army, Charlie had felt like she'd had no other choice than to run. Not just from her father. From him. He'd put her in an impossible situation as a confidential informant: against the family who protected and raised her. And he hadn't been there for her.

Granger wouldn't make that mistake again. Pooling a decade's worth of loss and shame into his next swing, he took down the tree in front of him. All her life, Charlie had been used—by her father, by Homeland Security, by him. Considered nothing but a tool rather than the strong, charismatic woman she was. Something to be discarded when she outlived her use. But she deserved to have someone in her life that fought for her. Just once. And he wanted to be that someone. "I'm coming for you, Charlie. No matter what it costs me."

Zeus charged through an opening ahead, out of sight.

"Damn it, dog. Wait for me!" Granger struggled to keep up.

A yip cut through the pound of his heart beating between his ears. Granger went on alert as he shoved through a barrier of trees the fire hadn't burned through. Smoke blunted his vision, and he tightened his grip on the branch. "Zeus?"

The K9 didn't respond.

He whistled in a tone only he and Zeus understood. And waited.

There wasn't a single time in Zeus's training that dog hadn't answered his call to heel. The glow of fire intensified behind him but barely cut through the haze of smoke ahead. Granger took a careful step—slow, calculated—as he relied on his senses.

Too late.

A glint of metal caught his attention.

Just before the blade of an axe sliced in front of his face.

Granger countered by throwing his weight to one side. Saving himself from losing a limb.

A growl escaped his attacker as the oversized frame of Henry Acker spun toward him. Something feral and dangerous bled from the man's eyes. The patriarch had lost all sense of age as he rushed Granger, axe at the ready.

Granger countered the onslaught. His back hit the tree behind him.

Charlie's father embedded the blade of the weapon into the bark of the tree beside Granger's head, then clamped a strong hand around Granger's throat. "I told you to leave, Morais. I warned you two to leave when you had the chance. So where is she? Where is Charlie?"

Latching onto the old man's wrist, Granger could've sworn his feet were coming off the ground. Given his size, weight and combat experience, it shouldn't have been possible. But this wasn't the same man who'd warned Charlie to leave town. This was the general of the most dangerous army in the country: one that'd taken its time shoring up its resources and didn't answer to the US government. The man was running on pure adrenaline. Granger struggled to breathe around the grip on his throat. Two more of Acker's soldiers left the safety of the trees, weapons aimed at Granger. "Shouldn't you…be asking your men who attacked…us?"

Henry Acker pressed his weight into the palm against Granger's throat with far more strength than should've been possible. "I never issued an attack order. My men are fighting to put out this fire."

Granger didn't have time for this. He slammed the base of his palm into Acker's inner elbow. The old man might've studied combat techniques, but there was no way in hell that experience matched Granger's government or private contractor training.

Acker's arm folded. Granger twisted his wrist one-hundred-and-eighty degrees and locked out the man's elbow, forcing Acker to his knees. All in the span of three seconds. The homegrown military general kept his scream to himself. Impressive. "I have a bullet graze on my ribs that says different, Acker."

Both of Acker's Army soldiers moved in to protect their leader.

Granger turned Acker to face them, using the old man as a shield in case this went south. "You shoot, and you'll only be killing him. Understand? Now where the hell is my dog?"

"You won't get away with this, Morais. She was safe, and you dragged her back. For what? To get to me? Something happens to her, I'll kill you," Henry Acker said. "I give you my word."

"You knew she was alive," Granger said. "How?"

Two gunshots echoed through trees over the roar on encroaching flames.

Granger loosened his hold on Henry Acker. *"Charlie."*

Chapter Seven

The bullet ripped across the side of her calf.

Charlie hit the ground short of the next cover of trees. Pain seared through her leg until she wasn't sure she'd be able to take her next breath. It was too much. Almost debilitating. But the thought of giving in to a cartel's demands when she'd fought to escape a life of control and punishment was stronger.

She dug her fingernails into the dirt ahead of her and pulled. Physical strength was a necessity of being a soldier of Acker's Army. No matter the situation, her father wouldn't have accepted anything less than her best at all times. Her training had started when she'd just been five years old, and it hadn't let up until she'd run the night of the pipeline explosion. Years of drills and weights gave her the strength to army crawl from her attacker as he advanced.

Only she wasn't fast enough.

A foot pressed down on her wound.

The resulting scream exploded through the trees and echoed back to her. Loud enough to scrub the back of her throat raw. White lights lit up behind her eyelids, brighter than the fire burning ever closer.

"I'm beginning to think you are unappreciative of my

offer, though I do appreciate the challenge you've presented me tonight." That same smoky voice that had tried to convince her to trust him was back. Edging underneath her armor, chasing back the pain in her leg. "Just for that, I'll personally make sure your father suffers before I kill him."

"Touch him, and it will be the last thing you ever do." The words hissed through clenched teeth as she fed into an anger she hadn't let herself fall victim to in a long time. Because there was a difference between Henry Acker serving a prison sentence for the lives he'd destroyed through his attacks on government property and someone killing him to punish her. "I give you my word, and if you know anything about me and the way I was raised, you know I mean that."

His laugh attempted to disregard her threat as nothing more than a temper tantrum. The weight of his foot disappeared. Strong hands wrenched her arm behind her, forcing her to turn onto her back if she didn't want to dislocate her shoulder. He stared down at her, his features clearer now that she'd gotten some distance from the fire. Sharp ears stood out from a pristine haircut that fanned over his forehead. Sweat had glued his dark hair around his temples and hairline, but it was his eyes she paid attention to. Softer than expected. Lighter too. A thin layer of facial hair spread from his sideburns down along his jaw, giving him a younger appearance. This wasn't a hardened soldier of a drug cartel, and yet he carried himself and spoke with far more authority than the soldiers in her father's army would dare. "You have no idea who you're dealing with, do you? Who I am or what I've done to people standing in the way of what I want?"

Charlie brought her head off the ground in an attempt to

make her point clear. "All I know is, right now, *you* are the man standing in my way."

Bullet be damned, she brought both legs up and wrapped them around his waist. In a move her father would be proud to see, Charlie hauled her attacker off to one side. She slammed his body into the ground and rolled on top of him. Adrenaline gave her a burst of fight as she rocketed her fist into his face. Once. Twice.

Blood spattered as bone crunched beneath her knuckles. His head snapped back, but not hard enough to knock him unconscious. Her attacker caught her third strike and twisted her arm in the wrong direction.

Her holler filled the trees around them, and she was forced to follow the arc of her arm. Charlie hit the ground, but she wouldn't let him get the upper hand. She rolled with everything she had as he struggled to pin her down. Dirt and ash drove into her mouth with every breath. Her leg screamed in protest, but she couldn't stop fighting. She shoved to all fours and tested her weight on her injured leg.

A third bullet pulverized the tree bark to her left. Her nerves shot into overdrive. Charlie froze, her hands over her head as though they could do anything to stop a bullet from killing her. There was no cover to hide behind. Nowhere she could run this time.

"My plan was to let you walk out of here on your own with me, Charlie, but it's not your legs I'm interested in. I just need that beautiful mind of yours, and my patience is wearing thin." Her attacker shifted his aim from the tree. To her. "I've given you plenty of chances to come to your senses, and I'm done playing nice. Now stand. We have work to do."

"You're making a mistake." Adrenaline drained from her

veins—faster than she expected. She felt its loss as though the earth's gravity had somehow intensified over the past minute. Charlie braced herself against the tree at her back. There was no way for her to hold her own weight. No way she was getting out of this on her own. She pulled out the knife she'd taken back from him and flipped the blade open. The one her father had given her on her twelfth birthday after she's won a fight against four boys her age. It'd been a training test. To prove she could overcome, and it'd gotten her to this point. A blade this size wouldn't stop a bullet, but it would keep her going. Keep her fighting. Because she deserved the life she'd created for herself, and no one—not even a drug cartel—was going to take that away from her. "Whatever you want from me, whatever you think you can force me to do for your organization…it won't work. I've spent my entire life being told what to do, and I'm stronger than you think I am."

A bark preceded the charge of the overweight bull terrier.

The gunman's attention cut to the K9 lunging at him from the right.

And Charlie had her chance. "Zeus!"

She summoned what was left of her adrenaline and shoved to her feet. Zeus bit into the cartel soldier's forearm and pulled the son of a bitch down. His body and his gun hit the ground as his scream exploded through the clearing. Charlie dove for the weapon.

He knocked it out of her reach as he fought off the dog with a bellow that outmatched hers. The gun disappeared into the bushes. Out of sight. Blood seeped from the wound in her leg. Unstoppable and pounding.

Her attacker unholstered his own blade, arching it down toward the determined bull terrier.

"No!" She didn't have any other choice. Charlie wrenched his arm back, trying to get a hold of the weapon. The blade sliced into her palm, but she didn't have the sense to get clear. Not as long as Granger's partner was in danger. "Zeus!"

The K9 released his target. The sense of relief flooding through her was short lived as a fist slammed into her face.

The momentum and pain knocked her backward. Her leg threatened to collapse right out from underneath her. She fisted both hands together and brought them down on the soldier's arm. Swiping her own blade toward his chest, she overcorrected as he dodged her attempt. Charlie made up for her imbalance and aimed for his gut.

He caught her hand an inch from the tip of her blade meeting the soft tissue of his stomach. Then slammed his head into her face. A strong right hook followed and threw her off balance. Images of that fight—of her facing off with four boys her age—threatened to superimpose on her current reality. She'd taken more than her share of strikes, but this…this was different. Back then, her father would've stepped in if things had gone too far. Now she was on her own. And she was losing.

Charlie's leg failed, and she dropped to her knees, her back to her attacker. He moved in, but she wasn't finished. Locking her arm, she rotated with the blade aimed backward. Only it didn't reach its target.

Gripping her arm, the cartel soldier stared down at her. Just before rocketing his knuckles into her cheekbone. "I didn't want to do this, but now you leave me no other choice."

She lost her balance and hit the dirt. Zeus's whine echoed through her head, as though the dog actually cared about what happened next. The crackle of flames grew louder in her ears. Growing closer. They'd outrun the brunt of the fire, but it was always meant to catch up to them. To her. Charlie gripped onto the only thing she had left of that old life.

And stabbed it into the soldier's foot.

He threw his fist into her side and knocked the air out of her lungs.

Charlie collapsed. Desperation told her to keep moving. She climbed to her feet, dizzy from blood loss and swiped at him again. Another strike took the last of her energy reserves, and she went down again. She couldn't breathe, couldn't think.

The fight slipped out of her as she stared up into the smoke-darkened sky.

Her attacker spit blood and saliva at her feet. Bending to meet her, he fisted the collar of her shirt and started pulling. Her remaining boot caught against rock and dead pine needles. "I have to admit, I didn't expect so much fight from you, Charlie. Maybe if your sister fought as hard as you, she wouldn't be dead."

Charlie reached for her abductor's hand, trying to get free, but she wasn't strong enough anymore. Maybe hadn't been in a long time. Zeus whimpered as he watched. His bark shook through her, but worse was the battle she saw in his eyes, as determination to go against his command took hold. "No."

"Don't worry, Charlie. This will all be over soon," her attacker said. "You and I are going to do great things together. You'll see."

"Zeus!" Where the hell was that dog?

"You expect me to rely on a mutt who can't control his

weight to find my daughter?" Henry Acker had called a temporary truce at the sound of those gunshots, but Granger didn't trust a single word out of the man's mouth. "What kind of agent are you anyway?"

They jogged to stay ahead of the fire while Acker's men worked to put it out from the other side, but the wind wasn't cooperating. Soon, this entire side of Vaughn would be nothing but ashes.

"I'm not an agent anymore, and Zeus is a purebred bull terrier. I'm the only one who gets to call him a mutt." Granger's heart pumped harder every minute they didn't have eyes on Charlie or his K9 partner. "And that mutt is a better hunter than you'll ever be, Acker. Dress it up any way you like, you need me and my partner to help find Charlie."

Henry Acker had no problem keeping up. Despite the grief from losing one daughter in the past week and the effects of age, the man had stayed physically fit. At least enough to keep up a panicked search for Charlie. "If we don't, the last thing you'll be worrying about is your dog."

Granger didn't have time for petty offenses. Charlie was out here. She had to be. Acker's men hadn't reported any conflicts with intruders other than Granger and Charlie in the past twenty-four hours, which meant those gunshots had been meant for her. And the thought of her out here—alone, possibly injured—pushed him harder. Socorro wasn't going to get here in time. He had to rely on Acker's Army to recover Charlie. "The *Sangre por Sangre* cartel has surveillance photos of Charlie. They've been following her ever since she came back to New Mexico three days ago."

Henry Acker didn't respond.

"But you already knew that, didn't you?" Granger pulled up short. As much as he hated to stop the search for Charlie, he had to know what they were walking into. He turned on Charlie's father as his anger built. The son of a bitch put his family at risk, and for what? To make a statement? For power? "You got into bed with a drug cartel. They came here tonight to get to her. All this time, you knew exactly what they were capable of, and you refused to protect your own daughters from falling into their hands."

Acker suddenly seemed so much smaller than Granger remembered. Unsure of himself. It was a mere glimpse of the man behind the army, but in an instant, that glimpse was gone. Henry Acker rolled his shoulders back, once again every inch the man Charlie had described. "The last thing I'm going to do is explain myself to the federal agent who used one of my daughters to get to me and the people I protect."

The accusation stabbed deep. Because Henry Acker was right. Granger had used Charlie just as her father had used her: to fight a war nobody could win. "What does the cartel want from her? What are they planning? What do they need her for?"

"It doesn't matter. They won't kill her. At least not until they get what they want." Acker maneuvered around Granger and picked up the pace. "Charlie is strong. She'll hold her own against interrogation just the way I taught her."

Granger had been put through interrogation training during his stint with Homeland Security, and he didn't want to think about Charlie strapped to a chair and physically tortured until she broke. And now she was potentially in the hands of *Sangre por Sangre*, the most bloodthirsty and brutal drug cartel Granger and Socorro had faced. There was nothing in the world he wouldn't give up to ensure Charlie never had to go through that kind of nightmare. "Everyone has a breaking point."

"If you truly believe that, then you don't know my daughter." Henry Acker kept moving, the topic reaching its end.

Movement registered up ahead. Granger reached for Acker's elbow, but the man was already slowing down to get a better read. A whine filtered in through the rustle of trees.

"Zeus?" The K9's yip spiked Granger's pulse. He maneuvered around Henry Acker and stepped into a clearing. Searching for signs of an ambush, he grabbed onto Zeus's collar. The bull terrier barked, unfazed by the appearance of his handler. "What do you have, bud?"

Another bark—louder this time—triggered a ringing in Granger's ears. Granger ran his hands over the dog's frame to check for wounds and turned Zeus's head toward him. A ring of something wet and dark disrupted the pattern along the dog's face. Granger swiped it from the K9's fur, rubbing it between both fingers. "He's got something." Granger shoved to stand, facing off with Acker. "Blood. Whoever Zeus attacked, he caused some damage."

"I'm starting to like that dog." Acker pushed ahead. "He's trying to tell you they went this way, but something is keeping him from following. Like he's been told to stay."

"Zeus doesn't listen to anyone but me." His confidence waned as he took in the K9's restlessness. Zeus had been trained to follow Granger's commands from the time he was a pup. Then again, Granger had never given anyone else the chance to try. It'd taken months for the bull terrier to establish trust in Granger. There's no way Charlie could've done it in mere hours. Right?

"A lot of people underestimate my daughter's influence." Acker shouldered his rifle and forged ahead. "Take it from me. I made that mistake once. Cost me something I loved in the end."

Granger found himself trying to keep up with the Acker patriarch. He whistled for his partner, and the K9 followed on his heels. "Go get her, Zeus."

The dog launched off his back legs and shot into the trees.

"These woods spill out onto barren desert in less than a quarter mile." Henry Acker called back over his shoulder. "My guess, they're trying to get her out of Vaughn from there by ATV or vehicle. The fire was a distraction."

And a damn good one at that. If what Granger believed about Henry Acker was true and the bastard had gotten into bed with a drug cartel, *Sangre por Sangre* had to know the kind of manpower and firepower Acker's Army carried. Threatening the town they'd die to protect was the only way to take the focus off the cartel's real intentions: getting to Charlie.

"Your daughter Erin." They moved by the light of the fire at their backs. Both in line as they followed after Zeus. "When the cartel couldn't find Charlie, they came for her, didn't they? They knew she'd been involved in the pipeline explosion, that she had her own expertise from the attack."

Henry Acker pushed the pace, refusing to confirm Granger's theory. "We're almost there. Be ready."

Battle-ready tension filtered down Granger's spine.

The trees were thinning up ahead. They broke through the border.

A pair of headlights skimmed across the desert.

Acker and the two soldiers behind them opened fire on the vehicle. Metallic pings sparked off the side of the armored SUV.

Return fire pulverized the dirt at their feet.

Granger grabbed for the old man and hauled him out of the way of the oncoming bullets. He threw Acker behind one of the last trees for cover.

"What the hell are you doing? My daughter is in there." Acker raised his rifle and got off another two rounds, but his rifle wouldn't be strong enough to breach through that armor.

Two more sets of headlights flared to life. Engines rumbled across the desert floor and exposed a game of hide-and-seek. Damn it. Charlie could be in any of one the SUVs. "I'm saving your life, Acker. *Sangre por Sangre* only moves in packs, and they don't travel light. Those vehicles are armored. You'll never get through."

"So you're just going to let them get away." Henry Acker took another shot from behind the tree.

"Hell, no." Granger pulled his cell phone from his pocket as all three SUV's shot into the dark unknown of the desert. A single bar of service lit up the screen. It was enough. He dialed in to Socorro. The line connected. "Scarlett, I need my SUV."

"Narrowing down your location." Static punctured through each of Socorro's security expert's words. "Got you. Sending it your way. ETA two minutes. Just enough time for you to tell me what the hell is going on. I can see the fire from here."

"No time to explain." Two minutes. Socorro was in route. They'd responded to Zeus's alert. Damn it. *Sangre por Sangre* was already moving at full speed. They didn't have that kind of time. "Redirect your approach on my position to intercept three hostile vehicles with a hostage inside."

"You got it." Scarlett ended the call just as a fourth pair of headlights cut into Granger's peripheral vision.

"Come on, old man." He pulled Acker out from the cover of the trees. The SUV pulled to a stop ten feet ahead of them, and Granger wrenched the driver's side door open. "Get in."

Henry Acker collapsed into the passenger seat, his weapon folded across his lap, jaw slack. "Had I known this thing could drive itself, I would've had the boys strip it for parts."

Granger threw the SUV into gear, chasing after three pairs of distinct brake lights a mile ahead. Momentum pinned him to his seat as they sped across the desert floor. "It's only accessible through Socorro's security system. Besides, I think you got enough of a donation from me out of the cargo area."

"And Acker's Army thanks you kindly." Acker turned in his seat as two more sets of headlights filtered in through the back window. "Those your people?"

"They're not shooting at us, so I think it's safe to believe they're here to help." He checked the rearview mirror, hit the radio tied into his steering wheel and floored the accelerator. He wasn't going to screw this up. Not like he had the night of the Alamo pipeline attack. Charlie was coming home safe. "Scarlett, you take the right. I've got the center. Tell whoever's with you to take the left."

"You got it." The SUVs on his tail maneuvered into position and raced ahead. Within seconds, each vehicle had cut off the *Sangre por Sangre* caravan and brought them to a halt.

"Stay in the vehicle." Granger pulled a weapon from underneath the seat, happy to know Acker's Army wasn't all that adept at searching for weapons.

"Like hell I am." Acker shouldered out of the SUV and

hit the ground, rifle raised as both Scarlett and another Socorro operative took the *Sangre por Sangre* drivers out of their vehicles.

"Clear," Scarlett said. Two Dobermans circled the driver on the ground with his hands on the back of his head.

"Clear." Recognition flared as Granger identified Socorro's forward scout, Cash Meyers, and his K9, Bear. "I've got nothing."

Granger approached the third vehicle. He reached for the vehicle's handle and nearly ripped the door off its hinges. Pulling the driver from behind the steering wheel, he planted the cartel soldier on the ground. "Where is she?"

Scarlett rushed to search the back of the third vehicle, lowering her weapon. "Granger... She's not here."

Chapter Eight

Her brain struggled to stay awake. She was so tired.

The vibration of an engine shook through her as Charlie stared up at the ceiling of the SUV. She'd tried replaying the moment everything had gone wrong, but it was just a waste of energy. Her attacker had won. In the end, she hadn't been strong enough.

Now Granger and Zeus were at risk.

Her father's life was in danger.

And she would be forced to do something terrible for the cartel.

Her frame bounced along the back seat of the vehicle, absorbing the uneven terrain. Every shift aggravated the pain in her body. The bruises were already pulsing. Her face most likely looked like a jar of spaghetti sauce. She could taste the blood at the back of her throat. And she had…nothing left.

Charlie twisted against the rope secured around her wrists. Seemed drug cartels knew better than to use zip ties. Too easily broken. The rope would take time for her to get through. Especially when she couldn't keep her eyes open.

After everything she'd fought to leave behind, the past refused to stay where it belonged. What had been the point of running? Memories she promised never to recall surged forward with the slightest effort. She didn't have the strength to stop them now.

That night had changed her life. And taken the lives of four others. She knew their names, had memorized their faces. She'd attended the funerals, out of sight, despite the risk of Homeland Security or her family learning she hadn't been caught in the explosion. She'd learned about the families they'd left behind and worked two separate jobs to send them money every month. It'd been the least she could do to help replace the income they'd lost after the attack. Though it could never be enough.

She'd seen Granger at every single one of the services to pay his respects, and his stoic grief had felt contagious and deep and uncomfortable. At times, she'd imagined that grief had been for her, and it'd taken years to convince herself that Sage was right. That she'd been foolish to believe he wanted her for anything more than a resource. His confidential informant. The nights they'd spent together—the secret rendezvous—had most likely been surveilled and authorized by Homeland Security, and she'd gone right along with it for the chance of having something for herself. Something nobody in her family knew about, something that made her more than a soldier.

I was in love with you too.

Had he really said that? It was hard to remember as the pain in her face and head peaked. The burning sensation in her calf told her the bleeding from the bullet had stopped but that she wouldn't get far if she managed to escape. Swirls of shapes danced behind her eyes. The kind that warned her she was about to fall asleep.

But she couldn't.

Because she believed him when Granger had said he'd

loved her. That he'd been searching for her. That he knew without a doubt she hadn't died in that explosion. He was out there, looking for her right now. Risking his and Zeus's lives for her in the middle of a forest fire. Not only against the people who took her but the terrorist army determined to bring down anyone associated with the US government. And she was just going to give up?

No. Granger deserved better than the woman who'd run at the slightest obstacle in their path all those years ago. She wasn't that person anymore. And she wasn't afraid.

"I'm going to be sick." Charlie fought against the momentum of the vehicle and coughed up the acid lodged in her throat onto the floor.

"Hey! I'm going to have to clean that up." Her abductor turned in his seat as she lost the contents in her stomach. The SUV's course deviated, and he jerked the wheel back in place.

She pulled at the rope around her hands to test the slack. Grainy fibers scratched at the thin skin there, but she managed to create space. Enough to slide one of the seat belt buckles between her wrists. If she pulled with enough force, there was a chance the metal could cut through the rope. "Stop the car. Please. I don't feel well."

Charlie started coughing again, ducking her head between the edge of the back seat and the rear of the front. Her abductor hit the brakes, and she had to plant her shoulder to keep from sliding to the floor. Only the SUV hadn't pulled to a complete stop.

Her abductor's swollen gaze moved to the rearview mirror. Blood crusted around his nose and face, and a small thread of victory charged through her. For as much damage as he'd done to her, she was pleased to see she'd gotten a couple shots in. The SUV lurched forward and exceeded its previous speed, as though he'd spotted something closing in. Or someone. "I recommend you swallow whatever comes up. We're not stopping."

For the first time, Charlie realized the interior of the SUV was darker than usual. No light coming from the instrument panel. Nothing ahead. They were driving without headlights. To make an escape. "Granger."

He was alive. He was coming for her.

The drugging effects of trauma dissipated slower than she wanted, but they were receding, second by second. Granger wouldn't be able to see the SUV as long as the headlights remained off.

If she wanted out of this in one piece, she'd have to earn his attention.

Charlie angled herself a few inches off the back seat. Her ribs screamed for relief, but she couldn't think about that right now. The rope caught against the empty seat buckle, and she pulled at it with everything she had left. Which wasn't much, but the threads were already coming apart. Holding her breath, she kept her gaze on the driver and tried again. Another bit of rope unraveled. At this rate, she'd secure the use of her hands after her abductor delivered her to the cartel.

She gritted through the pain flaring through her upper body. She could do this. She *had* to do this. For the sake of all those people who would pay the price if *Sangre por Sangre* won. Lightning struck behind her eyes as the last of the rope broke free. Feeling surged into her hands, and she took her first full breath since being hauled into the vehicle.

The driver wasn't going to stop. He wasn't going to slow down, but throwing herself from the vehicle was sure to finish the job he'd started back in those woods. She couldn't wait until they arrived wherever the hell they were going either, and the longer she thought it over, the less chance she'd have of escape.

This had to happen now.

Where Granger still might be able to get to her.

Charlie slowly brought her hands in front of her so as not to attract the driver's attention, keeping under his visual radar. Her breath shook through her as she considered the consequences of her next move. It was going to hurt. If she survived. Untwining the sections of rope from around her wrists, she reworked the longest piece between both hands.

And launched forward.

She hooked the rope around the driver's seat and over her abductor's head. He grabbed for the stranglehold she had on him, but Charlie used his own seat to protect herself. The fibers dug deep into his skin as gasps escaped. A part of his brain knew to keep one hand on the steering wheel while attempting to lighten the weight on his throat with the other. But his automatic need to leverage his weight into the seat floored the accelerator. They were speeding up. In complete darkness.

The rope cut into her hands. Just a few more seconds. She didn't want to kill him. She just needed him unconscious. Her abductor let his hand drop away from the steering wheel. The vehicle slowed without his constant pressure on the accelerator. He was losing consciousness.

Relief loosened the hold she had on the rope. It was going to work.

Her abductor pulled a blade. He sliced through the rope at his neck. His loud gasp punctured through the interior of the car.

Charlie fell back in the seat with nothing but two pieces of severed rope in her hand. The vehicle charged forward, pinning her to the seat, but she couldn't give up. She had to get out of here. She dove for the front seat.

The blade came up to meet her.

Hot steel sliced through her sweat-drenched shirt and across skin. Charlie fell into the passenger side door. She kicked at her abductor's wrist. The blade slammed against the opposite window with a crack. The window shattered, spewing tiny shards of glass into their seats. She kicked at him again. "Stop the car!"

But he wasn't listening. The driver blocked her next strike.

She went for the keys and knocked the steering wheel.

Shapes took form ahead through the windshield.

Rock formations.

They were driving straight into the side of a mountain.

"Look out!" Charlie grabbed for her seat belt and locked it in.

The driver's face lit up with panic.

Just before impact.

The SUV slammed into rock. The whole world turned upside down as the back of the vehicle vaulted upward. Charlie braced herself against the dashboard. Seconds seemed to turn into minutes as glass cut through the inside of the car.

The impact jolted through every cell in her body as the ceiling caved in. Metal screeched and ripped apart under the cutting edge of the rocks. The vehicle rolled. Once. Twice. The windshield cracked but held its own. Pain and nausea took control as the SUV jumped the formation and jerked downward into some kind of ravine. Gravity seemed to have lost its hold with each flip.

Until they weren't moving at all.

The SUV groaned as it settled. Charlie reached one hand out, looking for something to hold onto, but nothing seemed to be where it was supposed to be. The seat belt cut into her hips and shoulder, locking her in place upside down. She was conscious enough to realize she was still alive. That she'd survived, but the pain... Her body was trying to shut down to manage the trauma. Sooner or later, she wouldn't be able to fight it.

The smell of gas permeated her senses.

The fuel lines... They must have ruptured. She had to get out before any of the hot engine parts sparked a fire. Pressure built in her head as she reached for the seat belt latch. It released. She dropped shoulder-first onto the warped and torn metal ceiling with a cry. Tears burned in her eyes as she fixated on the passenger side window. It'd lost its shape in the crash. It wasn't big enough to crawl through. She'd have to find another way.

Charlie caught sight of the driver. Dead or unconscious, she didn't know, and she didn't want to find out. She forced her body between both front seats and clawed into the back. The cargo area had been saved. She could get out through there.

Every movement aggravated a deep pain she'd never experienced. Blinding and strong. But soon she'd made it to the cargo area. She tried the latch, but it wouldn't release.

Smoke filtered through the vents from the front of the vehicle.

She turned. Just as the SUV's engine caught fire.

GRANGER FLIPPED THE driver of the third SUV onto his back and took aim. "Where is she? Where is Charlie Acker?"

The soldier relaxed against the desert floor, laughing. "You'll never find her, *mercenario*. *Sangre por Sangre* owns her now."

"Like hell they do." Henry Acker fisted the driver's shirt and hauled the soldier up, slamming him against the car. "I'm going to give you three seconds to tell us where my daughter is, amigo, or you won't live to see the sunrise. Got it?"

"I'm willing to die for my cause," the cartel soldier said. "If you'd kept your end of our deal, you daughter wouldn't have to die for yours."

"What deal?" Granger closed the distance between them, both Socorro operatives and their K9s doing the same. The pieces were starting to fit together. Slower than he wanted, but sure all the same. "What the hell is he talking about, Acker?"

"Nothing." Contained anger slipped into Acker's eyes. "There is no deal. He's lying to stall us from getting to Charlie. That's his job. To slow us down."

"I don't have time for this. Scarlett, watch them." Granger shoved Acker away from the cartel soldier and confiscated the old man's weapon. He whistled for Zeus, and the dog targeted Henry Acker. The bull terrier latched onto the man's pants and dragged the patriarch to the ground. Zeus ripped and pulled back and forth.

"Get your damn dog off me!" Acker tried escaping the K9's hold, but it was no use. He kicked at the ground with both feet. Nothing but Granger's command would set the dog to release.

Scarlett and her Dobermans stood guard on the three drivers meant to distract them.

Granger stood over Acker as fear laced every aged line

in the man's face. Zeus could kill him if Granger deemed it appropriate, but right now, all he wanted was the truth. "Tell me about the deal you made with the cartel."

"There is no deal!" Acker struggled for freedom, but Granger wasn't finished with him yet. "I'll kill you for this, Morais. Every single one of you."

"And our little dogs too. I've heard it all before," he said. "Zeus, want to play your favorite game?"

The bull terrier's mouth curled into an excited smile as his tail started whipping back and forth. Zeus followed direct orders, launching his entire weight across Acker's torso. The old man's resulting groan for breath was enough to trigger an automatic inhale in Granger.

"Let's try that again, Acker." Granger crouched beside Charlie's father. "What deal did Acker's Army make with *Sangre por Sangre*?"

"Support. I agreed to supply them with manpower and weapons," Acker said.

"To do what?" The answer was already there, waiting for him to come to the realization himself. "You were going to attack the state capital building, weren't you? That's what was on those blueprints Charlie stole. All the notes you'd made. You and the cartel were going to raid the biggest government building in the state in an attempt to reestablish *Sangre por Sangre*'s cartel. That's what this is about. It's a power grab."

"No." Acker fought to breathe, but Zeus's massive weight wasn't going anywhere. "It's not the capital building they're interested in. That was just the first step."

"You put your daughter's life at risk for your own greed, Acker." The accusation burned hotter than the fire they'd just escaped. He pointed a hard finger into the man's chest.

"Whatever happens to her, that's on you, and I hope you live with that guilt for the rest of your life."

"Granger." Scarlett penetrated his peripheral vision.

"Not now." They were so close to answers. He and the rest of Socorro had run *Sangre por Sangre* into the ground. This was the final piece they needed to eradicate the cartel's influence for good.

"Granger, look." Scarlett's insistence was enough to break his focus on Acker.

He shoved to his feet. And caught sight of a fire in the distance. Instinct kicked him into action. What were the chances of two fires set in the middle of nowhere? His gut said whatever was going on had something to do with Charlie. That she was out there. That she was still alive. "Zeus, car."

The bull terrier released his prisoner and raced for the car. The K9's back feet slipped on the frame of the SUV, but he managed to get himself inside. Granger hauled Henry Acker to his feet and practically shoved him into the back of Scarlett's SUV. "You're staying here. I might've used Charlie in order to do my job all those years ago, same as you, but there's a difference between us. I'm the one who's trying to protect her now."

A flood of grief and shame replaced the anger that'd flared in the patriarch's expression, but Granger wasn't the person to offer anything comforting. This entire night had led to one goal: bringing Charlie home safe. "I'm going out there."

"You have no idea what you're going up against," Cash said.

"I'll be fine. There aren't enough of us to detain these drivers and keep Acker from doing something stupid." He dropped the magazine from his weapon with the touch of a button and counted the rounds left inside. Slamming the mag back into place, he holstered the sidearm on his hip. "Get what you can out of Acker. Tie him up if you have to. Stopping *Sangre por Sangre* from whatever they're planning is all that matters."

"Be careful out there." Scarlett stepped back, hugging her rifle to her vest. "We've got things covered. Just go do what you have to do."

Granger nodded goodbye and climbed into the driver's seat of his SUV. In seconds, he and Zeus were charging toward the glow of the fire. Because that worked out so well the first time.

The K9 whined from the front seat as Granger hyper focused on the fire less than a mile out.

He scrubbed his hand between Zeus's ears, but there was nothing he could do or say to neutralize the acidic worry in his stomach. "I know. We're going to find her. I promise. We're all she has left."

The thought of Charlie suffering alone had him bringing the SUV to its top speed. There was nothing but scrub brush, Joshua trees and dirt out here, but something had happened. Smoke filtered through his SUV's vents the closer he came to the fire. Only there was no visual sign of a source.

He carved the headlights along the rock formations guarding a drop on the other side. Chunks of metal and glass reflected back. Holy hell. Granger slammed his foot against the brake, nearly tipping Zeus into the front console. He shoved the vehicle into Park as dread pooled at the base of his spine. "No, no, no, no, no."

Granger shouldered free of the SUV, not bothering to close the driver's side door behind him, and ran for the wreckage. Glass crunched beneath his boots. The scent of gasoline filled his lungs. A single vehicle had rammed into the rock formation and tipped into the dried-up ravine. And now that car was on fire. "Charlie!"

She didn't answer.

Granger couldn't wait for his training to warn him about going into a deadly situation without knowing all the details. If she was down there, she had mere seconds to get out before the whole thing blew.

Flames crawled around the engine block and shot up into the sky. Fortunately, there was nothing out here to catch fire. Not like the woods around her childhood home. But an accelerated fire would explode if it reached the gas tank. Gravity pulled him down the incline to the bottom of the ravine.

Smoke had filled the interior and blocked out the windows. She was here. She had to be. Zeus's bark from the top of the hill echoed along the floor of the riverbed. The driver's side window had been pulverized, but there was no sign of a driver.

Granger checked each of the other windows, but it was too hard to see inside. The doors were stuck, too damaged from the accident. Unholstering his sidearm, he protected his face from the flames lashing out from the front of the vehicle. "Hold on, Charlie. Just hold on."

Granger slammed the butt of his weapon into the back driver's side window. The first strike merely cracked the glass. He tried again. The second shattered the protective layer, and a rush of smoke billowed into his face. "Charlie, are you in there?"

Black smoke cleared enough to give him a view of a single hand resting between the cargo area and the back seats of the SUV. Unmoving. Granger was already trying to rip the door off its hinges. The car refused to budge. "I'm coming for you. Hang on!"

He rounded to the back of the vehicle and brought the butt of his weapon up. There was a chance the glass windshield would slice through her clothing on impact, but Granger didn't have any other choice. He rammed the metal against the glass. Then again. And again. The glass was stronger here. Pain cut through his rib cage from the bullet graze, taking some of his strength. He was running out of time.

Zeus's incessant barking wouldn't let up. Every concerned sound notched Granger's nerves a level higher until he couldn't focus on anything but getting to Charlie.

He threw everything he had into the next strike.

The glass finally gave up the ghost.

Granger used the barrel of his weapon to knock the rest of the glass around the edge of the frame free and reached inside for the hatch. And pulled. The cargo door hydraulics kicked into gear, and he dove inside.

Dragging Charlie's lean body by both ankles, he hauled her over his shoulder and ran for the incline up to the rock formations. The bullet graze in his side threatened to rip wider, and a growl of pain escaped his throat. The fire was spreading along the SUV's frame. He had to move.

A hiss reached his ears.

A split second before the vehicle exploded.

Glass, metal and fire split in a thousand different directions. The pressure fanned out, and Granger was forced to dive for the side of the incline. He'd only made it half way to Zeus's position above. Right in the explosion's path. Curling around Charlie, he used his body as protection against incoming debris and fisted his hands into the dirt on either side of her head.

Heat fanned up the back of his legs and spine, but he wouldn't let any of it touch her. Ever. The fire seemed to suction back in on itself after another minute, and cool air filtered across his skin.

"Granger?" Her voice sounded so weak compared to the woman he'd found barricaded in her safe house.

Granger held the weight of his upper body away from her, staring down at the bloody damage she'd sustained fighting for her life. "It's okay. I've got you. You're safe."

She brought her hands up as the fire reflected off the glimmer of tears in her eyes. "The driver. He took me. He wants to use me to help the cartel. He wants me to do something awful. Tell me you have him."

Driver? Granger had checked the vehicle. "Charlie, there was no driver."

Chapter Nine

Her abductor had gotten away.

Charlie flinched away from the light shining in her eyes.

"Any headaches, nausea, vomiting, memory problems?" The physician cut the light to her other eye, looking for what, Charlie didn't know. Piel. That was her name. Dr. Piel. Socorro's on-call doctor. Though Charlie couldn't exactly remember coming to this place. The woman's gloved touch was gentle but probing around her broken nose and split lip.

"Would you judge me if I said yes to all of the above?" The pounding pain at the back of her eyes receded with the light, and Charlie was able to take in the room she'd woken up in. Crisp, clean walls and cabinets but comfortable-looking seating. The hospital bed itself didn't feel like the one she'd found herself in from time to time when her father's training had gone too far. Then again, the people of Vaughn relied on a single physician who lived within town and had committed himself to the cause. His idea of a recovery room was his teenage son's bedroom. A kid Charlie had beaten the crap out of more times than she could count while sparring. Not to mention that place didn't have anything close to a heart monitor or dimmable lighting. It was meant to be a way station. A temporary stop to make sure she hadn't sustained permanent damage. This place felt...good. Safe. Though she didn't know enough about Socorro or the people who worked here to come to that conclusion, she couldn't deny the sense of security she felt inside these walls.

"Not at all." The physician took a seat on a rolling stool. Long thin fingers made notes on a tablet resting in Dr. Piel's lap. Smooth black hair framed pristinely shaped eyebrows and almond-shaped eyes. The doctor was thin though Charlie couldn't ignore the way her arms filled out the sleeves of her white coat. A physician who worked for the top private military contractor in the country most likely knew how to hold her own in a fight. "I can definitively tell that you've sustained a concussion. Most likely from all the times you ran your face into someone's fist."

"Just couldn't seem to help myself." Though now Charlie was feeling the full effect of those punches. Effects from the car accident too. She tried to shift her weight to sit up straighter, but her hands, hips and legs weren't too interested in movement.

Dr. Piel smiled. "Don't worry. It isn't as severe as it feels. Concussions are something I see a lot of around here. If I was smart, I'd go back to school and shift my specialty to neurology for how many times operatives come in here with head injuries. You just need some rest. The smoke inhalation you suffered caused some lung irritation, but that should clear up in the next twenty-four hours, and as for the bullet graze on your leg, you'll survive. For now, I need you to stay awake. I'll be able to reset your nose when the swelling goes down in a couple hours."

That was when the fun would really start.

"I imagine it's nonstop around here, considering their

line of work." Charlie focused on the softness of the sheets rather than the fact her clothes had been taken from her.

"Pretty much." Dr. Piel rolled to a built-in desk on the other side of the room. "You'd think they'd learn their lesson, but they just keep coming back. Concussions, stab wounds, gunshot wounds. I've seen it all."

"What about Granger?" She shouldn't have asked, but the words had already slipped out, the haze of exhaustion throwing her common sense out the door. "Have you seen him for any of those?"

"That would be covered under doctor-patient confidentiality." Dr. Piel stood, her expression losing its humor from a minute ago. "But what I *can* tell you is that Granger and the rest have sustained a lot of wounds doing what they do. It's admirable really. How hard they fight for the people they care about and some they don't even know. I'm proud to be the one who helps them keep going."

Silence seeped between them as Charlie considered her words.

"Try to get some rest." The good doctor settled a hand on Charlie's shoulder in an attempt to offer some kind of comfort, but how was she supposed to come to terms with what she'd gone through just a few hours ago? "I'll bring you something for the pain and try to convince Granger he can wait a little longer before seeing you."

"He's out there?" A sliver of need charged through her.

"Has been this entire time." Dr. Piel turned her tablet toward Charlie to show her the screen. The doctor scrolled through what seemed like a thousand small blue message bubbles. "Keeps messaging me, asking how you're doing. Do you want to see him?"

"Yes. Please." Her emotions were starting to show. She

couldn't hide how much she needed Granger in the same room as her. To convince herself this was real. That she'd survived. That this wasn't some dream.

"I'll send him in." Dr. Piel gave her a knowing smile. Quick but warm. She headed for the door, pulling it open. "But I still want you to get some rest. No activities that take a lot of brain power. That means no TV, reading or general merriment in any shape or form. I'll be right back with that pain medication."

"Thank you." And before she was able to sit herself up in expectation of company, he was there.

Every bruise and laceration stood out under the overhead lighting. He looked battle-worn and on the verge of collapse, but Granger had waited outside her room until given the all clear to come in. He'd gone to war for her—up against her father's men and an entire cartel bent on using her for their own gain—and if he hadn't pulled her out of that SUV, she would've died. "Hi."

It was all she could manage in the moment, overtaken by the sheer sight of him. It'd been like that the moment they'd met. Having him here when she felt at her lowest was drugging and addictive and a relief.

"Hi." His voice weighed heavy with exhaustion, but Granger managed to close the distance between them. He angled himself onto the edge of the bed. "What's the diagnosis? Anything serious?"

"I'll live." Because going into detail was bound to send her into a tailspin if she wasn't careful, and Charlie didn't want to ruin this moment. She just wanted him. To feel something other than pain, to enjoy the fact they made it through one more day. Together. She brought her hand to his temple, where one of the soldiers from Acker's Army had clocked him. "How are you?"

"I'll live." His laugh rumbled down her hand and into her chest. Granger slid his calloused palm over her fingers, leaning into her touch. "Damn, you feel good."

"But I probably smell horrible." The scent of smoke and dirt and gasoline combined into a noxious odor on her skin and in her hair. He had to have sustained brain damage not to pick up on it.

"I don't mind." He turned his mouth into her hand and planted a kiss at her wrist. Right where the rope she'd been tied with had scratched her skin. "Nothing about you is as bad as Zeus's gas after one of his binge-eating episodes."

Her laugh caught her by surprise and aggravated the bone-deep pain running throughout her body. A piece of her wanted this moment to freeze. She wanted to pretend *Sangre por Sangre* hadn't almost killed her, threatened her father and might've had something to do with her sister's death. If it were up to her, she would ignore the pressure in her chest and stretch these precious life-affirming minutes out as long as she could. Because she deserved it. After a decade of isolating herself and looking over her shoulder, she just wanted a few minutes to remind herself she was human. But that wasn't how she was built. "Did your team find anything at the site of the crash?"

Granger lost the softness at the edges of his eyes. Threading his hand in hers, he dragged her hand into his lap. "Our logistics operative got Fire and Rescue out there to take care of the fire before it spread. Two other members of my team searched the area, but there was no sign of remains once the fire was out. Hard to tell with the rocky terrain, but it looks like whoever abducted you escaped."

"And they'll try again." She couldn't bury the shudder running from the top of her spine to her toes.

"Hey. You're safe here." Gravel seemed to coat every word out of his mouth. "I give you my word the cartel will never lay another hand on you."

"Except this isn't your fight, Granger." No matter how much she needed it to be. No matter how much she needed him at her side. "I came back to figure out who killed my sister. My father has plans to attack the state capitol, and a drug cartel wants to use me to put them back in power. None of this has anything to do with you. I'm the one who has to bring it to an end."

"Who the hell said you have to do it alone?" he asked.

She didn't have an answer for that. In truth, she'd simply taken it all upon herself. "You almost died out there in those woods. I just… I don't want to have to go through the process of losing you all over again."

It'd hurt too much the first time. She wasn't sure she could make it through again. If she could tolerate the isolation, the lies she would have to tell, the pain.

"I'm not going anywhere, Charlie." He stared down at their hands, intertwined. Ash and dirt and blood stained the fabric of his pants, and right then, Charlie understood it to be a perfect representation of their history. "You ran away from me once because you were afraid our relationship meant nothing to me. I'm not the kind of man who makes the same mistake twice."

He brought her hand to his mouth and kissed the thin scratched skin along the back. Warmth speared down her arm and tightened her insides. His next kiss was at her forearm. He moved closer, following the length of her arm with his mouth. The coarse hair along his jaw tickled her neck as he buried his face between her shoulder and jaw. And still he didn't stop.

Until he reached her mouth.

SHE TASTED JUST as he remembered. No. Even better.

It almost felt wrong to take advantage of her physical state right now, but the time without her—the past ten years, and the devastating hour during which she'd been taken—was about to destroy him. The only solution was this. This moment. This connection they'd lost themselves in once before. It'd been the only thing that'd grounded him the night of the Alamo pipeline explosion. That'd kept him from losing his mind, and he had the chance to feel that again. With her.

He couldn't fix what'd gone wrong in their lives. He wanted to. With every cell in his body, he wanted to make it so she wasn't in pain, so she didn't have this invisible target on her back. Maybe if he'd followed his gut and reached out the night of the attack, despite their agreement to keep their distance, he could've prevented all of this from happening. He could've protected her, and she wouldn't have gone through what she had tonight. She wouldn't have had to be alone these past ten years.

Instead, they were sharing a desperate kiss he couldn't seem to break. And she was kissing him back, pulling him deeper into an endless well of need he wasn't sure they'd ever be able to escape. Damn it, if he were being honest with himself, he didn't want to. Because this, right here, was his version of heaven. Free of fear, free of the weight of loss and loneliness. They deserved this. A small freedom from the terror that waited outside these walls, and suddenly, she was all there was, and Granger never wanted this moment to end, like so many others had.

They'd survived. Together. He'd lived despite every obstacle in their way. For this moment. For this woman. In this room, he no longer felt invincible as he had in the field, but very, very human. Alive. As though he'd just regained feeling that had been lost since the night she'd disappeared. Like he'd been waiting to breathe all this time.

Charlie speared battered hands through his hair, holding him in place, mirroring his need to hold her as close as possible. Her exhale shook through her, uncontrolled, caged. She broke the kiss and set her forehead against his. "I've missed you so much."

"I missed you too." Whatever happened after this didn't matter. Because this moment was perfect. It was theirs, and nothing in the world could take that from them. They weren't their pasts. The future didn't exist yet. He just needed to be here. "You have no idea how much."

Charlie bit down on her bottom lip then flinched against the pain of the split. "If you feel anything like I do right now, I think I might have some idea."

A throat cleared from near the door. "Perhaps you should wait before you start undressing each other." Ivy Bardot stood tall, chin parallel to the floor, as she waited for them to separate.

His chest felt as though it would break apart if he released his hold on Charlie. Granger peeled his hand from her arm, instantly aware of the empty sensation forging through him. He added a bit of distance between them but didn't bother removing himself from the bed. "You need me?"

"I wouldn't be interrupting your reunion if this weren't important." Socorro's founder didn't wait for an answer as she turned on her impossibly high heels and wrenched the door open before stepping into the hallway.

"I'll be right back." He needed Charlie to know that. That he wasn't going anywhere. That he would fight for her all over again. Granger pressed a kiss to her forehead. Though not for her reassurance. For his. Then he followed Ivy out. "I requested twenty-four hours off the clock. Last time I checked, I'm not on duty."

"Henry Acker isn't talking," Ivy said.

"He taught everyone in his backward army to hold up against interrogation. Charlie included." He nodded through the window looking into Charlie's recovery room. "From what I understand, he's damn good at it too. Stands to reason he'd use the same techniques in case of capture."

"Let me rephrase that." Ivy turned to face him, seemingly watching for every change in his expression, every unintentional tick. "Henry Acker won't talk to anyone but his daughter."

His gut hollowed as the events of the past twelve hours carved through his brain. "Charlie has been through hell because of that man. There's no way I'm going to make her face him after what she's gone through. He can sit in the interrogation room as long as it takes to get to him to open up. I'm not putting her recovery at risk."

"Is that really up to you?" Ivy cut her attention to the window, watching the woman on the other side. "You care about her, that much is clear. But Henry Acker knows details about *Sangre por Sangre*'s plans. There's a chance he's the only one who knows, and we need that information if we're going to carry out our mission here."

"You want me to use her to get to him." A sick feeling knotted in his gut as the past threatened to overtake the present. Charlie had just come back into his life. He couldn't risk losing her again. "I did that once, Ivy. I turned her into a CI who started working against the very people who'd raised her, and I lost her for ten years. How can you ask me to do that to her again?"

"I'm not asking *you*." Ivy kept her voice even. No emotion. Nothing but logic. "I'm asking her to the make the choice. The same choice you gave her all those years ago."

"I shouldn't have recruited her in the first place. If I hadn't, maybe none of this would be happening now," he said.

"Or maybe it would, and we wouldn't have a way to stop this attack. This game we're playing can't be won with what-ifs." Ivy crossed her arms. "I know what you're thinking, Granger. I know how important she is to you, but you have to remember what's at stake here. We have nothing but a set of charred blueprints of the state capitol with notes we can't decipher. Without Henry Acker's statement concerning the cartel's motives, we are operating blind. Everything we've done these past two years—everyone's lives that were lost in this fight to bring down the cartel—will be for nothing if we let *Sangre por Sangre* regain even an inch of ground. We've come so close, and I can't let us lose now. There's too much at risk. You have your orders."

Ivy's footsteps echoed off the black tile mazing through every square foot of this place.

"You mean our source inside the cartel is at risk." Granger didn't bother facing her. The click of her heels had stopped. He had never stood up to Socorro's founder before, but there was a piece of him that knew he could've protected Charlie better had he had the guts to stand up to his supervisory agent at Homeland. No one above him would sign off on labeling her as his CI. Too much of a risk. No matter how many times he'd tried to push the paperwork through, they denied him. So he'd done what he'd had to to convince her she was protected, that the government would have her back in case anything went sideways. He'd taken the risk on personally, knowing it wouldn't be enough. And in the end, he'd failed her. "That's what this is about for you, isn't it? Getting him out alive?"

Ivy didn't have an answer for that.

Granger turned, leaning against the window for support. His entire future seemed to balance on the edge of a blade. Tip one way and he and Charlie could make up the time they'd lost. Could start the life they'd always talked about together. Tip the other and his future with Socorro was secure. He'd continue his role as counterterrorism agent fighting the country's deadliest drug cartel and keep lives from being destroyed. But he couldn't have both. Not anymore.

"You didn't think I would do my own digging when I signed on with Socorro?" He'd done his homework on every operative under the Socorro umbrella. Cash and his determination to hide his brother's corruption from the DEA, Jocelyn and her drug addiction, Jones with his involvement in bringing down a state senator and Scarlett with her involvement in a military smuggling operation. He'd backed all of them up when they'd needed him, despite their dirty pasts and what had led them here, and now Socorro was going to make him choose between them and a woman he'd sworn to protect? Hell no.

"I know who your inside source is, Ivy. I know what he means to you, and that the only reason you're fighting this hard for closure is to get him out from under *Sangre por Sangre*'s control." Tendrils of resentment twisted in his chest.

"I would consider the next words out of your mouth very

carefully, Morais." The investigator she'd once been—the one who refused to stop despite direct orders from her superiors, the concerns of her partner and the cost of her family—shifted back into place. "Because the only reason we knew about the cartel's interest in Charlie Acker is because of that source. Do you really want to put his life at risk for a woman who cost you your job with Homeland Security?"

She was right. If Socorro hadn't gotten to Charlie first, based off that intel, she'd be dead right now. He had no doubt about that. The fight drained out of him. Whether due to exhaustion or logic, Granger didn't know. He didn't care. He just wanted to protect the one thing in this world that made him feel needed. Human. "No. I want to know if you would be willing to ask the same thing of him that you're asking of Charlie."

"I already have, Granger." A softness he wasn't accustomed to seeing bled into Ivy's eyes. As though she'd expected a fight and was relieved they hadn't crossed that line. "The minute we realized *Sangre por Sangre* was a threat the Pentagon couldn't ignore, he chose the greater good over a future with me. And I let him. Because I knew a lot of innocent people would die if I didn't."

Socorro's founder walked away.

Chapter Ten

She could still taste him on her lips.

That perfect combination of peppermint toothpaste and something she could only describe as Granger. Citrus and earth battling for dominance and grounding. Her mouth tingled from the aftereffects, and Charlie couldn't help but press her fingers to the sensitive skin to hold onto that feeling a little bit longer.

Stinging pain erupted instead. She memorized the bruising shapes and scrapes along the backs of her hands, knowing where every single laceration and injury had originated. Her abductor felt as close to her in this room as he had in those woods despite her isolation, and Charlie knew deep down the scar of her survival would stay with her forever.

It'd been like that after the Alamo pipeline explosion. Her guilt, the physical pain, the grief of losing Sage had stuck with her until it'd gotten hard to breathe at times. But now she had something to help her fight back, to keep her grounded in the here and now. She hadn't even let herself cry for Erin yet. There just…hadn't been time.

The hospital room door swung open, centering Granger beneath the frame. Where he'd charged in earlier to be with her, he seemed sunken now. In his slow approach, in the way he didn't meet her gaze.

Tension bled into her shoulders. "Something happened. What is it?"

She wasn't sure she could handle anymore. All she'd wanted to do was figure out exactly what'd happened to Erin, and they were nowhere closer to attaining that answer. Instead, she'd uncovered a plot on the state capitol, the involvement of a drug cartel and suffered through an abduction. Then again, if she'd learned one thing from her childhood, it would be that anything worthwhile was worth standing your ground for. And giving Erin justice was worthwhile.

"We have your father in custody," Granger said. "Along with three cartel members."

Air caught in her throat. Very few things could surprise her anymore, and yet Granger stood there as though the arrest of Henry Acker didn't call for some kind of celebration. This was what they'd wanted, what they'd worked for. Understanding bled through the haze of pain and ibuprofen. Though was a private military contractor allowed to arrest terrorists? Or did they have to call in the feds to take over? Either way, Henry Acker wouldn't talk. Not until it benefited him at least. "I take it from the fact you're not saying that with a smile that he's made conditions Socorro isn't willing to meet."

He rounded the end of the bed, keeping his distance, and collapsed into a chair on the other side of the room. Mere minutes ago, he'd brought the past back with a single kiss. Now it felt as though he wasn't allowing himself to come close. What had changed since then? "We're private military contractors. We have no authority to arrest him. Even if we did, we don't have any physical evidence linking him to what happened to you, your sister's death or any attacks he's suspected of carrying out."

"You have me." Didn't he understand that? A sliver of panic worked to get the best of her, to undermine every second she'd stood up to her father. Henry Acker wasn't the kind of man to take an arrest lightly. Socorro would be added to his list of grievances and would be a continuous target of Acker's Army from here on out, and now he knew of her involvement with them. What did that mean for her? Erin had been held against her will all these years, never able to leave for fear their father would make her pay. What punishment awaited for the daughter who'd managed to escape? "My account of that night. My testimony or statement or whatever you want to call it. I wrote it all down."

"You ran, Charlie. You convinced the US government you died in that attack. Anything you say now against Henry Acker won't be considered in court, and I don't work for Homeland Security anymore to back you up." An invisible hand seemed to choke his voice. "Everything that happened the night of the Alamo pipeline ten years ago can't be used against him. No prosecutor will touch the case if you're involved, and we have nothing to hand over to the local authorities."

No. That wasn't how this was supposed to work. They'd had a plan. They were going to make her father pay for what he'd done. For the death of her oldest sister and the innocent lives of those four other bystanders. But she'd run. She'd given into her fear that no matter which path she took—to return to Vaughn or return to Granger—she'd be the one to suffer. And so she'd made her own choice. She'd wasted so much time being scared, and now Henry Acker would never answer for the nightmares that haunted her each night.

Acceptance never came easy. Not for her. But she had to fix this. She had to make this right. "Socorro wants to know about the deal my father made with *Sangre por Sangre* and what the cartel is planning to do. My guess is he isn't talking. What are his conditions?"

Granger leaned forward, bracing his elbows against his knees. "He'll only talk to you."

"Right." She didn't know what to say to that, what to think. Confronting her father face-to-face—without the threat of his soldiers or her sisters as a buffer, without an escape plan in mind—went against everything she believed. Henry Acker was a dangerous man to many. But more specifically to the people he claimed to care about. "Where is he being held?"

"In one of our interrogation rooms on the first floor." Granger shoved to stand despite the injuries he'd sustained fighting for their lives. Warmth skirted up her arm as he secured his hand in hers. "I asked you to get intel on your father and his organization once, and it was a mistake. I made you believe all I cared about was bringing him down, that I was sleeping with you only because you could help me secure an arrest. I can't ask you to go through that again."

"You mean sleep with you? I mean, it wasn't all that bad. There were a couple times I had to fake it, but who doesn't when they're focused on impressing a handsome federal agent instead of the actual experience?" Her attempt to lighten the mood pulled one corner of his mouth upward. Charlie squeezed his hand, taking in the battered skin over his knuckles and the blisters along his forearm. Blisters like the ones that'd left scars on her forearms.

Her stomach dropped at the realization she'd come close to losing the only person who'd ever given her permission to be herself. Not the soldier her father had reared. Not a fugitive on the run. Just…her. "Granger, the whole reason I agreed to be your CI was to stop my father from doing something terrible. I still believe in that cause. I just lost sight of it for a while, but these past couple days have reminded me of what's at stake if I keep running. And I don't want to keep being the kind of person who had a chance to save lives and chose to look the other way."

"You're not that person." Granger crouched beside the bed, leveling his gaze with hers.

"I was. All those years of hiding, of pretending I was dead. I could've done something. Maybe then those families would've gotten the closure they deserve instead of being constantly reminded their loved ones aren't there to celebrate birthdays, and Christmases and anniversaries with them." Charlie pulled her hand from his and threw back the covers. The sight of her bruised legs gave her pause, but she'd reached the tipping point. The victims of her father's attacks deserved better than monthly cash payments as a sorry excuse for an apology. They deserved justice, and she was going to give it to them. No matter what it cost her. Because living with this feeling of corruption and defectiveness wasn't a way to live. And she couldn't take the weight of surviving anymore. "They're still wondering what happened. Because of me."

"What are you doing?" Granger shot from his crouch by the bed and rounded to the other side. Strong hands held onto her as she tried setting her weight on her own two feet. A headache reared its ugly head while the bullet graze in her calf threatened to rip her balance from her, but she held onto him. "You're in no shape to talk to him now."

"We don't have a choice." She braced herself against him with one hand and grabbed for a pair of scrubs Dr. Piel had left for her to change into from the side table. "If *Sangre por Sangre* is planning something with my father's help, we need that information now. Not after it's too late."

She raised her gaze to his, a ridiculous amount of height between the two of them, but while Granger was trained and honed for the single purpose of accomplishing his mission, he didn't intimidate her. Quite the opposite. He was the anchor to keep her from getting lost in the storm. Charlie fought the bone-deep pain in her side, raising one hand to his face. The coarse hair along his jaw pricked at her skin and elicited a reaction from her nervous system. The bruising along his temple had darkened significantly, but there didn't seem to be any permanent damage. She could do this. She could do anything with him as her partner. Hadn't they already proven that? They were always better together. "I know how to make my father talk. I need you to trust me."

A hint of acceptance softened the corners of his eyes. "All right. What do you need from me?"

"Can you just…hold me up while I try to get dressed?" She leaned into him—physically, mentally, emotionally—as they worked together to replace the hospital gown with a fresh set of scrubs. Charlie tried to brush her hair out of her face, suddenly conscious of the fact she hadn't undressed in front of a man for ten years. "Was that as painful for you as it was for me?"

His laugh escaped as a short bark. "You have no idea."

She couldn't stop her responding smile. Only it didn't last. "I've been so focused on coming home, Erin's death and just not dying, I didn't think to ask if…this mess is keeping you from whomever you have waiting at home." Nervous energy charged through her. She had no right to ask about his personal life. She'd given that up ten years ago when she'd cut herself off from him, but the words were there all the same. Tainted with hope and a little bit of desperation. "Though I'm hoping the kiss earlier was a good indication. If not, I hope she kills you and hides the body so not even Zeus can find it."

Granger stared down at her, his hands on both her hips. Whether to keep her balanced or because he felt the same overwhelming need for physical contact that she did, Charlie didn't know. "I'm not involved with anyone."

"Were you?" She couldn't force herself to look at him, to expose the answer she needed to hear, but it was cycling through her, out of control. "Ten years is a long time. I would understand if moving on with your life meant moving on with someone else. Forgetting about me."

"I tried to forget about you. Several times with several different women." Granger slipped his index finger beneath her chin, nudging her to look up at him. Her insides unraveled under his study. "But I'm only going to say this once, Charlie."

Her brain latched onto every shift of his expression, ready to disengage at a moment's notice. To protect herself from the rejection and the hurt.

"Nobody wanted to date me," he said. "Because I was still in love with you."

HE HELD ONTO her as they navigated through the oversized maze of the building.

"Black tile, black walls." Charlie managed one slow step

at a time. Brain injury had the ability to drop a person without provocation, not to mention a bullet to the calf, and he wasn't willing to push her harder than necessary to talk to the son of a bitch who'd given up his daughters for a chance to show his patriotism. "This entire building is ready for a funeral."

"Easier to clean up the blood we track in," he said.

Her smile told him she wasn't convinced, but there was a hint of truth to his answer. Socorro operatives charged into situations and engaged with threats that the US government couldn't or wouldn't risk anyone else for. That level of freedom and training came with costs. Mostly physical. Sometimes psychological.

They approached the elevator, and he hit the call button to take them down to the first floor. The shiny doors reflected their images. Her at his side, him ready to give his last breath for her. It was easy to imagine the years rolling by, of them as partners rather than resources for one another. The only one missing was Zeus. And he'd most likely gotten into another package of cookies while Granger paced the recovery wing. "You never told me what you've been doing while you were on the run. I'm guessing Charlie Acker hasn't been your name for a long time."

The doors parted, and Granger helped her into the car.

"No. It wasn't." She stared at the LED lights indicating the floor. "Living off the grid isn't as romantic as it sounds. The night of the Alamo pipeline explosion, I went back to Vaughn. I got the money I'd been saving for years between jobs around town and the cash you'd given me for intel—nearly ten thousand dollars—and I took off in one of the neighbor's cars."

The elevator dropped, and Granger's stomach shot higher

in his torso. "I remember. The neighbor reported it stolen. I found that car outside of Boulder City, Nevada, two days later. Wiped clean. Couldn't prove you'd been the one to take it though."

"What good is all this survival information in my head unless I use it?" She pressed her temple to his arm as the descending numbers on the LED screen lit up. "I spent the first few years stockpiling safe houses. Food, water, money, weapons, ammunition. I moved from place to place and switched up my car every time I stopped. Sooner than I expected, I ran out of money. I had to start working. Just here and there. Nothing permanent, and nothing that required a background check."

"I take it you're well-versed in breakfast foods then." The elevator pinged with their arrival, and the doors parted. He helped her over the threshold onto the first floor, doing everything in his power not to look at the spot where he'd nearly bled out from the gunshot wound three weeks ago. His shoulder was still sore, but putting eyes on where it'd happened intensified the pain. Granger didn't come down to this level, and if he did, he was sure to take the stairs on the other side of the building. His shoulder seemed to sense his proximity to the garage, as it had two days ago. Trauma was a given in his line of work, but ignoring the aftereffects would tear him apart from the inside if he let it.

"I might be. Maybe one of these days, you'll find out." Charlie's voice faded the longer he directed his attention to holding back the memories. "Granger?"

He rolled his shoulder back to counter the ache spreading down his arm. Damn it, his fingers were tingling. Going numb. He'd managed to keep himself in check since retreating back to Socorro by focusing on Charlie's needs, but his brain wasn't going to let him replace one gunfight with another and have him walk away unscathed. "Is that what you dug up at your safehouse the other day? Another cache you'd hidden?"

The attempt to focus himself failed.

Charlie centered herself in his vision. Brown eyes locked on him and refused to let him go. She followed him as he tried to turn away. "Granger, look at me. What's going on?"

"It's nothing." He shook his head, as though the simple action could erase the pressure building in his head. "The interrogation room is this way."

"I'm not going anywhere until you tell me what just happened." With one hand latched onto his arm, she hit the elevator call button just as the doors closed. "That asshole in Vaughn hit you pretty hard. Are you dizzy, nauseous? Dr. Piel said you guys come in here all the time with head injuries. She should take a look."

His pulse pounded hard behind his ears. Too hard. He closed his eyes, at the mercy of his own mind. The last place he wanted to be. "Keep talking. I just…need to focus on something else."

"Okay." Charlie slid one hand along his shoulder as the elevator doors tried to close on them, and the pain seemed to recede with her touch. Which he knew was impossible. Physical contact didn't change the sensitivity of pain receptors, but her touch was the distraction he needed. "Do you remember the night we met? How I almost shot you for walking onto my father's property uninvited? I was in the backyard skinning the jackrabbits I'd shot that day. My rifle was right there, yet you walked straight up to me with your hands up. I was ready to pull the trigger, but you said the one thing that convinced me to put down the rifle."

He gritted through the crushing loss of control determined to get the best of him. "I asked if you wanted some strawberry ice cream."

"It sounded so ridiculous." She smoothed circles into the back of his shoulder. Right where he needed her. "You told me you'd stopped into a diner on the way to Vaughn and ordered a strawberry shake, but they'd accidentally given you two. And you offered me one. Handed it to me and everything, and all I could think to myself was it was a good thing you'd come to me, because anyone else would've shot a stranger dead on the spot so late at night. Little did I know you'd been watching me for weeks by then."

The pressure in his head was draining with every word from her sweet mouth. Keeping him in the here and now, tethering him to reality. He wasn't back in the garage. He wasn't the only one standing between his fellow operatives and the *Sangre por Sangre* cartel. Charlie was there too. "I knew you liked strawberry milkshakes."

"They're still my favorite. Though I wasn't able to find anything that compared to the one you gave me that night. Then again, maybe it wasn't the shake I remember the most." Charlie's fingers dipped under the collar of his shirt, smoothing her fingers directly against the rise of scar tissue on the back of his left shoulder. Right where the bullet had been surgically removed. "Dr. Piel said that Socorro operatives have a dangerous job. I asked if you'd been to see for her anything other than a head injury in the past. She refused to tell me, but I'm guessing this isn't a scar from when you had the chicken pox as a kid."

Her other hand fanned the front of his collarbone, and Granger couldn't help but straighten. He grabbed for her hand, afraid of what she'd find beneath his shirt. "Charlie."

She slipped her hand out of his, using only her fingertips to study the healing wound, and suddenly it felt like she was the one holding him up. Her inhale hissed in his ear. "Smaller in the front, bigger in the back. Long distance. Fresh. No more than a few weeks old from the pliability of the surrounding tissue. But the exit wound feels...surgical. Not like a normal gunshot wound. Dr. Piel was able to remove the bullet?"

"Most of it," he said.

Charlie pressed herself into his arms, searching the floor. What she saw or what she expected to see, he didn't know. "You were shot. Here?"

He could breathe now. Odd. Memories from the past took longer for him to recover from, but there was something about Charlie—the way she seemed to center him and unbalance him all at the same time—that cut through the fear following him everywhere he went. "In the garage. I bled out here. We were under attack. I was the only one keeping them from penetrating the upper floors."

"Sangre por Sangre." Setting her forehead against his jaw, she held onto him. "Why don't you want me to see it?"

"Because then you'll finally see what kind of man I am." His mouth dried. "That I wasn't strong enough to protect you ten years ago, and that I might not be strong enough to shield you from what's coming now."

Charlie pulled back. The overhead lights were much brighter here, accentuating the bruise patterns, cuts and blood across her beautiful skin. Her broken nose. She pressed her finger over his heart. "I know exactly what kind of man you are, Granger Morais. You're the kind of man who runs into a fight that isn't yours to begin with. You have a hard time trusting people, but once you do, that trust lasts a lifetime, even when the person on the receiving end doesn't deserve it. You're committed and reliable and the only person who has ever considered what's best for me instead of exerting your power over me like everyone else. And nothing—not a bullet wound or any other injuries—is going to convince me you aren't the man I want at my side for what comes next. Your dog can come too. I'm sure we can bring snacks or—"

Granger crushed his mouth to hers. The last of his uncertainty fled, and he fed off the strength she'd lent him. He had survived the past three weeks on a mixture of adrenaline and duty, and for the first time since he'd come out of Dr. Piel's operating suite, he was beginning to feel whole. Duty wouldn't keep him moving forward. He had to have a hand in his own future. One of his own design. It was up to him. "Have you been practicing that speech?"

"Maybe a little." She smiled, kissing him again. Charlie intertwined her fingers with his, and it was as though they hadn't missed a step in the past ten years. "I have a few speeches on hand. Most of them are rewritten arguments I've had with my sisters, so I'm the one who wins."

Granger caught sight of Ivy at the end of the corridor. Waiting. "You got one of those for your father?"

She angled away from him, and her smile fell. This was it. What the past decade of her living on the run and faking her death had built to: giving those she'd hurt the justice they deserved. And Granger couldn't help but admire her strength. "No, but I'm sure I'll think of something along the way."

Chapter Eleven

Charlie didn't look back as she slipped through the door to the interrogation room. The man inside looked up at her, as though he'd expected Socorro to play into his hands all along. Knowing her father, his love of strategy and his ability to manipulate even the most seasoned preppers, she was probably right. "Dad."

"You came." His white-gray hair seemed to glow under the reflection of the overhead lights, aging him ten years if she didn't know any better. The lines spidering away from his eyes and mouth seemed deeper than even twenty-four hours ago, and she couldn't help but note the tension in his hands as he pulled against the cuffs securing him to a solid metal ring embedded in the table.

"Did I have any other choice?" Charlie forced herself to take a step forward, all too aware of the pressure of Granger's attention from the other side of the one-way glass. And he wasn't alone.

The interrogation room was exactly as she'd imagined. Though the ones she'd seen in her binge of movies and television she'd never been allowed to watch growing up came across grimier than this. If she'd stuck around after the attack at the pipeline, she might've gotten to see one herself.

Though Granger had told her he didn't actually have the authority to hold her father on charges, she couldn't help but wonder what would happen to him after their conversation. Would they let her father go back to Vaughn? Or would Socorro hold him indefinitely in the interest of public safety?

She pulled out the chair opposite her father and took a seat, unable to think of the last time they'd been alone together. Not as one of his soldiers waiting for their next mission assignment. As father and daughter. Charlie locked her jaw against the pain flaring in her legs and torso. The bruises on her hands were darker now. Impossible to ignore. "That woman, Ivy, said you wouldn't talk to anyone but me."

"I don't trust them." He set his cuffed wrists against the table, the metallic scratch of stainless steel on steel louder than expected.

"But you trust me?" she asked.

Henry Acker shut down any hint of what was going on in his head, pulling away from the table. His hands disappeared into his lap, the chain between the cuffs pulling tight. "I know they're listening. Watching us from the other side of the glass. Recording us too."

He nodded toward the camera installed in the corner of the room. The red light beneath the lens said he was right. She stared into the glass, unafraid of exposure now. It was a bittersweet feeling, contradictory to the way she'd lived her life these past ten years. There wasn't any more fear. Because she had a promise from a former counterterrorism agent that nothing would hurt her again, and she believed him.

"They want to know about the deal you made with *Sangre por Sangre*. And after fighting against a cartel member for my life, so do I." Because all of this—Erin's death, her own abduction, nearly losing Granger in that fire—could all be linked back to the man sitting across from her. Running hadn't changed anything. He was still the father who kept his emotional distance and favored punishment and duty over the stability she'd needed all her life. And she'd been a fool to think anything would change when faced with the consequences of his choices.

"I can't tell you about that," he said. "Not yet."

"Of course not. Because everything needs to be on your terms, doesn't it? What time I woke up and went to sleep, what I ate, how many hours I spent shooting, how I spent my free time, who I talked to, who I was allowed to date." She couldn't hold back the humorless laugh as the anger burned. Charlie stretched her interlaced hands across the table and shoved to her feet. Though not without a shot of pain in her calf. "Can you blame me for running when I had a shot at freedom?"

"It was for your own good." He notched that proud chin of his higher. Every ounce the man who'd molded her into exactly what he wanted her to be. "Everything I did, I did to protect you. To make sure you could protect yourself when the fight came to Vaughn."

"What fight, Dad? The people you hate so much haven't stepped foot in Vaughn since the night of mom's death. And from where I'm standing, you've brought this mess to your own door by making a deal with a drug cartel." She couldn't be in this room anymore. Not with him. Not ever again. "I can't believe I even came in here expecting a real conversation with you. You've never seen me as anything more than something to control. Me, Sage and Erin. We weren't your daughters. We were tools to be used for your own agenda, nothing more, and that makes you a real son of a bitch."

She turned to leave. For the last time.

"I couldn't lose you too." His voice warbled from behind. So unlike the man she'd feared growing up. "I couldn't lose any of you. You and your sisters."

Charlie had almost made it to the door with every intention of stepping through it and telling Socorro's founder to do whatever she saw fit with her father. But something in the way his voice crumbled held her still. "What are you talking about?"

"After your mother... I couldn't stand the thought of losing you the way I lost her." He flattened his palms on the table, staring down at them as though he didn't recognize his own hands. "I needed you to be stronger than she was."

A knot twisted in Charlie's gut. "Stronger how?"

"Your mother wasn't killed by police officers searching for a fugitive. I know what I told you girls, but she wasn't keeping them from searching the house. There was no struggle that led to her getting shot. She *left*, Charlie," he said. "She abandoned us."

What? She countered her retreat as a simmering heat spread under her skin, and her father seemed to melt right in his chair. "You're lying. You said we had to stay vigilant. That Acker's Army would protect our family and friends from a government that didn't care about who it hurt to get what it wanted. I believed you. For a long time, I believed you."

His voice barely reached over the thud of her pulse behind her ears. "I lied. To you and Sage and Erin."

A hot combination of fear and uncertainty urged her to leave, to put everything about the past few minutes behind her, but the thought of fear running her life a second longer held her in place. Bringing her hand to her mouth, she tried to stop the surge of acid as her entire life came apart. "Her headstone is in the backyard of your property. We had a funeral."

"You're right. I had it made when I realized she wasn't coming back. I just couldn't tell you girls the truth. I didn't want you to have to face the fact she left you behind." Her father tried to push away from the table, but the cuffs protested. "Before you were old enough to remember, I lost my job, then our house, our savings and everything else we owned. We had nowhere else to go. Vaughn seemed like a place to start over. Do things differently. But your mother was miserable from the moment we stepped foot in that house. She begged me to leave, but we couldn't go back. Every day I dug my heels in, the heavier her expression got. Until I didn't recognize her anymore. By the time I realized what I'd done, it was too late. She was gone. She'd packed her things and left in the middle of the night. Suddenly, I had three girls asking me where their mother was, and I didn't have any answers. I couldn't give you three answers."

Charlie didn't know what to believe. Everything she'd known about her father—why she'd been forced to adhere to his rules and commands, why she'd had to learn to protect herself—was a lie. "You could've told us the truth. We could've handled it. Instead, you raised us to believe our own government was responsible for killing our mother. You turned us into extremists willing to participate in your delusions. You lied to us about keeping the rest of our family safe. And for what, Dad? Why would you put us through all of that? Why would you carry out those attacks if you didn't really believe in what you were fighting for?"

"I did believe, damn it." The words were ground out through clenched teeth. He'd lost control, and for the first time in…ever, Charlie got a glimpse of a man who might be as human as she was. "My job, our house, our savings—all of it was taken by this government, Charlie. They laid off thousands during the economic crash. They took everything from us, and I couldn't let it go. I was bitter and angry and afraid we'd never recover." Her father sat back in his chair, trying to get his breathing level. "The night your mother left, we fought. She told me that at some point I had to stop being a victim. I had to step up and be a man and take care of my family. So that's what I did."

Charlie stood a bit straighter. Not really sure what to say to that, how to respond to the first hint of fear from a man who didn't seem to be scared of anything.

"That singular focus was the only sense of purpose I had." Her father's voice grew stronger. "We were forced to move to Vaughn out of desperation, but I did what was best for my family. I taught myself how to grow vegetables, preserve the harvest, how to shoot, hunt, survive the wilderness, if need be. I stockpiled supplies, weapons and ammunition to defend what little we had. The local church helped keep our bellies full, and I made sure to serve anywhere in the community I could for extra help. People appreciated it. Started seeking me out for advice on how to support their own families. That advice spread, and within a few years of us arriving, Vaughn had become a stronghold against the outside world. One I wasn't willing to risk losing. So yes, I recruited fighters willing to protect what was ours, and I built my girls to be stronger than their mother—stronger than me—and look at you now."

His rant had ended, leaving Charlie empty and cold and more confused than when she'd walked into this room.

"Yeah. Look at me now. Look at Sage and Erin." She

didn't know whether to believe him or not. Or if he was manipulating her to get what he wanted from her again. "Those little girls you promised to protect? We didn't want to be soldiers or answer to a general. We just wanted our father. To know that he loved us, and you failed. They're *dead*, Dad. Because of you. And I'm next unless you tell me about the deal you made with *Sangre por Sangre*."

"Don't you dare try to put Sage's death on me, Charlie Grace Acker. Had you followed through with your mission, she would still be alive, but you got involved with that federal agent out there and ran. Like a coward." Henry Acker pulled his shoulders back, sinking into his chair. Calm. Collected. "As for what happened to Erin, you don't have to worry about that. I've already taken care of it."

GRANGER WAS AT the door before Charlie could manage to pull it open.

Every cell in his body honed in on the despair in her eyes and wanted to assure her that anything out of Henry Acker's mouth couldn't be trusted. "Tell me what's going through your head."

She let the door close behind her, folding her arms across her chest. The motion set off a flinch in her expression. Whatever Dr. Piel had given her to counteract the pain was wearing thin. "I don't know what to think. My entire life my father told me one version of events, and now... I don't know what to believe. Except that I'm hungry."

"I can help with that." Granger pulled her into his arms, ready to be anything she needed in that moment. Support, a chef, someone to work through Acker's motives with. "I think Jocelyn just added some lasagna to the fridge. That is if Zeus hasn't already gotten to it. He's like Garfield the cat, except he doesn't know when he's full."

"Do you have any insight into *Sangre por Sangre*'s plan to attack the state capitol, or how they'll try to regain their standing?" Ivy Bardot had a job to do, and she wasn't wasting anytime in doing it, despite the obvious exhaustion in Charlie's face. "Anything actionable we can use?"

Granger tightened his hold on Charlie. She could only take so much before she crashed from what'd happened over the past couple days. She was running on empty with demands coming from every angle, and a second interrogation sure as hell wasn't going to make things any better.

"No, but I'm fairly positive he didn't have anything to do with Erin's death. The man who took me from Vaughn. He said something about my sister not fighting back as much as I had. My father is many things, but with what he's told me about his reasons for building Acker's Army, it's hard to imagine he would do anything to hurt the family he was so scared of losing." Charlie hugged herself, swaying on her feet. "Something is keeping him from telling us about the deal he made with the cartel. I'm not sure what it is, but you heard him. My father isn't the kind of man to take anything lying down. He's not afraid to stand up for what he believes or fight against a bigger and stronger opponent if it means keeping what he has. My guess? *Sangre por Sangre* is holding something over his head to ensure his cooperation and support."

"We know of three attacks that could potentially be linked to Henry Acker. He's thorough and strategic and, according to his history, has every reason to want *Sangre por Sangre* to succeed." Ivy stared into the interrogation room from behind the one-way glass. "What could a man like him possibly fear losing?"

Charlie's shoulders raised on a strong inhale. "I think he's afraid of losing me. When I mentioned that Sage and Erin were dead, and that I'm next, he reacted."

"I didn't see anything." Granger studied the man on the other side of the glass, looking for something—anything— that would give him an idea of what was coming.

"When you grow up in a culture of being prepared at all times and where mistakes are more deadly than the words you say, you learn to predict and read people's emotions in the smallest ways. You wouldn't have seen it, but the muscles on the left side of his jaw flexed. He was biting down," she said.

"Let's say you're right." Ivy faced them. "*Sangre por Sangre* can destroy your father with something in their possession, and they're using it to force his compliance. Maybe it's proof he and his army are involved in attacks like the Alamo pipeline. What kind of support would your father be able to provide to the cartel?"

"Weapons. Manpower. Supplies." Exhaustion played out in Charlie's eyes, to the point Granger wasn't sure how much longer she would be able to stand. She was pushing herself, driving harder than she needed, because this was how she believed she could make up for her mistakes. The truth was she couldn't. Not really. The five lives that'd been taken the night of the pipeline attack were gone. And they were never coming back. Even if they managed to prove Henry Acker was at fault—that Charlie was just a pawn in his game—that guilt wouldn't go away. She wouldn't let it. "But explosives are his specialty. He's been stealing them from construction sites across the state for years. Primarily C4. Sometimes dynamite. Nothing that could alert the ATF or tie back to him."

"That was why Homeland Security was never able to pinpoint where the C4 used in the Alamo pipeline attack came from." Granger should've known, but without alerts raised from those construction sites, he and the rest of his team had been operating blind. "That's how Acker kept under the radar."

Charlie set her hand against his forearm. "I'm sorry. I wanted to tell you, but…"

"You were the one tasked with getting your hands on the explosives." Hell. Did Henry Acker have no shame? Using his own daughter to commit felonies had kept him out of a federal prison, but at what cost? "If I had any proof of your involvement in the attack on the Alamo pipeline, not just that your blood was found at the scene, I would be forced to arrest you. You would be sentenced to federal prison for the rest of your life. Without parole."

A hint of fear etched into Charlie's features.

"Which is still a possibility, Ms. Acker. But considering your cooperation with this investigation, I'm sure I can put in a good word with Homeland Security when this is all over. Until then we'll assume *Sangre por Sangre* is in the market for explosives, which means their resources are still dwindling. That could work for us." Ivy Bardot brought their attention back to her. Time was running out. Whatever the cartel planned depended on Henry Acker, and without the support of Acker's Army, *Sangre por Sangre* might jump the gun. "I want eyes on the entire town of Vaughn. Acker might be stuck here, but that doesn't mean his subordinates aren't carrying out his orders as we speak. I'll send two operatives to keep us up-to-date. What about the blueprints you recovered from Acker's office?"

Granger's mind was already working through the snippets of handwriting he'd read on the thin paper in Henry Acker's office. He took out his phone and hit the photos app, bringing up the overhead view of Henry Acker's desk. "I got a clear photo of the notes, but they're unreadable. I don't know what the hell kind of language it's written is, but I've never seen it before."

He centered his phone between the three of them.

"It's a code." Ivy backed away, apparently not willing to waste her time trying to decipher it right then and there. "I've seen it before, years ago, but this one has been altered. My partner and I were assigned to a case of a young woman found murdered out in the middle of the desert, and this code was carved into her back. We weren't able to decipher its meaning before another woman was killed. We had a suspect that turned out to have a connection with an up-and-coming drug cartel called *Sangre por Sangre*. It was our first interaction with them."

"You think whoever made these notes might be involved in your original case?" Granger couldn't convince himself this was nothing more than a coincidence. "Did you make an arrest?"

"We were closing in, but the suspect escaped," Ivy said. "My partner at the time determined it was unlikely he'd resurface as long as the FBI was on the hunt."

"So he went undercover in the cartel to find the killer. He's your source inside *Sangre por Sangre*, the one who gave us the heads up on the cartel's interest in Charlie." Socorro's founder's past was beginning to make sense, despite her determination to shut everyone out and focus on the one goal they could control. "And given he's still there, I take it your partner hasn't found what he's looking for."

"Not yet." Ivy slipped her hands into her slacks, seemingly at ease, but Granger knew better.

There was an added tension at the corner of the woman's mouth, and he realized Charlie had been right. Learning to read people's masking behavior under pressure took time and a skill he hadn't been aware he'd picked up around his superior.

"What about the code? Were you able to decipher its meaning?" A brightness Granger hadn't expected entered Charlie's voice. As though this was the lead they'd been waiting for.

"Yes. In the end, our analysts were able to determine the three-letter key that unlocked the entire phrase," Ivy said. "Unfortunately, it was too late to save another woman from turning up dead."

"Scarlett is good at this kind of stuff. She might be able to narrow down the key and get us the answers we need." Granger had already sent the blueprints to Socorro's security consultant, but the last time he'd checked in, she hadn't been able to give him an update. "What were the three letters used in your case to unlock the phrase?"

"B, A and P." Ivy cut her attention back to Henry Acker, who'd slowly gotten to his feet. He was trying to get out of his cuffs. "The letters themselves didn't produce anything significant, but there was a reason the killer chose them. We were just never able to determine his motive."

"There's another option," Charlie said. "We recovered the blueprints from my father's office, but the notes aren't written in his handwriting. If we're right that *Sangre por Sangre* is using my father and Acker's Army in their plan, it means he should be able to read those notes. We can just ask him."

"The problem is your father isn't talking." Granger couldn't stand the thought of her going back in there to face the fact Acker had lied to Charlie her entire life. And given her exhaustion and injuries, she couldn't physically interrogate Henry Acker again. "He's shut down every attempt we've made to get the cartel's plan."

Movement caught Granger's attention through the one-way glass, where Henry Acker was currently bending over the table toward his hands. The man reached into his mouth and withdrew a thin rectangular piece of metal. "He's got a blade!"

Granger maneuvered around Charlie, pulling her out of his way as he charged into the interrogation room. Henry Acker smiled as he brought the blade to his neck and pressed it through the skin of his neck. "Stop them."

Granger bolted across the table, but it was too late.

Henry Acker fell against the table as his wound pumped blood onto the floor.

Chapter Twelve

The blood was still pooled on the floor.

Charlie couldn't make herself look away. "I don't understand. He was...sitting right there. This doesn't make sense."

"It happened so fast." Granger's voice had lost its sense of control. "I tried to stop him. I'm so sorry, Charlie. I don't know how it happened."

She knew. She'd watched the whole thing as though the recording of her life had somehow caught in the VCR she'd grown up with and froze on the single frame of her father ending his life. And she'd just stood there. Unable to move or stop him. In that single moment, her father had ignored the mountain of muscle coming right at him, and he'd looked straight at her.

Stop them.

All this time, all these years, she'd known Henry Acker as a man of conviction. One who'd never given in to threats from law enforcement, who'd never stood down from a fight or showed an ounce of weakness. What had changed?

Dr. Piel zipped the body bag closed over her father's face as two other Socorro operatives wheeled the remains out on the stretcher. Because that was what he was now. The monster of a man she'd feared would swallow her up and systematically destroy her was nothing but a shell now. Sympathy smoothed the physician's expression as Dr. Piel followed the team out of the interrogation room. "Charlie, I'm very sorry for your loss."

"Thank you." A heaviness she couldn't describe closed in around her. A disconnect between her body and her brain. The events of the past three days were starting to compound. How much more was she expected to take? And why couldn't she look away from the blood on the floor? "I just…don't understand."

"Unfortunately, that's not uncommon. Family and friends rarely have answers when something like this occurs, but I'm happy to request his medical records if that will help." The doctor bounced her gaze to Granger and back. "What's important is that you take care of yourself right now. You're injured and running on fumes."

"I don't care." The tears were back, and she hated them. She hated that she still felt something for the man who'd turned her into…whatever it was he wanted her to be. She hated that he still had this control over her, that he could get her to grieve for him. And she hated that he'd taken his deal with the people who'd abducted her into that body bag with him.

"Charlie." Granger placed a supportive hand under her elbow. "Dr. Piel's right. You look like you're about to collapse. You need some sleep and a few thousand calories to help you recover."

"I don't want to sleep, and I don't want to eat. I want to know what he meant by what he said." She turned all that building anger onto the man who deserved it the least. It flooded through her, out of control. Her heart rate spiked. She couldn't breathe, couldn't think. The only thought in her mind was that last image of Henry Acker holding a razor blade to his neck. Over and over. She'd fed off her drive to stay one step ahead of her father for the past ten years, and now he just got to leave? That didn't seem fair. "Stop them. What the hell is that supposed to mean, Granger? I have spent my entire life following his commands and cleaning up his messes. And now I'm just expected to…what? Take down an entire cartel at his suggestion?"

A rush of dizziness threatened to take her down. Charlie stumbled back into the wall. Low voices warbled in and out as Granger and Dr. Piel reached for her. Her legs gave out, and she collapsed. There were others closing in on her. Too close. "He wasn't supposed to die."

"She's likely dehydrated. We need to get her to my exam room for an IV. Now." Dr. Piel shoved to stand as strong arms threaded behind Charlie's shoulders and along the backs of her knees. "Let's go."

"I've got you, Charlie. It's going to be okay." Granger held onto her, and she couldn't help but want to bury herself in his strength. Walls and overhead lights blurred as he somehow managed to run with her weight at a full sprint. No matter the threat or the injury, he refused to back down, and she needed that right now. She needed his innate belief that the things they'd sacrificed could actually make the world a better place, because she was losing her grip. "We're going to get through this."

Her body hurt. She was tired. She didn't want to do this anymore. Every decision that'd led her to this point had been to get justice for the lives Henry Acker had ruined, but there was no justice to be had anymore. There was nothing she could do to give them closure. Except to make sure her father's deal with *Sangre por Sangre* never saw the light of day. "Put me down."

Her voice barely carried over the pound of her own pulse. Charlie held onto consciousness by a single thread as exhaustion pulled at her muscles and brain. Time seemed to slip by. Second by second, minute by minute, and she had no control over it. Her head ached, and she couldn't fight against the pull as her body tried to give up its fight.

Dr. Piel rushed ahead. "In here."

Maneuvering her headfirst through the door, Granger angled her down onto the examination table. Bright lights bleached Charlie's vision a split second before Granger centered himself over the source. "The doctor's just going to give you a saline drip. You're dehydrated and exhausted. You've got to give your body some time to recover."

"No." That single word slurred in her own ears. She tried to peel herself off the table, but Granger's hand held her in place. "I can't stay here."

Confusion deepened the three distinct lines between his brows. "Charlie, you can barely stand on your own."

"I don't care. I have to leave. Please let me leave." She fisted his shirt to haul herself upright.

"Granger, I need you to hold her still, or I'm going to puncture something I'm not supposed to." Dr. Piel moved in close. Stinging pain pricked at the soft skin of Charlie's inner elbow.

Her fight-or-flight kicked in. She ripped her arm back, tearing free of whatever the doctor had stabbed her with. Momentum forced her to overcorrect. The exam room blurred, and she hit the floor on the other side of the table. Adrenaline surged hot and fast. It replaced the pain spiking along her calf, and she managed to get to her feet.

"Charlie." Granger moved to intercept her, but the doctor held a hand against his chest.

"Don't, Granger. Give her space. She's not thinking clearly," Dr. Piel said. "Charlie, why do you need to leave?"

A massive migraine spread from the base of her skull. Charlie dared a step forward. Then another. She was capable of ordering her limbs to follow her commands, but something didn't feel right. A numbness had taken hold. Not just in her body, but her mind. Using the end of the exam table to steady herself, Charlie took in the concern etched into Granger's face. "Because my father was right. I'm the only one who can stop *Sangre por Sangre*."

"I told you before. You're not in this alone. I know it feels that way, but it's not true." He raised his hands out in front of him, as though approaching a wild animal, and maybe he was right to do so. Maybe Granger should think about himself first for once. "Every operative in this place will do whatever it takes to make sure the cartel never regains power. Especially me."

He wasn't going to let her go. That was clear now, and the tears burned down her face. Walking away from him had been the hardest decision she'd ever made in her life. Not becoming his CI. Not choosing to betray her father and everything he believed in. But leaving Granger behind. Because she'd been in love with him. Was still in love with him.

She wasn't sure why it'd taken her so long to realize that was the reason she'd survived her abduction. Something deep inside of her had wanted what they'd had back enough to fight for her life when the chances of surviving were the lowest. It'd been the possibility of being in his orbit that had driven her to attack the driver of a vehicle exceeding sixty miles an hour in the middle of the desert with no concern for the consequences. All she'd wanted these past ten years was to feel him again, to know she wasn't alone.

And she had to save that.

Because the longer he sided with her in this battle, the higher chance she'd lose him all over again. They'd come too close to death. He wouldn't survive the next time. She felt that truth in through the numbness, deep down into her bones.

So she had to hurt him. She had to make him see the truth. That there wouldn't be a future for them as long as she kept running. Was that what her father had been trying to tell her?

Charlie spotted an array of surgical tools on a rolling cart a few feet away. She darted for the scalpel, and both Granger and Dr. Piel backed up. There was only one way out of this, and damn it, he was going to force her to use it. She recalled the turns they'd taken to get to this room despite the fog working to shut down her cognitive function. She had to go. Now. "Let me leave, Granger."

"Why?" Understanding seemed to hit, and his expression crumbled right in front of her. Granger lowered his hands, facing off with her as he had the night they'd met. "Why are you doing this? After everything we've been through together, why can't you trust me?"

Her hand shook around the scalpel. Four words formed in her mind, and it took everything in her power to force them out. "That's the first lesson they teach you in Acker's Army, Agent Morais. I don't trust anyone."

Charlie rounded the end of the exam table and headed for the door. Without so much as a glance backward, she ran.

GRANGER STARED AFTER HER.

"I can alert Scarlett. She can use the security system to

shut down the building." Dr. Piel lunged for the phone at the desk shoved into the corner of the exam room. Raising the handset to her ear, she hit one of the buttons. "Charlie isn't going to make it far. She's—"

A tearing Granger had become all too familiar with clawed through his chest. It had nothing to do with the shrapnel in his shoulder and everything to do with the woman who'd left him behind. Again. "Let her go."

"We can stop her." Dr. Piel turned to face him. "She needs medical attention. If she doesn't get fluids, she might experience seizures, swelling in her brain and possibly lapse into a coma."

"Hang up the phone. Alerting security won't do any good." Granger headed for the door. "It doesn't matter how far she gets. We can't keep her here against her will."

"You survived a forest fire to find her," Dr. Piel said. "You risked your own life to pull her out of that burning vehicle. She just watched her father kill himself. She's obviously not in her right mind, and you're just going to let her go out there alone? *Sangre por Sangre* will find her, Granger. Doesn't that concern you?"

Granger didn't bother turning back. He'd spent years trying to locate a woman who didn't want to be found. And damn it, he was tired of the chase. He had a job to do: stop *Sangre por Sangre* from regaining their broken power. "Charlie made her choice."

Working through the maze of Socorro's headquarters, he made it to his bedroom and shoved inside. Zeus bounced off the bed and approached the door. Waiting. "She's not coming."

Granger unlocked the gun safe, pulling a weapon from inside. Acker's Army had taken his preferred sidearm, and there was a chance he was never going to get it back. He grabbed a few more pieces of gear and ammunition, including his Kevlar vest, and rammed it into one of the duffel bags he pulled from under the bed. The zipper scratched at the scabs along the back of his hand, tearing a hardened chunk of skin free. Blood dripped down his wrist, but he didn't have the patience to bandage the wound.

Sangre por Sangre had attempted to build an underground headquarters on twenty-two acres of land owned by one of its lieutenants, now long dead. There wasn't much of the building left after one of Socorro's operatives had literally torn the place down searching for the woman he loved after her abduction, but Granger couldn't think of a more fitting safe house for the few remaining members of the cartel. Off the grid, decommissioned and too dangerous to occupy.

He'd start there.

A trail of dust cut across his window. Granger straightened, watching as one of Socorro's SUV's sped across the New Mexican landscape, heading east. The entire team was grounded from assignments until the details of Henry Acker's death could be related to the local police. Which meant the driver was Charlie.

Granger shouldered his gear.

The bull terrier didn't seem to get the message Charlie wasn't going to walk through that door and grace Zeus with her presence. "Come on. We've got an assignment."

The K9 didn't budge.

"Zeus." The call came out harsher than Granger meant it to, and the dog turned on him with a whine. His heart—finally starting to piece itself back together these past few days—fractured at the sight of Zeus's sadness. He slipped the duffel strap off and let the bag hit the floor, lowering himself to the K9's level. "I know. I'm going to miss her too."

Granger allowed himself this moment of peace. Of him and Zeus hurting for the same loss. In a matter of days, Charlie had slipped back into his life and upended his world all over again. He didn't know how, and hell, it didn't really matter. Because there was no going back. "Come on, bud. We've got some cartel members to sit on."

But the truth was, he just felt tired. And watching Charlie leave hurt more than the bullet shard in his shoulder, except this one had gone straight through his heart. He was bloody knuckled, battered and bruised. Because of her. Because of his need to keep her in a life she never intended to stay in. It seemed no matter what choice he made or how he tried to make up for failing Charlie in the past, he would always be second best.

To her need for freedom.

Her need for justice.

And her need to prove herself as an individual rather than a soldier.

Granger collected his bag and headed for the door. Only to be stopped by the journal sitting on the edge of his bed. Erin Acker's journal. Charlie had broken into her father's house for it, risked her life for it. It didn't seem right to leave it here. He slipped it into one of the side pockets of his duffel and hit the hallway with Zeus on his heels. He took the stairs, uninterested in becoming another victim to the dark images and pressure in his head waiting to ambush him on the first floor. He mentally worked through the layout of *Sangre por Sangre*'s battered headquarters as he entered Socorro's garage.

To find Ivy Bardot standing in front of his SUV.

Understanding hit. "You gave her the keys and let her leave." Granger should've known. All this time, he'd wondered if his superior allowed herself to consider anything but the mission. Now he had his answer.

Socorro's founder didn't bother denying it. "You know as well as I do she's the key to the cartel's entire plan. There's something about her that *Sangre por Sangre* wants, and we need to know what that something is."

"So you gave her an SUV and sent her on her way." Son of a bitch. Ivy was going to use Charlie as bait. "You want her to lead us straight to the cartel."

"Wouldn't you have done the same in my position?" she asked.

Rage exploded through his chest and shot up his throat. Granger closed the distance between them as the last of his control slipped away. "I would've taken one look at her and realized she isn't ready for the fight she's walking into."

Ivy stared up at him, so damn calm. She wasn't the least bit intimidated by a man twice her size. She knew as well as he did she could put him on his ass faster than he could process the threat, and she wasn't afraid to prove it at the slightest provocation. "And yet you didn't stop her when she ran from Dr. Piel's exam room."

The accusation neutralized the fire in his veins, but it wasn't strong enough to quiet the concern pushing him to act. He wasn't strong enough. Charlie was gunning for a fight she wouldn't win alone, and there was nothing he could do to convince her otherwise. The night of the Alamo pipeline attack, he'd felt useless. Wondering where he'd gone wrong and how he could've changed the course of events. Losing his job at Homeland Security as a consequence of defying orders to let Charlie loose as his CI had only shored up that crack in his confidence.

This was worse.

She'd been right there, within reach, and he'd somehow lost her all over again. Granger tightened his hold on his gear. "You brought me into Socorro because I know the way terrorist organizations and the members inside them work. *Sangre por Sangre* might not fit the bill exactly, but they're desperate. This is their last stand, and I'm not going to let them use her like so many people have before. Like I have. So you can get out of my way or get in the vehicle, Ivy. Either way, I'm taking the fight to the people who started this. Maybe then Charlie will finally feel she's earned her freedom, and she can stop running."

"All right." Red hair escaped the tight bun at the back of Ivy's head, something Granger had never seen before in all the years he'd operated at Socorro. The former FBI agent had tried so hard to keep her hands on the reins, but something had happened. She was slipping. "But there's something you need to know before you charge straight at the cartel and start a war."

Ivy handed off her phone. "The coded notes on the blueprints. We weren't able to identify the owner of the handwriting, but Scarlett was able to decipher the notes a few minutes ago."

"How did she find the key so fast?" He read through the translated sentences. He took in times, dates and directions that didn't make any sense.

"It was easy after I explained there was a killer who'd used this code before he disappeared off our radar within *Sangre por Sangre*," Ivy said. "She took a chance on thinking of it like a calling card."

"He used the same key for both codes?" he asked.

"No. This code has been altered. There are only a few characters left from the original code. It's very sophisticated. Something that would've taken years to create." Ivy took a step into him. "But it did require a three-letter key. Just like the first. Scarlett believed it could be a set of initials."

The notes seemed to indicate a schedule of some kind. But for what? Or who? Henry Acker's name came to mind, but there was no way the general of Acker's Army would be able to waltz into the state capitol building with his face plastered all over federal databases. "Whose?"

"It was Charlie's, Granger," Ivy said.

Granger didn't understand. He pried his attention from the phone. "CGA. Charlie Grace Acker. Why would he use her initials to decrypt notes meant for Henry Acker? As a threat? To keep Acker from forgetting what was on the line?"

"We don't believe he did." The hardness in her voice

Acid surged up his throat as the pieces of Ivy's theory stitched together in the silence between them. "Tell me you're not saying what I think you're saying."

"There's a reason you couldn't find her for those ten years, Granger. Think about it." Ivy's gaze refused to let him go. "You approached Charlie in an effort to gather inside intelligence on Acker's Army. You recruited her to undermine and dismantle her father's organization with the promise to get her and her sisters out from under his control. But Sage and Erin are dead, and she blames him for their deaths. She's hurting. She's angry, and there's no way she can destroy him on her own. What better way to get back at him than by fighting fire with fire?"

"This is insane." Granger maneuvered around Ivy and

headed for his vehicle. "Charlie isn't working with *Sangre por Sangre*. They tried to abduct her. They nearly killed her."

"Unless it was a failed extraction. She survived, Granger. Against all odds. How do you explain that?" Ivy latched onto his arm to get him to stop, and he turned on her.

"Sheer will." He tossed his bag into the back seat and let Zeus climb inside. "She was raised to fight, Ivy. It's all she knows."

"You're right. Fighting is all she knows, except now she has no one to fight. So what do you think is going to happen next?" Ivy asked. "She refused medical care and ran, Granger. Why?"

He didn't have an answer for that.

"You have to move past your feelings and see the truth." Socorro's founder was waiting for him to see reason, but he couldn't. Not when it came to Charlie. "That code we decrypted tells me Charlie Acker is the one calling the shots. And whatever she's planning, she knows we're coming."

Chapter Thirteen

This was the only way to end the bloodshed.

Charlie had no idea if she was in the right place, but *Sangre por Sangre*'s dilapidated headquarters had made headlines over the past two years. There had to be something here that would help make sense of this mess.

She angled the SUV Ivy Bardot had let her take alongside what remained of a parking garage. Boulders of cement and rebar blocked any kind of entrance, but Charlie had snuck into her fair share of construction sites over the years. She knew what to avoid, how to spot a building's vulnerabilities and the general design of structures like this. Her head pounded as she stepped free of the vehicle.

Cool night air mingled with the sweat in her hair. She'd chugged three bottles of water and a couple of ibuprofen from the back cargo area to counter dehydration, but there was no guarantee her self-medicating would do any good. But tucking herself away in Socorro's fortress only delayed the inevitable, and she was tired of hiding. Of pretending she'd made the right choice by running ten years ago. Charlie took that first step toward the building, one of the flashlights she'd found in the back in one hand. She couldn't ignore the sick feeling in her gut that all of this—Erin's death, her father's suicide, the cartel's plan for her—wasn't as it seemed.

She needed the truth.

Hesitation wormed through her veins as she approached a hole where the cement hadn't closed off a section of the underground parking garage. The flashlight beam skimmed over hard cracked earth, not revealing much other than snake holes and ant mounds. No signs anyone else was here. Or that she was walking into an ambush. She'd watched the site from the broken chain-link fence surrounding the property. If the cartel was still working out of this location, they'd somehow masked their vehicles, their footprints and their perimeter security.

"It's now or never." Charlie angled the flashlight toward the largest break in the debris. Her body ached as she climbed through the mouth and into the belly of the expansive building. Darkness spread out in front of her as the structure seemed to groan. Dust fell from the ceiling and slipped beneath the scrubs she was still wearing. This was a bad idea, but it was her only option. To get the truth about Erin. To protect Granger.

Drops of water pattered somewhere inside the collapsed section of garage and echoed off the walls, and her skin suddenly seemed too tight for her body. A vehicle had crumpled beneath the weight of the ceiling coming down off to her left, and Charlie couldn't help but think one wrong move would deliver her the same fate. The sharp odor of fire and mold collected at the back of her throat. Parking garages didn't usually stand alone. There had to be an entrance in the main building.

Debris caught on the toe of her boot. She lost her balance for a moment and cut the flashlight across the room.

There. A corridor of some kind held its own against the weight of the collapsing structure. Charlie headed straight for it. "Here goes nothing."

Water seeped from the ceiling. Flooding must've occurred upstairs. That explained the cloying scent of mold. Shards of cement flaked off as she ran her fingers against the wall. She followed the hallway to a T, swinging the flashlight from left to right. If the cartel was here, they could come and get her. Finish this. "Hello?"

Her voice seemed to echo on forever, and she suddenly found herself colder than a moment before. There was no way for her to search this entire building alone. Not without getting lost or injured in the process. Her vision swam, and she realized she'd been holding her breath for the past few seconds. She'd made her choice. She'd left Granger and the rest of the Socorro team behind in a twisted attempt to protect them, but the truth was she couldn't even protect herself.

Not really. She'd expended massive amounts of energy trying to hide from the world, isolating herself, moving from one location to the next in an attempt to grant herself one more day of freedom. But it hadn't done a damn bit of good. Because now she was alone. She'd burned the bridges that had sustained her through the past ten years, and no one was coming to fight for her.

Not even the one man she'd trusted to do the job. Granger had slid back into her life as effortlessly as he had the first time. With promises of protection and concern and respect. He'd been intense—more so than her father—in all the right ways, and had given her something she'd never been granted before: choice. He saw the things she'd tried hiding from her family and the people she'd been raised around, even those she'd tried to hide from herself. Was that what had pressed him to approach her all those years ago and offer her an escape? Had he seen that somewhere deep down she'd never believed in her father's war, that she just wanted to experience the world outside of Vaughn for herself? Somehow, he'd come to know her better than anyone, and Charlie realized, standing in the basement of a crumbling building, surrounded by the putrid stench of death and destruction, she'd never really wanted to be alone after all. She'd just been waiting for him.

Because she was still in love with Granger. Recklessly, ridiculously and resolutely in love with the counterterrorism agent who'd gifted her more than an escape plan ten years ago. He'd given her strength and purpose and trust. Something far more valuable than the inside intel she'd handed over as his confidential informant.

And she'd thrown all of it away out of fear.

Just as she was doing now.

Granger prided himself on never making the same mistake twice. Why was it she couldn't learn from hers?

Charlie directed her attention to the left and followed the corridor as far as it would take her. The power was off, casting her into darkness aside from her flashlight, and it felt as though the walls were slowly closing in. Which was impossible. Her mind was playing tricks on her. Making her feel as though she were being watched. Like the floor was moving.

There was nothing here, and if there was, she wasn't sure she wanted to stick around to find it. She backed out the way she'd come.

She'd made a mistake coming here. She saw that now. Charlie picked up the pace, trying to remember the turns she'd taken. There were so many, just as there had been in the Socorro headquarters. The hallways weren't meant to make the building easier to navigate. They'd been designed to keep people in, and she felt as though she'd stepped into a prison of her own free will.

Panic clawed at the edges of her mind. Her bones ached, the muscles in her legs had tightened to the point they were pulling on the tendons in the backs of her heels. She couldn't see save for a few feet in front of her, and Charlie could've sworn the shadows up ahead had moved.

She was delirious. Most likely from dehydration and a head injury and the emotions that came from watching her father take his own life right in front of her. It'd all caught up with her, despite her determination to keep running. To never feel as though she couldn't win.

"Let me out of here!" Her own voice echoed back to her as she turned another corner. They all looked the same. Had she come this way? Why the hell hadn't she brought crumbs to mark the way out? Charlie misidentified a corner up ahead. Her shoulder slammed right into it, jarring her back into the moment. Cement crumbled in her hand as she pushed away from the wall. "I want out."

The building moaned as though it'd heard her pleas and mocked them back to her.

She wanted nothing more in that moment than the assurance of her partner and his obese dog. For Granger to tell her they were going to get out of this together. There hadn't been a single moment in the past three days she'd felt as empty and lonely as she did now. She'd always had her sisters or her father or the entire town of Vaughn on her side, even the counterterrorism agent who'd used her for nothing but information. But now? Now she truly had lost everything and everyone she'd convinced herself she could live without. And found she didn't want to. She didn't want to be alone anymore. She didn't want her freedom if it meant isolation. She wanted Granger and Zeus and even Ivy Bardot to have her back. She wanted to be the one the families of her victims could look at and forgive. She wanted a life. "Can anyone hear me? Hello?"

"I hear you," a voice said from the darkness.

Charlie recognized that voice. Though she'd hoped she'd never have to hear it again. She raised the flashlight, but there was no one there. It'd been so clear. So close. Swinging the beam to her left, she followed the corridor. Had her brain played another trick on her? Had she really become so desperate, it'd supplied something for her to focus on? No. It'd been real. "You know why I'm here. I want this to stop."

Her hand shook as she glanced back over her shoulder. The atmosphere had shifted. No longer cold and dark and damp, sweat built under her arms and at the back of her neck.

"That's not for you to decide, Charlie." The words filtered in from the right, but they couldn't have. Nothing but a wall faced her. He was playing games with her. "We're all just following orders here, even you."

"I don't give a damn about your orders." Charlie stopped dead as the corridor opened into a wide alcove. The floor was bare, but her flashlight beam picked up stains of brown spreading out from epicenters. Five, maybe six, in total. Blood. "So you can stop playing your mind games and tell me what the hell the cartel wants me for."

A whisper of an exhale brushed against the back of her neck. "But we were just beginning to have some fun."

Charlie turned, flashlight raised to defend herself.

Pain shot across her face, and the world went black.

Granger floored the accelerator.

The GPS in Charlie's SUV hadn't moved in the past thirty minutes. She'd headed straight for the abandoned *Sangre por Sangre* headquarters, feeding into the doubts Ivy wanted him to have. But Granger knew her. He knew her better than anyone on his team. "Give me an update."

The sound of Zeus's collar registered from the back seat as though the K9 was waiting for an answer too.

"The GPS hasn't budged." Ivy pressed another bullet into the magazine in her lap. Uneven landscape threatened to tip the ammunition and her weapon to the floor, but she'd done this thousands of times in a thousand different scenarios. She slammed the magazine into the base of her weapon and holstered it alongside her rib cage. "It doesn't mean she's still there, but we'll cross that bridge when we get to—wait. The signal just cut out."

"The cartel must've figured out the SUV is one of ours." Granger had never known Ivy to join any of her operatives in the field, but with the final stage of eliminating *Sangre por Sangre*, the agent had apparently taken it upon herself to see the job through. "She'll be there. And I'll prove she's not the one behind this."

"You're letting your emotions for Charlie get in the way of your assignment, Granger." Ivy kept her attention out the windshield, completely devoid of personality when faced with whatever waited for them at the end of this field trip. "You need to be prepared for the worst-case scenario."

"You're right. I *am* emotional, especially when it comes to her." Granger did what he did best: keeping his voice even while every cell in his body threatened to break apart. "It was my emotions that led me to take a chance on Henry Acker's daughter and turn her into a confidential informant.

Without Charlie, Homeland Security never would've gotten the intel about the Alamo pipeline attack and dozens more people might've been injured or killed in the process. It was also my emotions for her that kept me from turning into someone I didn't recognize after I lost my position with the government. She's the one I had on my mind when I heard about a private military contractor looking for operatives, and the one I thought about when I found Scarlett at the wrong end of a knife on that base four years ago. I let Charlie down when she needed me the most, and I promised I would never fail anyone else again. So yeah, I'm letting my emotions for her get in the way of my job. Because she's the reason I fight for people in the first place."

Ivy didn't respond to that and turned her gaze out the passenger side window.

"I know you believe our emotions shouldn't have priority when we're in the field, Ivy, and that policy might've worked for you to some extent when you were with the FBI," he said. "But if we're going to dismantle *Sangre por Sangre* for good, we can't be like them. We have to keep the parts of us that make us human, that make us better."

They drove the rest of the miles in silence.

Granger rolled up to the barbed chain-link fence standing as a warning to those who entered and surveyed the property. *Sangre por Sangre*'s headquarters had been built at the bottom of a manmade crater, a protective layer meant to mask the structure from satellite imagery and keep the cartel off law enforcement's visual radar. He could barely make out the curve of the roof from this distance, but something in his gut told him Charlie was still inside.

She was the key to this whole puzzle, and no matter what Ivy or the rest of his team believed, or how determined

Charlie had been to undermine her father's army, she'd never put anyone's life at risk to achieve that goal. The pain of her past mistakes wouldn't let her, and Granger loved her for that. Loved every fiber of her stubborn, perfectionist, passionate being. He was pretty sure he'd never stopped loving her, but these past three days had driven that reality to a point he couldn't shove it down anymore.

Because when it came right down to it, she would sacrifice herself to save someone else. How many operatives on his team would do that for the strangers they tried to protect? Charlie fought for what she believed in, but more importantly, she was afraid of being as corrupt as Henry Acker, and there wasn't a single cell in his body that could believe her responsible for this mess. Whatever was going on, she was just as much a victim as the innocent lives taken the night of the Alamo pipeline attack.

He loved Charlie, and he would do whatever it took to give her the future she deserved. One with him and a fat bull terrier at her side. If she would have him.

Granger let the SUV crawl forward, every instinct he owned on high alert. The south side of the building came into the windshield's frame, and his gut clenched. "This place is on its last legs. If Charlie's in there, she doesn't have long before the whole structure comes down on top of her."

"Then we better get moving." Ivy hit the dirt, using her door panel as cover until they cleared the path leading down into the manmade dust bowl.

Unholstering his weapon, Granger followed her lead as they skidded down the incline. Large chunks of debris and metal scattered across the eighth of mile between the edge of the crater and the building itself. A minefield perfect for an ambush. Except the closer they got to the building, the chances of a surprise attack decreased. "Cash sure made a mess of this place."

And Granger couldn't fault his teammate for that. Not anymore. Socorro's forward scout had literally torn apart an entire building to get to the woman he loved. And Granger would bring the rest of this place down if that was the way to get Charlie back.

They worked their way to what looked to be the remains of an underground parking garage. It was a miracle the structure hadn't collapsed in on itself in this condition, but he would take every second they had left. He and Ivy moved as one, her taking up the rear in case they were attacked from behind. He broke through the perimeter of the garage, dodging massive sections of cement twice his height, and scanned what he could see of the interior. "Clear."

Ivy carved a path over broken asphalt, debris and puddles of water. "There's an entrance on the back wall." She didn't wait for him to acknowledge, cutting across the remains of the garage, and took position at one side of the door. She waited for him, then nodded.

Granger raised his weapon at an angle. The battle-ready tension he'd relied on as he and Charlie had crossed the border into Vaughn snapped into place. Working the plan, learning who the players were and getting the upper hand—this was what he'd been trained for. What he was good at, and up until three days ago, he'd done his job on autopilot. Now he had a goal: to find the woman who made him want to keep going.

He whistled low to call Zeus to heel as the building seemed to swallow them. Hitting the power button to the flashlight along the barrel of his weapon, Granger lit up the few feet ahead of them. The scent of death and humidity burned down his throat. "Find Charlie, Zeus."

The dog trotted ahead, nose to the ground, his belly swinging back and forth with every step. There were so many competing smells in Granger's senses, he wasn't sure how the K9 would manage to pick Charlie out from among them, but Granger trusted his partner to make the connection.

A low ruff tightened the muscles down the bull terrier's back.

"He can't pick up her scent." Damn it. He'd known that was a possibility, but the stakes were higher than ever. Granger caught up with Zeus and scratched the dog between his ears. "There's too much interference."

"Then we're on our own." Ivy maneuvered ahead, coming up short of a T in the maze. "Which way?"

One wrong turn and they could lose Charlie forever. Granger wasn't willing to take that risk. "Every time we second-guess ourselves, Charlie is in more danger. We can't wander around in the dark. We need a plan. We need to split up. We'll cover more ground that way."

"And if you're wrong about this whole thing and Charlie is the one pulling the cartel's strings? We still don't know what *Sangre por Sangre* is planning." Ivy searched down the right corridor for signs of a threat. "Who's going to save your ass? Because the way I see things, your K9 would rather eat you than protect you."

"That's ridiculous. He's not a cannibal. He just has no control over what goes in his stomach and shaming him isn't going to speed the process along." Granger was avoiding the question, and they both knew it. He didn't want to acknowledge the possibility Charlie had led them into a trap, but he'd be a fool not to account for his own blind spots. "If you're right, and Charlie is the one behind this, I'll do what I have to. Until then, I'm going to operate on the belief she needs my help."

Ivy lowered her weapon and stretched out one hand. "That's one of the reasons I hired you. See you on the other side, Agent Morais."

"Agent Bardot." He shook her hand, knowing that his superior had been fighting her own internal battle since receiving the cartel's surveillance photos of Charlie. The man she'd known as her partner during her stint with the FBI hadn't resurfaced, despite the crumbling of *Sangre por Sangre*'s organization, and Granger couldn't help but think that meant one of two things. Either the agent had chosen to remain loyal to the people he was investigating, or she'd find him dead.

Ivy nodded before heading down the right corridor, leaving Granger to search the left.

"It's you and me, kid." He took the lead. The building seemed to come alive with a groan as they traveled deeper into its heart. Whatever waited for them at the end, Granger was ready.

His future was with Charlie.

And he'd fight like hell to keep it.

Chapter Fourteen

"I see you got my message." This voice was different than her abductor's. Familiar.

Charlie pried her eyes open, instantly overwhelmed in the center of a portable spotlight. Pressure built in her head to the point she wasn't sure her stomach could take it anymore. Then the spotlight cut out.

She faced off with the darkness, trying to see through the shapes her brain summoned to make sense of her surroundings.

The light burned her retinas a second time. Charlie pressed her head against the cold steel at her back. Her wrists were tied, her ankles bound with rope to individual posts. Zip ties would've been so much easier to break through.

The spotlight went dark again.

"What message? I don't know you." The assault to her senses was keeping her from focusing fully. Not to mention the severe dryness in her mouth and the migraine thudding hard at the back of her head. Her abductor. He'd been here. Watching her in the dark. He must've knocked her out. And now she had no sense of time or location. Charlie pulled at the rope, sawing through the first layer of skin at her wrist and aggravating the healing rash she'd sustained during her abduction. Her entire body felt as though it were on fire.

Movement cut across the spotlight as it flicked back on, and a smaller feminine frame was outlined in its glow. "Oh, Charlie. Of course you do. One could argue you know everything about me. Just as I know everything about you. My favorite foods, my favorite book I wanted to read every night before bed. How I hated the taste of homemade toothpaste, and my fear of being excluded from all the reindeer games my big sisters never let me be part of growing up."

Her brain struggled to connect the pieces. "I don't... I don't understand. Who..."

No. It wasn't possible. Charlie pressed her head back into the scaffolding holding her hostage. "You... You died."

The spotlight darkened, and everything inside Charlie wanted to turn it back on to confirm her worst fears.

Light blazed across the space.

And the woman was right there. Standing in front of her with nothing more than three feet between them. Back from the dead. "It felt like that the entire time I was waiting for you to keep your promise. It felt like dying. Over and over, a thousand times."

"Erin." Her sister's name left her mouth as nothing more than a whisper as she battled with logic and exhaustion and confusion. "What have you done?"

"I took control of my life, Charlie. Isn't that what you wanted me to do? Why you ran and left me behind?" Her younger sister sidestepped to Charlie's left, the spotlight highlighting the ten-year difference between the girl she'd known and the woman she'd become. Erin's hair was shorter, cut for convenience rather than inspired by the magazines she'd hidden under her mattress away from their father. Her face seemed thinner. Features Charlie had associated with the fifteen-year-old she'd loved no longer existed. Instead, there was something almost foreign about her. Detached. "There wasn't a single day of the past ten years that I didn't think about you. Not one moment that I didn't wonder if you thought about me."

"Of course I did. Everything I did, every choice I made, was to help you escape Vaughn." Charlie forced herself to stare into the spotlight in order to adapt her vision faster. Another glow pulled at her attention, near where Erin stood. "To finally get you out. But when I heard you'd died... I thought I was too late."

The spotlight went dark.

Leaving the familiar outline of her sister's shape.

And the glow of a barrel fire.

Metallic scraping got her attention and raised goose bumps along Charlie's arms.

"There's that promise again. The same one you told me the night we set the charges on the Alamo pipeline. You were going to find a way out of Acker's Army. I lost count of how many times I went to bed with that hope." Erin's voice had changed. No longer familiar and soothing, but dark. "But instead, you ran away, and you left me and Sage there to die. I managed to escape before police got to the scene. Barely. I waited, you know. For you to come back. For you to keep your promise. But you never came."

The spotlight found a new life.

Exposing the steel rod in Erin's hand. The tip glowed orange, flickering with heat—like a brand—as her sister neared. Erin angled the rod closer to Charlie, letting her feel the scalding heat against her face. Her sister's features took second priority as Charlie focused on the threat of feeling that rod on her skin.

"Erin, you don't have to do this. Please. Dad is dead. You can leave." Her voice shook. Charlie pulled against the ropes as the final conversation between her and her father filtered across her mind in a desperate attempt to come up with something—anything—to neutralize her sister's hatred.

"I already have, Charlie. Don't you understand?" Erin waved the steel poker back and forth, illuminating her own face in the process. A dreamlike daze seemed to relax her sister's expression. "Once I realized you weren't going to keep your promise, I devised my own plan to escape Daddy's control."

Understanding hit. "*Sangre por Sangre*. But how?"

"You remember those construction sites our father used to send us to for explosives?" Erin said. "Every single one of them was owned by the cartel through a number of shell corporations. Upper management may have discovered who was responsible a few months ago after Daddy accidentally let the information slip. The cartel may have then sent one of their lieutenants to take care of the problem. And I may have convinced him we could work together. I would help them salvage what remained of their organization, and, in exchange for that help, they would destroy Acker's Army."

"He knew, didn't he? Dad knew." Why hadn't she seen it before? Why hadn't she put the pieces together before now? "That's why he wouldn't tell me about the deal he made with *Sangre por Sangre*. He was willing to provide manpower and weapons because of you. In his mind, everything he's done has been for our benefit. Yours, Sage's and mine. And giving you up wasn't an option."

Erin stared at the glowing tip of the steel rod. "A mistake

on his part. I always thought our father was a hard man who demanded perfection at every turn, but in reality, he was very easily manipulated if you managed to hit the right buttons. And now he's dead."

"That means you're free, Erin. You can live your life without him hanging over your head." Charlie tried to wiggle free from the ropes around her wrists, but her sister had known exactly what she was capable of. The scaffolding she'd been bound to shook, and for the first time since she'd regained consciousness, she realized she and Erin weren't alone. A man stood behind the spotlight. Most likely the one who'd knocked her unconscious in the first place. She lowered her voice to a whisper. "Whatever it is the cartel has planned, whatever they're making you do, you don't have to be a part of it. We can leave. We can start over. Together. You just have to loosen the ropes. I can take care of everything else."

The spotlight died, casting her back into darkness and stealing the hope that'd held her upright.

A laugh Charlie didn't recognize echoed off the walls.

"You still don't understand, do you?" Erin's voice seemed distant now. Alien. Sparks shot up from the floor as her sister dragged the end of the poker along the cracked cement. "*Sangre por Sangre* isn't forcing me to do anything against my will, Charlie. That day the cartel sent a lieutenant to kill our father, I proposed a different plan. To use him and his army to our own advantage. Much the same way that Homeland Security agent approached you."

"What?" Charlie asked.

"You didn't think I knew about him, but it was so clear to anyone who bothered to notice. I noticed," Erin said. "The late-night disappearances from your room. The way you'd smile throughout the day when you didn't think anyone was looking. You changed. You lost your touch during sparring. Like you were distracted. You were more compliant to our father's commands, and I knew something had changed."

The spotlight lit up again, burning Charlie's retinas.

Erin was holding the steel rod back over the edge of the barrel fire, twisting it this way and that, as though she had all the time in the world. "So I followed you. I waited as you slipped out of your bedroom window and met him in the trees. I didn't recognize him at first, but it wasn't long before I realized you'd been selling us out. All of us."

"For you, Erin. I only agreed to give up information on Acker's Army and our father in exchange for the three of us to get free." Didn't she understand that? She'd put her own life on the line for her sisters. Only she'd been too late to save Sage. But she could still help Erin.

"You can tell yourself that all you want, dear sister, but I know the truth." Erin brought the rod back up in front of her. "We were a team, Charlie. You, me and Sage. It was supposed to be the three of us against our father. We were supposed to be together forever, but I saw how you looked at that agent, how much you wanted to please him, and it seems like nothing has changed. You're terrified that he'll be disappointed in you, that he won't have any use for you. You're as weak as he was, you know? The man who raised us. All I have to do is push the right buttons. Fortunately for you, I have a way to fix that."

"What do you mean?" Charlie lost her focus on escape as Erin came back, the steel poker between them. The heat bled through her scrub top. "Fix what?"

"I have a use for you. I can give you purpose again. I

can make the past ten years disappear as though they never happened. I have the explosives, thanks to my friends here. All I need from you is your skills in directing the blast," her sister said.

"The blueprints I found in Dad's office." Charlie rushed to make sense of the cartel's motives. "You wanted him and Acker's Army to attack the state capitol. Why?"

"There's something we need." Erin's voice had taken on a wispy quality again. Lighter than it should be, considering the circumstances. "Evidence that was taken from us by the DEA. We know it's being stored in one of their facilities. We just don't know which one, and I'm kind of in a hurry."

"You mean drugs." She couldn't believe this. Her little sister—the perfect innocent girl she'd helped raise—had sided with a brutal, unforgiving drug cartel. "That's what all of this is about?"

"I gave my word, Charlie. I promised the cartel I would do whatever it took to help them put their organization back together, in exchange for helping me dismantle Daddy's life's work." Erin pulled at the collar of her shirt, exposing angry and twisted scaring along her collarbone. "But first, I need to know you're one of us. That you won't betray me again."

"Erin, please." Survival kicked in. Charlie wrenched her wrists and ankles, but there was no give in the rope.

"Don't worry, Charlie. The pain only lasts a minute." Erin lowered the steel rod against Charlie's shoulder.

The heat burned through her scrub top and past layers of skin. Every muscle in her body fought against the scalding pain of hot steel, but there was no relief. Her scream ripped up the back of her throat.

Erin pulled the poker back. Satisfied. "Then you and I are going to get to work."

THE SCREAM PIERCED through the heavy rhythm of his breathing.

It tunneled past Granger's focus and pulled him up short.

His gut tightened as pain, agony and hopelessness combined into a hot rage in his veins. "Charlie."

Granger picked up the pace. Zeus hadn't been able to pick up her scent yet, but they were getting close. He could feel it. His heart rate hit out-of-control levels the harder he drove himself, but he had no other option. He wasn't going to lose Charlie. Not again. "Go on, Zeus, go get her!"

The bull terrier vaulted ahead despite the extra thirty pounds on his frame. He disappeared around a corner up ahead, and Granger had to trust the K9 would lead him true. The muscles in his legs protested with every step and aggravated the wound along his rib cage, but there wasn't anything in the world that would stop him from getting to her.

Not when he was so close.

Granger rounded the corner, following Zeus's trail.

A gunshot exploded from down the corridor.

He slowed his momentum and listened. Silence seeped through the walls as he waited for a response. Damn it. He'd rip this place apart if something had happened to his K9. He whistled low enough for Zeus to pick up on, a specific tone only the bull terrier would respond to. Granger approached the corner and rounded it without hesitation

A fist flew at him.

He dodged out of the way and threw a right hook at the attacker who'd been waiting for him. His knuckles screamed at the contact, pain vibrating up his wrist and into his arm.

Granger palmed the side of the soldier's head and slammed the bastard into the wall. The man collapsed. "Seems I'm in the right place after all."

Another attacked from behind. He managed to block the strike coming straight at his face, then latched onto the soldier's shoulders and threw the second attacker to the cement.

"I've been looking forward to this moment, Agent Morais," a voice said. "Please give my regards to Agent Bardot."

Ivy? Strong arms wrapped around Granger's neck from behind and threw off his balance. He stumbled back, at the whim of a third soldier tasked with slowing him down. His shoulders hit the wall a split second before a fist rocketed into his face. Lightning struck behind his eyes as momentum threw him to one side. The taste of blood coated the inside of his mouth as another soldier joined in the fun. "The hell do you want with Ivy?"

"She and I go way back." Recognition flared as memories of the attack in the woods surrounding Vaughn rushed to the front of his mind. The man who'd taken Charlie, the cartel lieutenant. "Didn't she tell you? Perhaps when this is all over, I'll pay her a visit myself. Until then, I've been asked to keep you here. Dead or alive—it doesn't matter to me."

"Good luck with that." He kicked at the attacker to his right and jolted the son of a bitch back and gained a bit of freedom in the process.

Granger launched his elbow into the soldier's rib cage. The bastard doubled over and gave Granger the perfect opportunity. Grabbing for the attacker's boot, he threw everything he had into getting the man off his feet. Only the soldier fisted Granger's clothing and brought them down together. Aches charged through his system as he tried to get his bearings. The bullet graze in his side screamed in response. Not to mention tore at the healing muscles in his shoulder. His vest kept him from taking a full breath and only added to the dizziness trying to get the best of him.

A moan filtered through the overactive race of his pulse. He threw a fist into the soldier's face beside him, knocking a piece off the board. Granger struggled to get to his feet, unsure of his own weight. Just as the next strike forced him back down. Pain erupted from his mouth and nose in a blinding flash of heat and agony, but he wasn't going down. Not until he found Charlie.

Granger cocked his elbow back and targeted the son of a bitch in front of him as exhaustion undermined his control. His fist streaked past the soldier he was aiming for, and Granger couldn't help but follow. Faster than he expected, his attack shoved him into the opposite wall of the corridor.

Hunched down, the third soldier angled his shoulder into Granger's gut and hauled him off his feet. One step. Two. Gravity released its hold on him as his opponent slammed him to the floor.

He barely had a second to make sense of his attacker's next move before a knee slammed into his face. The world threatened to spin as Granger tried to regain control of his body. A boot carved into his rib cage and stole the oxygen from his lungs despite the protection of his Kevlar vest.

Granger summoned the last of his adrenaline reserves and put everything he had into getting off the floor. He dug his fingers into the wall for support. Throwing his shoulder into the nearest attacker, he lunged at the man standing between him and Charlie and pulled the soldier off his feet. The muscles in his legs burned as he hauled the added weight through a thin door on the other side of the corridor. They spilled into the room and hit the ground as one.

His mouth filled with blood. Granger spit it out as the pain in his head tried to warn him he was shutting down. Red stains spewed in every direction, creating miniature Rorschach tests on the floor.

Granger pulled a blade from his ankle holster. He arched his arm and buried the tip of the knife into the soldier's thigh. With a twist, he inflicted as much pain as he could to take the cartel member out of commission. Only the bastard wouldn't go down. Granger fisted both sides of the soldier's collar and threw him into the floor face-first.

The cartel lieutenant he'd left in the hallway had come around. He shot straight for Granger's throat and squeezed, pinning him against the floor. "Do you know how many women I've killed for challenging *Sangre por Sangre*? Your FBI agent Ivy Bardot doesn't even know about all the other bodies I buried. She only found the ones I wanted her to find. Now imagine what I'm going do to Charlie when I'm finished. How long do you think it will take you to find her? You and your team of dogs will have to search the entire state to put her back together."

"No." The visual was too much. Pressure built in his head with every second his brain lacked oxygen, but he hadn't come this far to stop now. He maneuvered one hand around the soldier's wrist, broke the suffocating contact with his throat and twisted until the bones of the man's hand snapped.

A scream echoed off the walls as the cartel member dropped to his knees, and Granger rocketed his fist into the son of a bitch's temple to put him down. "You'll never touch her again with that hand."

The final rush of adrenaline seemed to drain right out of him then, and he stumbled toward the door and back out into the corridor. His brain had a hard time making sense of direction, but there was something pulling him deeper into the building. He sucked in as much air as his lungs could hold, and still, it wasn't enough. Peeling off his Kevlar vest, Granger discarded it on the floor to get a hold of himself. "I'm coming, Charlie. I'm coming."

His boots kicked up chunks of cement as he used the wall to keep him upright. All he had to do was take that next step. To keep moving forward. "Just hang on."

The corridor emptied him out into alcove lined with scaffolding. Spotlights cast too-bright light around the room. A barrel fire burned at one end with a steel poker discarded nearby, its tip still red from heat. The scream. He caught sight of severed rope hanging from one section of the scaffolding and crossed the room. Pulling it free, he rubbed the fibers between his fingers and scanned the rest of the room. Empty. His chest filled with all the longing and grief and rage he'd felt after her disappearance and honed it into a single word. "Charlie!"

The building moaned in response. Dust fell in streams. Then a single chunk of cement from above. The rock exploded upon impact and sent shards in every direction. The entire structure seemed to be suffering right along with him.

A bark cut through the tremors vibrating through the walls.

That single sound washed the failure from his veins and focused his attention to a doorway across the room. Granger discarded the section of rope, jogging for the exit. "Zeus?"

The door dumped him into an area not mapped on satellite imagery. Weapon raised, he cleared each door he passed along the corridor. The scaffolding. There was a reason *Sangre por Sangre* wouldn't let this building fall apart and die where it stood. They were still building in secret. Under the radar from law enforcement and Socorro. Damn it. How long had he and his team let them restructure without notice? Wood beams braced up the ceiling, preventing the shaft from falling in on itself. The unpaved ground slopped downward, and the only place Granger could think where it led was straight to hell.

An earthquake shook the corridor and knocked Granger into the wall. Despite the cartel's determination to keep this building on its last legs, the whole place was about to come down around them. Dirt slid beneath his shirt and into his hair, pushing him to pick up the pace.

He had to move fast.

Granger followed the shaft deeper into the earth as one of the beams fell out of place. A landslide of dirt cascaded behind him. Within seconds, the way he'd come was sealed. Another bark sounded from the darkness ahead. He couldn't focus on a way out right now. All that mattered was getting to Charlie and Zeus. They were his team—his future—and he would do whatever it took to reach them.

He breached an anterior room off the main shaft. And froze.

"It's so nice to finally meet you, Agent Morais." The woman held Charlie at gunpoint. A hint of familiarity pricked at the back of his mind, and Granger found himself looking at a dead woman. "We have so much to talk about."

Chapter Fifteen

Charlie struggled to pick an emotion to feel.

There were just too many, all vying for her attention. The burn on her collarbone screamed with every move of her fingers interlaced behind her head, but no amount of pain could keep her from taking her gaze off Granger.

He'd come for her.

After everything she'd said—everything she'd done—to protect him, he'd once again risked his life in favor of saving hers. A sob shook through her at the thought but cut short as dirt from the ceiling rained down in handfuls.

"You pull that trigger, and it's the last thing you'll ever do, Erin." Granger was slowly closing the distance between them. There was nowhere for them to go. This place was about to cave in, and the three of them would be buried if they didn't leave now.

"Funny. I was about to tell you one more step and I'll pull the trigger." Erin pulled back on the weapon's slide and loaded a round into the chamber. "My father raised me to be the best, Agent Morais. Do you really think you can cross this room before Charlie dies?"

The barrel of Erin's weapon scratched against her scalp, and Charlie closed her eyes to clear her head. Instead, her mind forced her to face a black pool of ifs and whys. "Erin, please. You can still walk away from this. I know you're scared. I was too when I first got out from underneath Dad's control, but you can do this. We just have to—"

Erin fired a shot into the ceiling. Dirt hit the ground from above, and a crack spread out from the bullet's entry. "Stop trying to convince me we're a team. You were never any good at it, Charlie, even before you disappeared. No. Here's what's going to happen. Agent Morais and his doggy sidekick are staying here while you and I have some quality sister time. On your feet."

Her sister wrenched her arm up, bringing Charlie to stand. "If you so much as move in our direction, I'll shoot her. If you call your dog, I'll shoot her. There is nothing you can do to save yourselves, Agent Morais. I'm the one—"

Charlie wrenched her elbow back into Erin's stomach. She turned as her sister brought the weapon up. Ramming her shoulder into Erin's belly, Charlie tried to knock the gun from her hand. And failed.

"Charlie!" Granger screamed.

Erin buried the heel of her boot in Charlie's chest. The back of her sister's hand made contact and knocked Charlie off her feet. They'd trained together. They'd learned to fight from the same source. There wasn't anything Charlie could do that wouldn't be met with equal or greater force. And, in truth, she didn't want to. She didn't want to hurt her baby sister. Not when she had so many memories of helping raise her. Guilt for not saving her as she'd promised.

She stared up at Erin from the ground as the betrayal and loss and grief she'd suffered at the news of her sister's death washed over her.

"You can't beat me, Charlie. I'm not the same girl you

knew back then." Erin buried her boot into Charlie's gut. "I'm stronger than you'll ever be. I always have been, and there's nothing you can do to stop me or *Sangre por Sangre* now."

Her ribs threatened to break under another assault. Charlie gasped for breath, but her lungs refused to inhale. She curled in on herself to relieve the pain sparking through her. Her cough bounced off the failing walls and ceiling.

"Stop!" Granger took a step forward, holding his bull terrier partner back. "Erin, stop. She's your sister."

Erin took aim. At him. "You did this to her. You corrupted her. You turned her into something weak with promises of protection and love. Does she even know Homeland Security never authorized you to make her a confidential informant? Does she know how you failed her, that if something had happened, she wouldn't have been protected at all?"

Granger didn't seem to have an answer for that.

And Charlie didn't care.

Because she would've still taken the risk. Just for the chance to start her own life, outside of Vaughn, away from her father. To go to a movie in a theater and drink as many strawberry milkshakes as she wanted. To see the world and work diner jobs. To be with someone who loved her. She'd make that choice over and over. Granger had given her that chance. He'd given her everything.

"You'll never be free this way, Erin. Dad's still controlling you. It's just with your own fear." Charlie kicked her heel out with everything she had.

Erin's feet swept out from underneath her. Her sister managed to keep herself upright, but the gun hit the ground. Erin had been right. The little girl Charlie had known all her life was gone. Now there was only an emptiness.

Grabbing for the weapon, Charlie brought it up. Her finger slipped over the trigger. Ready to bring all of this to an end.

Erin crushed her hand against Charlie's forearm, and her aim went wide. Her sister regained control of the gun and reached out, latching onto Charlie's neck. And squeezed.

She circled both hands around Erin's wrists as the life drained out of her, but there was no relief. The burn on her collarbone protested even the smallest movements.

Granger rushed forward.

"Now, I'm starting to lose my patience with you both. So here's what's going to happen next." Erin took aim. And pulled the trigger.

A groan registered from behind Charlie. And it was then she knew Granger had been hit. Every cell in her body honed in on letting go of the feelings attached to her sister. She twisted out of Erin's hold and gasped for air.

Just as nearly a hundred pounds of K9 weight vaulted over her.

Zeus collided with Erin and brought her down. The bull terrier did what he did best while playing his favorite game and sat on her sister's chest with his full weight. The gun knocked free of Erin's hand and skittered out of reach.

The ceiling shook above them, bringing Charlie's attention up. "Granger, we've got to get out of here." She didn't hear a response, cutting her gaze to the unmoving man on the ground. Her heart shot into her throat. "Granger!"

Dragging herself upright, she let gravity lead her way to him and collapsed at his side. Blood spread over the same shoulder he'd taken a bullet in two months ago. She pressed her hand to the wound, watching as a pool of blood seeped out the back. It was a through and through. Easily treated as long as they got out of this mess.

"Why do people keep aiming for this shoulder?" His attempt to lighten the mood worked better than she wanted it to. "Hasn't it been through enough?"

The shaft walls started to crumble around them. Zeus sneezed from the added dust in the air.

"Come on. You need to stand. We've got to go." Taking his weight, Charlie angled her shoulder beneath his arm. His face had been battered. He seemed to be covered in blood no matter where she looked, but he was alive. They were both alive. For the time being. "Zeus, let's go."

The K9 obeyed, leaving Erin gasping for breath.

Her sister clawed for the weapon just out of reach. "I'm not finished, Charlie. You owe me. You owe me ten years of waiting!"

"No, Erin. I don't. Because you're still stuck in the past, and I was brave enough to go after my future." Charlie turned to face her as the ceiling collapsed directly onto her sister. Dust billowed out from the hole in the ceiling and spread faster than she expected.

"Run!" Granger clutched onto her hand and pulled her through the opening. He kept her at his side as the walls seemed to disintegrate right in front of her eyes.

Her legs protested with each step, but they couldn't slow down. They couldn't stop. Zeus raced ahead of them like that reindeer she'd read about as a kid helping Santa through the fog on Christmas Eve.

Except part of the shaft had collapsed in front of them.

She could see the other side. Light permeated from the other end of the tunnel, but there was no way for them to get to it. Wood beams and an oversized mound of dirt had cut them off. "Start digging!"

Zeus took the order with enthusiasm and started using both paws to dig. Charlie bit back the pain of her branded shoulder and the relentless pain in her skull as she grabbed for handfuls of dirt from the top of the mound.

But the ceiling was still caving in. With every scoop they got out of the way, the earth seemed to want to fill the void, and they had to start again. Dirt kicked up into the air and drove down into her lungs. If tens of thousands of tons of earth didn't crush them, they would die of suffocation. A rumble shifted the ground underneath her feet, and Charlie looked back to see the shaft collapsing in on itself.

"Granger." His name left her mouth as nothing more than a whisper. They'd run out of time. No matter how many minutes they'd made up for these past three days, it was never going to be enough.

"Don't give up." Granger secured her in his arms as the wave of dirt and debris drew near. "I love you. I'm always going to love you."

"I've loved you ever since that night you offered me a strawberry milkshake. You changed my life for the better, and I'll never be able to thank you for that," she said.

"Granger!" A voice cut through the low groan of the building coming down on top of them. A single hand drove through the mound of loose dirt. "Grab hold of the rope!"

Someone had offered them a lifeline.

"Go!" Granger maneuvered Charlie up the side of the mound, and she wrapped the rope around her wrist. "Pull!"

Charlie took a deep breath as though she were about to dive for the Olympics. Her arm stretched through to the other side as thousands of pounds of dirt threatened to crush her, but there was another force on the other end. One that wanted her to live.

She broke through the wall of debris to find Ivy Bardot on the other end. Untwisting the rope from around her wrist, she shoved it at Socorro's founder. "We need to get them out of there!"

"Granger, rope!" Ivy speared the ratty fibers back through the wall of dirt as the ground shook beneath their feet.

"Pull!" Granger's voice boomed through the space on the other side, and Charlie and Ivy worked together to get Zeus through the limited opening.

The bull terrier shook layers of dust from his coat and sneezed three times before circling around Charlie's feet. Untying the knot on his collar, she drove the end of the rope back through the mound. "Granger!"

Only there was no response.

The rope remained slack, and the seconds slipped through her fingers as easily as the grains of sand through an hourglass. "Granger."

She drove both hands into the mound, searching for a sign he'd survived the collapse.

And pulled a single hand free.

Two days later...

DYING IN A shaft collapse hadn't hurt so bad.

Granger tried to sit up in the recovery bed, but the mattress and pillows were too damn soft. He kept sinking down into the middle as if he'd been ordered to recover in the middle of a marshmallow.

The lights were too dim. His body kept trying to go to sleep on him, but he wanted to stay awake for updates from the team.

Two bodies had been recovered in the bowels of *Sangre por Sangre*'s headquarters. The third soldier who'd attacked him—the one intent on making his relationship with Ivy clear—hadn't been found. Seemed the son of a bitch was good at dodging death. Though Socorro's fearless leader didn't seem bothered by Charlie's description of her abductor, Granger was fairly certain the man Ivy and her partner suspected of killing those women all those years ago and the one Granger had knocked unconscious were one and the same. Which meant Socorro's undercover source within the cartel couldn't surface. At least not yet.

Scarlett had decrypted all of the notes written in the margins from the blueprints taken from Henry Acker's office, including the cartel's final goal: retrieving the massive amount of fentanyl pills confiscated from *Sangre por Sangre* less than a month ago. Turned out, the government had only been on the lookout for the pills because of a sample collected by Scarlett in a warehouse raid to save a DEA agent's son. Six million dollars' worth. Enough to put *Sangre por Sangre* back on top of the drug hierarchy, so long as they were able to liquidate their inventory.

A knock registered from the door, and Charlie—in all her gauzed and bandaged glory—leaned against the doorframe. "Up for some company?"

"As long as it's you." Granger relaxed back against the pillow, taking in everything he could about her.

"This is killing you, isn't it? Having to lay here and recover like a good operative," she said.

She wasn't wrong. "Doc had one of my teammates drag me back when I tried to leave. Said she'd sedate me the next time."

"Patience has never been your strong suit." She brushed

a section of his hair off his forehead, exposing the gauze beneath her shirt collar. "Mine either. I think that's why we get along so well."

Her smile took his attention off the ache in his shoulder, but more, it gifted him a knot of hope. That they could move on from this. Together. "How are things in Vaughn?"

"Chaotic, but Acker's Army has officially dismantled. Once I informed the residents my father was dead and why, there didn't seem to be any interest for anyone else to step forward." She skimmed her fingers down his arm, raising goose bumps in her path. "His legacy is dead, and the families of the people he hurt will be able to move on now. Just like we always dreamed of."

"I'm sorry about your father, Charlie. I know a part of you still loved him," he said.

"Yeah. Deep down, I believed him when he told me everything he did, everything he put us through, was meant to make us stronger, so we didn't have to suffer like he did. That's what fathers are supposed to do, right?" Her expression smoothed over. She was retreating again, holding herself back from having to feel the grief that came with losing a parent. In time, Granger trusted she would learn to deal with it, but for now, he'd let her grieve how she felt she needed to. "But at the same time, look at what happened to Sage. What happened to Erin." She straightened. "Were they able to recover my sister's body?"

"Yeah. Turns out that tunnel wasn't the only one. Once the engineers were able to map out one that ran parallel, they managed to get the excavators in and clear out the collapse." He'd been lucky. Just a few more seconds and Granger would've suffocated right along with Charlie's sister. Lost forever. But she'd pulled him out. "She's with the medical examiner in Albuquerque."

"Good. I know what she did was terrible and hurt a lot of people, but she didn't deserve to stay down there," she said. "I guess I'm the one who gets to choose where she goes."

"You have a place in mind?" he asked.

"She tried to get out of Vaughn her entire life. I don't think it would be fair to take her back."

"What about your safe house?" He twisted his torso toward the nightstand on the other side of the bed. The bullet graze along his rib cage didn't like the movement one bit, but this was important. "Maybe this could be buried with her."

He handed her Erin's journal, the one she'd taken from her sister's room the first night she'd come back to New Mexico.

"We used to write each other notes in a journal like this. In a special code only the two of us knew. Just in case Dad started snooping." She flipped through the pages, landing on the last entry. "She kept it up. Even after I left, she was writing me notes."

"Come here." Granger brought her head to his chest, below his newest bullet wound. "She was going to kill you, Charlie. I couldn't let her take you from me again."

A line of tears glistened in her eyes. "I know. I just wish she hadn't decided to let her anger and fear make her choices. Maybe then she'd still be alive."

"Maybe," he said.

The click of nails echoed down the hallway. A thud slammed into the recovery room door. The entire frame threatened to break under whatever had hit it.

"I'm going to take a wild guess that Zeus is here to see

you." Charlie pried herself from the edge of his bed and answered the door.

The bull terrier took the invitation without hesitation and launched himself onto the bed. Granger's legs instantly regretted the added weight as he wrestled with the K9 one-handed. "I missed you too, buddy. I hope Charlie's been taking good care of you these past couple days."

"Well, he really took more care of me than I did of him, isn't that right?" She scratched Zeus between his ears, and the dog seemed to melt.

Great. Granger was never going to be able to get out of this bed between the two of them.

"How's the shoulder?" she asked.

"No shards left behind. Seemed the second bullet pushed the shrapnel from the first out. Dr. Piel called it a shot in a million." Granger settled back in the bed, no longer feeling as though he needed to leave. Instead, he wanted to remember everything about this moment. "I'm feeling better than I have in a long time. Then again, maybe it has something to do with the possibility of seeing you once I get out of this bed."

Her smile chased back the numbness starting in his toes and reinvigorated his nervous system. It was a smile only he saw, a spark that couldn't be contained. And he was lucky enough to witness it now. She leaned over the edge of the bed and pressed her mouth to his. "I didn't realize I had such an influence on your recovery. Maybe I should visit more often."

"I like the sound of that," he said.

"I just have one question for you before I agree to anything." There was a brightness in her eyes he hadn't seen in far too long, and Granger couldn't help but lose himself in it. "Do you like strawberry milkshakes, Agent Morais?"

"I would kill for a strawberry milkshake right now, but I think I'm beginning to like this even more." He fisted her jacket and pulled her in for another kiss. The taste of her spread across his tongue and quieted all of the violent memories he'd held onto these past few weeks. It wasn't the mere physical act of having her here but the connection. To her.

"I think I can come around to your way of thinking." She whispered the words against his mouth. "For a price."

"Whatever it is, I'm willing to pay it." There was no arguing about that. He didn't care what she required of him. He would do whatever it took to keep from losing her again. "As long as it gets me you."

"Tell me you love me," she said.

"I love you, Charlie." He set his uninjured hand against her face, and Zeus instantly took that to mean he needed attention too. The dog army-crawled up Granger's chest and set that wet nose against his chin. "I think I fell in love with you the night I met you in your father's backyard with a rifle pointed at my heart, and I was too much of a coward to say it."

It wasn't sudden. It was three months of trusting her as his confidential informant, ten years of building her up in his mind and four days of fighting with her at his side. No matter the circumstance, she'd been right here with him. "And I want you to know, official paperwork or not, I never would've let anything happen to you while under my supervision. Ever."

"I knew, Granger. I knew Homeland Security wasn't going to consider me an official confidential informant because of my relationship to my father." Charlie pressed her face into his hand, planting a kiss in his palm. "Your superior contacted me. He tried to convince me to sever my contact with you, but I didn't care. I made the choice to trust what you were doing. Because we were a team."

"Then and now." And he wouldn't have it any other way.

"Forever," she said. "So, Agent Morais, how about that milkshake?"

He searched the window facing out into the corridor and clocked the security camera posted outside. "We can have all the milkshakes you want if you get me out of this room without anyone else finding out."

"Good thing I have experience with disappearing." She kissed him again. "You've got a deal."

* * * * *

CORRALLED IN CUTTHROAT CREEK

JUNO RUSHDAN

To the heroes who may not know where they fit in,
but who are never afraid to stand up for justice.

Chapter One

Her gut twisted. She wasn't alone. Someone else was in the house.

More floorboards creaked somewhere downstairs.

Summer Stratton couldn't tell exactly which room the sound had come from since she wasn't very familiar with the place, only having been inside it on a handful of occasions. The house belonged to her longtime best friend, Dani Granger, who was now deceased.

Murdered.

Summer refused to believe that Dani's death had been a convenient accident.

Was the killer the same person creeping around now?

In the upstairs primary bedroom, Summer stared at the box under the bed. Checking the contents would have to wait. Switching off the heavy black flashlight, she stood up and stilled. The only thing sparing her from being plunged into total darkness was the moonlight filtering in through the parted curtains of one window.

Something crashed downstairs in the back part of the house, making her jump. Whatever it was had been big and heavy. Must've been knocked over. Possibly in the kitchen.

Then silence.

Despite the July heat trapped in the house, cold sweat trickled down her spine.

Wind hissed through the old house, causing its bones to rattle and squeak. Branches from the trees around the place clattered, scraping against the siding. A storm was gathering. The massive evergreen close to the window stood like an ominous sentry in the shadows.

She had hoped to find what she was searching for, sneak out and make it back to the small cabin she'd rented on the outskirts of Cutthroat Creek before the rain started and without being discovered.

Two fails.

But could this one misstep cost her life?

A thump echoed in tandem with a screech downstairs. Glass or porcelain shattered. Maybe the intruder had bumped into something. Had the noise come from the living room?

That was the one space in the house crammed with tchotchkes and collectibles on every surface like mini booby traps.

The noises had started in the kitchen and were now coming from the living room, she supposed. He was working his way through the house, from back to front.

She wasn't sure if she should move and try to hide. The old floorboards might give away her position.

Rain pitter-pattered on the roof. Pulses of lightning flashed outside, illuminating fat beads of rain quivering down the windowpanes. The wind picked up, rustling the branches, and the mixture of noises made it hard for her to pinpoint the location of the footsteps in the house.

Thunder cracked. The rumble was in the distance, shifting closer. As the sound faded outside, another one rose inside—the groan of the stairs.

A shiver scuttled over her body like a legion of icy spiders.

He's coming up.

Summer glanced around the bedroom for her purse that had her pepper spray. She never left home in Seattle without a canister of Mace and had been sure to pack several in her bags, even putting one on her key chain during the seven-hour drive from Washington to Montana.

No handbag in sight. She swore to herself as she remembered where she'd left it.

Her purse was downstairs. With her Mace. On the coffee table in the living room. Right along with her cell phone and the keys to her car that she'd hidden in the woods.

Another slow creak from the weight ascending on the risers set her pulse pounding.

The man creeping up the stairs stood between her and all possibility of calling for help and getting rescued. Between her and the sole weapon she'd brought to defend herself. Between her and freedom—the only way to escape.

Standing there, she was rooted in place by fear, with a virtual bull's-eye on her forehead. The guy in the house could be there to simply scare her away, give her a more forceful warning.

But deep down she suspected that was wishful thinking. The reality was she'd already been warned. Several times.

Anything could happen to her out here. *He* could do anything to her. Hurt her, or worse.

Kill her.

She shook her head, needing to calm down and think clearly. Shuffling around in haste and leading him straight to her wasn't a much better option either. She strategized, planned, thought things through ad nauseam.

Rushing always led to a regrettable choice.

Lightning flashed again. Within seconds, there would be thunder. That was when she'd hide. Hopefully, the noise would be enough to mask the sound of her movements.

Summer waited. The storm was drawing nearer. Thunder would come sooner than the last time.

Down the hallway, a door squeaked open. He was up on the second floor.

A boom bellowed loud enough to rattle the windows.

Summer gave in to the flight response flooding her system and dashed across the room on the balls of her feet to the back wall, where there were two closets. She chose the second one, closest to the windows, farthest from the door, and ducked inside, shutting it as quickly and quietly as possible.

The primary bedroom was the last one at the far end of the hall. Eventually, whoever was skulking around inside the house, searching for her, would make their way down there and find her.

Then what?

Panic flared hot. She felt around gingerly, frantically, for a baseball bat. A golf club. A shotgun—not that she knew how to use one. Something she could use to protect herself, doing her best not to knock anything over by accident. Only clothes and hangers in the closet.

No weapon within easy reach. Her heart sank.

She'd been warned to stay away, to stop poking her nose where it didn't belong, to go back home to Seattle. Better to be safe than sorry. That was what she'd been told.

The house was being watched or she was. Either was

bad. But it was undeniably clear that one, most likely both, were under surveillance.

Going to the Granger house late at night, under the cover of darkness when she'd normally be asleep, had seemed like a good idea. Until now.

Breathe. Think. Going off the deep end isn't going to do you any good.

No help was coming. She hadn't told anybody that she was going to the house tonight. Not her sisters or her parents. None of them lived in Montana. It wasn't as though they could run over in the nick of time even if she had her cell phone to call them. Or 911. Not that a call to the local authorities would go well, because technically, the sheriff would consider her a trespasser.

There weren't even any neighbors within screaming distance for her go to, provided she could get out of the house. In fact, the closest one was a couple of miles down the road.

Her stomach lurched as the hopelessness of her predicament set in. She was all alone in the middle of nowhere, with someone in the house who wanted her to stop investigating.

Dani had already been silenced. Maybe this time the murderer wouldn't hesitate to kill her, too.

Tightening her sweaty grip on her Maglite, she tamped down her despair. She needed to think of a way out of this. Alive and hopefully unharmed. Clutching the flashlight to her chest, she clenched her fingers around it. The long handle was thick and heavy-duty and might suffice as a makeshift weapon in a pinch. She was certainly in a sticky situation. One she intended to survive.

This was costing her everything. Summer was on the brink of losing her dream job with a top law firm and possibly her life, all for the sake of exposing the truth and for justice. For Dani.

She took a deep breath and forced herself to focus.

Get out of the house by any means necessary. Grab keys. Mace. Run to the car.

That was the plan, albeit a flimsy one, but it would have to do.

Floorboards near the bedroom groaned. Heavy footfalls entered the room and stopped. Adrenaline swamped her, and she struggled to listen through the roar of her drumming pulse in her ears.

A jarring screech made her flinch. Sounded like he moved something. The bed? She covered her mouth with a hand to keep from screaming.

Footsteps crossed the room. Toward the corner, on the other end of the wall. Hinges squeaked as a door opened. Hangers scraped on the metal rod. He was checking the closet.

A cold tightness threaded through her sternum while a greasy sliding sensation took hold in her stomach. He would move on to the next closet and find her. Impossible to hide.

Fight and run. Stick to the plan.

Thunder roared overhead, making the house shudder, the loud booms resonating in her bones. Through the fading rumble, the sound of footsteps thudding across the hardwood carried. Each one drawing nearer. Steadily. Slowly.

The walls closed in. Her stomach roiled.

Oh, God. She could do this. Had to. No other choice.

Summer braced herself, holding the flashlight tight, and prepared to attack whoever was on the other side of the door.

The heavy footsteps edged closer, approaching the closet,

and stopped in front of the door. A dense knot swelled in her throat. Hands shaking, she tasted acid fear on her tongue.

The doorknob twisted with a creak.

She shoved on the door with all her might before he fully opened it as a cry cracked loose from inside her. The surprising force jostled the person back. Then she saw him. A man wearing a ski mask.

Summer swung the flashlight, hitting him in the head. She kicked him, going for the groin. The guy doubled over with a grunt and cursed her. She swung the Maglite again, whacking the back of his skull and knocking him to the ground. She didn't waste a second. Whirling around, she bolted for the door. Dashed from the bedroom.

Bang! A blast of gunfire split the air, the deafening sound chilling her to the bone.

Was she hit? She wasn't sure but didn't stop running.

It took a second to register that she didn't feel any pain. She kept moving. Down the hall. To the stairwell.

Summer grabbed the railing and hit the steps as another shot exploded, the bullet striking the wall, bits of plaster erupting with debris hitting her face. Screaming, she hunched and instinctively covered the back of her head with the hand that held the flashlight.

She might not be so lucky if he fired again.

Footsteps pounded after her, closing the distance between them. The terrifying sound made her stomach clench and bile burn her throat. Could she make it? She didn't stop racing down the steps, one hand gripping the rail to prevent her from tumbling down face-first. Adrenaline pumped hot in her veins. She was almost at the bottom of the stairwell.

Then came two more blasts.

And her luck ran out as searing pain slashed through her.

LOGAN POWELL HAD pulled his truck up in front of his cousin's house and cut the engine when he heard the unmistakable sound.

Gunfire!

Even through the rain and the low music in the cab of the truck, he was certain it had been a gun's report and not a clap of thunder.

But no one was supposed to be in the house. His cousin Dani was dead, as well as her parents. Her next of kin was their uncle, Ric Granger, who was back home in Wyoming, and Dani's friend Summer Stratton was staying in a place she'd rented near town.

He jumped out of the truck into the pouring rain so fast he didn't take the usual precautions of calling 911 first. Drawing his service weapon from the holster on his hip beside his badge, he charged toward the porch, getting soaked.

Bang. Bang.

In the quick muzzle flashes that lit up the darkness inside the house, he spotted someone running from the bottom of the landing, being chased by another person barreling down the stairs.

Logan stormed up the porch, his steps soft and stealthy, and almost kicked the door inward. But he had the element of surprise to his advantage and didn't want to give it up unless necessary. He tried the doorknob. It turned. Unlocked. With his Glock at the ready, he swept inside the house.

Noises of a violent struggle came from the living room—grunting and panicked screams, flesh being hit, items clattering to the floor. He hurried deeper inside, glancing at the stairway and noting bullet holes in the wall, and rounded the corner into the living room.

A guy dressed in all black with a ski mask covering his

face grabbed a woman from behind and yanked her around. The woman was fighting back. She stomped on the guy's foot and threw an elbow into his gut. The guy swore, hurling threats, but didn't let her go.

The two were locked in a deadly tussle. Logan didn't have a clear shot—no way to guarantee he didn't hit her by accident. He holstered his gun and charged forward, his boots crunching on broken porcelain.

The assailant whirled at the sudden noise, letting the woman go.

Logan tackled the gunman and rammed him hard enough to send them crashing to the floor, but the woman fell with them. Her legs were caught beneath them as they fought.

Blow for blow was exchanged. Needing to prevent the other guy from shooting him, Logan kept the masked man's wrist holding the gun locked in a tight grip. Still, Logan took a solid hook to the jaw and tasted blood, but he didn't pay attention to the pain since he was more focused on delivering his own. He managed to grab the guy by his shirt and yank him to the side.

Free, the woman scrambled up from the floor. She was panting, her dark hair wild, scanning the room as though she was looking for something. He caught a glimpse of her face.

Summer?

He'd met her once, years ago, but couldn't be sure it was her in the dim light and the frenzy of the attack.

Logan threw a knee in the masked man's stomach and punched him in the face while the woman scooped something up from the table and dashed toward the kitchen. They wrestled, the two of them both trying to climb to their feet. The assailant smashed his head into Logan's face, nearly breaking his nose. The blow left him reeling. His hand loosened on the man's wrist, and he reached out to steady himself. The edge of something bit into his palm.

A glint of silver flashed in the moonlight as the masked man raised the gun.

Logan wrapped his fingers around the object his hand had found—a long, broken shard—and swung it around, stabbing the man in his wrist.

Howling in the pain, the guy staggered back, but didn't drop the gun on reflex. He lashed out with the pistol, giving Logan a sharp rap across the head with the weapon. Stunned, Logan dropped to a knee and pulled his Glock at almost the same time.

In a blur, the masked man spun and ran for the front door. His footsteps pounded down the steps, the sound fading beneath the rain.

Logan swallowed blood and stood with a groan. For a second, he worried that the woman had fled out through the back door and might run into whoever had attacked her. He hurried through the dark house to the kitchen.

The refrigerator had been knocked over. With the top resting on the edge of one of the counters, the fridge blocked the back door. She was up on top of the counter, prying open the window above the sink.

"Hey," Logan said, hurrying up behind her, and touched her arm. "Are you hu—"

She kicked back, throwing a foot in his gut and whirled, her right hand raised.

Logan registered the can of pepper spray in her grasp. Too late.

The blast of stinging mist him in the eyes and nose. "Oww!" Flinging his hands up, he ducked away, trying to avoid the worst of the spray. Still, some got into his open mouth. Gasping for clean air, he couldn't haul in enough. He stumbled backward, his stomach heaving. Through the burning that blinded him, he yelled, "Stop." Sucking another sharp breath at the combination of his stinging eyes and his skin on fire, he coughed and choked. "I'm a cop."

Chapter Two

A cop?

Summer stared at him in disbelief. "Prove it." With a trembling hand, she kept the pepper spray pointed at the stranger's face.

The man gagged and coughed, trying to catch his breath. He unhooked a badge from his waistband and held it up.

She climbed down from the counter and winced from the pain in her arm. The bullet had grazed her shoulder, leaving a bloody, sore mess, but she was thankful the injury wasn't serious. Cautiously, she approached him, and took his badge for closer inspection. Looked real enough.

Special agent with the Wyoming Division of Criminal Investigation.

He *was* a cop, but that didn't automatically make him a good guy. Not in this town. "Now prove you don't want to hurt me." The last time she came to the house, the sheriff had *coincidentally* showed up shortly thereafter—as though someone had called him, or he'd been the one following her—and intimidated her.

Best to leave well enough alone. It's better to be safe than sorry, the sheriff had told her right before he threatened to arrest her for trespassing, insisted she hightail it out of town and go back to Washington.

"What?" With his head lowered, he wiped his eyes and coughed like he was hacking up a lung. "Why would I hurt you? I just saved you from that guy."

True, but she'd learned you couldn't be too careful. "What are you doing in this house? Who are you?"

"This is my family's house. I'm Logan Powell. Dani Granger's cousin."

"Oh my gosh. I thought you were..." Summer stepped closer, putting the pepper spray away inside her cross-body purse. "Sorry. I didn't realize."

Once she had learned about Dani's death, she'd flown out to Cutthroat Creek. She'd missed the funeral, but she had a chance to talk to Dani's closest living relative, her uncle, Ric Granger. He happened to still be in town, deciding what to do with the property. She'd convinced him that Dani had been murdered and asked him to hold off on selling. Ric had promised to send someone to help her investigate, possibly his son, Matt Granger, a cop whom she'd met previously. He hadn't mentioned when someone might show up or that someone else might come in Matt's stead. Much less that it would be Logan Powell.

"A little help over here," he said. "Where's the sink? I need to rinse the pepper spray out of my eyes."

His eyes were watering, and his nose didn't look too good either. He took a half-blind step toward her.

"We should get out of the kitchen." Pepper spray lingered in the air, irritating her eyes and throat as well, simply from being in the area. Taking him by the arm, she led him from the kitchen.

The living room was in shambles. Many of the trinkets

and collectibles, items she'd consider to be dust collectors, were in pieces, scattered on the floor. At least Ric Granger wasn't attached to anything in the house and had been uncertain what to do with everything.

"I'm so sorry," she said. "I was terrified." She guided him through the living room and to the stairs since there wasn't a powder room on the first floor. "I thought the other man might kill me. Then you came up behind me and I panicked." She put his hand on the railing and kept her palm on his arm. "It's dark and I had no idea who you were or why you were there. Whether you'd attack me, too." And in the dim light from the window, his muscular shadow was more than a little frightening.

"I get it. Totally understandable." His tone was gentle when she wouldn't have blamed him for being irate. "I just need some water so I can rinse my eyes out."

Picking up the pace, she led him to the hallway bathroom, the second door on the left, and flicked on the light. "Thanks for taking this so well."

"Sink?"

"Oh, right." She steered him to the sink and turned on the spigot. "Sorry," she apologized for a third time, feeling awful for hurting him by accident.

He bent over and splashed handfuls of water onto his face again and again, rinsing out the Mace from his eyes and nose. Another palmful he scooped into his mouth, swished it around and spit.

In addition to the chemicals, blood hit the sink. She guessed it was from the fight in the living room. Several times more he repeated the process.

Summer sagged with a mix of shame and embarrassment. Her nerves were on edge. It was hard to tell who the good guys were anymore. Guilt prickled her for being the cause of his hissing gasps of discomfort. She put a hand on his back, not knowing what else to do to help him. His taut muscles flexed under his drenched T-shirt and in his exposed, sinewed arms.

The sheer strength of his body took her breath away. He was ripped.

Logan shut off the water and stood upright. He was six feet easily, maybe an inch or so taller. Curly dark blond hair glistened like gold in the bathroom light. And he was built like a freaking Viking.

Or maybe she had been watching way too much of the History channel.

Tearing her gaze from him, she looked for a towel. She went to the linen closet, grabbed a hand towel and gave it to him.

"Thanks." Wiping his face, he trudged over to the bathtub and plopped down on the edge.

She sat beside him. "You should've told me who you were instead of creeping up behind me like that." The situation had demanded that she act first and ask questions later.

"The guy who attacked you fled out the front door," he said. "I was worried you might run into him outside. Figured I'd make sure you were all right and stayed safe before I bothered with an introduction."

"Oh." That made sense, which in turn made her feel even worse. Not only had he saved her, but he'd been worried about her safety. "Sorry I nailed you with my Mace."

"No need to apologize. Again." He blinked rapidly. "You were scared and didn't know who I was."

Why did he have to be so nice about it? His kindness only compounded her guilt.

"Let me get you a bath towel," she said, rising to her feet. "You're soaked through." Not only was he drenched from the rain, but she was certain his shirt had absorbed a good deal of the pepper spray. The chemicals would continue to bother him.

She hurried back to the closet and pulled out a large, fluffy beige towel for him to drape around himself.

Turning around, she staggered to a halt as he grabbed the bottom of his T-shirt and hauled the wet top over his head.

Her jaw dropped, and she gaped at him, at all that exposed, tanned skin. At his bulging pecs. At his rippling abs. At his long, lean legs that were clad in wet denim. He wasn't overly bulky with muscle. Lean and sculpted. A well-honed physique too impressive to ignore, though she tried and failed.

"Wow," she breathed. Smart, good-looking men with an athletic build were her type. Add in chivalrous and she'd never encountered such an alluring combination.

"Huh?" He raised his head and looked up at her, squinting red, irritated eyes.

"Um, nothing." But he was definitely something. Unexpected in more ways than one.

"My vision is still blurry," he said. "Those sprays are oil-based. Hard to get off. Can you grab some soap for me?"

She slung the towel over her good shoulder and picked up a container of oat milk bodywash from the side of the tub. Turning on the bathtub faucet, she passed him the soap. He leaned over, washed his face twice and rinsed it thoroughly before taking the towel from her. She sat back down beside him.

He dried his face and ran the towel through his hair.

"That's better. Let's try the introduction one more time. Logan Powell." He proffered his hand as he wiped his eyes.

His grip was strong and steady, his palm warm.

"Summer Stratton. We met a few years back when Dani's mother passed away." She had died suddenly from heart disease. The death had devastated Dani, and Summer had done everything possible to lighten the load for her friend and Dani's dad, who had been heartbroken. After the funeral, once exhaustion set in, she and Logan had shared a quiet moment alone together on the back porch. She'd sipped a glass of wine while he nursed a beer. Chatted in a way that she never had before with a man—open and vulnerable, simply herself.

"I wasn't sure if you'd remember me," he said. "It was so long ago. I didn't want to presume and be wrong."

"You're hard to forget." Rare to find a man who had all the four *C*'s. Confident. Capable. Cute *and* considerate.

He'd been easy to talk to, things flowing naturally between them. In the crowd of strangers who'd come by to pay their respects, Summer had felt like an outsider. Until that moment alone with Logan. The two of them had been in a calm bubble out on the back porch, a little haven where she felt like she was home.

She'd wished he'd asked for her number. But what kind of man picked up a woman at a funeral?

Besides, her life was in Washington and his in Wyoming.

"I could say the same about you," he said. "The way you took charge, organizing and handling things from the flowers to the food. Dealing with problems without making a fuss. Impressive." Logan draped the towel on the side of the tub. "Wish we were meeting again under better circumstances, Ms. Stratton." Shifting in her direction, he looked at her. No more squinting. Direct gaze.

Piercing eyes so blue they were simply stunning met hers and then he smiled. Even those dimples were unforgettable.

Oh, my.

Chapter Three

A surge of intense awareness struck Logan like lightning as he stared at the brown-skinned beauty. Her face was stunningly familiar despite the fact that it had been several years, five to be exact, since he'd last seen her. As if he'd spent the brief time that they had been together memorizing each feature.

An oddly disturbing thought. Still, he continued to stare at her. Luminous, dark almond-shaped eyes. Smooth complexion. Lush, full lips. Her shoulder-length hair was tousled and wild, yet sexy with bouncy curls.

Why did death keep bringing him back together with this gorgeous woman?

"Please don't call me Ms. Stratton. It makes me feel like I'm at work. Summer is fine. My dad calls me Sunshine, but that makes me feel as though I'm eight years old instead of twenty-eight."

"I like Summer. As a season," he said, thinking of the first swim of the year in the lake, the busiest time on the ranch, the big Fourth of July celebration his family always hosted, his birthday and ideal weather, "and also as a name. It's beautiful." Like her.

"Thanks."

Blood on her shoulder caught his eye. It had soaked through the sleeve of her top and was dripping down her arm. "You're hurt."

This entire time she was tending to him, making sure that he was all right while she was injured. Bleeding. A wound she no doubt sustained because of the man he'd fought off. Anger rose and he tried hard to control his temper but seeing her hurt… Knowing that man had been the one to harm her. And for Summer to ignore the pain and focus solely on him with no thought of herself had Logan gritting his teeth.

"Why didn't you say anything?" he asked and reached for her.

But she cringed, making him lower his hand.

"It slipped my mind after I pepper-sprayed you," she said. "I was a little preoccupied worrying about your eyes and hoping I didn't blind you."

"What happened?" He gestured to her arm.

"That guy shot me. I was lucky. He nearly took my head off. I think a bullet only nicked me."

"Any idea who he was?"

"No," she said and glanced at her shoulder. "It hurts like the dickens."

"Thought it slipped your mind."

"Well, you've brought it back to the forefront, and now I know you're going to be okay."

His face stung, and would for a while, but he was fine. She was the one in need of medical attention. "Permission to touch you, so I can take a look?" he asked.

She nodded. "I don't mind you touching me."

Their gazes locked and silence fell. A pleasant moment of quiet brought another pop of awareness—a gut punch—

something so hard-hitting it took the air out of his lungs and weakened his knees.

Summer shook her head and quickly added, "I was nervous about the pain when you reached for me. I have a low tolerance for it. Never dealt well with physical discomfort."

Moving from the tub, he dropped to a knee on the other side of her where he could see the wound better. "I'll go slowly. If it hurts too much just let me know." He grabbed the hem of her short sleeve shirt and peeled it up. She winced, but didn't complain. "A lot deeper than a nick. But it passed right through. I can clean and bandage it for you, but you're going to need stitches. Otherwise, it'll leave a nasty scar."

Summer sighed. "I hate hospitals and with a gunshot wound they're going to call the sheriff."

"You say that like it's a bad thing." He got up and opened the cabinet under the sink. A medical kit peeked out from behind a stack of toilet paper, and he grabbed it.

"The sheriff hasn't been too helpful. In fact, I'd say he's been the opposite."

Law enforcement officers tended to get territorial and didn't appreciate civilians meddling in their investigations. Despite their good intentions, private citizens sometimes mucked things up or put themselves in harm's way. At the moment, he was inclined to place Summer in the latter category.

"We need to report what happened earlier anyway," he said. "Do you think the guy who attacked you was a burglar?" Cutthroat Creek had a few affluent areas. This wasn't one of them. Mostly farmland with owners making ends meet. Yet something had provoked the guy to break in wearing a mask and gloves and to carry gun. "Or was there more to it?"

"He wasn't a burglar," she said with such conviction that it was hard not to believe her. "He was here to stop me from nosing around by scaring me or…killing me."

His protective instincts flared hot again. "Once shots are fired, things have escalated beyond a scare tactic."

"Either way, the sheriff won't do anything about it. I don't know if he's being paid off or if he just thinks I'm delusional about what happened to Dani."

Logan sat beside her, where he could easily tend to her bloody shoulder. "I came up for her funeral with my uncle Ric and his son, Matt." Not only had he wanted to support Matt, but he had also been confident Summer would be there to say goodbye to her friend. Surprise, surprise, she had been a no-show. "The sheriff told my uncle and Matt that Dani was drunk and crashed into a tree." Logan had gone to get groceries while they went to the sheriff's office. Based on everything he'd heard, the circumstances were tragic but had appeared straightforward to him. Uncle Ric had stayed behind, trying to decide what to do with the property. Finally, he'd returned to Wyoming under the impression that Dani might have been murdered. His uncle had insisted someone with a badge needed to go to Cutthroat Creek to help Dani's friend, a lawyer, investigate and discover the truth. "I take it you don't think that's what really happened."

"No, I don't."

He opened the med kit. Took out gauze and saline solution. "Mind sharing your theory?"

"How well did you know Dani or about how much trouble she was having out here?"

Dani was only a cousin through marriage and with her living in another state, there wasn't much cause for them to be close. "I've only been here a couple of times." Every instance had been to keep Matt company. Logan and his brothers had grown up alongside Matt, thought of him as a brother for all intents and purposes. When they were younger, Matt had a hard time fitting in, feeling as though he didn't belong anywhere. Logan did what he could to show him family would stand by him through anything. "Honestly, I didn't know her well at all." Wiping the blood from her arm, he worked his way up toward her shoulder. "As for the trouble she was having, I heard she lost her father last year." Uncle Ric's brother had passed from cancer. Work had prevented Logan from attending the funeral. "Things weren't going well on the farm, and she was having financial difficulty. Something to do with a problem with her cattle." He squirted saline solution in the wound, and she flinched. "Sorry."

"It's okay." Her gaze lifted to his, her brown eyes glowing with a softness. "I kind of deserved it for Macing you."

Logan grinned. Not that getting pepper-sprayed in the face was a joking matter. Her tone was so apologetic, her eyes so full of remorse—she was sweet, for a lawyer—that he wanted to make her feel better. Simply couldn't help it.

For a second, he was awed by the realization that he couldn't shake the bizarre feeling of connection to this woman. It had been the same way five years ago. There'd been the preparations, a wake, the funeral. And through it all, Summer had been at Dani's side. Then at the repast later at the house, they'd stood out on the back porch talking. He'd been mesmerized by her. Warm and charming and completely at ease with herself. Even after he'd returned home to Wyoming, the young, whip-smart attorney had stayed on his mind.

"Ric told me Matt might come up to investigate," she said. "He didn't mention the possibility of anyone else. I'd say this was a nice surprise, but…" Her voice trailed off.

No need for her to finish the sentence.

He wrapped gauze around the wound, bandaging it. The best that could be done until she got stitches.

"Matt is on vacation with his fiancée. He's had it planned for a while and didn't want to cancel," Logan said. Matt and Hannah weren't the types to take downtime often. No one in his family was. Workaholics the lot of them. Logan wanted the two lovebirds to get away, unwind, and have some fun for once instead of working their *day jobs*—a relative term since both Matt and Hannah were cops—while also putting in time on the ranch. "My brother Jackson, he's a US marshal, wanted to do it. He actually lives nearby but he's traveling right now on a fugitive recovery assignment. Uncle Ric felt the situation was urgent and couldn't wait. So, I stepped up and volunteered."

Everyone else was busy these days. Falling in love. Getting married. Having babies. Everyone except for him and his youngest brother, the marshal. They all joked that Jackson was the forgotten one. Left home as soon as he turned eighteen and just visited for a special occasion—wedding, christening or funeral. Only their mother kept track of him with regular phone calls. In many ways, Logan admired how his little brother had forged a path apart from their family, away from home, outside of Wyoming. Heck, Logan still lived on the ranch, along with his brothers Monty and Holden, and his cousin Matt. His other brother, Sawyer, only left last year after love led him to Virginia. The ranch had been Logan's home all his life. One day he'd leave, if he ever found the right reason.

"I've met Jackson," she said, slight hesitation in her voice. "We both attended the funeral for Dani's father last year. Your brother, he's not..." her lips flattened in a tight line, like she was choosing her words carefully "...a people person. Not like you. I don't think he would've been quite so understanding about the pepper spray."

"Jackson can be standoffish with strangers." Downright cold and curt, to be honest. "He doesn't have the Powell family charm." What his brother lacked in people skills, he made up for with fierce loyalty and ferocious tenacity. Once he fought for a cause or a person, he didn't back down. No one ever said that Jackson Powell didn't have determination.

"It's generous of you to take time off and come out to investigate on behalf of a cousin you barely knew."

If only his reasons had been entirely selfless. His ulterior motive had been to see Summer Stratton again. This time he knew for certain that she'd be in Cutthroat Creek. Logan's interest in her had been stirred from the moment they were introduced, and had intensified during the events surrounding the funeral. Still, he'd realized there was a possibility he would be disappointed when he came back here.

People changed, sometimes drastically over five years, and were often different at funerals than their usual, day-to-day selves.

Not Summer. She was the same genuine, kindhearted woman he remembered.

But he was unable to admit his selfish cause for being in Cutthroat. He stayed quiet, letting her believe he was a better man than he really was.

"You and your uncle Ric must be close."

"Not really," Logan said, sadly. The distance between them had been entirely his uncle's choice. "Uncle Ric helps manage the Shooting Star-Longhorn Ranch at home, but he acts more like an employee than family."

"Why is that?"

Logan shrugged. "The situation is complicated. I'll tell you another time. Let's just say coming out here was the right thing to do. I might not have known Dani well, but if her death wasn't an accident, she deserves justice and my uncle needs peace of mind. Figured I'd put some of the leave days I've got banked to good use. Only problem is I'm not really sure what I'm here to investigate."

The sheriff's office had closed the case. Logan didn't have the faintest idea why his uncle and Summer thought it should be reopened beyond a hunch.

"Dani was my best friend," Summer said.

Logan recalled that they had gone to college together and had been roommates throughout all their undergrad years, starting on campus and eventually sharing an apartment close to the school.

"We always stayed in touch, talking several times a month," she continued. "A couple of years ago, she contacted me with suspicions that her cattle were being poisoned."

"By whom?"

"Einhorn Industries. They own the paper mill and waste recycling plant in town. Einhorn manufactures fertilizer from biosolids. They claim it's safe, but it isn't. Dani discovered it was making her cattle sick and convinced her father not to buy it anymore."

"Did it make a difference when they stopped using it?"

"Unfortunately, no. Einhorn has a facility not far from here. Dani suspected the chemicals from the biosolids were polluting the creek that not only runs through this property but is also adjacent to the waste recycling plant. At my firm in Seattle, I've helped work on class action lawsuits against companies like Einhorn as an associate. I told her how to go about collecting evidence to see if there was a possible case. She found four other farmers having similar problems. I helped convince them to become plaintiffs as well. We were getting close to nailing Einhorn. We had almost everything we needed. Then I found out Dani was dead."

"The timing is a bit suspicious, granted, but her blood alcohol was 0.3." For a woman Dani's size, that was dangerously high and could've been enough to kill her even if she hadn't gotten behind the wheel of a car. "She shouldn't have been driving the night of her accident." The only positive thing was that nobody else had been killed. Way too often it seemed that passengers or the innocent occupants of other vehicles bore the brunt of the trauma while the drunk driver walked away with barely a scratch. "I get that you two were best friends and you might've been close to finding something on Einhorn, but her death doesn't sound like a homicide."

"There's something you don't know. Dani was an alcoholic," she said as though the statement refuted the facts.

"More proof that substantiates what I'm saying."

"You don't understand. She's been sober for seven years. No relapses. Worked the program consistently. Went to meetings once a week like clockwork. There's no way Dani was drinking and driving."

"Alcoholics relapse all the time. Addiction can be a daily struggle for some."

Summer sighed, shoulders slumping, brow creasing, mouth twisting into an expression that tugged at something inside his chest. "I'm used to the skepticism from everyone in town, but I didn't think I'd get it from her family who was sent here to help."

"Yes, I'm family. I'm also a cop." A good one, too. He'd worked for the DCI, a division of the Wyoming State Attorney General's Office, for ten years. At thirty-one, he'd dedicated a third of his life to law enforcement. It was a part of who he was. "I need to look at this objectively. Filter out emotion. The fact is Dani had the added pressure of losing her father and the strain of the farm not making money. Stressful reasons that could drive someone to fall off the wagon. I can't ignore it."

Summer put a hand on his forearm. "I loved Dani like a sister. I knew her. We told each other everything. No matter how embarrassing or shameful. You have to believe me. She wasn't drinking."

No one could say with certainty what a person did alone at home behind closed doors, no matter how well they knew the other person. Countless times he'd seen family members and friends of victims and criminals who were shocked to learn the truth about people they loved.

But he hadn't come all this way to simply shut Summer down. "Let's say you're right and there was foul play. Why would Einhorn Industries kill her?"

"Einhorn has a foothold in the northwestern region. They recently signed a huge government contract. Losing a class action lawsuit would expose them to billions of dollars in damages that they don't want to pay and give the government grounds to terminate that lucrative contract. They're not a behemoth like some other companies who can afford to take that kind of hit or hire lobbyists to champion their side in Washington, DC. This would bankrupt Einhorn."

"That's definitely a motive. I'm sure the list of suspects

won't be a short one." It would most likely include the entire executive leadership: CEO, CFO, CCO, CIO, etc. "Not that any of the suits would get their hands dirty. They would delegate the unpleasantness to someone on the security team or a freelance person. All hard to prove *if* a homicide had been committed." A big if with a capital *I*.

Summer tightened her grasp on his arm. "I realize you're inclined to believe Dani's death was an accident. The story is a good one. A recovered alcoholic has a relapse, drinks an abnormally high amount, gets behind the wheel and plows into a tree. Simple. Easy. Won't raise any red flags. Unless you knew Dani. If you did, you'd see it as a *great* cover story for murder. She didn't deserve to die so young."

"No one does."

"I was almost killed tonight because I won't stop asking unwelcome questions about Dani and Einhorn. You saw the guy for yourself."

Someone had tried to kill her and may have very well succeeded if Logan hadn't arrived when he had. That was irrefutable.

He wanted to know who'd attacked her and why. Motives weren't always obvious. Part of him considered telling her to go home and let him handle it, but Summer didn't strike him as the sort to be easily dissuaded.

"I did see him and there's no denying he wanted to do you bodily harm. Assuming the gunman's intent was to silence you, he'll try again."

Danger could even follow her back to Seattle. Logan couldn't let that happen. Whoever it was had messed with the wrong woman and the wrong cowboy.

"You're skeptical," she said, "and I understand why, but

you came here anyway. All I'm asking is that you help me get to the truth. No matter where it leads."

Her hopeful expression tugged on him. He couldn't remember when he'd last felt needed. *Crucial.* As one of six boys—including his cousin—he was a middle child and had often gotten lost in the shuffle. Never could find his place and had to carve one out for himself. He filled in the gaps. Served where he could when he could.

But this came down to him. Either he helped Summer see this through and kept her alive in the process, or no one else would. "I'll stay and I won't stop digging until we find the truth. Together. I give you my word."

Chapter Four

On a scale of one to ten, this was…unquantifiable. How could she rate this kind of nightmare?

Her best friend had been murdered, she'd been attacked, and a skeptical, distractingly handsome cowboy had agreed to help.

Ouch. She winced when the ER doctor brought the needle near her arm again.

Then she had stitches to add to the list of the things that lowered the scale on the wrong side.

"I haven't even touched you yet," Dr. Payne said.

An apropos name.

Summer stared at the doctor, wishing he'd show her some sympathy. "The thought of the needle going in hurts."

"The anticipation of pain can trigger cortical systems involved in the experience of pain." Dr. Payne drew in a deep breath, his patience beginning to wear thin on his face. "Try looking away."

Summer turned her head and glanced up at Logan.

He gave her a sincere smile. "I could hold your hand if you think it'll help."

"Let's give it a try. Can't hurt. Pun intended."

His smile deepened, along with his dimples, warming something inside her chest as he took her hand.

She squeezed her fingers tightly around his. Staring at his handsome face while touching him should've been enough of a diversion, but it wasn't. She pictured the needle drawing closer, the sharp tip pricking her skin, and flinched.

Dr. Payne sighed. "I still didn't touch you."

"It's going to be okay," Logan said, patting her leg. His boyish grin was charming enough to sell ice in Antarctica.

She did her best to fix a matching smile on her face, but only managed to give a grimace.

"Since the wound isn't very deep, can you use liquid stitches instead?" Logan asked the doctor.

"I can," Dr. Payne said with a curt nod. "But they're triple the cost. Most folks either can't afford it or don't want the unnecessary expense. So, I don't usually mention it."

Summer didn't realize those were even an option. Anything was better than a needle. Except for a skin stapler. She shivered at the prospect.

"I'll take the liquid stitches," she said. To heck with the cost.

She saved and invested forty percent of her money, a lesson her mom and dad had drilled into her. Another twenty percent, she sent to her parents, to repay them for their contribution to her law school fees, so they could enjoy retirement. Although she denied herself luxury purchases such as designer handbags, a fancy car and thousand-dollar suits, this was one splurge that was worth the expense.

"Okay." The doctor pulled off his latex gloves in a bit of a huff and tossed them in the trash. "Give me a minute and I'll go grab the surgical glue." He pulled back the curtain in the emergency room bay, but he caught a nurse passing by and asked her to get it for him. Folding his arms, he turned back to them. "So, you're the hotshot lawyer from Seattle out here stirring up trouble."

Here we go.

No matter where she went in Cutthroat Creek she received the same unwelcoming spirit. Originally from a small town in Texas that was just outside of San Antonio—a diverse area in the US—she had wondered if the cold shoulder in Montana was because she was a Black woman on her own. Yet, she'd never had a problem when she'd been with Dani. After being here for a couple of weeks, she realized her ethnicity and gender didn't matter. Whenever she ventured out of Cutthroat to a nearby town, like Bitterroot Falls, she was greeted with a smile and treated hospitably. The moment she mentioned Einhorn, however, everything changed, like a glacier magically materialized, frosting over the conversation.

She had hoped there wouldn't be any need to worry about a confrontation at the hospital.

Apparently not. She was right not to let the doctor anywhere near her with a needle.

Summer straightened. "I'm not here to cause any trouble. Only to get to the truth, which shouldn't be a problem for anyone, unless they have something to hide."

"I'm friends with the coroner. He's a good man. Not corrupt like you've insinuated."

"Even good men can falter," she said, "and succumb to pressure." No one was perfect. She'd seen firsthand in other cases just how far and deep the poisonous influence of a big corporation could taint a community.

"Dani Granger's tox screen wasn't tampered with," Dr. Payne said. "The woman was drunk. If crashing into a tree didn't kill, alcohol poisoning surely would've. Fortunately, she only killed herself in the process. Even though the truth is simple and plain to see, I hear you're hell-bent on twisting it to suit your own manipulative purpose."

Gossip spread faster than Ebola in this small town.

Stiffening, she prepared to set him straight about her motive and her theory.

"Dr. Payne," Logan said before she could get a word out, "it's an ethical and legal violation for the coroner to discuss a case with his pals."

The nurse returned and hesitated near the curtain, picking up on the tension in the medical bay.

"The facts were printed in the *Bitterroot Beacon*," the doctor said, referring to the one paper that serviced the entire area of Bitterroot Lake, including Cutthroat, "and he only discussed it with me after the case was *closed*. Officially, I might add, by the sheriff. As I said, he's an upstanding man."

The nurse cleared her throat. "Excuse me, Doc, I have the surgical glue you requested. If you'd like, I can apply it and free you up to handle other things."

"Thank you, I need to call the sheriff and see what's taking him so long to get here to look into this gunshot wound. He should've been here by now." Dr. Payne threw a scowl Summer's way and left.

"Hi," the nurse said, coming in, "sorry about that." Her name tag read Kimimela. She was Native American, at least part Native American, with light brown skin and long hair that flowed down her back in a glossy black sheet. The nurse set the glue on a stainless steel tray and grabbed a set of latex gloves. "I got the impression it might be better if I stepped in."

Her intervention was appreciated. "Thank you. I'm glad I passed on the regular stitches."

Kimimela tugged on the gloves and inspected the wound the doctor had already cleaned. "Don't worry about Doc." She removed the top to the glue. "He would've given you nice clean stitches even if you did imply that his golfing and hunting buddy was corrupt."

"You'd think I took out a full-page ad in the *Beacon* declaring as much. I only mentioned the idea to one person."

"And who was that?" Logan asked, still holding her hand like it was the most natural thing in the world.

"The sheriff." Assuming he was on the side of justice, Summer had told him far too much.

"This will sting." Kimimela held up the pen-shaped tube of Dermabond glue. "But it won't last long. I'll line up the edges of the wound and seal it. Should take less than sixty seconds, but the glue needs two to three minutes to dry."

"Should I look away?"

"I overheard how squeamish you were with Doc." The nurse gave a sympathetic look. "While I fix you up, why don't you look at his baby blues?" She gestured to Logan.

Summer met his gaze. He flashed her another easy smile, standing beside her, at ease and composed, with a dark brown cowboy hat on his head and wearing a fresh change of clothes he'd pulled from a duffel bag that looked like it had seen better days.

Since she'd gotten to Cutthroat Creek after Dani's death, her stomach had constantly churned with anxiety and fear while her head filled with ideas of who the murderer could be. With Logan now by her side, for the first time she experienced a sense of calm, a stillness inside. It was as if some great emotional roller coaster, up and down and twisting and turning, had finally stopped.

"Only takes one person," Logan said, "to act as the town crier and then everybody knows your business. It's the same way back home. Small towns have that in common."

A burning sensation flared in her arm, and she grimaced.

He tightened his fingers around hers. "You're almost done and handling it like a champ after the night you've had."

Emotion knotted her throat at his kind words. She drew a quick breath, trying not to notice his sexy lips, the strong jaw, the thick curly hair that fell over his forehead.

Maybe she needed to think of Logan as a bodyguard, keep a good solid emotional wall between them. "I'm more like the biggest wimp, but I appreciate the encouragement."

"Finished. We just need to let it dry," Kimimela said, stepping around to the other side of the stainless steel table.

Logan moved in front of her, leaned over and blew on her shoulder the way her mom used to whenever she got a boo-boo. It helped. A lot.

He really was sweet. Sexy, too.

And cracks already started forming in that wall.

"I read about your lawsuit," Kimimela said. "Is it true about Einhorn products not being safe?"

"It's true. Dani's family stopped using their products, but runoff from their facility contaminated the creek her cattle drank from. The cattle started dying. Tumors. Black teeth. Some of them acted crazed. The ones that lived had to be put down and her father died from cancer."

Summer was tightening the threads that connected directly to Einhorn. Not a simple, quick or straightforward task. After filing the lawsuit, Einhorn had complied with the discovery process and sent her boxes upon boxes of documents she still had to finish going through.

"Einhorn's facility isn't far from the Bigfork Reservation," Kimimela said. "The Snowberry Creek that runs through the Granger property and right next to the facility feeds into the Bigfork River. Is it possible people on the reservation could be poisoned?"

Summer nodded. "It's possible."

"You should be careful if you're planning to stay in town." Kimimela unwrapped a bandage and put it on Summer's arm, covering the liquid adhesive stitches. "You're upsetting the wrong people. Powerful people."

"People willing to kill Dani Granger to silence her?" Logan asked.

The nurse rocked back, her face paling. "I'm not saying that. It's just…" Kimimela peeked out of the bay and looked around. "I knew Dani. We weren't close friends or anything, but we spoke in passing, asked each other about our families. I'd see her around all the time." Kimimela hesitated, pressing her lips in a grim line.

Summer had questioned enough witnesses to know when someone was taking the scenic route to get to the destination of what they wanted to share. "It's okay. Whatever you have to say will stay between us."

Kimimela leaned in and lowered her voice. "I don't know about the tox screen or if Dani was drinking that night, but it was odd she was driving that old Ford pickup."

"The green one?" Logan asked, and Kimimela nodded. "Why would it be odd?"

"That truck was her dad's. Dani never drove it. Not once in the past twelve years since we all got our licenses, around the same time, have I ever seen her behind the wheel of it."

A chill washed over Summer. During the times when she had visited, Dani hadn't used the green truck. In fact, she hated it and had told Summer it represented everything that was wrong with Cutthroat Creek. *Old body style and engineering that was a nose-thumb to social consciousness.*

Logan let go of her hand and stepped closer to the nurse. "Why would the coroner lie about her death?"

"I'm not saying he lied. For all I know, Dani was blitzed out of her mind and made the regrettable choice to drive when she shouldn't have. All I'm saying is Dani wouldn't have done it in that truck. Listen, no one questions the coroner's assessment. Ever. Greg Genberg has been around a long time. Like the sheriff. And this is an election year. Einhorn is a major campaign donor to parties they—"

"Kimi Anne Wheeler." Sheriff Tofteland entered the bay, his voice stern and booming with authority. "Dr. Payne thought you'd be finished by now. He needs your assistance. A young man was just brought in with a broken arm and busted jaw. Brawl in a bar. That's what delayed me in getting here."

The nurse flushed. "I was just, um, explaining the lay of the land."

"No need to do that, Kimi Anne. If you're done in here, you should get going."

The nurse nodded. "Yes, Sheriff." She looked at Summer. "Keep the wound dry for the next few days. The stitches will fall off naturally after it has done its job. Good luck." She hurried off out of the medical bay.

Then Lester Tofteland turned his full, steely focus on Summer. The sheriff had a menacing air of authority to him that made her want to cringe, but she refused to be intimidated, scared off, or browbeaten.

Straightening, she faced him. She wasn't leaving Cutthroat Creek until she decided it was time to go.

THE SHERIFF STARED at Summer and shook his snow-white head with a look of disapproval.

Tofteland, who Logan took to be in his late sixties, cut the very image of a vintage cowboy with his barrel chest, sweeping walrus-style mustache that was equally white, and pale green eyes lined with wrinkles from all the years of squinting beneath the rim of his campaign hat.

A shadow of anxiety passed over Summer's face as she stiffened, and Logan found himself taking a defensive posture at her side before he even realized what he was doing. He was glad he'd changed his clothes prior to coming to the hospital so he didn't have to face the sheriff looking like a drowned cat.

"Miss Stratton, it appears that you just can't stay out of trouble. This is a sure sign that it's time for you to pack your bags, get out of my town, and go home, missy." The condescending tone grated on Logan.

Two things he couldn't stand: inappropriate assumptions and bullies. Especially bullies wearing a badge.

"Thank you for responding to the gunshot wound as quickly as possible," Logan said, drawing the sheriff's gaze. "*Ms*. Stratton was attacked and nearly killed." *Miss* sounded just as patronizing as *missy*, coming from the sheriff. "I sustained injuries myself during an altercation with the gunman. We'd like to file a report."

Tofteland raised a bushy white eyebrow. "And you are?"

"Logan Powell." Rather than shake hands, he unclipped his badge from his waistband and held it up. "A special agent with DCI."

The sheriff's gaze lasered in on the seven-pointed star. Then he studied Logan for a moment and narrowed his green eyes. "You're outside of your jurisdiction, son."

"That may be, but I'm not your son and she's not a missy. We'd like to file a report about the attack."

"An attack, huh?" The sheriff stroked his mustache. "Where did this alleged attack take place?" he asked, pulling out a notepad and pen.

Summer folded her hands in her lap. "I was inside the Granger house when—"

"Hold on." The sheriff raised his palm. "Let me stop you right there because we seem to have a failure to communicate. The last time you were out there, I told you that you were trespassing and to steer clear of the Granger property. Otherwise, I'd arrest you."

"Ric Granger called your office," she said, "and left a message that I had permission to be in the house."

The sheriff shrugged. "I never got the message and I can't just take your word for it, little lady."

Logan clenched his jaw, letting the man dig a deeper hole.

"That's why I also advised Mr. Granger to email you. He cc'd me. I'd be happy to pull it up for you."

"I would need to see signed documentation." Tofteland put a fist on his hip. "Emails can be hacked."

What on earth was he implying? Whatever the illicit insinuation, it was ticking Logan off. "Fortunate for you, Sheriff, I'm here."

"And how is your presence fortunate, Mr. Powell?"

"I forgot to mention I'm Dani Granger's cousin. In the glove compartment of my truck, parked just outside, is permission for both me and Ms. Stratton to have full access to the property," Logan said. "Signed by my uncle, the current owner, notarized and witnessed by the mayor back home." He left out the part about the mayor being his mother.

"Also done under my advisement." The distinct hint of satisfaction in Summer's voice almost made Logan smile.

He had thought the document was overkill, along with the limited power of attorney his uncle had given him, but it was coming in handy now.

"I see." The sheriff stroked his mustache again. "Well, let's hear your statements."

They both explained what happened, giving as many details as possible without mentioning anything after the assailant ran off, when Summer had pepper-sprayed him.

"Neither of you got a look at him or noticed any identifying marks, is that correct?" Sheriff Tofteland asked.

Summer nodded.

"That's correct, but I stabbed him in the right wrist," Logan added. "He'll have a wound."

"Not much else to go on besides the assailant's injury." Tofteland hurriedly flipped the notebook closed. "I do have one more thing to ask you, Miss Stratton. What on earth were you doing in the house, creeping around in the dark, at eleven thirty at night?"

The first good question from the sheriff. Logan looked at Summer, wanting an answer as well.

"I was in the dark because I believed the house was being watched. Or I was being followed. I wasn't sure."

"The reason you were there?" Tofteland pressed.

Summer squared her shoulders. "I missed Dani," she said with a little hike of her chin. "We had a pair of blue jeans we used to share, sending them back and forth to each other over the years. I figured I'd get in, find them and go back to the place I'm renting. It was sentimental and silly, but I needed those jeans." Emotion vibrated through the words that flowed smooth as silk from her, like a prepared oral argument.

Frowning, the sheriff shook his head. "Women," he said under his breath, not nearly low enough.

The sheriff might have bought her story, but Logan didn't. He imagined that was how Summer presented herself in court. Confident and calculated, only showing enough emotion to be persuasive.

Tofteland shoved his notebook and pen in his pocket. "You're ruffling a lot of feathers in this town with your lawsuit and your questions. I'm telling you again, for your own safety, you should go home."

"And if she doesn't?" Logan asked.

"This is big sky country. We don't take kindly to outsiders wreaking havoc. I'm not sure I can guarantee her safety unless she leaves."

To Logan, big sky country meant untamed landscape and Old West values—loyalty, respect, justice—where someone's word was their bond—and the folks were warm and welcoming.

Not lawlessness without consequences.

"We're only asking you to do your job," Summer said.

"Whoever broke into the house and attacked you was probably just trying to scare you," the sheriff said. "Next time, their intent could be more deadly."

Logan shook his head. "The intent was clearly deadly tonight." Summer was right. The sheriff wasn't going to help. "Who in town would want to hurt her, other than someone on Einhorn Industries' payroll?"

Sheriff Tofteland laughed. The sound was deep and scathing and devoid of humor. "Boy, you're way out of your depth. Most of the town is on Einhorn Industries payroll. The others who aren't reap the benefits of the company being here in some form or fashion."

Logan met the man's hard stare and held it. "Does that include you?"

"Watch yourself," the sheriff said, pointing a finger in his face. "Do me and yourselves a favor. Leave. Special Agent Powell, go home, where you've got jurisdiction. And as for you, little lady, fight your lawsuit in Seattle. No need to wage war in my town."

"I have every reason to stay," Summer said, not backing down, "and no intention of leaving until I get to the bottom of what really happened to Dani." The glimpse of vulnerability she'd shown minutes earlier was gone, replaced by fiery determination. "Why didn't the coroner perform an autopsy?"

"An autopsy is only carried out when a death is suspicious." The sheriff's ferocious scowl deepened. "What happened to Dani Granger is unfortunate. Poor woman just drank too much. Died in a car crash. She had a blood alcohol level that could strip paint. Case closed." Tofteland crossed his arms over his chest as if to punctuate that statement. "You ought to be careful poking your nose where it doesn't belong in Cutthroat Creek. Never know who'll poke back. You two drive safely." He tipped his campaign hat at them and left.

Logan turned to Summer. "Was he serious that it could've been anyone from town who attacked you?"

"Not only who attacked me, but also killed Dani. The list of possible suspects is longer than you might think," Summer said. "After being here for a couple of weeks, I don't know if it was Einhorn for certain or simply someone in town who was angry at Dani for pursuing a lawsuit."

This conspiracy theory was growing, getting more concrete and feeling less like a far-fetched plot. "Why would a lawsuit against Einhorn make someone in town angry enough to kill Dani and attack you?"

"Dani and I spearheaded this. Einhorn practically owns Cutthroat Creek and dozens of other small towns just like it. Here, the paper mill and the waste recycling plant do in fact provide seventy-five percent of the town's jobs. If Einhorn lost a lawsuit that's worth billions, bankrupting them, it means a lot of people here would lose their jobs and wouldn't be able to feed their families. I've learned there are plenty of folks in town who will do anything to prevent that from happening. Who hold us responsible."

"Another valid motive, but—"

"No more buts."

"I believe you that there's more here than meets the eye. *But* we need evidence."

Summer got down off the hospital bed. "We're not going to find it here tonight. It's after one in the morning. We need to get some sleep."

"Agreed. Your car is still in the woods near the house. Why don't you just stay there with me tonight. Take one of the guest rooms or Dani's. That way I know you're safe. In the morning, I can follow you over to the cabin you rented."

Summer hesitated like she was going to fight the issue, but to his surprise she said, "Okay." She grabbed her purse. "Let's go."

"Hey," he said, putting a light hand on her uninjured shoulder. For some reason, he just couldn't stop touching her. "What was with that story about the pair of jeans?"

"What makes you think it was a story?"

He gave her an incredulous look. "Come on."

"It was from a movie that Dani and I watched together one night in college. *The Sisterhood of the Traveling Pants*. Ever seen it?"

"Sounds like a sappy flick for teenage girls."

"Don't knock it until you've tried it." She smiled, and he barely resisted the urge to push back stray curls veiling one eye.

They were practically strangers, but the sensation that he'd known her forever crashed through him. Like they'd been something more in a past life. Not that he put a drop of credence in any of that woo-woo pishposh.

She was beautiful. Had the kind of face he could look at forever. And nice. Brave, too, the way she'd attacked him, trying to defend herself.

Still, it was more than a primal attraction. He just couldn't quite put his finger on what *it* was. Maybe all the adrenaline flooding his system induced this visceral reaction, making him feel something that wasn't real.

Only one way to find out. Digging into the circumstances of Dani's death alongside her meant he'd get a chance to know her better.

"The movie has a little something for everyone," she said. "At the heart of it, it's about learning to appreciate what's right in front of you as well as new experiences."

He didn't need a movie for that. Only more time with Summer. "So, what were you really doing in the house, close to midnight and in the dark?"

"The part about being followed or the house being watched was true. Before Dani was killed, she believed someone was following her, too. Her house was even broken into. Everything she had on the case was either in the dining room or stored in the garage. Someone took files, destroyed samples she had collected on her cows, and stole her laptop. Anyway, she started hiding things. *In the house.* I was looking for evidence. Dani told me that she got the last thing we needed. In essence, the smoking gun with Einhorn's prints all over it. We just need to find it."

Something told Logan that would be easier said than done.

Chapter Five

Spending the night at the Granger house had been a good suggestion by Logan. Summer had been reluctant to stay there after Dani's death, but it had been tolerable in the guest room. She still hadn't slept soundly, tossing and turning throughout the night. Although, with Logan close by, just in the next room, she'd had one less thing to worry about.

All her personal things were back at the rented cabin. She'd had to borrow one of Dani's nightgowns to sleep in. A long, white one dappled with yarrow and coneflowers, and with spaghetti straps and ruffles at the bottom. The nightgown had been one of her best friend's favorites. Unlike the fake story about a pair of blue jeans they'd shared, wearing the nightgown had somehow made her feel closer to Dani.

Summer finished changing into her clothes from the day before. Aching to shower and put on a fresh outfit, she tied her hiking boots.

Having slept with her hair up to maintain her curls, Summer pulled out the pins and tossed them back in her purse. As she left the bedroom, Logan was coming up the stairs and had reached the top landing.

Face flush and chest bare, he wore running shorts and sneakers. His tanned skin glistened with sweat.

Summer quickly popped a piece of peppermint gum in her mouth. "I didn't hear you leave the house," she said, doing her best not to ogle him.

"Went for a quick jog around the property. After my eleven-hour drive up here from Laramie last night, I needed it. I didn't want to wake you, but I left a note for you downstairs so you wouldn't worry," he said, once again reminding her how considerate he was.

Little things like that mattered. She'd had a date stand her up one time, leaving her sitting in a restaurant waiting for almost an hour because he got caught up at work and forgot about her.

A respectful, thoughtful man such as Logan would've called.

"How did you sleep?" he asked.

"Pretty good." She looked past him at the hole in the wall. Last night that bullet had nearly killed her. "Considering." She gestured to it, one of many.

"The sheriff didn't even bother to come out, take a look, collect any evidence. There are bullets and cartridge casings, ballistic fingerprints all over the place."

She'd warned him. "We can't expect much from Sheriff Tofteland."

"Unfortunately, you're right. That's why I called my boss first thing this morning and explained the delicate situation. Asked him to reach out to DCI here in Montana to see if they'd be willing to investigate the attack since they're neutral and a special agent was involved. Once he's done talking to someone in investigations, he'll let me know if they're willing to step on some toes out here."

"Very clever." A lot to admire about Logan Powell. When he stood up to Sheriff Tofteland in the emergency room there'd been a steel gleam in Logan's eyes, an unshakable confidence in his tone, a core of strength that she found very, very appealing.

Right along with the rest of him. Her gaze wandered over the sweat-slicked landscape of his body, and she moistened her lips. He was in incredible shape. Muscular arms. Broad shoulders. Tapered waist. Well-defined legs. She'd never seen calves so sculpted.

Being near him stirred sensations and curiosity she did not need stirred. Not at a time like this, when she needed her sole focus to be on investigating. But his good looks and his kindness and strength and the fact that he'd saved her from the masked gunman had her thoughts careening in a sexually charged direction.

At twenty-eight, she was still a virgin and proud to wait for a meaningful experience rather than give in to a carnal moment she might regret. For her, she didn't see anything wrong with waiting rather than rushing, even though her sisters thought she was being ridiculous.

But this was the first time she'd entertained the idea, for a moment anyway, of sleeping with a man she wasn't in a relationship with.

"I'll take a quick shower," he said, "then drive you to your car and make sure you get back to your rental safely. There's fresh coffee downstairs. I made a pot before my run. Should still be hot."

"Thanks." She skirted past him on the landing, catching the scent of him—sweat and musk and all male—and headed down the stairs.

"Don't clean up while you're waiting," he said, and she glanced back at him over her shoulder. "Just in case the

Montana DCI decide to come out. It's best to leave the scene as intact as possible."

"Smart thinking. I probably would've tidied up. I hate a mess."

"I'm a clean freak, too." A lopsided grin tugged at one corner of his mouth, highlighting a single dimple.

She had to grab the railing to steady herself on the stairs. "One thing we have in common."

"I'm sure there are many others. Like I remember you told me you were close to your family. Especially your sisters. All of you named after seasons."

How did he recall that after five years?

Summer did miss being near her family in Texas, having weekly dinners with them. Her parents were about to retire and planned to spend the next three years living on a cruise ship, sailing around the world. Winter, a detective with the San Antonio PD, was going to relocate to Seattle to be closer. Her other sister, Autumn, who was a forensic psychologist, was ready to leave the congestion and high prices of Los Angeles, where she currently worked. But Autumn complained Seattle was too rainy and too large and would prefer someplace with small-town values: community involvement, neighborliness, quality family time, resilience and inclusivity. The type of cornerstones they had growing up.

"I'm tight with my family, too," Logan said.

Except for his uncle, but that was a conversation for another time. "All boys, right?"

"Yeah, but almost everybody is engaged or married, so there are plenty of daughters-in-law."

"Does that also include you? I mean, are you engaged?

Married?" she asked, noting he didn't have on a wedding band. Not that the lack of one meant he wasn't married. "Attached?"

"Comfortably single."

Nice to know. "Oh. Me, too."

His grin spread into a deep smile.

Why did she say that? Just because she wasn't dating didn't mean she was available for a long-distance relationship and just because he was a nice guy didn't mean he was interested anyway. He did say that he was comfortable being single.

Nothing wrong with getting to know him and being friends with someone she also happened to be attracted to.

"I'll hurry," he said. "I won't be long." He disappeared into the bathroom and the shower started.

It was a good thing she was staying in a cabin on the outskirts of town. She was already going to be attached at the hip to him while they dug deeper into the circumstances surrounding Dani's death. Spending countless hot, sultry nights under the same roof as him, too, would only spell trouble.

The living room was an even bigger disaster in the morning light than she had first imagined. Impossible to get to the kitchen without stepping on something.

She grabbed a mug and poured a cup of hot coffee.

Remnants of pepper spray lingered in the room. To let in much-needed fresh air, she cracked open the window over the sink, which she realized she'd left unlocked after attempting to make her great escape.

Sipping on her coffee, she stared at the fridge, still at an angle, resting between the counters and blocking the back door.

The gunman who broke in had gone through a lot of trouble to push it over that way. Not to mention the noise he had made in the kitchen and the living room. Had he done all that to spook her and draw her out into the open?

"Ready?" Logan asked, appearing in the doorway. He was fully dressed, in a white T-shirt and jeans, his curly hair damp from his shower.

"Sure." She finished the coffee in her mug, set it in the sink, then closed and locked the window. "We can go."

He let her walk out of the kitchen ahead of him. Passing him on the threshold, she couldn't help taking in the clean, woodsy smell of him that taunted her senses with promises of safety. He trailed behind her through the living room.

Near the front door, she noticed the console table for the entryway. Unopened mail was on top beside a small porcelain bowl with owls painted on it. Inside were Dani's keys.

She picked them up, ran her fingers across them and clenched them in her hand.

"What is it?" Logan asked.

Ideas spun in her head, but she said, "Nothing." She put the keys in her purse.

Outside, they climbed down the porch steps. As they headed toward Logan's big silver Dodge Ram, she stared at Dani's pickup. Black and beat up, it was a Chevy like the old, green two-seater Dani had supposedly been driving the night of her accident, but large enough to haul several passengers along with plenty of farm supplies. Still, it was certainly smaller than the massive Ram they climbed into.

Although it was only nine thirty in the morning, the truck was already steaming hot. Logan rolled down all four windows. The cross breeze was nice as they drove down the driveway and turned onto the road.

Summer took Dani's keys out and stared at the keychain with the name of their alma mater engraved. Shifting in her seat, she angled toward Logan. "I can't stop thinking about what the nurse, Kimi, told us."

"About Dani never driving the green truck?"

"Yeah. It wasn't until she mentioned it that I realized Dani hadn't used that truck during any of my visits. Always steered clear of it. Told me once she hated the old thing."

"I've never known her to use the green truck either, but that doesn't mean that she didn't climb behind the wheel drunk."

"Or maybe someone put her behind the wheel. Someone who grabbed the wrong set of keys from the bowl in the entryway."

"It's also possible Dani took the wrong keys. By the time she stumbled outside, maybe she was too inebriated to care which truck she was driving."

Glancing out the windshield, Summer swallowed a jolt of frustration and shoved Dani's keys back in her purse. "There has to be a way to convince you that Dani didn't have a relapse."

"Actually, there might be," he said, and she looked at him, waiting for him to finish. "If Dani went to meetings regularly, then she had a sponsor. Someone who could verify her consistency and possibly provide firsthand insight about her state of mind in the days leading up to the accident."

Another good idea. "How do you propose we do that? AA is anonymous for a reason."

"This is a small town. Can't be too many meetings. We go to one, around the time it's supposed to end, and talk to the person leading it." Logan slowed, stopping on the road alongside her car.

She had parked her navy sedan off the shoulder in the grass, nestled between two trees.

"You didn't do a very a good job of hiding your vehicle," he said.

In the daylight, it was plain to see. "At night, I figured it wouldn't be so easy to spot since it's a dark color."

"That's true, but when I pulled down the road, your license plate reflected my headlights, and I noticed the car. I didn't put much thought into it at the time since it was late and I was bone-tired from the drive, but anyone looking for you would've seen it. Not only that but with the rain you could've gotten stuck in the mud. Parking there wasn't a good idea all around."

If she had made it to the car last night only to get stuck in the mud, she would've been a sitting duck. A seasoned cop, like her sister Winter, never would've made such a careless mistake. Then again, Winter had warned her not to go to Cutthroat Creek at all. *Better to hire a private investigator.* But a PI would not have been personally invested in the outcome. "I'm a lawyer, not a cop. Staying under the radar isn't really my forte."

"I get it." He flashed another dazzling smile her way. "Stars weren't meant to hide. They were made to shine."

Was he flirting with her? "That's the nicest compliment anyone has ever given me." Even if it was a little cheesy.

"I find that hard to believe. I'm sure you draw compliments like bees to nectar."

Her cheeks heated and she lowered her gaze. "Believe it or not, I don't."

"Guys must tell you that you're beautiful all the time."

He thought she was *beautiful*?

She looked back up at him. "Sometimes. Usually they

just say pretty." Not beautiful. "But I've also been called a prude and—my least favorite—a tease." Several men had even been threatened by the fact that not only was she attractive but also an attorney at the top of her game.

"Nothing wrong with being modest and taking things slow. I know a few guys who think that if they buy a woman dinner, they're entitled to more after the meal. In my book, *more* should be hard-earned, like respect."

She tended to keep her virginity a secret from the men she went out with. Never lauded it as a prize for someone to win. But the idea of intimacy being hard-earned, like respect, resonated.

Men who felt entitled were the worst. She had once dated a professional athlete who had demanded sex after their third dinner, insistent to the brink of violence. To this day, she shuddered to think what might have happened if she hadn't been carrying her Mace.

"I dated a guy for four months and we never made it past second base." The words flew out of her mouth without thinking, like a defense mechanism to keep from talking about the close call with the athlete that was now at the forefront of her mind.

"Oh," Logan said, his eyebrows rising like they might jump off his forehead.

"He smelled like oatmeal, and I couldn't get over it." The guy had checked all the boxes on paper. From a good family. Parents still married. Six-figure job with a big tech company. Attractive. Nice. Interested in marriage and kids. She kept hoping things would finally click. But then there'd been that odd scent, and her inability to let her guard down around him, and how he never shared anything deep about himself, like nothing truly deep existed, and the complete lack of any *zing* between them.

Her list of intangible cons exceeded the number of checked boxes.

She didn't buy into the fairy-tale notion of romance. She understood that perfection in a partner wasn't possible, but she did expect a spark. Passion.

At least butterflies.

And a man needed to smell good.

Even sweaty, Logan smelled tempting enough to contemplate third base.

"Four months is a long time to some people," he said, "but good things come to those who wait."

Thankfully, she had the sense not to mention that she'd never made it beyond second base with *any* guy.

What was it about Logan that had her mind dredging up the past, loosening her lips and pushing her out of her comfort zone?

"Was that your longest relationship?" he asked.

"Yes," she said, and his brows jumped up again, his eyes growing wide. Enough of her dating résumé. If she continued any longer, he'd think she was defective. "So, you'll follow me to the cabin?"

"Yep."

With a nod, she hopped out and hustled through the low brush over to her vehicle. She pulled on the door handle, and it opened without her hitting the key fob.

The door was unlocked. An unnerving feeling swept through her, but maybe she had been in such a rush on her not-quite-so-clandestine mission that she'd forgotten to lock it.

She got in and pushed the start button, turning on the

engine. Music flooded the car, contemporary pop from a local station. The same one playing in Logan's truck. He was watching her, tapping his fingers on the steering wheel to the beat. She lowered the volume, cranked the air conditioner and rolled down the windows to let in a breeze on the drive until the AC kicked in, cooling things off.

Summer fastened her seat belt. Putting her hands on the steering wheel, she was about to press on the brake and shift gears when she sensed movement and then felt something brush the cuff of her jeans.

Tensing, she looked down. A snake slithered over her foot—sand-colored with a triangular head and beady, black eyes—hissing as it slunk between her boots.

Her heart seized. A scream lodged in her throat.

Move and you die.

She forced herself to stay still as stone, warring with the fight-or-flight instinct pumping through her system.

"Logan!" she called out, drawing on every ounce of courage she had to remain calm. Slowly, she turned her head, careful not to move any other part of her body, and met his gaze.

"What's wrong?" he asked, peering over at her through his passenger-side window.

"Snake!" Fear fractured the word into three syllables.

Logan jumped out of his truck and was at her door within seconds. He poked his head inside the car, looked down at the footwell and cursed.

"Is it poisonous?" she asked, praying the answer was no.

Please tell me it's a harmless garden snake.

"Venomous, and yes. Highly. Don't move," he said, but he didn't need to tell her that. Logan reached inside the vehicle, hitting the button to unlock all the doors, moving quick as a ghost. Running around to the other side of the car, he yanked open the passenger's side doors, the back followed by the front. Then he moved back around to the driver's side and slowly opened the one behind her. "Listen to me very carefully."

"Okay."

"I'm going to get you out of the car."

Panic threaded through her veins. "No. If I move, it'll bite me."

"You're not even going to lift a finger. I'll take you out, slowly. As long as there are no sudden movements, we'll be fine."

We? She was the one stuck in the car with a deadly snake. "Just call animal control or something."

"That could take an hour. Maybe longer for them to get here," he said, and something inside her chest squeezed, sucking the oxygen from her lungs. "You can't hold still that long."

Stay strong.

Then she glanced back down. The snake's forked tongue stabbed the air, as a spine-tingling hiss curled in her ears. Terror prickled her skin and she nearly flinched.

Blocking it all out, she took in a deep gulp of air, held it a moment and blew out the shaky breath, clearing her head. Logan was right. She couldn't keep that up for an hour, or possibly longer.

"Shoot it," she said, slowly enunciating each word, determined not to let hysteria overrule reason. Damage to her car didn't matter, only staying alive.

"Killing it with a headshot on the first try in tight quarters is not likely." His voice was calm, steady. "I'll only end up aggravating it and provoking the darn thing to bite you. But don't worry. I'm going to do everything possible to make sure nothing happens to you."

"Logan." His name left her lips in a desperate whisper.

"Do you trust me?"

For some reason, the answer was clear and bright as the sun on a cloudless day. "Yes."

"Close your eyes. When I tell you, I want you to go limp and let me do all the work. All right?"

What choice did she have? "Okay."

Fear wormed down her spine. Her heart jackhammering against her sternum, she put her faith in a man she barely knew and shut her eyes.

Chapter Six

A prairie rattlesnake.

Looked to be about five to six feet long. Even though the rattler was deadly, the nature of all snakes was the same. They were defensive rather than offensive creatures. Leave them alone and they sought to avoid confrontations with larger animals such as coyotes, wolves, bobcats and humans.

He'd opened the car doors to give it an escape route. The vast majority of snakebites occurred when people attempted to kill or otherwise catch one.

Then again, he doubted there were any statistics on individuals trapped inside a car with a snake.

Logan grasped the handle of the driver's door and gently lifted it until he heard the soft *click* of the mechanism disengaging. Then slowly, centimeter by centimeter, he opened the door wide. Fortunately, he had almost a full ninety-degree opening to work with.

Crouching low, he watched the rattler slither between her feet, the scaly body trailing over her toes. Its forked tongue darted out as the snake slid under the seat, heading toward the back.

Summer was wearing thick hiking boots. The ridge of the top stopped above her ankles from what he could tell beneath her jeans. A small layer of protection that might make all the difference once he moved her.

"Do nothing," he reminded her. "Let me handle it."

"Got it." Her voice was soft and low.

He inched closer to the frame of the vehicle. Slipping the fingers of his left hand under her thighs, he wiggled them deftly deeper along the seat, one inch at a time, not making a sound, and got a firm grip on the outer edge of her leg. All the while he listened for the warning sound of the snake's rattle, which would tell him if the creature felt surprised or threatened.

So far, only the blissful beat of the music.

Sweat beaded his forehead and rolled down along his temples. Summer held so still she seemed to be holding her breath.

With his other hand, he carefully pried her fingers from the steering wheel, lifting her left arm, and draped it around his neck. He nestled his shoulder up against her side while tracking the snake. The tail had disappeared. Even though the rattler was out of sight, he was 100 percent certain that it was directly under her seat.

He repeated the same process he used to get a hold of her legs, sliding his right hand between her back and the seat and finally under her arm. Once he had a firm grip on her side, right at her rib cage, he said, "Now."

Rigid tension left her body as she sagged against him, her other hand merely cupping the steering wheel now rather than holding it in a death grip.

Gradually, he lifted her from the driver's seat, moving inches in what felt like strained minutes. The distinctive rattle rose from underneath her seat, warning him to stop. It sounded like the buzzing of a large hornet. If the snake had been coiled, giving it height and increasing its striking distance, with the rattled tail completely off the ground, the sound would've been more like that of a pepper grinder.

The rattler was limited in its current position. Better to keep going rather than leave her in the car.

Standing from the crouched position, holding her and shifting her out of the seat—doing so painfully slowly—taxed every fiber of the muscles in his legs and back. Summer was soft, slender and svelte, with the lithe physique of a dancer. He was grateful she was as light as she looked and that he spent so much time getting in hard workouts on his family's ranch.

His muscles quivered. Perspiration dripped down his back. He almost had her free when the rattler struck.

The snake's fangs nipped the sole of her boot as he rushed backward. He got her clear of the car frame and out of striking range, shuffling her a safe distance as quickly as possible on the off chance the snake left the vehicle.

At the front of his truck, he stopped. Holding on to her, he set her feet down on the ground. She opened her eyes and went limp in his arms, her knees buckling. He picked her back up, carried her around to his open driver's-side door and sat her down on the seat.

He cupped her face in his hands. "Breathe. You're going to be all right."

She nodded, but fear still glistened in her eyes.

His heart was racing. He'd never been so terrified of making a mistake in his life as he'd been in the last few minutes. "I'm going to call someone to get the snake out of your car. Okay?"

Another silent nod from her.

But he couldn't let her go yet. He pushed her hair from

her face, longing to give her a hug or a kiss, any physical comfort to ease her lingering stress and make things better.

His reaction to her was unsettling. While working he never had trouble disconnecting when dealing with a victim or handling a case. But this was different.

Summer threw off his entire center of gravity.

Get a grip and focus.

Finally, he forced himself to pull away. He hurried back to her vehicle and slammed the doors, keeping the rattler contained inside. Once someone came to the scene, he wanted an official report of the snake being in her car.

He whipped out his phone and placed a call to animal control.

By the time he was back beside her, his shirt was damp with perspiration.

She climbed over into the passenger's seat, making room for him. He hopped inside, closed the door and rolled up the windows.

The air conditioner blasted cold air from the vents, cooling them both off. Not only from the July heat but also from the boiling tension of the too-close encounter with the rattler.

"Are you okay?" he asked. The silence from her was concerning.

"Yeah. Fine."

But she didn't look fine at all. "Someone will be here soon to take care of the snake. There's an agent already in the area. Something to do with a bear."

"Thank you for coming to my rescue. Again. Twice in two days."

Less than twelve hours apart, to be more precise. "Starting to become a habit."

She grimaced. "Let's hope not. As much as I appreciate you being there for me, I'd prefer not to be in a position where I need to be saved."

Thinking about it, he had to agree. "I can't believe how still and calm you were through that."

"Calm?" she scoffed. "What you witnessed was barely contained hysteria."

"Could've fooled me. Faced with a scary, life-threatening situation like that, people often panic and do something stupid." Her levelheaded reaction was a testament to how well she was able to perform under pressure.

"Thank you, I guess."

It was definitely another compliment. "You did good," he said. "Seriously."

Summer was tough. On the outside, she appeared ladylike, almost delicate, but she had a backbone of steel.

"No, you're the one who did great," she insisted. "Getting me from the car without a single bite."

"Well, you did get one. On your boot. Good thing you were wearing those thick-soled hiking shoes, and that rattler couldn't coil under the seat and strike up."

Luck had been on their side. If the snake had still been in the footwell, Logan wouldn't have been able to get her free from the car safely.

"Once you got me out, why didn't you just kill it rather than calling animal control?" she asked.

"Two reasons. First, I want it officially documented by someone other than the sheriff's department that the snake was in your car. And second, it didn't mean any harm. Snakes are good for the environment. They help prevent diseases from spreading and play an integral role in maintaining a healthy ecosystem."

"Of course, a cowboy from Wyoming would know all about them. Fortunate for me. I don't know what I would've done if I had been alone."

The notion of losing her was enough to make his stomach churn. He reached across the console and took her hand. She threaded her fingers with his. The connection between them was already growing and he wanted to see what it could blossom into.

"What's the survival rate for a snakebite?" she asked.

"Depends on how many times you're bitten and how quickly antivenom is administered. Even if you survive, you're looking at days, possibly a week in the hospital."

"The entire time you were trying to get me out of the car safely, I kept wondering how that snake got in my vehicle in the first place," she said. "What are the odds of that happening by chance? Some weird fluke? Is that normal for a snake to be able to get into your car?"

"There are nine or ten snake species in Montana." More in Wyoming, eighteen that he knew of. "But the only venomous one is that prairie rattlesnake that was in your car. I'd say that'd put the odds at zero of it being a fluke." Making documentation of the incident all the more important.

Squeezing her eyes closed for a moment, Summer pressed her lips in a firm line. "Do you think the guy who attacked me at the house put it in there?" she asked, looking back at him.

"Working a case is often like piecing together a jigsaw puzzle. While I was out on my run this morning, I thought about the disarray in the house and the way you were attacked. Pieces that make more sense now. To answer your question, yes, I believe whoever attacked you planted the snake in your car. I think he never intended to graze you with the bullet. His goal was to get you moving. He blocked the back door in the kitchen to force you to flee from the front and head straight for your vehicle. When you came down the steps, why didn't you run out of the house?"

She dropped the back of her head against the seat. "I left my purse and car keys in the living room. I had to go in there to get them."

"A hiccup the guy probably hadn't counted on. Much like me showing up." Thank goodness he arrived when he did. That he hadn't made an extra pit stop to refuel and stretch his legs and instead had pushed on through to get to the house. Ten minutes later and the outcome might have been far different. "He probably figured you'd be scared half to death, racing for your car, that you'd hop in and speed off in the dark, not aware that you had a deadly passenger on board until it was too late. Either the snake would've killed you or a frenzied car crash."

Logan needed to update his boss. He let go of Summer's hand and started typing him a text message. In case DCI here in Montana needed a bigger push to investigate, this latest incident should be enough to get them involved.

"There's one thing I can't wrap my head around. Why would that guy go through all the effort when he could've simply shot me, put a bullet in my head and been done with it?" she asked.

"Then the sheriff would've been forced to do his job." No way to turn a blind eye to cold-blooded murder. "If your theory is correct that Dani wasn't drinking and driving and was really killed, then I guess it would be for the same reason. The coroner, Genburg, would've signed off on your death certificate, ruling the cause a snakebite or another fatal crash, and your murder would've looked like an accident. Like Dani's."

She wrapped her arms around herself and rubbed her arms. "This is worse than I thought."

Summer had no idea how ugly this was shaping up to be, and he wasn't sure if he should share his suspicion.

The high level of planning involved, blocking the kitchen door with the fridge, shooting to scare her rather than kill her, deliberately slipping the venomous snake in her car, and the high likelihood that she had been followed, all pointed to one thing.

He didn't want to jump to conclusions, but his gut told him that a professional, someone accustomed to eliminating targets, had Summer in their crosshairs.

Chapter Seven

The animal control agent had confirmed that—while it was easy, though not likely, for a snake to get into the engine bay, seeking a dark place to hide from predators—it was near impossible for the prairie rattlesnake to get inside the cabin of the vehicle. Unless Summer had left the windows down or doors open in a wooded area for an extended period of time.

None of which she had done.

Summer parked her car in front of the small guest cabin she'd rented through Airbnb for the month. The place was nestled between Cutthroat Creek and the town of Bitterroot Falls, close enough to the former for folks to consider it the outskirts.

It was peaceful out here and one of the most scenic parts of Montana, though there were quite a few to choose from. Far prettier than back home in Texas and drier than Seattle. The cabin was adjacent to the owner's main house and faced a massive, pristine lake with crystal blue water and a backdrop of majestic mountains and cherry orchards. The sight of the water rose up to meet her, the lake only a stone's throw away. Staying here lightened her grief over Dani and helped her reconnect to her cowboy roots. A culture she missed after years trapped in Seattle with horrible traffic, earthquakes, prevalent homelessness and high housing costs.

Once the lawsuit was done and she'd gotten to the bottom of Dani's death, maybe she'd come back on vacation and soak it all in. Take the chance to enjoy herself. She hadn't had a fun break since graduating from law school. It was long overdue, and this was as close to paradise as one could get.

She got out of the car and inhaled. The air was perfumed by bougainvillea and clematis growing around the cabin.

"Amazing view of Bitterroot Lake and the mountains," Logan said, coming up alongside her. "I bet the fishing is great." He turned to her. "Do you fish?"

"A little. More so when I was younger and spent time on my cousin's ranch." The Kings on her mother's side. "They had a huge pond full of fish. I remember it being quite relaxing." Fond memories of being on the ranch. They had their fair share of snakes in Texas, harmless and venomous alike. Not once had she come across one and certainly no deadly encounters. "I believe there's trout and bass in this lake."

"If I lived out here," he said with a bright smile, like he was fantasizing, "I'd go fishing once a week during the season. Food always tastes better when you catch it yourself." He took a deep breath. "This is a little slice of *paradise*."

She'd thought the exact same thing. The sun shimmering on the vast expanse of the water. Flowers and blooming trees near the shore. Mountains not too far in the distance teasing the idea of a long hike. Sunset was primetime perfection. "That's how I feel." Maybe it was time to update her checklist on what she was looking for in a partner. Include a box for someone who saw the world the way she did and wanted a similar lifestyle. "Pictures online didn't do the place justice." She was fortunate to have stumbled on it during her search.

Logan looked around, his attention landing on the main house. "Are the owners around all the time?"

"No. I haven't seen them since I checked in," she said, walking down the driveway to pick up a copy of that morning's *Bitterroot Beacon*. "They delayed their trip to visit family in Florida to give me the keys and show me around a bit. They even took me to lunch at a fantastic lodge down the road within walking distance." Then she'd shared her reasons for her indefinite stay. Their smiles had faded and their demeanors turned icy. "The food is so good I've eaten there every day."

A worried expression crossed his face. "You're out here by yourself?"

Yes and no. "The neighbors are fairly close. Not quite shouting distance, but easy enough to reach." She could at least see their houses. "And the owners here were kind enough to introduce me before they left." Everyone was lovely. At first. Standoffish once they realized who she was and why she was there, but she believed they'd help her if she had to turn to them in a bind.

Logan scrubbed a hand across his jaw like he was thinking. "I need to look into Einhorn's top brass, see if I can find any leads for us."

"Done. I already have a file on them. Started digging after Dani told me she thought she was being followed."

"Good." But he didn't sound relieved as he kept looking around the property. His phone chimed. He took it out and read the text.

"Is that your boss getting back to you?" she asked.

"Uh, no," he said, like the question had pulled him from his thoughts. "On the drive over, I heard back from him."

"And?"

"The Montana DCI has agreed to investigate the attack last night. My boss requested someone not originally from these parts, if possible. They're going to send Special Agent Declan Hart. He's from Colorado and has been with the department five years. The text message is actually from him. Agent Hart plans to be at the house at three o'clock today to collect forensic evidence."

"At least that's a spot of good news." She went to the front door, unlocked it and let him go in ahead of her.

He crossed the threshold, staggered to a halt and stared at the piles of boxes she had stacked everywhere. "What's all this?" he asked.

"In order to help get proof against Einhorn, I filed the lawsuit and this is one result."

"Don't you need proof before you sue a company?"

Once again, the answer was yes and no. "Dani had already been collecting evidence on her end, but it wasn't enough," she explained. "When you file a lawsuit, it triggers the discovery process that forces a company to disclose everything." She waved her hand at the boxes crowding the small cabin. "And they sent me absolutely everything. I've been going through it on my own for months. My firm hasn't been too happy with me. I was on the fast track to becoming the youngest partner until all this." Now she was in danger of losing her job. She'd already taken two pay cuts as this case sucked up all her time. "Since I didn't know how long I was going to be out here investigating Dani's death, I had the records shipped here, so I could continue working on them."

"You barely have any room to walk around. There was no place else you could store them?"

"I filed the suit in conjunction with a local attorney. The one guy willing to risk attaching his name to it over in Bitterroot Falls. Jeff Arbuckle. He was supposed to help me find somewhere to put everything, but I haven't heard back from him yet. I should check in and see if he's found any possibilities."

"I might know someone who could solve this problem for you," Logan said.

"Really? Who?" she wondered.

"Chance Reyes. He's a lawyer, like you. Works for Ironside Protection Services. IPS has an office in Bitterroot Falls. Chance and I grew up together. His family's ranch is adjacent to mine. In fact, the two have been combined since his sister married my eldest brother, Monty, last year." His brow crinkled, giving her the impression that there was more to the nuptials that didn't make him happy. "I'll give him a call and see if he can help us out."

Us. She liked the idea of not being in this on her own. "You get along with Chance, but not his sister?"

"Amber? No, she's great." Deep creases etched his forehead again, this time accompanied by a tense smile. "We're, um, good friends."

Huh. Maybe there was a problem with the in-laws. Plenty of books and movies dramatized how disastrous those relationships could be. "Are the Reyes parents a nightmare?"

"They're deceased, but when they were alive our families were both quite close."

Odd. She couldn't help feeling like she was missing something.

Logan started taking pictures with his cell phone.

"What are you doing?" she asked.

"When I tell Chance that we need storage room, I want him to know what to expect."

We. She smiled. "Good idea. The only problem is that I have a system." Only she knew which boxes she'd already sorted through, which ones she considered a higher priority. "I'll need to label them or put sticky notes on them so that they don't get all mixed up."

"I'll text Chance the pictures and give him a call while you freshen up."

"Right." She took the narrow path through the maze of boxes from the living room to the kitchen. "Do you want me to start a pot of coffee before I shower?" she asked. Summer could drink coffee all day long. It was a great appetite suppressant that kept her focused.

"No, thanks," he called out from the front of the cabin. "I figured we could grab a bite to eat once you were ready to go."

Sounded perfect. She was famished. "Want some water?" she asked, peeking around a stack of boxes to see him as she waited for an answer.

He took out his phone and started dialing. "I'm all right for now. No need to worry about me but I appreciate you asking."

Opening the fridge, she took a bottle of water out and sipped it. After the incident with the snake her throat was achy and dry.

"I got his voicemail," Logan said. "I'll leave a message."

Summer slipped off the rubber band from the newspaper while Logan left a brief voicemail that conveyed the urgency of the situation. Flipping through the paper had become a part of her morning routine since she'd been there. She glanced at the front-page headline.

Local Man Drowns in Bitterroot Lake.

She turned to the story and choked on the water sliding down her throat.

"Oh my God." A glacial chill went through her as if someone had walked over her grave. She couldn't believe what she was reading.

"Are you okay? Something wrong?" Logan asked, putting his phone away.

She hurried over to him, winding her way through the labyrinth of obstacles, and showed him the front page of the *Beacon*. "Jeff Arbuckle, the lawyer I was working with, is dead. He drowned in a boating accident while he was out on the lake two days ago."

Logan took the newspaper from her and glanced over the story. "Says he was alone. Fishing at night."

"How much do you want to bet that it wasn't accident?"

"Some people fish at night. Plenty of species are more active at that time, like bass," Logan said.

Sighing, she bit down on her impatience.

He looked up at her. "But I agree that another supposedly accidental death is too much of a coincidence. I don't think that it's a good idea for you to stay out here alone."

"All the documents are here. We don't know if Chance has space for them. I usually review what I can at night until I'm ready to go to bed. The place is paid for until the end of the month." She might have spent one night at Dani's house, but she wasn't mentally prepared to stay there for however long this was going to take.

Logan put a hand on her arm and rubbed, the gesture a comforting one. "We'll work out the logistics of everything. I promise," he said. "Whoever attacked you last night may be tying up loose ends and I don't think he's done with you. Pack a bag. After everything that's happened, you can't be here alone."

Chapter Eight

Sitting in his truck, parked behind a church, Logan read through the file on Einhorn higher-ups that Summer had compiled. Summer kept track of the time. At one o'clock, a local AA meeting was scheduled to let out. In case it ended early, they planned to head over a few minutes beforehand to the auxiliary building where the group met.

Logan glossed over the information regarding the CEO and founder Evan Einhorn and COO Todd Collins, along with the rest of the usual suspects. No doubt if Einhorn was producing toxic fertilizer, the leadership was aware of it and might have even taken steps to make the problem disappear. Billions were at stake. But the suits weren't the ones doing the dirty work. They needed to find the gunman to connect the attack to Einhorn, or whoever was responsible.

He focused on the last name in the file. Emma Einhorn. CSO—Chief Security Officer. "What is Ms. Einhorn's relationship with the CEO?"

"Emma is his daughter."

Logan nodded. "Then this is more than a job for her. It's personal. With her father as the founder and CEO, the company is her family's legacy. A powerful thing that many people would go to ugly lengths to protect."

"You sound as if you have firsthand knowledge of something like that."

"I watched my own parents push moral boundaries to ensure the Shooting Star Ranch survived for future generations. They conspired with Mr. Reyes to force Monty to marry Amber." That was the simplest explanation.

"I thought the marriage was happy."

"It is. Now. This was ten years ago. Caused a lot of pain. Mostly for Amber. But it all worked out in the end. She and Monty are deeply in love. They have a beautiful son. The two ranches are also joined. The Shooting Star-Longhorn. Everything worked out the way it was supposed to, but sometimes even the best people will cross the worst lines to preserve a legacy."

"Okay, Emma Einhorn has a motive beyond money, her family's legacy, but she may also have the means." Summer took the sheet of paper from him, turned it over and pointed out a paragraph in her bio.

"Emma used to be a detective with the Pondera Pines PD. Okay, so what?"

"The entire security team has four people, including her. Charles Boyd, the deputy CSO, Alex Pope and Tyler Higgins. Guess what they all have in common?"

An answer popped into his head, but that couldn't be right. "They're not all former cops, are they?"

"They are. Guess what else?"

"You've got me waiting in suspense." Shifting in his seat toward her, he leaned closer, truly riveted by the sparkle in her eyes and what she had to say next.

Summer rested her forearm on the console between them, angling to face him, giving him a tempting view of her cleavage in the pale blue V-neck top that clung to her frame like a second glove. Her perfume scented the cool air of the cabin. Sensual sandalwood, freesia and jasmine. Complex and sophisticated without being overpowering. Suited her perfectly.

"Go on, tell me," he prompted.

"They were all fired. At the same time."

She definitely knew how to pique his interest.

"Any idea why?" he asked.

"I did some digging."

"Of course you did." His gaze dropped to her slender, shapely legs exposed in sexy pleated shorts. Her skin looked smooth as satin. He bit the inside of his cheek, longing to run his hand along her thigh to see how soft and supple it really was. "And you found?"

"An article came out in the *Beacon* six months prior to their dismissal. Two suspects died under suspicious circumstances while in police custody, while in their custody to be more specific. They were subsequently suspended during the investigation. Rumors of corruption filled the paper. The county coroner, ole Genburg, stated the manner of death was an accident. The families filed a civil suit for wrongful death. As a result, PPPD fired the officers for not following police procedure. A settlement was reached with the families for an undisclosed amount. But would you like to know for how much?"

"Didn't you just say it was undisclosed?" he said while daring to put his arm on the console beside hers, skin to skin. She was warm and soft.

"I did." Crossing her legs, she flashed a coy smile.

Beautiful. "How did you find out?"

"I visited one of the families and simply asked. A widow. Each family received a quarter million dollars."

"Surely they signed NDAs." Such deals were usually made in the shadows on the condition that no one leaked the details.

"I told the woman to give me a dollar, thereby retaining me as her lawyer, which made her free to disclose the amount to me under attorney-client privilege."

"Shrewd. I like it." He liked her. *Very much*.

"A month after the settlement was announced, Evan Einhorn donated a half million to Pondera Pines."

"Convenient."

"I think it's a little too convenient. Then he hired his daughter and her cronies."

"When did all this take place?"

"Four years ago." She glanced down at her watch. "I think it's time we should head inside."

As they climbed out of his truck, his cell phone rang. He pulled it from his pocket. "Hey, Chance," Logan said, walking beside Summer toward the auxiliary building located behind the church. "Thanks for getting back to me."

Never a doubt in Logan's mind that Chance would. Not only were they close friends but their families' histories were also intricately woven together. Chance always appreciated how Logan supported his sister Amber, had her back no matter what. Growing up, Logan had thought he was in love with Amber, would've done anything for her, but she had only had eyes for his older brother Monty. She'd made her choice painfully clear a lifetime ago. Logan had had ten years to lick his wounds from the rejection. It no longer stung. Now Monty and Amber were married and had a baby. He wished his brother and sister-in-law every happiness. They were meant to be. If only he wasn't forced to see it every day on the ranch, where they all lived.

He was ready for a clean slate. One in which he defined his identity, and nobody thought of him as lovelorn Logan. As Monty's little brother. As Amber's spurned admirer. As the one son who didn't have the joy of ranching flowing in his veins. As the family stopgap.

A new place that felt like home, where he could crawl out from under the Powell shadow.

"Sorry I couldn't return your call sooner," Chance said. "We just wrapped up a couple of cases."

"Satisfied clients?"

"Always. I took a look at the pictures. Heck of a lot of files. But I can make room for you over here at our IPS office."

Logan and Summer stopped at the entrance of the building and waited since AA meetings were usually closed to members. They had no desire to violate anyone's privacy. They only wanted information.

"Are you sure? I don't want to impose."

"Of course you do. That's why you called asking for a favor," Chance said, his tone lighthearted, and Logan chuckled.

The door of the auxiliary building swung open, and people began moseying out. Perfect timing.

Summer pulled someone off to the side and spoke to them.

"Do you and the lawyer need any help going through the files?" Chance asked. "And what's her name again?"

"Summer Stratton. And I'm sure any assistance you can provide would be appreciated. We're going to have our hands full looking into the death of Dani Granger and investigating Einhorn Industries." The two of them shouldn't have to sacrifice sleep to comb through boxes of information when Chance was gracious enough to offer help.

"Give me the address and we can pick everything up for you."

Logan rattled it off. "We're about to interview someone. As soon as we're done, we'll leave the key under the mat by the front door. Should be there in less than an hour. Lock up when you're done and take it with you. We'll pick the key up at the office."

"Sounds good," Chance said. "See you later."

Logan hung up, putting away his phone, and turned to Summer as she thanked the woman she was speaking to and joined him.

"We want to talk to Mike Johnson," Summer said, and Logan was reminded how there was no such thing as anonymity in small towns. "Tall. Beard. Glasses. She said we can't miss him."

They headed inside.

Cleaning up a table lined with doughnuts, cookies and other refreshments, Mike was easy to spot. Several members chatted with him, and others stacked chairs.

"Excuse me," Summer said, drawing his attention as the conversation ended, "do you run the AA meetings?"

"Sure do. Well, most of them. I'm Mike." He offered them a pleasant smile that reached his eyes. "What can I do for you?"

The guy was taller and fitter than expected. Despite the short graying hair and silver-speckled beard, he didn't look older than his late forties.

Logan remembered seeing him at Dani's funeral, but they hadn't been introduced. Mike had clearly been grieving. On the verge of tears.

"I'm Summer Stratton and this is Logan Powell. I was Dani Granger's best friend and he was her cousin," she said, and recognition of the name dawned across Mike's face. "I'm the attorney who filed the lawsuit against Einhorn on Dani's behalf. Now we're looking into the events surrounding her death."

The man's smile faded as he nodded solemnly. "You were at the funeral, weren't you?" he asked Logan.

"Yes, I was." He shook Mike's offered hand. "But we didn't get a chance to speak."

"Dani talked about you, Summer, on more than one occasion. Very highly, I might add. I know you two were very close."

"I wish I could say the same, but she never mentioned you."

"That's the nature of AA," Mike said. "We keep this part of our lives separate from the rest unless we're making amends or asking a loved one to attend a milestone celebration. How can I be of help?"

"Can you tell us if Dani regularly attended meetings," Logan said, "and if so, did she miss any around the weeks leading up to her death?"

"Ask anyone here." Mike gestured to the handful of people still hovering nearby. "Dani attended a meeting every single week. Not always the same day and time. But she came here for AA even when there were Sundays she missed church service."

"I told you," Summer said, giving Logan a sexy, know-it-all look.

"Did Dani show any signs of depression? Stress?" Logan asked. "Any reason you think she might've been drinking the night of her alleged accident?"

"I was her sponsor." Mike pushed the sleeves of his Henley shirt up to his forearms and shoved his hands in his jean pockets. "When she was feeling low, she told me, so I could check in with her more frequently. That happened after her mom and later her dad passed away. But she always bounced back. Never had a relapse. Sobriety was a part of her everyday life. Right along with trying to prove that Einhorn was responsible for killing her cattle and for her father's death. Especially in the last four to six months. She became a woman on a mission. The news of what happened to her hit us all hard."

Summer stood a bit taller, confidence radiating from her. "Dani did talk about you, but not by name. I guess because it's AA. She told me that her sponsor gave the best hugs and that you were a great listener. That talking to you over a piece of pie was better than a drink ever was when she felt stressed."

Mike smiled but it was full of barely contained grief. "Thank you. For telling me that. It means a lot."

As much as Logan wanted to share in Summer's satisfaction that she was right about Dani's state of mind, Logan didn't want to jump to conclusions prematurely. "Did Dani's behavior change at all in the last few months or weeks?"

Mike considered the question for a moment. "Well, she did start acting a bit obsessive about Einhorn and kind of paranoid. Started talking about how someone was following her. I thought she was losing it, but then she called me scared one night. Claimed someone broke in and stole evidence she was collecting. I went by to take a look. Sure enough, somebody had painted the word *Stop* in big, red letters on her dining room wall and had cleaned out her garage. That sent her spiraling to a dark place."

"One of depression?" Logan wondered.

"More like desperation." Mike sighed. "Dani was willing to cross any line to get what she wanted."

Folding her arms, Summer narrowed her eyes. "What do you mean by that?"

Mike shrugged. "Dani blamed Einhorn for destroying her family's farm, for her father's cancer. She wanted proof they were responsible. I got the impression she'd do anything to get it."

"Even break the law?" Logan asked.

Summer gave him a pointed look. "Dani would never do that."

"I wouldn't be so sure." Mike looked around and lowered his voice. "Several months ago, Dani broke into Chip Boyd's place, convinced he was the one who took all her stuff, and stole his computer. Got someone to hack into it for her."

Logan glanced at the gawkers paying more attention to them than the refreshments or putting away chairs. "Are you talking about Charles Boyd, the deputy CSO over at Einhorn Industries?" he asked.

"One and the same, but he goes by Chip. The entire Einhorn security team is dodgy."

"But that doesn't sound like Dani." Summer shook her head. "She'd never break the law."

"Desperation can drive people to do unpredictable things they wouldn't normally consider," Mike said. "Even things that run counter to their morality."

Concern flared in her eyes as she pressed the heel of her hand to her forehead. "Do you know if she found anything on Boyd's laptop?"

"I don't think so, because she only spiraled harder after that," Mike said. "Things started heating up on all sides for her. I told her to leave it alone. But Dani was so headstrong, she wouldn't listen."

Nodding, Summer frowned. "The obstinate part sounds exactly like her."

"Other than the leadership at Einhorn," Logan said, thinking specifically about the security team, "is there anyone else in town who might've had cause to silence Dani?"

"Besides half the town in general, the only other person who comes to mind is Roy Nielsen."

"The name doesn't ring bell," Summer said. "What would be his motive?"

"Money. Plain and simple. Since the lawsuit was made public, Roy has made it known he's not too happy about it. Turns out he's a major shareholder in Einhorn Industries. Something like thirty to forty percent."

Fairly significant.

"Nielsen stands to lose a lot if the lawsuit doesn't go in Einhorn's favor," Mike added. "Ever since his son, RJ, Roy Jr., came back home, he's been a constant thorn in Dani's side."

"Came back from where?" Logan asked.

"The army. Did twelve years. Special Forces hotshot," Mike said with a deep undercurrent of disdain. "I hated the way he treated Dani."

An older woman with a weathered face and auburn hair pulled up in a tight bun had steadily edged down along the refreshment table, moving closer to them. Now she wasn't even trying to hide the fact that she was eavesdropping as she gave Mike a hard side-eye.

Mike must've sensed the woman staring, because he glanced over his shoulder at her. Then he quickly jerked his head back around like the sight of her standing within earshot scared him. He cleared his throat. "Just so there's no misunderstanding, I'm not accusing RJ or Einhorn of anything. I don't need any trouble."

Logan was used to small-town busybodies hungry for gossip, but it occurred to him that interviewing Mike here, with so many members still lurking, might've put him in danger. "Can we get your phone number in case we have any follow-up questions?"

"Sure," Mike said and gave it to them.

Summer entered the number in her phone. "Out of curiosity, when was the last time you saw Dani?"

"Three days before the accident. We celebrated her five-year sober anniversary, and I gave her the coin she had been eagerly waiting for. The big five, she called it. She was so happy. Proud. And she had every right to be. Hang on a second." Mike took out his cell, brought something up on the screen of his phone and showed it to them.

A picture of Mike standing next to Dani, his arm wrapped tight around her shoulder, hers curled around his waist, his cheek resting on the top of her head as she held up the coin that had a prominent number five in the center. Dani's brown eyes sparkled with pure joy. Her cheeks were flushed a rosy pink. She and Mike were both beaming.

"Between you and me," Mike said, his voice a sad whisper, "my guess is that Dani crossed the wrong line, with the wrong person, and it got her killed."

Logan intended to make sure the same thing didn't happen to Summer.

Chapter Nine

By four o'clock, they stood out on the broad porch of the Granger house while Special Agent Declan Hart finished collecting evidence inside.

Summer left the key to the rented cabin under the welcome mat for Chance Reyes before heading over to the house with Logan. She had already packed a bag earlier after Logan insisted that she couldn't be there alone. Although the cabin was cozy, with the best view in town, it was a little too cozy for two. It only had one bedroom and the *sofa* was little more than a love seat, not nearly long enough to comfortably accommodate Logan's long frame.

Standing on Dani's front porch, forced to stay in her house, all for protection from an unknown assailant who probably had also murdered her best friend, had pressure swelling in Summer's chest. Her mind kept spinning around all the things Mike had told them. Now she couldn't escape the memories, the grief, the strain of the lawsuit. Not even for an evening. Not stuck out here on the Grangers' land, where Dani had spent her last days. Terrified. Alone.

Obsessed.

"Thinking about Dani?" Logan asked.

Always.

Summer looked over at him. Dark brown cowboy hat on his head, a form-fitting white T-shirt that showed off his athletic physique, sculpted arms, broad shoulders and narrowed waist. The battered denim he had on emphasized his muscular legs. Scarred, sturdy work boots that matched his personality. Rancher's hands—strong, tanned, calloused. He was the type of good-looking that would make any woman take notice, more than once, but the best parts about him were more than skin-deep.

"The things Mike said about her." She shook her head, still trying to process everything, finding it hard to accept. "It didn't sound like the woman I knew. Breaking and entering. Stealing a computer."

Logan strode closer and put a hand on her shoulder. "She was desperate. Probably at her wits' end for closure after two years of fighting this battle."

Her heart sank, near breaking. "But I was fighting it with her." Putting everything on the line. "She wasn't in this alone."

"Maybe she still felt alone," Logan said, his voice soft and supportive in a see-both-sides kind of way. "Here. In Cutthroat Creek. Surrounded by vipers who wanted her to stop digging. Who were harassing and intimidating her. Sounds like it drove her to extreme measures."

She appreciated his empathy. As a lawyer, often working with the worst of the worst, it was a hard-to-come-by trait she highly valued. It had been a long time since she'd been around a man like him. Simple but not basic. Tough yet sweet. Ethical and good-hearted and so darn hot it was a distraction to be near him.

"Even if she had found something on Boyd's laptop," she said, "we would've had to tell the court how it was obtained. That's why I insisted that Jeff Arbuckle track everything Dani brought in. I didn't want any nasty surprises later on in court."

"Would it have been admissible since it's a civil lawsuit and not a criminal case?"

"The defense would've challenged any illegally obtained evidence. If the court allowed it to be introduced, Einhorn could use it as grounds for an appeal, not to mention how it would've exposed Dani to charges of theft and a potential lawsuit for damages." Doing the wrong thing for the right reasons still made it wrong. The ends didn't always justify the means.

"She probably didn't realize that. Or she didn't care, so long as she nailed Einhorn."

"Maybe it's my fault she took such drastic steps. I complained to her about spending sixteen hours a day going through the discovery files Einhorn had turned over and the pressure I was under at my firm. I didn't even tell everything. How bad it was getting for me. About taking two pay cuts because I wasn't bringing in new clients. I worried that I not only wasn't going to make partner like this, but might end up losing my job. Dani was used to me being the strong one who had it all together. I shouldn't have burdened her. But I was so frustrated trying to search for a needle in a haystack in the dark with just a flashlight. I told her that if only I knew what I was looking for, an email, a report, a test, something proving Einhorn Industries was aware of the chemicals in the fertilizer, the damage it could do, and simply didn't care that it would've been a hundred times easier to find it in the discovery." Tears stung Summer's eyes. She never should've dumped her stress onto Dani's shoulders when her friend was already under more than enough strain. "What if she was doing that? Taking a dangerous shortcut. Illegally looking for the smoking gun to steer my search through the files for legal evidence."

"You can't assume what she was thinking. It'll only torture you."

"But she did find something concrete." And it was probably hidden in that house somewhere. "I wish she had talked to me." Tears fell from her eyes and she quickly whisked them away, not wanting to break down in front of him or ruin her makeup. "Confided more. Trusted me."

Logan stepped forward and silently wrapped his arms around her in a hug. His embrace was warm and soothing. She sagged against him, resting her head on his shoulder, digging her fingers into his muscled arms, and his reassuring presence closed more tightly around her.

Poor Dani. Only twenty-eight. Never had a chance to become a veterinarian the way she'd planned. To fall in love. To get married. Start the family she had wanted.

Her death filled Summer with a nasty mix of guilt, grief, deep regret and anger that Dani's shining light in the world had been extinguished.

Life is fragile and so very short.

"Dani loved you," he said. "She did trust you and confided in you. But she probably knew that you would've told her not to take the last-ditch measures she was set on. I'm sure Dani didn't want to show you that side of her because she didn't want to disappoint you."

He couldn't possibly know that. Summer pulled back from him. "Those are pretty big assumptions. You barely knew Dani."

"But I think I've got a fairly good read on you. Easy to love. Loyal to the point that you're risking your job. Sacrificing salary. All to help your best friend. You have high standards, Summer Stratton, which is good, but with those come equally high expectations. For yourself as well as for others. If *I'm* worried about disappointing you, I'd say it's safe to assume so was Dani."

His words stroked over her senses, leaving her heart aching and tender. Stunned by his razor-sharp assessment, blown away that he was worried about disappointing her when she was merely grateful to have him here, she stared at him.

At his warm blue eyes. At his chiseled features.

Logan brushed hair back from her face, his calloused fingers caressing her cheek, gentle and featherlight, but also weighty. A sad smile tugged at his mouth and the way his lips curved sparked a deep yearning that spread all the way through her stomach. To know what his lips would feel like pressed to hers.

His cell phone chimed. He dropped his hand, reaching into his pocket. Taking out the phone, he looked at the screen. "Chance has all the boxes loaded and is hauling them back to the IPS office."

"Already? That was fast for one man. There are fifty heavy boxes." Her back protested every time she moved one.

"Well, he does have three guys helping him."

"What exactly does Ironside Protection Services do?" Summer asked, needing the conversation to focus on something other than how she might've driven her best friend to reckless actions. "Are they bodyguards for hire?"

"They can be if necessary. Depends on what the client needs. IPS employs a lot of ex-military. Chance being an exception because of his legal expertise. But they offer security services that run the gamut from protection details to risk management and all sorts of investigative and intelligence work."

"If that's the case, then why didn't you or Ric ask Chance to look into Dani's death with me instead of coming all the way out here yourself?"

His lips twisted in a lopsided grin. "Sick of me already?"

Smiling, she stepped closer into his personal space, testing the boundary between them. Instead of moving away, he leaned in.

"Not at all," she said. "I wasn't complaining. Only curious."

"Ric wanted family to handle it since Dani was his niece. He thought someone in law enforcement would be better suited than him to do it."

"You mentioned that you two aren't close. Why not?" Dani never really talked about her extended family and Summer never had a reason to ask. "Doesn't he live on the ranch with you and the other Powells?"

Logan lowered his gaze like he didn't want to discuss it.

"I'm sorry if I'm prying. You don't have to tell me." She rocked back on her heels, giving him room to breathe. "I didn't mean to overstep."

He caught her wrist and tugged her back toward him. "You didn't. I promised to tell you and I'm a man of my word," he said, his thumb stroking her arm.

The topic was clearly a difficult one. After her summers at her cousins' ranch, she had witnessed plenty of family drama. More than enough to understand the discomfort that could come from explanations. "Doesn't mean you have to do it now."

"Won't get any easier later." He glanced out at the land. "Matt's mother, Ric's wife, Ivy, ran off with another man when Matt was little, leaving their family to deal with her gambling debts. Ivy is my mom's twin sister," he said, and she stiffened at the surprising news. "Not only did Ric show up at our ranch in dire financial straits, hat in hand needing a job, but then, every single day, he was forced to look at a carbon copy of the woman who'd skipped out on him. On the outside, my mom, Holly, and Ivy are identical except for how they wear their hair. But in all the other ways that matter, they're polar opposites. Ric steered Matt toward us, asked for him to live in the main house, while my uncle stayed in the bunkhouse with the other ranch hands. There's always been this weird distance between us. I could never fully grasp the difficulty of Uncle Ric's position. Although now I think I understand it much better than when I was a kid."

"Complicated is an understatement." Summer imagined what it must've been like for Ric, jagged claws sinking into his chest every time he set eyes on Holly, seeing the face of the woman who'd walked away with another man, abandoned their child and left him with her gambling debts to boot. The man must've been truly destitute to swallow his pride and turn to his sister-in-law for help. "Good parents make extraordinary sacrifices for the sake of their children. To give them a better life."

Her parents had taken out a second mortgage on their house to pay for Autumn's doctorate degree and used what they had left to help put Summer through law school.

"Matt grew up wanting for nothing," Logan said, "but ironically resenting everything."

As tough as the situation must've been for Ric, it must have been just as confusing and hard for Matt. "It was still really nice of you to unburden Matt, let him enjoy his vacation and come out here to help. Very generous."

He looked up at her. "If I'm being completely honest, I didn't do it just for him. I wanted—"

"I think I've got everything I need," Special Agent Declan Hart said, stepping out of the house, wearing latex gloves and carrying sealed evidence bags.

Logan let go of her wrist and swung around to face the other man.

Declan strode closer, authority radiating off the Montana agent like sunbeams, the antithesis to Sheriff Tofteland. Declan was a handsome man. Rich brown skin smoother than mahogany, soulful brown eyes, a trim mustache. Six feet tall and buff, he wore a mint green polo shirt tucked into jeans that had nary a wrinkle, and a cream-colored cowboy hat. He was both polished and rugged at the same time. Bad-boy swagger packaged with good-guy vibes. A dichotomy she found bothersome, but one that she was certain her sister Autumn would've been drawn to.

"I'd say I'm shocked the sheriff didn't come out to do this," Declan said, "but I've had some dealings with Tofteland." He pulled off the latex gloves. "You think the attack is related to the death of Dani Granger?"

"We do," Logan said.

"I'm certain of it," Summer said. "We have strong reason to believe that she wasn't drinking that night and the car crash was no accident like the coroner declared."

"In the past twenty-five years, since Genburg has been the county coroner and Tofteland the sheriff, you know how many autopsies Genburg has requested the medical examiners perform?"

Neither Summer nor Logan ventured a guess.

"Five," Declan said, providing the answer.

"What?" Logan sounded aghast. "You can't be serious."

"Unfortunately, I am. From what I can tell, Genburg tends to rubber-stamp the death certificates based on Sheriff Tofteland's findings." Declan sighed. "Are you Dani Granger's next of kin?" he asked Logan.

"No. My uncle is."

"If you can get a power of attorney, we can exhume the body and request an autopsy from the medical examiners who work for the state. That would be faster and easier than trying to get a warrant to make it happen."

"I have power of attorney. Summer recommended that my uncle get one for whichever relative was going to come out here to look into Dani's death," Logan said, stroking her arm.

Only doing her due diligence after face time with Sheriff Tofteland and him issuing a warning to have her arrested for trespassing.

Declan glanced at the point of contact between her and Logan. His look was direct, penetrating. She guessed that he didn't miss much.

"Smart to get the power of attorney," Declan said. "Let's use it. I can call in a favor with the forensic science division. They're only two floors above me. I can have the body exhumed tomorrow and ask them to expedite *everything*." He held up the bags of evidence and shook them.

Finally, the wheels of progress were turning after being stalled for weeks.

"Since we think the lawsuit that Summer and Dani filed against Einhorn Industries is related to all this," Logan said, "we're going to go over there and question a couple of people on their security team. Emma Einhorn and Chip Boyd. Though any of them could be behind it. Any interest in coming along?"

Declan frowned. "I'd say my presence is a necessity. Otherwise, they'll simply stonewall you. The Einhorns are used to doing what they want when they want. Trying to go about this on your own is not the way. I'm the only one with real authority here. Maybe take a step back from this and let me do my job."

"I came here to investigate," Logan said. "*With her*. We intend to do so."

She had to admire Logan's determination to keep his word and not simply hand things off to Declan Hart. "Just as any private investigators would," she added.

"But we'd rather do it with you," Logan said, tagging back in. "I want and requested Montana DCI's involvement. But not your hindrance."

Declan seemed to weigh their words. "I get it. If I were in your shoes, operating in someone else's jurisdiction, carrying a meaningless badge for all intents and purposes, I'd feel the same. I don't do powerless very well either."

The tension in Logan's shoulders eased and his brow smoothed out. "Thank you."

"Roy Nielsen and his son, RJ, are also on our list of people to talk to," Summer said. "Do you know them?"

Declan shook his head. "Not personally. I've never had any interaction with either, but the name Nielsen is well-known around these parts. RJ is a bit of a local celebrity for all the wrong reasons, if you ask me. He was in the Special Forces. Came home with the Distinguished Service Cross for heroism. Can't stop bragging about how many people he killed. Also, all the Nielsen farming equipment stores in the state belong to his family. His father has deep pockets."

"Roy Nielsen is also a major shareholder of Einhorn Industries," Logan said.

"The plot thickens." Declan grimaced. "When questioning the Einhorns and Nielsens, we need to tread lightly. What we don't want is for them to lawyer up and pipe down. With the assault against the two of you last night, I understand this is personal for you."

"The murder of my best friend makes this personal," Summer clarified.

Declan took a deep breath, and she could tell he was trying to handle this delicately. "If you're too close to the situation to remove emotion," he said, "then it would be best for me talk to them alone."

No way were they going to be sidelined. "Logan and I are capable of being professionals about this." He was a DCI special agent and she was chief counsel for the lawsuit against Einhorn. "Emotion won't cloud our judgment or get in the way." That was more of a hope than a guarantee. The people in Cutthroat Creek had a way of getting under her skin.

Declan gave a curt nod, then looked at Logan.

"You heard the lady."

"All right. But bear in mind that we are not approaching this as a team effort. I'm allowing you both to accompany me as a professional courtesy only," Declan said, his face serious as he studied them. "Got it?"

Not a team?

They'd found these leads, which they didn't have to share and could've pursued on their own.

But Declan was the one with the badge and legitimate authority, she reminded herself. They needed to do this by the book. Once they found Dani's killer and whoever had attacked them, Summer didn't want the person getting off on a technicality because they had gone rogue.

Work the system. If she did as she'd been taught, there wouldn't be any risk of a miscarriage of justice. She needed to do this the right way, for Dani.

Logan glanced at her.

Summer nodded. "Yes, understood," she said to Declan, speaking for them both.

"Let me get a photo of your power of attorney for the paperwork to have Ms. Granger's body exhumed. Hopefully, first thing in the morning. The sooner we get the autopsy done, the better. I'll make it my top priority and get the ball rolling on that and ballistics. In the morning, I'll give you a call, letting you know what time to meet me at Einhorn Industries." Declan handed her a business card. "My personal cell is written on the back. Logan, you already have my number," he said, and she recalled the text message Declan had sent Logan. "Now, I want you two to tell me everything you know about this case, so we're on the same page. No detail is too small. Don't leave anything out."

Summer took comfort in having another ally in this. She and Logan might not be leading this investigation anymore, but they weren't stuck on the sidelines, watching from the bench. They were on the field, in the game. Exactly where she preferred to be.

Chapter Ten

Logan drove through Bitterroot Falls, the town on the other side of the lake, heading to IPS.

"It's generous of Chance to give up space at his office to store all those files," Summer said, seated in the passenger's seat. "Not to mention the manual labor of hauling everything over."

Logan couldn't agree more. "Yeah, I owe him for this."

Asking for a favor was new territory for Logan. He was usually the one always ready to oblige. Ready to put his own wants and needs on the back burner. Never leaning on others. Never thinking twice about helping out family or a friend.

Though, in this case, he considered Chance Reyes to be both.

The Powell and Reyes families were meant to be joined through marriage. Once upon a time, Logan had assumed he'd be the one to marry Amber. A silly teenage fantasy that had distorted his judgment, obscuring the reality that he had only been an afterthought for her. Someone who might've been her second choice if fate hadn't stepped in, saving them both from settling for less than they deserved.

He had no regrets. The experience had taught him what

he was really looking for, what he needed in a partner. And through it, the years he'd spent watching out for Amber and never being the one in his family to hurt her—when his parents and Monty had, all in a complicated, manipulative effort to get the Reyes land—he and Chance had formed a unique bond. A close friendship that couldn't be fully defined. Or broken.

Logan was the brother Chance never had.

And Chance was the buddy Logan never had in his own brothers.

"Thank you for going out of your way to help me like this." Summer's smile was sad around the edges. "I know it's not what you signed up for when you agreed to come here. After dealing with that rattlesnake, you probably wish your brother Jackson had been available instead."

Not for a second. "I like the unexpected. Keeps me on my toes," he said, and this time the smile reached her eyes. He was also glad that he was getting to know Summer better and spend time with her, as he'd hoped.

"Sorry you have to play babysitter. I'm sure I'd be fine in a big hotel with security cameras in Kalispell or Missoula."

He could use a security system at the house, as well as better locks. "Both are an hour away." One to the north, the other to the south. "Besides the expense, it's an unnecessary inconvenience. Also, hotels tend to give people a false sense of security. That guy could grab a maid's universal room key, slip inside and wait for you. Or knock on your door, pretending to be hotel security. Once you open up, all he has to do is shove his way inside."

She frowned. "That's grim."

"That's reality. Staying in a hotel also won't stop someone from tampering with your car, like cutting your brakes," he said, putting on his blinker. He made a left turn at the light and parked in front of the office of Ironside Protection Services. "Or putting something worse than a rattler inside."

"What's worse than a rattlesnake?"

"That you wouldn't see or expect?" He shrugged and put his arm on the console, angling toward her. "Off the top of my head, a black widow. Their venom is fifteen times more potent than a rattler's."

Summer shivered, rubbing her hands over her arms. "I'd rather avoid both."

"I guess we have to stick together. In the interest of mutual safety."

"I guess so."

"Think of me as your bodyguard. Here to serve and protect, and the best way for me to do that is to keep you close." The task his uncle had asked of him was to investigate, but the primary mission had become keeping her safe, and that was everything. "If you can put up with me."

"I think I can manage the hardship." She grinned. "Seriously, you're the one making the real sacrifice, putting yourself in harm's way by helping me." She reached over and took his hand. "Thank you," she said, giving it a half shake and a half squeeze.

The gesture was friendly and warm, but she didn't let go.

"It's not a sacrifice," he said. "I want to be here. Doing this. For Dani. My uncle. *For you.*" He felt good in her presence, being near her. Seen and appreciated. More alive and awake than he had in months, and it had nothing to do with the danger and everything to do with her.

They stared at each other for a long while, her hand lingering in his. He couldn't bring himself to break the silence or to let her go. Then she chewed on her bottom lip with a look in her eye, a mix of nerves and possibly heat, and he wanted to bring her closer and kiss her.

"I've been thinking about the lawsuit," she finally said.

"Not about dropping it, I hope," he said, tightening his fingers around hers.

"No. Never. Just that I need to warn the other farmers who are plaintiffs. They've heard about Dani and soon they'll know about Jeff, if they don't already. I need to tell them to keep a low profile. Better yet, to get out of town for a while."

"If they are anything like the ranchers back home, they won't be inclined to leave their land and go into hiding."

"No, they won't, but I also need to make sure nothing happens to them. Too many lives have already been lost. My conscience can't handle another."

"We'll figure something out," he said, lifting his left hand to her face, and caressed her cheek. Continued to stare into her eyes. "Maybe they can be persuaded to take a vacation."

"I hope so." Her voice was soft, her eyes searching his.

He leaned in, slowly, testing the boundary.

A car horn beeped beside them, making them jerk apart.

HEART THUDDING, Summer looked around, annoyed at the jarring disruption. The loud, short noise was the sound of someone ensuring their vehicle was locked.

A man stood in the IPS office window, holding up a key fob, watching them. Smiling, he waved.

"That's Chance Reyes," Logan said with a grin. "We should go in."

"Yeah." She nodded, wishing they were back in that little bubble where nothing and no one else existed and he was about to kiss her.

They exited the vehicle. Logan held the door open for her and they entered the air-conditioned building.

"You could've given us a minute," Logan said, hugging Chance.

A mischievous smile curled on Chance's mouth as they pulled out of the embrace. "I was generous and gave you ten. You're welcome."

He'd been watching them the entire time?

"Thanks for all your help," Logan said.

"Anything for you, brother. All you have to do is ask, and if it's within my power to give, you shall receive."

Strong words. For some reason, he seemed like the kind of guy who would back it up with action.

"This is Summer Stratton," Logan said, turning to her.

"A pleasure to meet you." Chance shook her hand.

His grip was a little too strong, but the smile offset it.

"Trust me," she said, "the pleasure is all mine. I really appreciate your assistance."

"We both appreciate it," Logan added.

"No problem at all. I only wish you had given me a heads-up you were going to be in my neck of the woods. Especially if it was to *unleash chaos*." Chance's mouth quirked again. "No fair you have all the fun, not bothering to invite me to the party."

The man was tall, tanned and, in a word, debonair. It wasn't simply the luxury watch on his wrist, the handcrafted Lucchese boots—she'd been given a pair as a law school graduation gift, they stood out—or the tailored shirt that fit him like a glove.

She got the impression that he would somehow look suave wearing a burlap sack.

"This party has been deadly," Logan said. "Not quite

what I was expecting. I didn't intend to rope you into this at all."

"The road to hell is paved with good intentions. I prefer transparency," Chance quipped back, amusement on his face. "Speaking of deadly, can we help on the security side of things?"

"It's not safe for Summer to stay at the place she rented by herself, so we'll be at Dani Granger's house together," Logan said, and Chance gave them a coy smirk that made Summer squirm. "I'm going to buy new locks for the house, but the place will still be vulnerable. You don't happen to have a high-tech security system that I can install tonight, do you?"

"We have something you could use. Not the level of security you probably want, but we can set up a few cameras to cover blind spots for you. I'll have one of the guys install them today."

"Give me the system, instructions, and I can do it," Logan said.

"This is our bread and butter. We can have it taken care of in under an hour. No instructions necessary." Chance patted him on the shoulder. "I'll show you where we set up the files. This way." He led them through the one-story building to a large conference room in the back. Boxes were lined up in stacks around the perimeter of the room, and three other men were inside, sitting at the table. "This is the motley crew. That's Bo Lennox, Tak Yazzie and Eli Easton," he said, tossing out introductions. A diverse bunch. "Logan Powell, brother from another mother, and Summer Stratton, attorney brave enough to go up against Einhorn Industries."

They exchanged handshakes and made a little small talk. "I hate to impose on you like this. Won't you need the space in here for meetings?" Summer asked. "Or for briefing your staff?"

"Staff." Bo chuckled, leaning back in his seat and putting his feet up on a nearby chair.

"We prefer team," Chance said. "I may technically be in charge of the office, but we all work together. As for meetings, we can hold them in one of our offices. Trust me, this is not an imposition." He turned to the boxes. "Your discovery process has proven fruitful. Einhorn sent you the whole kit and caboodle in response to your RFP."

A request for production of documents could include almost anything. Contracts, emails, medical records, lab tests, financial statements, maintenance logs, photos—all discoverable when relevant.

"They're trying to bury me in it," she said. "I found Christmas cards dated ten years back, recipes, notes about what color to make the packaging of their products. Garbage to waste my time."

Chance shrugged, appearing unfazed. "That's the nature of the beast, is it not?"

Her own firm had used the very same tactic numerous times when defending corporations such as Einhorn. "It is, but being on the receiving end sucks."

"The boxes you have marked as reviewed are on this side." Chance gestured to the right. "The rest far outnumber the others."

She stared at the daunting stacks. "I've been going through them all by myself." Normally, she had a team of paralegals assisting her.

"Aren't you working with a local attorney on the lawsuit?" Chance asked.

"I was, with Jeff Arbuckle." Which reminded her that

she needed to contact his assistant to get into his office and collect everything he had regarding the lawsuit.

"He's dead," Logan said. "Drowned in an alleged boating accident."

Eli leaned forward in his seat, resting his arms on the table. "I read about that this morning in the *Beacon*. Didn't realize he was a lawyer attached to the same case as Dani Granger. It wasn't mentioned in the paper."

"Summer was also attacked," Logan said, "shot." He gestured to the bandage on her arm. "And someone put a rattler in her car."

Tak sucked air through his teeth with a hiss. "Nasty business, rattlers."

"Hence the urgency of the message I left you," Logan said.

Chance sighed. "You skipped a few important details."

"Someone wants this lawsuit to disappear and they're tying up loose ends by making the deaths look like accidents." Logan turned to Summer, concern heavy in his eyes. "I'm going to make sure she stays safe." He spoke to the room, his gaze never leaving hers.

But she wasn't the only one in danger. "There are four other farmers as plaintiffs. We need to give them a heads-up about what's going on."

"Hold on." Bo put his feet on the floor and sat up. "If whoever is behind this wants it to look like everyone had an accident, why shoot her?"

"I don't think he meant to," Logan said. "The guy blocked the back door, leaving the front door clear. I believe he shot at her to force her to run to her car where the rattlesnake was waiting. He grazed her by accident."

"Was Dani Granger the kind of person to be easily intimidated or to take a bribe to back off?" Tak asked.

"No." Summer shook her head. "Never."

"Three accidents might be plausible," Tak said, moving his head from side to side as though he was thinking it through. "But not seven, and surely, these farmers have families. Bodies start piling up and a deadly cover-up becomes obvious. To everyone. With Granger, Arbuckle and you dead, the other farmers could be pressured into accepting a small settlement to leave it alone."

Chance rubbed his clean-shaven jaw. "I was going to ask how we could help further, but I think I know how. Give us a list of the farmers and we'll reach out to them to let them know about the potential danger. Just in case. Summer, you need a local attorney attached to your lawsuit. Use me until you find someone else better suited to avoid any unnecessary delays in the lawsuit. As for this heap of discovery, tell us what you're looking for in all these boxes and we'll pitch in."

"Oh, I can't ask you do that." Summer glanced around the room at the eager faces.

"You didn't." Chance grinned. "I offered and if you're worried about our expertise, let me set your mind at ease. I've been practicing law for a decade and these fellas are some of the best investigators you'll ever come across. Bloodhounds. Give them a whiff of what you're looking for and once they've got the scent, they'll find it."

Smooth talker. Persuasive, too.

Logan was already doing so much when he barely knew Dani, wasn't even close to his uncle, and owed Summer nothing.

Now, through extension of him, four more were going

to step in to help her when they owed her absolutely nothing either.

"I can see the apprehension written all over your face. For a bigwig attorney you're not very good at hiding your emotions," Chance said, the insult pulling her from her thoughts. "How well does that work for you in court?"

She reminded herself to breathe.

Chance Reyes was a lot to take in.

Too much.

"In the courtroom, I use a persona," she said without thinking, letting one of her secrets slip. It was all about preparation and acting.

"An alter ego?" Chance asked, grinning. "Like Sasha Fierce?"

"Not quite." Summer was no megastar Beyoncé with a powerful alter ego such as Sasha Fierce, capable of captivating sold out arenas.

"Give us a minute," Logan said, putting a hand on her shoulder. "To talk about it."

"Only to talk?" Chance raised an eyebrow. "If so, you can use my office across the hall. But if you were interested in finishing what you started while parked out front, it might require a different kind of room."

Way. Too. Much.

"The hall is fine." Logan ushered her out of the room, closed the door and steered her a few feet away from the conference room. "What's your concern?"

"The use of their time." In her world, time was money. Billable hours were everything. They reigned supreme. She'd had none for almost a year, was burning through vacation days out here, and was about to lose her job because of it all unless she managed to get a huge settlement from this lawsuit. "They must have other things to work on."

"How long would it take you and me to finish going through the rest of those boxes, after a full day of investigating, at night, when we're not sleeping."

She shrugged. "Months."

"Exactly. With the four of them working on it full-time, they could get it done in weeks. Possibly days. Using them frees us up to focus on what really happened to Dani and Arbuckle and find out who is after you."

"But…but I can't pay them what their time would be worth."

He clutched her shoulders, drawing closer. "You're not coming out of pocket for this, and it's not like they get paid by the hour anyway. They're salaried. If they weren't available to help, believe me, Chance would not have offered. In fact, they just wrapped up a couple of cases. IPS is going to pay those guys whether they're working on this or not."

"What if they had planned to take time off? Relax. Recharge."

"That's not how they're wired. Especially with two people dead and you under fire."

She had no clue how they were wired, but they were still people with lives and needs beyond work. On the other hand, what he said made sense about allowing them to sort through the documents to save precious time that was running out, but… "I feel bad."

"We need help. You need help. How much sleep have you been getting?"

"Not much. Usually four hours." If she was lucky. She was making do, testing her limits, on the brink of exhaustion nearly every day. But long hours without complaint was her norm.

"It's unsustainable. We need to be well-rested. Focused. Situational awareness plummets when someone is exhausted, and we can't afford that. Not in Cutthroat Creek, when we don't know exactly what we're up against. I'll be damned if I'm going to let something happen to you because we're spreading ourselves too thin."

Putting her hands on his chest, she leaned against him. "I'm so used to being independent, doing everything for myself, it's sometimes hard to let others step in without feeling beholden."

"What about with me?" He cupped the back of her neck, caressed her cheek with his thumb, stirring tingles low in her belly.

She looked into his eyes, so very blue and bright, and the rest of the world faded away. There was only him and her and this feeling she couldn't explain. "You're different."

"How?"

He wasn't simply giving his time and expertise when he didn't have to. He was standing by her, standing *with her* through this, risking his life. And not once had he made her feel indebted.

But he did make her *feel*. Emotions, sensations, desires she was struggling to rein in.

"If I owe you," she said, "then I need time to pay you back." Time for this. To know more about him. To touch him. To explore this yearning for more with him.

"I like the idea of collecting." His thumb brushed her bottom lip, sending a quiver through her. "Slowly."

Then what?

They'd each go back home to their respective lives,

a thousand miles apart. And they would never see each other again.

A strange panic settled over her. An overwhelming, rattled sensation. She wasn't dating Logan, hadn't kissed him, and yet, the thought of never doing either sent a surge of nausea through her. Even worse, the idea of doing more than kissing—much, much more—and then not being with him after made her physically ill.

Someone cleared their throat, loudly, deliberately, and they both looked down the hall.

"I'd say a different kind of room is definitely required." Chance flashed a sly grin, and she pulled away from Logan as heat rushed over her face. "What's it going to be? The choice seems rather simple to me, but it is your choice."

Logan stared down at her.

No denying it, she needed more help. How could she refuse when there was so much at stake?

Summer shook off her embarrassment, headed back down the hall to the conference with Logan and faced everyone. "I'll walk you all through the case, show you what I have so far, go over what I hope to find in those boxes and explain why I may need to expand the lawsuit."

"Expand it how?" Tak asked.

"The contaminated creek that runs through Dani Granger's property feeds into the Bigfork River. It's likely that the people on the reservation are being poisoned."

"Sounds like we're in for a long night," Chance said.

"We'll need takeout." Bo stood. "I'll grab the menus."

Summer marveled at them. Their efficiency. Their dedication. All without complaint. "You're going above and beyond. Thank you so much." She turned to Logan, gave his arm a squeeze and mouthed another *Thank you*. If not for him, none of this would be happening. Montana DCI's involvement. Ironside Protection Services' assistance. Security cameras for the house. Logan was amazing.

"All right," Chance said, waving a dismissive hand at her. "Enough of that. Let's get to work."

Chapter Eleven

Even though it was late, Bo was kind enough to come out to the house and install the security cameras after Summer had finished explaining the particulars of the lawsuit to the IPS team. With Logan assisting and learning, Bo put up four cameras on the outside of the house, covering the doors and most of the exterior, but there were still a few troubling blind spots. While Bo checked the system and set up the tablet that could be used to monitor everything, Logan installed two more cameras inside the house.

People with nefarious intentions might spot the exterior cameras anyway and maneuver to avoid them. But almost no one would expect security cameras inside of an old farmhouse. One he positioned in a corner in the living room, to overlook the windows of the dining room and the window above the kitchen sink, where Summer had tried to escape. The last camera he placed to cover the foyer as well as the bottom of the stairs. In the event someone made it inside the house and attempted to sneak upstairs, he'd see them coming and it would give them a fighting chance.

"You're all set," Bo said, handing him a smart tablet that would enable Logan to keep an eye on things at all times.

"Give me your cell phone. I'll download and sync the app for you."

Logan passed it to him. "Chance mentioned that you guys are all veterans."

"Yep. Prior US Air Force. Eli, Tak and I served together. Chance recruited us at our last duty station. The 819th RED HORSE Squadron at Malmstrom Air Force Base. That cunning devil knew exactly what he was doing. He'd just opened the IPS office. The owner, Rip Lockwood, had offered him a modest bonus for recruitment with double the money if he got vets to join, since Lockwood is a veteran himself. Chance scooped us out somehow, specifically eyeing people from RED HORSE. He was up-front. Told us that he'd cut us a generous percentage of his bonus as a new hire incentive. Chance got the three of us in one fell swoop, making IPS history to be the fastest to fully staff an office with all vets."

"That's Chance for you," Logan said, with a chuckle. "I've heard about RED HORSE." Rapid Engineer Deployable, Heavy Operational Repair Squadron Engineer. Always wartime-ready, they rapidly mobilized people, equipment, and provided heavy repair capability, construction support and combat engineering anywhere in the world. "My cousin Matt talked about how your squadron was critical during one of his missions for aircraft recovery and engineering support for some weapon systems."

"Your cousin must be Special Forces."

"As a matter of fact, he was."

"Those guys are the only ones who ever talk about us."

"Was the transition to IPS hard?" Logan wondered.

"Making the switch to civilian life was. We're used to being ready to deploy at a moment's notice. Doing sixteen-, sometimes twenty-hour, days under pressure, indefinitely. As engineers, we're used to investigating problems. Working a case is fairly similar. Out in the field, we had to take care of our own security, even in war zones. So, we're capable of handling ourselves, protecting people and infrastructure. The rest we've picked up along the way." Bo gave him back his phone. "You're good to go. There's a five-minute tutorial that'll walk you through the features."

"Appreciate you taking the time to do this."

They shook hands.

"No problem," Bo said. "Have a good night."

Logan let him out. Locking the door, he chided himself for not getting a new dead bolt yet. *Tomorrow.*

Every time he thought about tomorrow, conducting this investigation alongside Summer, unease threaded through him. She was already the target of an attack. Thrusting her further in the spotlight, having her front and center as they questioned people, might make matters worse.

Not that she was going to back down, even if he asked her to.

He walked through the living room, Summer had tidied up while he and Bo were installing the security cameras. He found her in the kitchen, working her way through the pantry, checking boxes and cleaning out cabinets. "Hey, I thought we agreed to search the house tomorrow, for whatever Dani might have hidden." In the daylight, when they were fresh.

"We did, but this still has to be done." She gestured to the cabinet full of spices and the essentials in the pantry that would never be used. "I'm already in cleaning mode. I figured we could at least get through the kitchen. Comb through it while cleaning it out. Scratch one room off the list."

Wearily, he nodded. "All right." He went over to the radio on the counter, flicked it on and scanned for a good station. "Always easier to do something when you're doing it with music."

IT WAS ALMOST MIDNIGHT, and fatigue crept through her. The day had been never-ending. Listening to the radio while they worked made the task far less dreary and tedious. But something weighed on Logan. He was too quiet, too stiff.

Summer helped him carry the last of the filled garbage bags to the trash bins outside. They passed the five-hundred-gallon propane tank that kept the hot-water heater, stove, dryer and refrigerator running. An essential in some parts of Montana, especially in the colder months. Light from the kitchen window provided enough illumination for them to see clearly. Music wafted out through the open door, carrying a sultry tune.

He dumped the last bag and turned back to the house.

"What's wrong?" she asked, stopping him.

"I'm tired."

She searched his face. "Is that all?"

He didn't answer, only nodded.

Her throat grew tight with nerves, and she swallowed against it. "I feel like you're holding something back from me. If you are, you can tell. I don't want secrets between us. Whatever it is I can handle it. Promise."

He grimaced. "I worried going forward with this investigation, with you, might be a mistake," he said and hesitated.

"Why?" She stared at him, waiting for him to explain. Not wanting to push him or hurry him.

"Letting you come to Einhorn Industries to speak with the security team will only expose you further. It might reinforce some sicko's idea that you're a problem. The more I turn it over in my head, the more it worries me that it might make things worse. Maybe you should spend the day at IPS and focus on the lawsuit. Let me and Declan poke around. Draw the town's ire away from you."

"Don't you see, the lawsuit is the problem." She ran her palm against his sandpapery cheek, over the day's stubble. "What do you think I've been doing for the last two weeks? Sitting in that cabin under wraps, not daring to question anyone or show my face in public, too scared to announce who I am and why I am here? Everyone in Cutthroat Creek already knows that I'm a threat. The only way I'll stop asking questions about Dani, and now Jeff, or drop the lawsuit is if they kill me."

He clutched her arms and tugged her closer until her chest pressed to his. "I won't let that happen."

"I know." She slid her hand up his shoulder, to his neck and into his hair. "And tomorrow, they all know it, too. This is progress. Not potential failure. You are not endangering me by *letting* me come. Not that you can stop me," she said, and that brought a grin to his face. "We're going to show them that no matter what they do, I won't back down and I'm no longer alone."

"They'll have to come through me to get to you."

She believed him. With every fiber of her being.

He reached up and cupped her cheek, brushed his thumb across her bottom lip. Her breath caught in her throat, pulse fluttering unsteadily through her veins.

Every particle around them ionized.

"I like you, Summer. More than I've liked anyone in a really long time. I care about you," he said. "I'm attracted to you."

Holding her breath, unable to speak, she nodded.

Me, too.

"I wish tragedy wasn't bringing us together again," he said. "I wish that I had asked for your phone number that afternoon when we spoke outside on the porch."

Me, too. "It was a funeral. Probably would've been weird if you had." Weird but in a good way.

"I wish *this* was happening under normal circumstances."

"What would that normal look like?"

"I'd ask you out. Take you to dinner. Someplace with great food. On the water. Eat while the sun is setting. Maybe have a little wine."

Sounded like a perfect start. "And then?"

"We'd go dancing."

He wrapped his arm around her waist, and they swayed to the slow music coming from inside the house. She slid her arm over his shoulder and curled her hand on the back of his neck.

A slight breeze blew, rattling the branches of a nearby tree. She shivered, but not from the cold, and pressed her body even closer to his. He looked down into her eyes and she discovered an awareness that matched her own.

Electricity and heat flared between them.

And she wanted to feel more. To feel everything.

As they moved together to the music in perfect step, in complete harmony, alarm bells rang in her head. Warning her to stop. Demanding that she use caution.

But she didn't listen. Because she didn't want to.

Life was too fragile, too darn short not to take the smallest of risks. What she wanted was to know what it would be like to kiss him. Just once.

She glanced at his mouth, swallowed her nerves and rose

up on her toes. But he angled his face away, lowering his head while keeping his arm snug around her.

His breath feathered over her neck, and her whole body tingled, coming alive. His lips brushed her jaw, then higher on her cheek—like he was giving her time to reconsider, a chance to run—and finally he kissed her. She sighed softly with longing, and his tongue answered, gliding into her mouth. She tasted him, savored the feel, the flavor, shivers spreading over her.

The kiss was sweet and slow and tentative.

But also, something deeper.

Something softer.

Something so much more profound. Unlike any other connection she'd had.

Because Logan was the one kissing her. This man, who'd chosen to make her fight his, risking his life, vowing to protect her, was the one holding her, touching her.

She closed her eyes and relished every second, memorized the feel of his lips against hers, his hands on her body, his breath flowing and mingling with hers. He angled his mouth across hers, and she opened willingly, tangling her tongue with his, reveling in this moment.

They swayed to the music and shared their breath and heat and presence. His arms tightened around her, his palm sliding lower. A small groan tore from his throat, and she wanted to cling to him. Wanted to feel his hands and mouth everywhere.

His other palm made its way to her breast, molding the cotton of her top and the lace of her bra over her flesh.

Warmth, heat and desire fired through her body, hot enough to reduce her to a pile of ash right where she stood.

Wake up! You live in Washington, and he lives in Wyo-

ming, a thousand miles apart, the cold logical voice in her head pointed out. *This is a reckless moment in time, nothing more.*

This can be nothing more.

Reality hit her like a bucket of ice water, and the romantic mental cocoon shattered. She pulled away. "I like you, Logan. The attraction is mutual, but I'm..." Her voice trailed off as she wondered whether or not to tell him she was a virgin. "I'm not interested in a casual hookup."

He blinked several times, the image of innocent confusion. "Neither am I."

Then what were they doing?

"I know this has been fast, with a lot of fear and adrenaline mixed in, but I care about you, Summer. Truly, deeply," he said. "I wouldn't try to sleep with you just for the sake of sex, especially if you weren't interested." He spoke the last part like it pained him.

She'd craved genuine emotion, a real connection with someone for a long, long time. One guy she had dated had told her he loved her after three weeks. Something about the words or the man didn't feel right. Struck her as hollow. It didn't take too long before she realized, with an excruciating sting to her heart, that his idea of *love* was nothing like hers. When someone really loved you, they didn't let you down. Much less have sex with other people because she wasn't ready to sleep with him.

This wasn't the same thing in any way.

Logan was different. A man of his word who didn't say hollow things with some hidden agenda. So far, she believed everything he said, even the part about him caring for her. Their situation was different, too. He'd proven she could trust him with her life. Why not her heart? Her body?

But Summer was a relationship type of woman with a capital R. Okay, if she was being brutally honest, the whole word was in all caps.

Where could this go?

His eyes darkened with affection and hurt, but she looked away, emotion squeezing her chest so tight she was finding it hard to breathe.

She cleared her throat. "I'm sorry." For starting something that she wasn't able to finish. *Flirt. Tease.* Her eyes became all teary, blurring her vision. "But I can't."

"Can't what?" he asked.

For years, she'd thought perhaps she was missing the whole libido thing since most of the kisses she had experienced to that point had been enjoyable, certainly, but nothing to crave. The longer she waited to have sex, the more she had built it up in her mind, one checkbox after another of a man's necessary qualifications, layers upon layers of conditions and rules, until it had become this Mount Everest. A monster of a mountain to climb. The world's tallest. One of the toughest.

A deadly peak men should steer clear of rather than try and conquer.

An unattainable objective. One she'd never achieve.

What could this ever be with Logan besides some hot fling that would end in heartache, leaving her filled with regret?

That was why she couldn't.

"If you can't tell me *what*, at least tell me *why*," he pleaded. "Why can't you?"

Because every time he touched her, stared at her with that intense look in his eyes, Summer finally started to get an inkling of what all the fuss was about. Because his kisses could fuel fantasies.

Because I could love you, Logan Powell. Maybe she was already falling. Too hard. Too fast. How could she feel so much, want so much with a man she'd known for such a short time?

She'd cared about some of the men she'd dated, but she'd never truly fallen for any of them. Never this feeling that she had for Logan. Even that moment out on the porch with him five years ago had been intimate without touching, immediate, startling in its intensity.

"Summer, did I do something wrong?" He reached for her.

Backing away, she met his gaze and emotion lodged in her throat at what she saw in those blue eyes. She yearned for him to hold her again. But it would only lead to more kissing and touching and to other things she'd regret. She looked down at the ground instead.

"You didn't do anything wrong." Tears welled in her eyes. "It's really late. We're both tired," she choked out. "We should probably call it a night. Get an early start in the morning to search the house for whatever evidence Dani might have hidden."

Spinning on her heel, she ran inside on shaky legs before tears escaped her eyes. She was caught in a trap of her own making. A prison of standards she'd built and couldn't simply bulldoze overnight. Not even for Logan.

She fled up to the guest room, closed the door and sank to the floor with her heart quivering in her chest.

Chapter Twelve

The morning was tense. Awkward.

Logan hated it.

Grinding his teeth, he had no idea how he'd messed everything up last night. One minute, he and Summer were having a moment. Lighthearted. Romantic. Passionate. Then the next minute, she'd simply shut down and withdrawn from him.

Talk about a sour end to an evening.

Summer had gotten up right after dawn, the same time as him, and was doing her best to avoid him. No eye contact. No conversation. She wasn't even interested in the breakfast he had gone to the trouble of making for her.

As he stepped out of the room he'd been bunking in, she came up the stairs with a mug of coffee in hand. Wearing jeans, hiking boots, a tank top covered by an unbuttoned cotton shirt, she was practically fully covered today.

A stark contrast from yesterday, when she'd shown a tantalizing amount of bare skin.

She passed him in the hall without saying a word.

The scent of her sultry perfume curled around him, teasing his senses. Being near her brought their kiss back in vivid detail. The way her mouth had fit his, her taste, the snug press of her curves against his body. Every cell inside him had been cheering, *Finally*.

"I'm going for a quick jog," he said to her, and she stopped and turned around. He needed to put in a few hard miles. He wasn't a fitness nut. Far from it. The fresh air, working up a sweat, getting his heart pounding, cleared his head. Running was like meditation for him. He did it for his health, physical as well as mental. The one habit he couldn't do without. "Here's the tablet so you can monitor the security cameras while I'm gone."

She took it from him, not meeting his gaze. "I'm going to get a head start on searching the house for any hidden evidence until it's time to go meet Declan at Einhorn Industries."

"Stay upstairs and set the cameras to *Away* mode. Any movement will send a notification to the tablet and my phone." He held up his cell and tucked it in his pocket. "I'll have it on me."

"Okay."

"And take this." He pulled his gun from the back of his waistband and handed her the Glock. "You know how to fire it?"

"My cousins taught me. Out on their ranch in Texas. Do you really think this is necessary?"

"Just in case. Better to have it and not need it, than need it and not have it." For that exact same reason, he had a folded knife in his pocket. Killing with a blade wasn't as easy as they made it look on television and in movies. It was hard work and more time-consuming. But slashing tendons could be done in a heartbeat. "I won't be gone long." Today, he'd limit the run to three miles. "Twenty minutes max."

She nodded and disappeared back inside one of the guest rooms.

All she wanted was to search the house to find the evidence.

This smoking gun.

He should've wanted the same thing. Focused on the reason why he came to Montana. But Summer was an intricate part of that and right now she didn't want anything to do with him.

They'd have to leave later today to meet Declan. Maybe he would try talking to her in the truck on the drive over. Not as if she could skirt away from him then.

Avoidance wasn't going to fix the problem. Not that he had a bead on what that problem was in the first place.

Turning for the front door, he strode outside onto the porch in the muggy heat. The movement felt good even though he'd only gotten in a stretch so far. He locked the door, gritting his teeth at how flimsy it was. Anyone with half-decent lockpicking skills could get in with little effort. In less than sixty seconds. Not a decent dead bolt or chain on either the front or back door. Today, he'd rectify that. In the meantime, they had the cameras in place.

He slipped the spare key in his pocket, hopped down the porch steps and headed toward the trees. The woods surrounding the house were dense. Easy enough for someone to hide out there, watch from afar with a set of binoculars. During his jog, he'd look for signs to see if anyone had been camping out. Cigarette butts. Trash. Any item that hadn't been there the day before.

Throughout the night, he'd checked the security cameras every couple of hours and hadn't spotted anyone prowling around the house.

His phone beeped. He whipped it out of his pocket and glanced at the screen.

Summer had set the security cameras to *Away* mode.

Good. She might not be too talkative with him but at least she was still listening to him.

Get moving, slacker.

He took off on the trail through the trees. His feet pounded the compact earth. Under the shaded canopy of the trees, the temperature dropped a couple of degrees. Settling into a brisk pace, he regulated his breathing.

On his first visit out to Cutthroat Creek, he'd found this five-mile trail in the woods. Every occasion he'd come here, he preferred to use it over jogging out in the open on the country roads. The good thing about this particular trail was that it looped around the Granger property, allowing him to keep an eye on the house for most of it.

Sweat beaded on his skin. His lungs, his arms, his legs, all pumped hard. Fluid. In and out, his breath flowed in a solid rhythm. One mile into the run, he'd gotten into the zone, gliding along the path, when a flash of light caught his eye.

Logan stopped and peered through the trees. A few seconds later, he spotted that same glint. Like light bouncing off something. He looked around the area. Saw nothing else unusual. He listened to the silence. To the birds. The droning buzz of cicadas. The wind rustling the leaves. He stepped off the well-worn trail into the thick copse of trees.

Another flash of light.

Keeping his gaze on a swivel around him, he headed toward it, weaving his way around the trees rather than taking a direct path. Drawing closer, he noticed an object dangling.

A mirror.

Somebody had tied string around a small pocket mirror and hung it from a tree limb.

His skin prickled. He suddenly got the uneasy sense he was being watched. A branch or twig snapped at his three o'clock. Spinning toward the sound, he crouched at the same time.

Something whizzed past him overhead, right where he'd been standing, and hit the trunk of a tree.

A dart, .50 caliber.

Like the kind used to tranquilize an animal.

His blood pressure spiked along with adrenaline. The mirror had been bait, and he'd fallen for it, allowing himself to be lured in. Suddenly, he felt like a moth caught in a spider's web.

Click.

Click.

The sound of someone reloading. Tranq guns only held one injection. They used them on his cattle ranch back home.

Logan dropped to the ground and rolled just when another ballistic syringe tipped with a hypodermic needle, loaded with some drug, struck where he'd been positioned.

He needed to move while the man reloaded.

Jumping up, he sprinted closer to his assailant. *Click.* He still didn't have him in sight. Tracking him only by sound. Staying low, Logan crept to another tree. He peeked around the base of it. Waiting. Weighing his options. Not knowing how many darts the guy had left.

Click.

Logan ducked behind the trunk. A third tranquilizer dart bit into the bark of the tree he used for cover.

Peeking out again, he spotted the guy.

A man stood a few feet away. Dressed in woodland camouflage with a dark green balaclava covering his face. He opened the back part of the air rifle, making the first c*lick*. Pulled another dart from his cargo pocket.

Bolting up from his concealed position, Logan took off at a dead sprint straight at him as the guy shoved the dart inside the chamber of the air rifle and snapped it closed.

Click.

Logan tackled him, taking him down to the ground hard. The air rifle dropped. Scrambling to his feet, Logan kicked the tranquilizer gun away.

The man straightened up, his fist coming clear, clenched around a combat knife with a serrated edge.

Logan squared up in the narrow space between two ponderosa pines as the other guy shuffled forward. His eyes narrowed. Logan kept his gaze on the fighting knife, waiting for it to rise, but the masked man held it low at his belly.

The man spun the knife in his hand with a skilled proficiency that told Logan he needed to take care, or this guy would carve him to pieces.

A knife fight wasn't the answer. That would be a losing battle for the home team.

Instead of drawing his folding knife from his pocket, Logan charged the man, who in turn brought his knife hand up, preparing to rip Logan open.

Logan faked in, causing the guy to slash early, and then dodged the sweeping blade. Almost. The knife sliced across Logan's bicep.

Gritting his teeth, he swallowed a groan of pain, ignoring the burn in his flesh. All his focus was on taking this guy down before he could bring his hand back up for another try. Before he could hurt Summer.

Logan stepped in close to eliminate his assailant's leverage and snatched his knife arm in a bruising grip. Controlling the blade, Logan ducked under the man's arm, bringing the knife with him while wrenching his attacker's arm into a pretzel. The guy yelled in shock and pain. Logan twisted the arm up and back, then locked his other arm around the man's neck and squeezed tight.

Locked in his grip, the man clawed at Logan's arm with his one free hand. If Logan could keep the choke hold, cutting off the blood flow in the carotid arteries, he could render the guy unconscious.

But the man threw the back of his skull into Logan's face, nearly breaking his nose. A move Logan should've anticipated.

The camouflaged man rammed an elbow into Logan's gut, causing pain to snatch his breath. Then the assailant took off running through the woods.

Eyes watering, Logan blinked away at the spots dancing across his vision. He was about to take off in hot pursuit when his phone buzzed in his pocket.

Terror seized him. The security cameras at the house had detected motion. He'd set the notification to vibrate his phone rather than chime and make noise.

Was there a second guy? Another one sent to go after Summer while Logan had been lured and baited in the woods?

Without taking the time to look at his phone, he tore through the trees, snatching one of the darts along the way. He sprinted, running flat out, his legs eating up the distance back to the house.

She has a gun.
She'll be okay.
She'll be okay.

He repeated the words over and over again in his head like a mantra, while listening for the sound of gunfire.

A good one-mile time for him was six and a half minutes.

He made it back to the house, taking the porch steps two at a time and racing through the door in under five. "Summer!"

LOGAN.

The sound of him screaming her name set her heart pounding. Summer dashed from the kitchen to the foyer with the gun in her hand. "What's wrong?"

He grabbed her by the arms, his frantic gaze flying over from head to toe, his brows pulling together as he hauled in ragged breaths.

"Are you all right?" she asked.

"Me?" he said, breathless, sweat pouring from him. He nodded.

A punch of relief hit her. "What happened?"

"Notification. Triggered." More ragged breaths. His chest heaving. "Motion detected. On cameras."

"Oh, goodness." Squeezing her eyes shut, she was mortified for having worried him. "I forgot it was set to *Away*." She looked back at him. "I went downstairs to get another cup of coffee. I'm sorry."

A muscle clenched in Logan's jaw. He bent over, grasping his thighs, and breathed.

Blood ran in a stream down his left arm.

"You're bleeding." She took his uninjured arm and led him upstairs. "What happened?"

"Trap. Set for me in the woods."

"Are you okay?" She led him into the bathroom and steered him to sit on the side of the bathtub.

He held up a dart with a bushy orange tail. "Tranquilizer."

She grimaced. Someone had set a trap for him. Intended to sedate him and then do what? To him and next her?

An icy shiver ripped through her at the prospect. She ached to touch him, to hold him, grateful he was okay and had made it back to the house. Back to her. But she'd changed the dynamic between them. Had drawn a line in the sand, for better or worse, and couldn't erase it now. No matter how badly she might want to.

Turning, she pulled out the first aid kit from the cabinet. She sank to her knees in front of him and looked at the wound. "It looks deep. Are you in a lot of pain?"

Logan's face remained pale with worry and fear. "I'll be fine."

"I'm so sorry I forgot about the sensor on the cameras." She took out a bandage and gauze. "That you had to run back in a panic."

"You're unharmed and safe." His gaze held hers, and her heart tumbled over in her chest. "That's all that matters."

She lifted the gauze to clean the wound and he caught her wrist.

"I don't want to put you through the trouble of tending to me," he said.

The hurt look in his eyes was like a knife in her gut. "It's no trouble. Really."

"I need to shower first anyway." He took the gauze from her, lowered his hand and his gaze. "I can wrap it."

"It might need stitches," she said softly, not wanting to do more harm.

"As long as it stops bleeding, I won't worry about it. I don't have a problem with scars, and when Declan calls us after he's done exhuming Dani's body, I don't want to be the cause for delay or the reason he conducts the interview without us."

"Logan." She didn't know what to say. So, she was simply honest. "You're important. Your health. Your well-being. If you need stitches, then that takes priority."

His cheeks flushed but it looked like frustration. "I guess you've got to keep your bodyguard in fighting condition."

"You're more than that to me."

"Really." He scoffed. "Can we talk for five minutes? No dodging. No evading. No running off. Five minutes of cold, hard truth."

He stared down at her, and she sensed his tension. Saw the heat in his eyes. He was frustrated and angry, and it wasn't just about what happened to him in the woods.

Summer swallowed against the sudden flutter of nerves in her chest. She owed him that much. With a nod, she said, "Yes."

A LOOK OF dread and conflict filled her eyes, but he didn't care. His objective was to get answers.

Taking a breath, he decided it was best to cut straight to it. "I messed up last night. I did something wrong, something to upset you, but I need to know what it is because I don't want to walk on eggshells or make the same mistake twice."

She dropped her gaze and wrung her hands in her lap. "You didn't do anything wrong, Logan."

"We were dancing and kissing and then everything changed. Now there's some kind of problem. Distance between us that wasn't there yesterday. I'd like to know why." Because he couldn't bear it to continue.

Face still turned away from him, fingers twisting into knots, she was silent.

"Did I go too far? Overstep in some way?" He thought he'd been a perfect gentleman. Well, maybe not *perfect*. He'd been carried away by the kiss and had perhaps gotten a little handsy, but he didn't think he'd been aggressive. "Did I misread you or the moment? I got the impression that you wanted me to kiss you. To touch you. If I was mistaken and—"

"You weren't mistaken and didn't misread anything, but I was wrong for encouraging it. I shouldn't have."

"Why not? It was only a kiss, Summer." He waited for an answer that didn't come. "You said you didn't want any secrets between us and here you are keeping one from me."

She looked up at him. "It felt like more than a kiss. Made me want a whole lot more than that with you. Maybe I'm so naive that I didn't realize it meant nothing to you and wouldn't lead to anything else."

Logan would be a liar if he said he hadn't felt the same way. The entire time he was kissing her, he'd imagined what it would be like to strip off her clothes, to hold her close with nothing between them, to be buried deep inside her. Making her groan with pleasure and cry out his name.

Even now, the thought of it was getting him hot and bothered and had him adjusting the way he sat. He'd been attracted to plenty of women but wasn't into hook-up sex anymore. It always left him feeling cheap and more alone than ever. Only one woman had held a special place in his heart. Amber Reyes. Who was now Mrs. Montgomery Powell, the mother of Logan's nephew.

His feelings for Amber as anything more than a friend had been dealt with and died out a decade ago, after he'd learned she only had eyes for his brother. Not that he and

Amber had ever gotten physically close. Hugs and a few shared caresses, but not a single kiss.

Even back then, he had never experienced this bolt of instant chemistry. A gravitational pull to another human being. Not until Summer Stratton walked into his life.

Something about this woman called to him, touched him on a deeper level. This was the first time in his life that he'd had this kind of connection, and he didn't want it to end.

Logan wanted to take hold of her hand to stop her from twisting it into a pretzel, but he resisted the urge. "We both wanted more last night. Because we click." Which in itself was rare. "The chemistry is right." Off the charts. "What's the problem with a kiss leading to more?"

"My best friend is gone. So is Jeff Arbuckle. Because I convinced both of them that pursuing this lawsuit was the right course of action. Instead of having my full focus on finding out what really happened to them and making the person responsible pay for it, I'm dancing under the stars and kissing you. I didn't come here to get distracted with a fling that will only fizzle out once you go back to Laramie and I go home to Seattle. That's not who I am. It's not what I want. Two people are dead. Finding their killer has to come first. Can we please agree to concentrate on what's most important and drop any ridiculous ideas of romance?"

Taken aback by the punch of cold, hard truth, he nodded, silent for a second, letting his heart catch up to his head. "Yeah. Sure. You're not interested and that's fine," he managed, but he needed to set her straight about one thing. "Despite what you might believe, Summer, you're not the reason Dani and Jeff are dead. Filing the lawsuit was the right thing to do. Grief is natural and it's important to feel it. Misplaced guilt, on the other hand, is a distraction, too.

Maybe you should work on letting it go while I keep my primal impulses in check." He wasn't an animal. He could keep his hands and lips to himself. "We'll continue investigating together and I'll keep you safe. Like I promised." He swallowed the bitter taste in his mouth. "Just as friends. Nothing more."

Chapter Thirteen

Just as friends.
Nothing more.
The words still rattled in Summer's head two hours later. When she asked him to drop any ridiculous ideas of romance, he'd looked as though she'd reached out and slapped him.

In that moment, she'd almost crumbled. Almost kissed him. Almost decided to settle for a hot fling. Take what she could have with this incredible man for whatever time they had together.

But once she got back home, she'd have regrets. Big-time. She wished things were different.

That they lived in the same city, brought together by common interests that had nothing to do with death and violence and fear, and could simply date. Like normal people.

But they couldn't. They weren't.

The lack of sleep wasn't helping either. She was going on day twelve without a solid night, and her nerves were frayed. Because someone was trying to kill her. Now both of them.

The stakes were already too high, trying to find Dani and Jeff's murderer, doing their best to stay alive while her professional life was unraveling.

These were not the kind of circumstances in which to make a life-altering decision.

Yet, she couldn't stop thinking about Logan, no matter how she tried.

After Declan called, she changed her clothes into business attire suitable for the temperature. A good pair of high heels always made her feel powerful, ready to conquer the world.

During the car ride, Logan didn't force conversation, which she appreciated, but the defeated expression on his face made her chest ache and her temples throb.

She switched on the radio, filling the silence between them, and stared out the window.

It didn't take long to get to Einhorn headquarters.

Logan parked in the lot and shut off the engine.

The things he had said, the things he thought, weighed on her. "Hey, hang on a second." She turned to him. Wanted the awkwardness swelling between them like an inflating balloon to just pop and dissipate into nothing. For a moment, she considered telling him that she was interested in him, very much so, and that was the real problem, but it would only start another conversation they didn't have time to have. "We're not just friends." She patted his forearm, and his jaw hardened. "We're a team. In this together. I know you've got my back, but I've also got yours. We're partners. Okay?"

He stared at her. For a long, long time.

Felt like hours, but it was only minutes. Seconds, really.

She watched him, heart drumming.

He laughed, and she felt a twinge of hurt, but tried not to let it show.

Leaning across the console, she risked taking his hand in hers. Friends could do that. Hold hands. She'd done so with Dani many times when one of them needed comfort, the physical support. "You *are* important to me." His gaze dropped to her mouth, and it was there again, that hot flare of undeniable attraction. "I wouldn't want to do this with anyone else," she said, meaning every word. "Okay?"

He sighed, sounding resigned. "Okay. Partners."

LOGAN AND SUMMER met Declan Hart out in front of Einhorn Industries at ten o'clock sharp.

"How did it go this morning?" Logan asked, shaking the agent's hand.

"Smoothly. The medical examiner is going to give me a call when they're ready to start the autopsy on Dani's body. I want to be there for it. Also, Forensics assured me that they're going to run ballistics today as soon as they can."

Summer shook Declan's hand, looking chic in a buttoned pinstripe vest that accentuated her small waist, slim matching pants and high heels that Logan guessed were for Einhorn's benefit. Her outfits were like a little visual treat for his soul.

"We appreciate it," she said. "Thank you for not dragging your feet on this."

Declan gave a modest smile. "Only doing my job."

"When we're done inside, I have something to give you. Someone tried to shoot me with a tranquilizer gun," Logan said, and Declan raised an eyebrow. "Set a trap in the woods where I jog. I have the dart for you to analyze. We had a scuffle, and he gave me this." Logan gestured to the bandage on his arm. "Unfortunately, he got away."

"Sorry to hear about the altercation and that our suspect is still on the loose," Declan said. "Are you two ready?"

They both nodded.

Declan's expression turned stark. "Before we go inside, let me be crystal clear. You will follow my lead. You will not color outside the lines. You will let me conduct the interview. When I say it's time to leave, we go. Can you work with that?"

Logan and Summer exchanged glances. "Yes," they said in unison.

"Okay. I will hold you both to it." Declan led the way inside.

The lobby of Einhorn Industries was bigger than Logan had expected. Glossy. Polished. Walls of glass. Gleaming floors of marble. Dominating the space was a long reception desk made of a log with geometric cuts, illuminated from the inside and encased in glass. The wood must've been hollowed out with the lights added inside. Otherwise the weight of it would be massive.

As Declan approached the front desk, Logan hung back beside Summer. He was thankful they hadn't been assigned an agent who was a hard-boiled stickler for the rules. This guy was seasoned, no-nonsense, but flexible. Someone Logan could work with. He was certain it helped that they were both agents for the justice department, even if they were under a different attorney general. There was a camaraderie that translated across state lines since this particular job often drew a certain type of person. Required them to take on cases that regular local law enforcement couldn't handle for one reason or another. They operated in the backyards of others, where they sometimes weren't welcomed. It forged a shared bond that extended beyond the badge.

"Hi, I'm Special Agent Hart with DCI of the Montana Justice Department," Declan said, holding up his badge for the receptionist, "and these are my associates." He gestured to them over his shoulder. "We'd like to speak with Emma Einhorn and Chip Boyd from security."

The young woman's eyes widened. "One moment, sir." She picked up the phone, pushed a couple of buttons and whispered into the receiver. A minute later she hung up. "Someone will be with you momentarily. Can I get you anything while you wait?" she asked.

"No, thank you," Declan said. "We're fine."

Declan joined them as they waited.

A large digital screen hanging on the wall behind the desk projected idyllic images, set to cheery instrumental music, showing how Einhorn Industries made the world a better place. Sunshine and blue skies. Kids frolicking in the grass. A Nielsen farming spreader laid down fertilizer. Adults smiled as they harvested ripe crops. A family gathered around a table outdoors, eating. The screen panned out, showing pallets of stacked bags of Einhorn fertilizer and then zoomed in on the front of a bag. The montage ended with three lines in big, bold letters, each highlighted separately before fading to the next one:

EINHORN FERTILIZER RICH IN NITROGEN, PHOSOPHOROUS AND POTASSIUM

SAFE AND ORGANIC

NO WASTE GOES TO WASTE AT EINHORN

"What exactly is the fertilizer made from?" Declan asked. "And what's the basis for your lawsuit?"

"They make the fertilizers from raw sewage sludge, known as biosolids," Summer said. "Our claim is that there are high levels of polyfluoroalkyl substances, PFAS, or forever chemicals, in the fertilizer. The product is contaminating Snowberry Creek, which runs through the Granger property and a few other farmlands. Dani convinced four other farmers to join the suit. The chemicals killed their livestock, decreased property values and may have even given some of them cancer."

"Can you prove it?" Declan asked.

"Some of it. Most of the evidence that Dani collected was stolen from her house, but she had already taken liver samples from one of her stillborn calves to be tested out of state to prevent tampering, along with samples from the other plaintiffs' livestock and water from the creek."

"Did the tests find anything?" Logan asked.

"They did," she said with a nod. "PFOS, which is the most toxic PFAS. Two years ago, the US Environmental Protection Agency proposed a limit of four parts per trillion for PFOS in drinking water. The samples from the livestock as well as the water in Snowberry Creek contained more than 600,000 parts per trillion of PFOS."

Declan gave a low whistle. "That's staggering. If samples have already been tested and you can trace it back to Einhorn, what would killing Dani Granger, Jeff Arbuckle, or you for that matter, solve?"

"As it stands now, we go to trial with only this, sure Einhorn would say mea culpa. But then we have to prove that it's causing cancer and killing people. Even then, they'd face paying nominal damages."

Logan raised an eyebrow. "Nominal being relative, I'm sure."

"Yes, but I know we can do better. Much better. I don't want them keeping this quiet, forcing farmers to sign NDAs in exchange for pennies. I don't want Einhorn to get away with making superficial changes to how they use biosolids. In my experience and that of my mentor, companies like this usually know about the potential harm but do nothing because it would crush their bottom line. If we can prove that Einhorn was aware there is a dangerous level of PFOS in the fertilizer," Summer said, "and have known for quite some time, neglecting to do anything about it, then we've got them on the hook for billions in damages. Enough to bankrupt Einhorn and put an end to their fertilizer making for good."

Down the hall, a door opened and a stern-looking man strutted out. Middle-aged. Receding hairline. Sturdy build. He adjusted his bolo tie, sliding a medallion set with turquoise in the center along the leather cord up to the collar of his dress shirt. His cowboy boots clacked against the stone floor, echoing through the lobby as he headed toward them with a sense of purpose in his step.

Another guy emerged from the same room down the hall and hurried after him. Younger. Midthirties. Lean but muscular.

Both wore earpieces.

"I'm Chip Boyd," the older man said, extending his hand. "And this Alex Pope."

"Special Agent Hart with DCI." Declan shook it. "This is Special Agent Powell from DCI Wyoming, and Attorney Stratton," he said.

Logan appreciated the use of Summer's professional title in this situation.

"Thank you for giving us a few minutes of your time," Declan continued. "Will Ms. Einhorn be joining us shortly?"

"Afraid not. She had to leave on other business. What can I do for you?"

"We have a few questions regarding an ongoing investigation," Declan said.

Chip Boyd folded his hands in front of him. "Is that so? It was my understanding that the Dani Granger case was closed."

Declan flashed a wan smile. "I never said this was regarding Dani Granger."

Logan studied the former cops. They both had deadpan expressions and stood still as stone. Boyd focused on Declan while Pope was assessing everything else, namely him and Summer.

"Where were you two Wednesday night between eleven and midnight?" Declan asked.

It wasn't until then that Logan noticed Declan Hart hadn't taken any notes. Not a single one. Not yesterday, when he had questioned them about the attack or when they had passed along every pertinent detail they could think of regarding the case. Not even now.

Logan wasn't sure what to make of it. Everything indicated the DCI special agent was taking this case seriously and throwing the full might of the agency behind it. Yet, capturing details accurately was rookie 101 stuff that Declan wasn't bothering to do.

"I was at home." Boyd remained composed, but his clasped fingers tensed.

"As was I," Pope said, his expression inscrutable. "Sound asleep."

"Why do you want to know?" Boyd asked.

"Can anyone corroborate your whereabouts?" Declan ignored the man's question.

Boyd's gaze narrowed slightly. "My wife."

"And you, Mr. Pope?" Declan's gaze swung to the younger man.

"No," Pope said with a shake of his head. "I was home alone."

Boyd lifted his hand to his earpiece like he was listening to something. Then he leaned over and whispered to Pope. "You'll have to excuse Alex. He needs to attend to an urgent matter." Boyd gave him a hand signal to leave, and the guy strode off down the hall.

"Is there a fertilizer crisis?" Logan asked, not able to help himself, and Declan slid a warning glance his way.

Boyd simply smiled at Logan and turned to Declan. "If you want this interview to continue, I suggest you tell me why you're asking about our whereabouts."

This was the problem with questioning cops or former ones. They knew how the game was played, understood the rules better than the average civilian and could stop playing whenever they decided.

"I was attacked last night," Summer said. "Someone shot me."

Declan flattened his mouth into a grim line.

"You look pretty good for someone who took a bullet," Boyd said, raking his gaze over her. "Appears as though you only got a scratch." He indicated the bandage on her arm. "But I think you had it coming."

Logan bristled. He had had his fill of menacing looks and anything that sounded remotely close to a threat. He was prepared to draw a line under it, but he also wanted to keep his word that he wouldn't jeopardize the case or make Declan reconsider their active involvement in the investigation.

"And why did Ms. Stratton have it coming?" Declan asked.

"Oh, I'd say that'd be the general consensus around town." Directing his gaze away from Declan back to Summer, Chip Boyd grinned again, and Logan's spine stiffened. "I know exactly who you are. Meddlesome lawyer from Seattle who decided to come to Cutthroat Creek," he said, a hint of Montanan twang showing on the last word that he pronounced as *crick*. "Only to kick a hornet's nest. After years of representing corporations just like ours, you've turned traitor, taking everything that you know about how companies such as ours operate and using it against us like some no-good, dirty informant."

Something in Logan rose up like a beast, ready to pounce, and he stepped toward Boyd, but Declan put a cautionary hand out, silently telling him to back down.

"How do you know about the cases I've worked on?" Summer asked, eyes wide with surprise.

"Do you really think you're the only one who can do research?" Boyd sneered. "Dig around and find something that stinks. You should be ashamed of yourself for getting Dani Granger riled up. Putting fanciful ideas in her head. Dangerous ideas that apparently caused her to relapse and drive into a tree. Ideas that made Jeff Arbuckle take a terrible tumble into the lake. You're the reason they're both dead."

Summer reeled back, her jaw dropping, as though the words had slammed into her like a physical blow. The pain in her face cut Logan to the bone.

"That's enough," Logan said, pointing at Boyd as he stepped in front of Summer to shield her from any more vitriol.

"Yes, it is." Declan cast both him and Summer a sidelong glance for an uneasy moment. Then he turned back to

Boyd. "Would you please roll up your right shirtsleeve and show us your wrist?"

"What for?" Boyd asked with a look of contempt.

"Humor us and we'll be on our way." Declan motioned to his arm. "It'll take less than thirty seconds."

"Fine." Boyd unbuttoned his cuff, rolled up his shirtsleeve, held out his right arm for them to see. He then flipped his arm over, showing them the other side as well. "Satisfied?"

"Thank you for your time, Mr. Boyd. You and the rest of the security team should stay close to town for the time being. Don't leave the county without letting us know. We'll be in touch." Declan gestured for them to leave.

Logan put a hand in the middle of Summer's back, ushering her through the lobby. Once they got out of the building, he realized the physical contact he shouldn't have initiated and dropped his hand.

At the edge of the parking lot, Declan stopped them. "You violated your end of the agreement." While his voice wasn't hard, it was direct.

"I apologize," Logan said. "For losing my temper." Working a case, he was always tactical. Never emotional. But this blurred the line between professional and personal.

"That *man*—" narrowing her eyes, Summer took a breath and pointed back at the building "—provoked us."

Logan put a hand on Summer's shoulder, urging her to calm down with a gentle look. Giving him a nod of understanding, she took another breath, this one deeper, and held it along with her tongue.

He turned to Declan. "It won't happen again."

"You're right. It won't. A second chance is just another opportunity for someone to repeat the same mistake. I don't believe in them and I don't offer them. I'll speak with Mr. Nielsen and his son without the two of you."

Things hadn't gone as planned, but not so far astray that Special Agent Hart needed to hijack the case. "I have a concern with that," Logan said, not wanting to raise the issue, but it had now become necessary.

"Which is?" Declan asked, his patience beginning to wear thin in his tone.

"You don't bother to take any notes and you don't even use a recorder. After the interview with the Nielsens you might forget to pass along essential information." Other agents could handle their cases, interviews, note taking or lack thereof, as they saw fit. None of his business. Unless it involved him, and this time he had a personal stake in the matter. "We need to be there to hear the answers firsthand."

"No need to worry in that regard," Declan said easily, as if there was no need to elaborate.

"And why is that?" Summer asked before Logan had the chance.

"I don't need to take notes because I don't forget. Ever."

Logan scoffed. "The devil is in the details. Everyone forgets something at some point."

"Not. Me." Eyes hard as stone, Declan was deadly serious.

"Do you have a photographic memory or something?" Logan countered.

"No," Summer said, shaking her head. "That's the ability to recall something exactly as seen or read." She turned to Declan. "You have hyperthymesia?"

"Hyper-what?" Logan asked, feeling more clueless than he preferred.

"It's a super memory." Awe laced Summer's voice.

"When a person is able to remember nearly every event in their life with great precision."

"They don't call it that anymore." Declan's tone was matter-of-fact. "It's simply HSAM now."

Logan glanced at Summer.

"Highly superior autobiographical memory," she said, explaining the acronym.

"Oh, yeah." Logan nodded like he'd heard of it.

At the sound of a chime, Declan pulled his phone out. "One of the medical examiners is ready to start the autopsy on Ms. Granger's body. They're waiting since they know I want to be there for that. I'll let you know what it turns up in addition to what I eventually learn from the Nielsens. In accurate detail. As for Chip Boyd, he wasn't the guy who attacked you, but he was lying."

"About what?" Summer asked, brushing hair back behind her ear, now looking like she'd fully regained her composure.

"Emma Einhorn didn't leave early. She's in the building."

Logan wasn't sure if he was buying the whole HSAM thing. Even if he did, that didn't translate to the other agent knowing Emma Einhorn's whereabouts. "How do you know?"

"Her car in the lot." Declan hiked his thumb over his shoulder. "Pearl gray Hummer parked in front of the sign labeled Chief Security Officer."

Logan had been far too focused on Summer when they arrived and had neglected to even notice the basics. Setting aside his emotions and concentrating on his surrounding environment was usually one of his sharper skills.

"She's avoiding us for some reason," Declan said. "Probably the same one that made Boyd get rid of Alex Pope. It rubs me the wrong way how they don't even care it's obvious they're hiding something."

Logan really wanted to call BS on Declan's memory thing. Or at least test it. "What's her license plate number?" No guarantee that he had seen it, but if Declan had noticed that much already, then, as a cop, he had looked at the plate.

Declan rattled off the license plate number like one did their birthday.

"When you questioned us yesterday, you asked us both for our home addresses." Logan held his unwavering, stony gaze. "Mind repeating them?"

The Montana DCI special agent spouted those out too with a bored expression.

"What was the name of the nurse in the ER who spoke to us?" Logan pressed, and Summer put a hand on his forearm, now giving him a look of her own. Message received. He'd back off.

"Kimimela Anne Wheeler." Declan sighed. "If the autopsy turns up anything suspicious, then we'll have reason to haul the entire Einhorn security team in for questioning, including Ms. Einhorn."

"Please keep us posted," Summer said.

"I will," Declan said. "Let's go to your vehicle, so you can pass along the tranquilizer dart." They started walking through the parking lot. "Did you know that Snowberry Creek feeds into the Bigfork River?"

"Yeah." Summer let out an unsteady breath. "We found out from the nurse, Kimi."

"The reservation uses it for their drinking water," Declan said.

Logan nodded. "The nurse was concerned that it could be making people on the reservation sick."

"You need them," Declan said. "You need as many plaintiffs as possible. A team of lawyers helping."

"I've considered it, given it serious thought." Summer's brows drew together. "I just don't want to endanger anyone else. Two people are already dead." She raked a hand through her curls. "And an attempt was made on my life. I'm reluctant to drag more innocent people into this mess."

"You have to. No other choice," Declan said, straight to the point. "They're innocent, but they're also victims who deserve justice. Ultimately, you have to make this lawsuit so big, with so many parties involved, that it's unstoppable. Unkillable. They can't silence everyone with a convenient alleged accident. Strength in numbers. It's the only way to keep you safe."

But that would take time.

Time they might not have unless they could figure out who murdered Dani and Jeff Arbuckle and was now targeting Summer.

At his truck, Logan opened his glove compartment, pulled out the resealable bag with the dart inside and handed it to Declan.

The agent took it. "Call me if you find out anything else."

"Sure." Logan nodded. "Hey, out of curiosity, do you really remember everything, no matter how long ago, even feelings?"

"Yes. Simply seeing a date can trigger a vivid memory. Down to how I felt at that moment, like no time has passed."

Logan couldn't fathom being haunted by graphic details of things he wanted to forget, of Amber Reyes and all their interactions, each conversation, every close moment, what it had been like to want her. The striking granules of a thing kept it alive, an animate snapshot inside your head and heart. The adage that time healed all wounds was true.

Memories were meant to fade for good reason.

"Sounds like a blessing and a curse." Logan pitied the guy.

A grim expression crossed Declan's face. "You have no idea."

Chapter Fourteen

Back at the house, Summer needed to keep busy. Her hands moving. Her mind active—on anything other than how she'd messed up at Einhorn Industries with Chip Boyd.

Logan gave her space. Didn't push. Didn't force the conversation. Instead, he'd suggested that they search the house for any evidence that Dani might have hidden.

But it only led to a merry-go-round of frustration that lasted for hours.

They'd turned the place inside out. There wasn't any place left to check. They had searched every cabinet and loose floorboard and paint can. Rummaged through boxes. Probed for false-bottom drawers. Explored inside the stair treads. Looked in the plumbing pipes and vents and the cavities of every household item.

Turned up nothing. Besides weapons.

Dani had them stashed all over the house, except in the one closet where Summer had hidden on the rainy night she was assaulted.

They found a shotgun, knives, baseball bat and a revolver. Dani had been armed like she was prepared for war.

After the past couple of days, it wasn't hard to understand how Dani had grown fixated on this case until it took over her life.

Until it killed her.

"There's nothing in any of the rooms upstairs, including the bathroom and attic." Summer plodded down the steps barefoot, wanting to scream her disappointment.

Logan finished putting on the dead bolt and chain door guard and turned toward her. "You're in a mood."

"I thought for certain Dani would've hidden whatever she found in the house. Are we missing it somehow?"

Once she reached the bottom of the stairs, he gazed down at her, his brow furrowed. "You were upset before we got back to the house and started looking. Ever since we left Einhorn Industries. What is it?"

He hadn't blamed her for Declan cutting them out of the investigation. Not one harsh word from him. No shouting. No condemnation. No criticism.

Which only made her feel worse about the situation.

Her stomach growled, embarrassingly loud.

"Are you hangry? Is that it?" he asked. "We should really get something to eat anyway."

"No, it's not that. I am hungry. And angry. At myself. I'm sorry I let Chip Boyd get to me," she said, clenching her hands at her sides. "I wasn't prepared." For Boyd's viciousness, for his cruelty.

Guilt thrummed through her, strong as the pulse in her veins. She couldn't help but feel responsible for what happened to Dani and Jeff Arbuckle. If she had never suggested the lawsuit, told Dani how to go about collecting evidence, enlisted Jeff's help, they might both be alive.

Logan curled his warm hands around her arms. "It's okay. He got to both of us."

How could he be so nice and understanding about this?

A partner in her firm would have unleashed verbal hell on her while doing their best impression of Satan himself.

"It's not okay," she admitted, taking responsibility. "There were consequences. Declan Hart benched us because of me."

No second chances.

What kind of heartless person didn't give someone a second chance?

A man with a highly superior autobiographical memory who couldn't forget that every time he had given someone another chance it had backfired. That's who.

"We're not benched. We're simply playing in a different field on our own," Logan said with such conviction that she stared up at him. "We're still going to investigate Dani's and Arbuckle's deaths, using the lawsuit as our cover. Trust me on this?"

She trusted him with her life. Everything else was easy. "I trust you."

But he didn't let her go and his gaze didn't waver from her. "I didn't realize your firm represented companies like Einhorn. For some reason, I assumed you had experience working for the plaintiffs of class-action lawsuits." There was no judgment in his voice.

Still, she hung her head, her cheeks burning with shame. "There's a lot we don't know about each other."

"That's true."

"Representing the defendants, big corporations, in cases like this is not something I'm proud of. I went with the firm that made the best offer after law school. They paid off the rest of my student loan." Her parents didn't have enough to cover the full cost. "The salary was nothing to balk at and there was an attorney who fought to get me on board.

Marty." Her mentor. "In so many ways, it was the right choice at that time. He took me under his wing. Taught me so much. Put me on the fast track to becoming a partner. And now…" She swallowed the rest.

"And now? I'm listening." His voice was kind and patient. Gentle.

She looked up at him, at his laser-sharp focus on her, as he listened, really listened like he was soaking up every word. Something about it made her chest tighten. Made her want to let her guard down and let him see all the messy, scary parts of her. "And now I'm throwing it all away. Because I'm here pursuing this case against my mentor's advice. In spite of warnings from the partners."

"Do you regret being here? If you do, you can go back home. Go back to your job. To your life. I'll handle everything. Continue the investigation whether Declan Hart likes it or not, though I'd rather not get on his bad side again since he'll remember it." The corner of his sexy mouth ticked up in a grin. "Chance can help me find another lawyer and a different firm to take over the suit. We can figure out some kind of protection for you in Seattle until it's resolved. You don't have to do this anymore. You can leave Cutthroat Creek."

Protection for her?

What about him?

If he was going to continue poking around in places where he wasn't welcomed, it meant he'd also be a target.

Summer had started all this. She couldn't hand it off to someone else. Ask another person to pick up a deadly mantle she wasn't willing to carry.

She stared at Logan. Even if she did go back to Seattle and he worked out protection for her, he still wouldn't be safe.

The thought of leaving him behind, in danger, while she scurried off with her tail between her legs and hid was… unbearable.

Unconscionable.

Besides, she was no quitter.

He was still focused on her, waiting. *I'm listening.*

"I belong here, waging this war," she said. "Dani lost her life because of this, because she believed in the lawsuit, in making Einhorn pay, in ensuring that they admit to what they've done. She believed in me. I started this with her and I need to be the one to finish it. No matter the cost to me."

His hand trailed up, brushing her shoulder, his fingers settling on the back of her neck, and a wave of profound connection washed through her.

"And you gave me your word we'd get to the bottom of her death together," she said. "That kind of commits me to stay."

"There are a lot of ways for us to still do this together, without you being here, in the fray."

"Are you trying to get rid of me?"

His mouth curved, a sad smile tugging at his lips. He brought his other hand up and caressed her cheek.

She pressed her face against his palm. Absorbed the feel of his touch. Tender. Warm. Full of reverence. More intimate than any kiss she'd ever shared with another man.

"I don't want to get rid of you, Summer. I want to keep you safe. The thought of you getting hurt any more, any worse…" His voice trailed off and he shook his head. "I wouldn't be able to stomach it."

Running and hiding wasn't the answer. "Someone killed

Dani because she was alone. Jeff was out on that lake, supposedly fishing, alone. I was attacked because I was also alone. The same with you in the woods." Someone was picking them off, one by one, weak when separated from the herd. "But I'm not anymore. Now I have you by my side. Watching over me. Do you trust anyone else to do a better job at protecting me?"

And who would watch his back?

Logan groaned. "No one else will care as much as I do."

"About the case? About doing the right thing?" She took a breath and dared to ask what she really wanted to know. "Or about me?"

"All of the above," Logan said without a second of hesitation. He held her gaze with an intensity that made her lower belly tingle.

"Then that settles it once and for all. We stay together, get through this, and keep each other safe."

"You're a brave woman." The sincerity in his voice touched something deep inside her. "Brave and beautiful."

The tingle spread to her thighs. He had such an effect on her. But if it was like this just being close to him, how would it feel if he ever really touched her?

"I'm not brave." And she certainly didn't feel beautiful. On good days, rather attractive, sure, especially when men took notice, but not much beyond that. Maybe because her mother had taught her it was far more important to focus on what was in her heart and head than what she looked like. But she loved it when Logan called her beautiful and sounded like he meant it. "I'm terrified."

"But you're staying. You're fighting. Not running when you could. That takes guts. You're remarkable. You remind me of my brother Sawyer. He was a firefighter before he became an arson investigator. It takes something extraordinary, something special to choose to run into a burning building when every instinct tells you to do otherwise. Whatever that thing *is*, you have it in spades."

Wow. He really did give the best compliments of her life. "Thank you."

She stepped closer.

Heat sparked in his eyes, and he slid his hand down, wrapping his arm around her waist. "Summer."

"Yes."

"When you look at me like that, you make me want things."

She swallowed hard. "What things?"

"Everything."

Ditto.

He lowered his head toward hers. She held her breath in anticipation. He was going to kiss her.

One kiss had stirred up this much trouble between them. What would another do? But she didn't move away. She watched his mouth draw closer, heart thudding.

His phone rang, the noise penetrating the haze, and they separated.

He fished it out of his pocket. "It's Declan."

"Would you put it on speaker?"

Nodding, he did so. "This is Logan. Summer is with me. We can both hear you."

"The substance in the dart you gave me tested positive for ketamine. Enough to put down a man your size rather quickly. Also, ballistics came back. You're not going to believe this. Turns out that the same gun was used in multiple homicides," Declan said. "In Atlanta, Georgia. Houston. New York. Las Vegas. And Los Angeles."

Summer's stomach knotted. "I don't understand. That's all over the place. What does it mean?"

Logan grimaced. "The guy is most likely a professional."

She staggered back a step. "What? A hit man?"

"That's what I was thinking," Declan said.

"The use of a contract killer changes things," Logan said.

"And not in good way." The gravity of Declan's voice carried over the phone. "Tomorrow, I'm going to haul in the entire Einhorn security team and the Nielsens for questioning. I'll do what I can to find a connection. Also, I have preliminary results back from the autopsy. There were bruises on Dani's wrists and ankles consistent with being restrained. She was tied down and struggled. The ME found minor lacerations inside her throat and a great deal of alcohol still in her stomach."

"But she wouldn't have been drinking," Summer said. Couldn't have been.

"The ME believes something was shoved down Dani's throat."

Logan's jaw clenched. "Like a funnel. Someone tied Dani up. Shoved a funnel inside her mouth and forced alcohol down her throat to make it look as if she'd been drinking."

"My thoughts exactly," Declan said. "She also has a head wound. A fracture on the side of her skull. The blow is what killed her. Blunt force trauma. She was dead before someone placed her in the truck and staged the accident. This gives me plenty to get a warrant to have Jeff Arbuckle's body exhumed and an autopsy performed on him as well."

Everything inside Summer tensed, her stomach roiling. This was the news she'd been hoping for. Proof that Dani had been murdered. But it left her unnerved and reeling.

White noise roaring in her ears. "Who did that to her? This contract killer?"

"That's what I'm thinking," Declan said.

Cold dread gripped her. "The same person who murdered Jeff. The same person who's now coming after me."

Logan put a firm hand on her shoulder. "I'll keep you safe. Or die trying. I swear it."

Chapter Fifteen

The question was: Who hired the contract killer?

Who set this entire murderous plot into motion?

They weren't going to get any closer to the answer until tomorrow. After Declan interrogated the security team.

Once Logan and Summer had a chance to process all the news from Declan, Logan convinced her that they still needed to eat a little something. They had been so focused on searching the house and cleaning up afterward that they had skipped lunch, and she hadn't eaten breakfast. He didn't want her passing out from low blood sugar.

For a late dinner, they drove to The Wolverine Lodge that Summer couldn't stop raving about. He hoped it might lift her spirits a little.

The place was popular but small. The parking lot was practically full; every table was taken, and there was an hour's wait to be seated. They chocked it up to it being a Friday night.

Summer insisted they place a to-go order since she wasn't in the mood to sit in a crowded restaurant. Another time, after they caught the hit man who murdered Dani and Jeff, they could come back, grab a seat outside with a view of the water and watch the sunset as they enjoyed a relaxing dinner.

Logan stood in a corner inside the restaurant. With his back to the wall, he kept an eye on the front door, on the hostess station where their food order would be dropped off once ready, and on Summer as she paced back and forth while speaking to Karen Perkins, Jeff Arbuckle's assistant, over the din of the restaurant.

An older woman with auburn hair, the same one they'd seen yesterday at the AA meeting, came out of the kitchen, carrying two white paper bags. She made a beeline to the hostess, exchanged a few words and hustled back to the kitchen.

"Thompson," the hostess called out.

A guy seated on the bench got up, took the bag and left.

The hostess took note of the name on the second bag, glanced around and set it inside the podium in front of her.

Logan hoped that wasn't their food, but the hostess seemed to be searching for someone in particular.

"Thank you, Karen. That's perfect. We'll see you tomorrow." Summer hung up, put her phone away in her purse and came closer to him. "The poor woman is devastated. I suspected she and Jeff might have been in a relationship, the way she took care of him, reminding him to take his vitamins, or how he playfully complained about the green smoothies she made him drink."

Logan glanced around, making sure no one else stood close to them. "Did she say anything about Jeff's death?" He kept his voice low.

She nodded. "Karen said that he often fished around sunrise or sunset but never after dark. He was supposed to come over to her house that night. Jeff was her official taste-tester, and she was trying out a new recipe. Spaghetti carbonara with homemade pasta. Of course, he never showed. She started to get worked up, crying. I didn't want to push with more questions. Not over the phone."

Summer was kind. Sensitive. Putting the feelings of others first came naturally to her.

Although she didn't have that killer edge, the show-no-mercy kind that Chance had, Logan didn't doubt that she would be tough when taking Einhorn to court.

"When we see Karen tomorrow, can we share what Declan told us?" she asked. "About Dani?"

"No. Declan is going out on a limb for us because I'm a fellow DCI agent. We can't talk about the details of an ongoing investigation with anyone else."

The door opened and a guy breezed in. Average height. Muscular build of a man dedicated to fitness. He wore a tight T-shirt, jeans, and a compression sleeve from his wrist up past his elbow on his right arm. Gazes swung in his direction and stayed locked on him. A woodland camo cap that hunters wore was pulled down low, but folks seemed to recognize him anyway. He took long, confident strides up to the hostess, who beamed at seeing him.

"RJ!" she said brightly, fluffing her hair like a peacock preening.

Logan and Summer exchanged surprised glances.

Do you think it's him? she mouthed.

He gave her one quick nod.

"Shouldn't you be out on a hot date?" the hostess asked. "It is Friday night."

"Some of us are focused on more important things, Molly."

She reached into the podium, pulled out a bag, and stepped around to face him. "Physical connection *is* important."

RJ looked over her skimpy black dress and grinned. "Can't deny that."

The auburn-haired woman emerged from the kitchen again, carrying another bag, and hustled to the podium.

The hostess held up a palm. "One sec, Hattie," Molly said, hurling the words over her shoulder.

Hattie rolled her eyes, dumped the bag on the podium and was about to leave when she spotted Logan and Summer. Her brows drew together as she stared at them.

"How about I deliver dessert after my shift ends?" the hostess asked RJ.

"Not tonight. I'm busy." RJ took the bag from her, and Molly's smile deflated. "Some other time." He turned on his heel and headed toward the door.

Molly twisted her mouth into a sour expression.

A kid in his late teens stopped RJ and asked to take a selfie with him. RJ obliged, getting into a pose.

Molly snatched the bag from the podium and glanced at the name. "Powell!"

"Are you thinking what I am?" Summer asked.

"Yes." Logan rushed over to the podium as RJ strode past them outside. "I'm Powell."

The hostess handed him the bag.

"Hey," Hattie said with a grimace. "You two were talking to Mike about Dani Granger at the church."

"It was nothing. He didn't have anything worthwhile to say." Logan hoped that would satisfy her enough to leave Mike alone and drop it. He hurried to the door.

Summer was already outside, beckoning to him.

By the time he made it through the front door, she was down the steps, approaching RJ.

"Excuse me," she said, stopping him from climbing into his truck. "Are you Roy Nielsen Jr.?"

His eyes narrowed. "Yep. What do you want?"

"Do you know who I am?" she asked.

"Everyone knows who you are." RJ called her an indecent word and tossed his bag inside the vehicle.

Picking up his pace, Logan rushed up alongside her. "I'm Logan Powell and that kind of talk won't be tolerated."

"What are you going to do? Wash my mouth out with soap? You're welcome to try."

Logan wanted to rip his tongue out and shove it down his arrogant throat. "We're both working on the lawsuit against Einhorn Industries."

RJ pursed his lips. "A baseless lawsuit that's a waste of everyone's time and energy, if you ask me."

"We didn't ask." Summer squared her shoulders. "We're also investigating the murder of Dani Granger."

Adjusting the cap on his head, RJ lowered the bill. "I don't care about dead Dani Granger any more than I care about your unjustified lawsuit. The only thing I do care about right now is that my dinner is getting cold. So, what in the hell do you want?"

What a nice guy. Real American hero who should be celebrated.

Logan pulled out his badge and flashed it. Quickly. "I'm with DCI. Would you mind answering a few questions and we'll be out of your hair?"

RJ folded his arms across his chest. "I would mind." He looked at Summer. "You realize you're going to fall flat on your face in court and this little lawsuit will come to nothing, so now you're trying to turn an accident into a murder. Is that the best you can come up with?"

"Einhorn's fertilizer made from biosolids is toxic," Summer said. "We have the evidence to prove it. Gathering more and strengthening our case every day. Someone killed Dani Granger and Jeff Arbuckle to stop the lawsuit. But they failed. Because I will not rest until Einhorn pays for poisoning Snowberry Creek, Bigfork River and countless people."

"We'll see about that." RJ grinned. "Time will tell."

She took a single step closer to the man, the look in her eyes chilling. "Dani and Jeff's murderer will be brought to justice. No amount of money or power or influence will prevent it."

"Now, that's where you're wrong, again," RJ said. "Einhorn is untouchable. Us Nielsens are untouchable, too. I'd wish you good luck trying, but you'll need a miracle."

Logan moved in between them. "No one is above the law. No matter what your last name is. Might take a little longer, but in the end, the bigger you are only means the harder you'll fall."

RJ spit on the ground near their feet. "If you have any more questions, you can ask them with my lawyer present." He hopped in his truck and sped out of the lot.

Once his vehicle was out of sight, Summer's shoulders relaxed as she let out a long, audible breath.

"Was that the alter ego you use in the courtroom?" Logan asked, working a casualness he didn't feel into the words.

"Yeah," she said with a little nod, trembling. "It was."

He wrapped an arm around her shoulder, the way a brother would with a sister, he told himself. But when she sagged against his chest, his body's reaction was anything but brotherly. He wondered how long they were going to continue this farce, pretending that there was nothing romantic between them. "Very convincing," he said. "You made me quake in my boots."

"Did not." She gave him a playful punch to the stomach. "I didn't faze RJ at all. Only made him angry. How upset is Declan Hart going to be when he finds out that we questioned him?"

On a scale of one to ten, Logan guessed a seven.

He shrugged. "We took advantage of a chance run-in. It's not like we went to the guy's house and interrogated him. A little unfriendly chitchat in a parking lot, that's all."

"When I mentioned Dani's murder, he didn't go into a rebuttal about it being an accident like half the town."

"I noticed that, too. Right along with the compression sleeve covering his right forearm. The same arm I injured on the attacker."

"You don't think it's possible that RJ is the murderer, a contract killer for hire, do you?"

Anything was possible. "Stranger things have been true. He's got the right background for it. One thing they teach those guys in Special Forces is how to kill efficiently. But I do think RJ is going to lawyer up and remain silent."

A bigger concern was that by standing up to Roy Jr. and Chip Boyd, Summer had painted an even larger target on her back. If there was ever any doubt that she was a threat, to Einhorn interests and the murderer on the loose, after today, that uncertainty had been erased.

All this didn't lie solely on her shoulders. He shared in the responsibility. They had agreed to do this together when the best way to protect her was to keep her out of the spotlight. Hidden. Silent.

Something she wouldn't have stood for, and he couldn't have forced her to do.

He could only hope she was right, that having him at her side would be enough of a deterrent to keep anyone from trying to take her life again.

Chapter Sixteen

The sun rose far too soon Saturday after another night spent tossing and turning. After hurrying through a shower, Summer threw on jeans and a tank top, then grabbed her purse and met Logan downstairs.

"How did you sleep?" he asked.

She shrugged. "More or less the same since I've gotten to Cutthroat Creek." Restless. Her mind churning. About the lawsuit. Dani and Jeff's murders. The professional hit man. The tranquilizer dart.

Logan.

When she closed her eyes at night, her thoughts started and ended with him. She even dreamt about him. Being in his arms. At ease yet aching for more all at the same time.

"I heard you moving around a lot," he said.

"Which means you didn't get much sleep either."

"Comes with bodyguard territory." Logan grinned, and she had to fight very hard not to grin back.

"You need rest, too. We could both use a solid eight hours."

"Maybe that'll happen once we're done here and go back home."

She only wished home was in the same city for them.

"We should leave. I don't want to be late and keep Karen Perkins waiting." It was kind of Karen to offer to meet them at Jeff's office after she was done making funeral arrangements. If it took her longer than expected, Summer would prefer that they be the ones to wait.

They left the house and climbed into his truck.

"I might need to be at Jeff's office for most of the day to go through everything he had on the lawsuit. Is that all right?"

"We'll stay as long as necessary." He sped off down the long drive and stopped, waiting for a tractor lumbering down the road to pass.

Summer glanced out the window. Dani's mailbox was jam-packed. The little black door could barely shut and looked ready to pop open. Summer hadn't checked it once since she'd arrived.

"Give me a second to get the mail," she said.

Logan nodded, and she hopped out.

Things were still flowing, quite literally, in Dani's life, though she was cold in the ground. They were getting closer to the truth. Summer wouldn't rest until she got justice for her friend. And Jeff Arbuckle.

She opened the mailbox. Grabbed the thick pile of envelopes. Cradling the mail in her arm, she slid back into the truck.

As Logan hit the road, heading into town, she sifted through the stack. Plenty of bills. Most stamped Past Due in red. Others looked to be letters from collection agencies.

One envelope stood out. From the United States Postal Service. She opened it and scanned the contents of the letter.

"What is it?" he asked, glancing over at her.

"A renewal notice for a post office box. Number 135." She couldn't hide the confusion in her voice.

"Any idea why she would need one?"

"None that I can think of. Dani never mentioned having it. I don't know why she would bother with the extra expense when things were already so tight for her financially." She looked back at the letter. "Dani was renting it three months at time. This is the third renewal."

"The thing about post office boxes is that you can leave mail sitting there for as long as you like. If you keep the box paid for. Otherwise, the post office will eventually return it to the sender."

"So, what?" she asked, not following his train of thought when they'd been in so in tune before.

"Makes it a good hiding spot with easy access that doesn't draw any attention. No one thinks twice about someone going into a post office. After all the trouble she had with people breaking in and stealing stuff to sabotage the case, she probably wanted a more secure hiding spot. Maybe Dani mailed herself the evidence for safekeeping."

Counting back nine months, it made sense. "She started renting the PO box after the samples and files were stolen from her house."

Summer grabbed Dani's set of keys from her purse. Looking over several on the metal ring, she stopped and held up a small brass one that was engraved U.S.P.S. DO NOT DUPLICATE. "We've got the key and with the notice we know which box to check."

He glanced at his watch. "We have a little time before we need to meet Ms. Perkins. Let's stop there on the way."

The detour was worth the time. She nodded.

At the traffic light, Logan made a U-turn going in the

opposite direction from Jeff's office but headed toward the part of town where the post office was located. Within ten minutes, he pulled into the lot and parked.

"Come on." He shut off the engine.

They got out of the truck, hustled inside the post office and scanned the boxes.

"There." He pointed to a medium-sized one.

Number 135.

She inserted the key in the lock and opened it. Two manila envelopes were inside. Nothing else. She took them out and showed them to him.

The return address on both was Dani's house.

"You were right," she said, her pulse picking up. "Dani did send these to herself." She closed the box door, locking it and tucked the envelopes under her arm.

THEY HURRIED BACK to the truck, and he started the engine. "See what's inside the packages while I drive."

She tore open the first envelope, pulled out some pages and began reading through them.

With dark circles under her eyes, Summer looked as exhausted as he felt. Logan had only been here investigating for a few days while she had been doing this on her own for two weeks. Hard to imagine how dog-tired she must really be.

He pulled out of the lot and raced toward Jeff Arbuckle's office, without going over the speed limit. Surely, Karen Perkins was waiting for them by now and they didn't need the additional delay of getting a traffic ticket.

His gaze flicked to the rearview mirror to see if they were being followed. After his deadly encounter in the woods and learning that a contract killer was targeting them, there was no such thing as being too careful.

Summer was silent, reading the pages one by one, her attention completely dialed in.

"What did you find?" he finally asked.

"Precisely what Dani was talking about." A cautious smile spread across her face but there was worry in her eyes. "The smoking gun. There are printed emails between Einhorn leadership. The CEO, his daughter, Chip Boyd and others. They knew about the PFOS in the fertilizer. They've known for over five years and deliberately tried to bury it."

"But how did Dani get those emails? Mike Johnson told us that she didn't find anything on Boyd's computer."

Summer's smile faded. She glanced at the front of the envelope. "It's dated ten days before she died."

The smoking gun that got his cousin killed.

"But Mike said that she broke into Chip Boyd's house several months back." Summer spoke while staring at the front of the envelope. "If she had found something on his computer, wouldn't she have mailed it to herself sooner rather than risk hanging on to it?"

That was a good point, especially if Dani had grown paranoid and was taking extra precautions. "What about the other envelope?"

She opened the second manila packet, peeked in it and made a face. Then she dropped something into her lap. An old, beat-up cell phone with a red case.

"This looks just like the one she used way back in college," Summer said. "Of course, it's dead."

He lifted the three-in-one multi-charging cable he had attached to the car lighter USB adapter. "One of those should fit."

The cable for the type-C port worked and the phone started charging.

She reached into the envelope, pulled out more pages and flipped through them. "News articles." She scanned the stories. "They're all about the same thing. The death of a man named Nikolai Azarov. He was a member of a Russian crime syndicate in Atlanta, Georgia. The articles are dated more than twenty years ago. And guess what else is in here?" She held something up for him to see.

Pulling his attention from the road for a second, he glanced over at it. "A bearer bond?"

"Two," she said. "Worth *one hundred thousand dollars*. Each."

Shock washed over him at the amount. "They're probably worth a heck of a lot more than that. The US government stopped issuing them back in the 1980s because they're far too easy to use for illegal activity like money laundering, tax evasion and drug trafficking since they're not registered. The main appeal was the anonymity they provided, but the treasury department will still honor them. They collect something like five or six percent interest a year."

"Why would Dani sit on this kind of money?" Summer stared down at the bearer bonds. "Do nothing with it when she was going bankrupt and couldn't afford to pay her bills? Why wouldn't she say anything to me about it?" Hurt laced her voice.

"More importantly, where on earth did she get them? What's the date on the envelope?"

Summer gasped. "She mailed it to herself *six* months ago. For six months, she was hiding this and lying to me about whatever she was doing. Oh, Dani, why wouldn't you tell me?" Summer picked up the red cell phone that was charging. "It's at eight percent." She turned it on and waited while he kept driving to Arbuckle's office.

"Do you know her passcode?" he asked.

"If it's the same phone she had in college and she didn't change it." Summer entered a four-digit number. "It worked," she said, sounding surprised. "I'm actually in."

"Maybe that's why she used that phone, for whatever purpose, so you would be able to access it." In the event something happened to Dani.

Almost as if she knew that whatever she was doing might get her killed.

"But what am I looking for? Phone numbers? Voicemails?"

"Maybe pictures," he said, thinking aloud. "Those are the three things most people use their phones for."

She tapped the camera icon and then the symbol for the photo gallery and scrolled. "Oh my God."

"What is it?"

"Pull over," she insisted, gesturing to the side of the road. "Now. Hurry up."

He did as she demanded, stopping on the shoulder. After putting the gear in Park, he hit the button turning on his hazard lights. *Guess Karen Perkins will have to wait.* "What did you find?"

"You have to see this. Easier than explaining it." She showed him the screen.

Pictures of tattoos. On a man's back and chest. Not just any tattoos. Familiar ink. "Those are tats only the Vory v Zakone wear. Russian mob. Those are thieves' stars." He indicated the eight-pointed stars on either side of the man's chest near his shoulders. "When worn only on the knees, the stars are a sign of someone who commands respect."

I will never get on my knees in front of anyone. "But only the most respected can wear the thieves' stars on the chest. Means a high rank."

She pointed to a tattoo of a woman's face with roses around her neck. "Does that mean he was in love with someone?"

"No, it's the symbol that he was initiated into the Vory."

"How do you know so much about the Russian mafia?" she asked, meeting his gaze.

"I worked a case involving them once. Drug trafficking." One of the toughest he ever dealt with and rather early in his career with the DCI. "The media focuses a great deal on Mexican cartels and illegal immigrants, but the Vory have been entrenched here for decades. Their children and grandchildren born on US soil right into their illicit empires. They run a lot of drugs. Have pockets of power in expected as well as unexpected places. Like Los Angeles, Houston, Las Vegas, Atlanta, New York, even Colorado and Wyoming. They really are everywhere."

"So, our hit man is probably a part of this Vory or works for them."

"Based on this," he said, gesturing to the phone, "probably."

"What does the Russian mob have to do with the lawsuit?"

"Maybe they're a silent investor in Einhorn Industries with something to lose like the Nielsens. Or someone with a stake in this hired the mob to take care of the problem." Suits never wanted to get their hands dirty. "I don't know. Yet." But they were going to piece it together, one step at a time.

She looked back at the photos. "What does the skull with the teeth bared mean?"

"It's a sign of standing up against authority." There were plenty of others. A dagger. A spiderweb. A snarling tiger. Also, something written in Russian on the center of the back in bold letters. Whatever it meant was significant. But another detail in the picture caught his attention. "Looks like the guy is lying down on a bed."

Summer swiped between a few pictures. "But the sheets are different in the photos of him on his back from the ones with him on his stomach."

"For Dani to have taken these means she was intimate with this guy."

"Or it means someone sent them to her," Summer said, her tone defensive. "There's more than one way for a person to get photos that are on their phone." She opened a text message.

"What are you doing?"

"Sending copies of the pictures to myself as a backup." She hit Send and moments later her phone chimed. "See, now I have photos of a half-naked man on my phone, too, and I didn't have to sleep with him to get them." Then she snapped pics of the bearer bonds.

Logan reached out to put his hand on top of hers, but caught himself, dropping his arm on the console between them. "I don't like the idea of her bedding this type of person either, but we have to consider every possibility."

The most disturbing was that Dani had gotten herself mixed up with the Russian mob.

Chapter Seventeen

Entering Jeff Arbuckle's small office, located in a shopping center sandwiched between a Mexican restaurant and a coffee shop, Summer went up to Karen.

"Sorry we're late," she said, giving the older woman a hug.

Despite Karen being in her late sixties, she always had youthful energy. An eagerness and spring in her step that Summer had envied. Now, even though she appeared a bit haggard, there was an undimmable light in her sad eyes.

"I'm the one who should apologize," Karen said, leading them over to Jeff's desk. "I should've been the one to call you and tell you about his death. It's just that it was such a shock." She pressed a hand to her chest. "I still can't believe that Jeff is gone. That I'll never see him again." Tears sprang up in her eyes. "Talk to him. Make him a smoothie. Fight with him to take his medication and vitamins."

Summer guided Karen to sit in one of the chairs opposite the desk. "The shock and your grief are understandable." She sat beside her. "We're sorry for your loss. How long were you and Jeff together?"

"Eight years. We met after I left my husband. Jeff was the one who helped me with my divorce. I didn't have the happiest marriage. Swore I'd never hitch myself to anyone again. Jeff was okay with that and my need for space a few nights a week. It wasn't the hot kind of passion of my younger days, but we found something special, something true, that we made work for us. Took care of each other. Loved each other. Deeply."

Summer glanced at Logan and found him staring back at her. But looking into his eyes, she struggled to find her center of gravity, lost in the depth of blue that was the same shade of the ocean on a sunny day. There was no denying or escaping the affection in his expression that made something in her chest shift and squeeze.

And ache.

Just as friends. Nothing more. She repeated the words in her head, reminding herself to stay focused.

Turning to Karen, Summer put a hand on her shoulder. "Did you talk to the sheriff about the circumstances surrounding Jeff's death?"

"Of course, I did." Karen nodded vehemently. "First, Dani Granger has a drinking and driving accident and then my Jeff drowns," she said, choking up. She grabbed a tissue from the box sitting on the desk and dabbed her eyes. "But Sheriff Tofteland insisted that Jeff had been drinking too much while out on the boat, must've fallen into the water, and wasn't wearing a life vest."

"Did they run a tox screen?" Logan asked.

Karen shook her head. "No. The sheriff told me that an empty six-pack of beer was found on the boat and that there were no signs of foul play."

Logan sat on the edge of the desk in front of Summer but stayed focused on Karen. "Was he a beer drinker?"

"Sure, he liked to relax with a beer at night. But Jeff

wasn't a heavy drinker. My ex-husband was and I was sensitive to it. Jeff had a max of two and I've never known him to drink on the boat while fishing."

"Did the sheriff tell you what brand they found?" Logan asked.

"No, but I had the presence of mind to ask. I wanted to point out anything suspicious, but it was the IPA Jeff drank. Outlaw Brewing. He won't touch anything else. Always has some in his fridge." She sniffled and blew her nose. "I insisted on an autopsy anyway. The timing alone of Jeff's death, so close to Dani's, demanded it in my opinion. But the sheriff told me that I wasn't *family*, that I wasn't in the position to make any such demands, and there were no grounds to spend the taxpayer's money on an autopsy. Lester had the audacity to say that to me. That Jeff's death happening less than two weeks from Dani's was an unfortunate coincidence. Nothing more. Looked me in the eye and warned me to *leave it alone*. For my own good." Karen swore under her breath.

They had both lost people they loved to this fight.

Summer shared in the woman's outrage. "Shortly before Dani's death, she found what she called a *smoking gun* to use against Einhorn Industries. Do you happen to know anything about that?" They had agreed to find out how much Karen knew before sharing what they had discovered in the envelopes.

"I know plenty. I remember that day well. It was the first time in a long time that Dani came in so happy. Over the moon. You would've thought she won the lottery or something. That girl was pleased as punch with herself. But she was also worried about telling you." Karen said, gesturing to Summer.

"Why was she worried about me?"

"I can't say for certain, but I think Dani wanted to make sure she was right. That the evidence was solid before letting you know about it. Putting together the little things, she said." Karen sighed. "Dani seemed concerned that you were under a lot of stress. Working yourself to the bone to help her with the lawsuit, and she didn't want to get your hopes too high. Didn't want you to worry."

Guilt pressed in on Summer for all the mistakes she'd made. Chiefly, making Dani feel like she couldn't tell her the truth and needed to hide things from her. "Dani was risking her life with…unsavory people, doing unsavory things but didn't want me to worry. Told Jeff but cut me out of the loop."

"Summer, you two were best friends," Logan said as he moved closer. Crouching down in front of her, he reached for her hand, stopped himself and gripped the arm of the chair instead. "More than that. Like sisters. When you love someone, you want to protect them. Not add to their stress. Part of loving someone is not wanting them to worry. Not wanting them to hurt. She wasn't trying to leave you out. She was trying to spare you."

"Maybe she did you a favor by not telling you," Karen said.

"How so?"

"You're still alive, honey."

Logan gripped her arm, like he couldn't help, and nodded in agreement.

"You're right," Summer said. "She didn't tell me to protect me." *To spare me.*

"Did Jeff agree that the evidence was solid?" Logan asked Karen.

"He had some issues with it, if I recall correctly. Questions about how she obtained the emails and such. Jeff needed to depose the person who gave her the thumb drive."

Summer and Logan shared a glance.

"What thumb drive?" she asked.

"It's locked away." Karen pointed across the room to one of the five-drawer filing cabinets lined against the wall. "But I downloaded copies of everything for Jeff." She got up and sat in front of Jeff's computer and logged in.

Summer and Logan moved around the desk behind Karen and watched as she brought up the folder marked *Einhorn Class Action*. Inside, she opened another folder.

There were twenty files listed, each labeled as a date with NT at the end.

"Did you name these files?" Summer asked.

"No, that's how they came on the thumb drive. I downloaded them as is. Jeff and Dani reviewed them together, and she asked him to print out copies of the ones she dubbed the smoking gun. She took those with her."

Summer leaned in, taking a closer look. "Who was Jeff going to depose?"

Karen brought up a spreadsheet simply marked Evidence.

Summer scanned through it. Chip Boyd's computer was listed, and Dani was noted as the source. Below it was the thumb drive along with the date and name of the source:

NovaTech Data Center, Mike Johnson

"What a minute." Pressure welled in her chest. "Do you see this?" she asked Logan, pointing to the name.

"Yeah, I see it." He glanced down at Karen. "Does Mike Johnson work for the data center?"

"Work for it?" Karen said, raising both eyebrows. "No. He owns NovaTech. The company pretty much runs itself at this point. He doesn't need to be hands-on. It's the reason he has all that free time to run the AA meetings."

Logan turned to Summer. "We need to talk to Mike again."

That was precisely what she was thinking.

It was after seven o'clock when Logan and Summer arrived at IPS. The guys helped him unload all the files Summer had deemed pertinent and brought from Arbuckle's office.

Tak had been the only one missing but finally walked through door.

"Where have you been all day?" Chance asked.

"At the reservation, taking initiative," Tak said. "People have been getting sick. Weird stuff. They're willing to discuss the possibility of joining the lawsuit, but I think they'll need to be convinced. By a lawyer."

Chance looked at Summer. "I can be quite convincing. I'm happy to go there tomorrow, knock on some doors and round up more plaintiffs unless you'd prefer to do it yourself."

"We've learned some questionable things about what Dani may have been involved in. I think my focus needs to be on that. Figuring out what really happened to her. Besides, I believe in your power of persuasion," she told Chance.

"There was something else," Tak said. "The local water district sent everyone on the reservation a cagey and curiously worded letter." He handed it to Summer.

Logan moved in beside her and read the letter along

with her. "The water district already knows there's PFAS in the water?"

Summer sighed. "This is a game to Einhorn. This letter is a strategic move. They must have spoken with the water district after I filed the motion for discovery. Admitted that there's PFAS in Snowberry Creek and Bigfork River because they know we have evidence proving it. I had to turn over the results of the samples that were tested on our end during discovery."

"But the letter only states that there's 'low concentrations' in the water," Tak said. "Makes no mention of the potential damage."

"Why would Einhorn essentially admit that the river has chemicals in it and have the water district send out this letter?" Logan asked.

"Starts the clock on statute of limitations for those on the reservation to sue," Chance said.

Summer nodded. "My firm has used the tactic." She looked back at the letter. "It's dated a little more than eleven months ago. In less than thirty days, Einhorn won't have to worry about the unsuspecting men, women and children living on the reservation becoming plaintiffs. With Dani and Jeff dead, and they hope me out of the way as well, they can easily offer the four other families already attached to my suit a small settlement and be done with this problem."

"We're not going to let that happen," Logan said.

"No. We're not," Chance added.

Summer appreciated the support. She glanced at her watch. "We need to go meet Mike soon."

"Why didn't you have him come here?" Bo asked.

"I don't want anyone else to know that IPS is involved," Logan explained, "or that we're stashing everything here.

We're only meeting him a couple of minutes away at a café he picked. Said they have excellent pie."

Eli smiled. "That must be Fowler's. I highly recommend the strawberry rhubarb or huckleberry pie. Nothing like sweet and tart wild Montana huckleberries."

"I'm not in the mood for pie," Summer said.

To be honest, neither was Logan. "We better get going. Thanks for everything, guys."

They took off, went straight to Fowler's, and found Mike sitting in a cozy booth in the back, enjoying pie à la mode. There were only a couple of other diners seated closer to the door.

Logan let Summer slide into the booth first and then sat down across from Mike.

"Do you guys want anything?" Mike asked. "The huckleberry is out of this world. It was Dani's favorite."

Karen Perkins had picked up sandwiches, salads and kombucha for dinner and they'd eaten at the office. "We're fine."

As the waitress approached, Mike gestured to her that she wasn't needed. "Is meeting here okay?"

"This is fine, if you're good with it," Logan said. "We just wanted you to feel free to talk without fear of reprisals in case someone else overheard our conversation."

"They'll give us space here at Fowler's. Dani and I used to come here together after meetings a couple of times a month. Pie instead of drinks. So, what follow-up questions did you have?"

"Why didn't you tell us that you gave Dani incriminating information on Einhorn?" Logan asked.

"The walls had eyes and ears at the church when we spoke. There was no way I could've announced my involvement for everyone to hear. Do you have any idea what kind of liability that would expose me to? Einhorn is one of my clients."

Logan put his forearms on the table and leaned forward. "You could've mentioned that you own the NovaTech Data Center. An important detail considering how you were able to get the information."

"Everyone knows I own NovaTech," Mike said. "It's not a secret."

"Why would you jeopardize your business?" Summer asked. "Open yourself to a potential lawsuit and loss of clients by giving Dani illegally obtained information?"

Mike set his fork down. "Dani was desperate. Doing things that scared me. Made me afraid for her life. I figured if I helped her, gave her just enough of what she needed, then she would stop putting herself at risk."

"Weren't you worried about the ramifications of breaking the law?" Logan asked.

"Of course, I was, but she had a hacker friend. Told me she could get him to make it look like there was a data breach at NovaTech in a worst-case scenario, to keep me out of trouble. She told me that you guys would only use the information to identify the emails in some boxes. Something about how it was easier to find what you were looking for if you knew what it was. You told her that," Mike said, gesturing to Summer.

Logan didn't want this to add to Summer's guilt. "Mike, how did you afford NovaTech?"

"I was already in the industry for years. When my father died and left me some money, I invested my inheritance in Bitcoin, back in 2012. Did really well. Used some of my profits to build the first data center in the area eight years ago," he said, and Logan studied him carefully. "Took a lot of legwork in the beginning to recruit clients but the business runs itself now and I can spend time helping people. Why do you ask?"

Logan weighed how much to say. "Dani had some things in her possession that has raised a lot of questions for us."

"What kinds of things?" Mike asked.

"For starters, bearer bonds," Summer said.

"Bearer bonds?" Mike's brow furrowed. "Isn't that an Old West thing? They still make those?"

Logan shook his head. "No, they don't. They stopped before she was born, which is what makes it so perplexing."

Mike considered it a minute. "Maybe it has something to do with her boyfriend. The hacker."

"The hacker was her boyfriend?" Logan asked, and Mike nodded. "You didn't mention that before."

Hunching forward, Mike lowered his voice. "The less I say about that dude, the better."

"If she was dating someone," Summer said, "she would've told me."

"Like she told you about breaking into Chip Boyd's house and stealing his computer? Or that she had those bearer bonds you found?" Mike sounded crestfallen, like he'd been through hell the last few months with Dani.

Summer clenched her fingers under the table, probably hating how much her best friend had kept secret.

Logan wanted to cover her hand with his, pat her arm, give her some small gesture of comfort. He only dared pressing his knee to hers, and she didn't pull away. "Why didn't you tell us she had a boyfriend?" he asked, circling back to it. *A boyfriend who happens to be a hacker.*

Mike shook his head as he paled. "I didn't say anything

about him and still don't want to because I'm more afraid of him than the Nielsens and the Einhorns combined."

"Why?" Summer and Logan asked in unison.

"The guy is trouble. Serious bad news. I'm talking brass knuckles, scary tattoos, steel-toed boots, has friends who can make people disappear. I think he might be in the mob or something."

"What's his name? How did Dani meet him?" Logan's questions were rapid-fire.

"She didn't really talk about him a whole lot. I think it's because she knew I didn't approve," Mike said. "His name is Kirill Luzhin. She met him in Moscow."

Summer stiffened. "Dani never left the country."

"Not Moscow, Russia," Mike said. "Moscow, Idaho. I think she met him when she took her samples to be tested out of state. She mentioned a bar and grill called the Kremlin."

Summer put a hand on Logan's forearm. "She did have the testing done in Idaho, but I didn't focus on the exact location, only the name of the lab. She thought it'd be safer to do it anywhere out of state than here in Montana."

"There's a group of Russian mobsters in Moscow. When Dani started talking about her hacker boyfriend being *connected*, I thought it best that she steered clear of him. But she kept telling me how she had things under control."

"She used to say that all the time." Lowering her head, Summer squeezed her eyes shut for a long moment. "How she had everything *under control*. The moment I started to get a bad feeling in my gut, I should've pressed her for answers."

"Don't beat yourself up," Mike said, his expression pained. "Dani wasn't in the right state of mind to listen to anyone. Believe me, I tried. She was too determined. Obsessed. Nothing and no one could have stopped her."

"And it got her killed." Summer covered her mouth with her hand. "If only I had known." She shivered, shoulders hunched, looking wracked with emotion. Tears leaked from her eyes.

Logan put his palm on her back and rubbed—a reflex he needed to curb. But she leaned against him, accepting his comfort. He lifted his arm, wrapping it around her, letting her rest her head on his shoulder. He searched for the right words as a weight sank through him. A dark heaviness that drained him. Because he didn't know how to make this better for her. No matter what he told her, it wouldn't bring the easement of guilt she deserved and needed. "This isn't on you," he said, his voice low, his tone gentle. "Okay?"

Letting out a shaky breath, Summer grabbed a paper napkin from the metal holder on the table. She wiped her eyes and nodded. Then she seemed to realize they had crossed the newly established boundary and jerked away from him. "Do you think Kirill Luzhin had anything to do with her death?"

Mike shrugged. "If he was her boyfriend and was helping her, why would he hurt her?"

Of female victims for whom the relationships to their offenders were known, 50 percent were murdered by their husbands or boyfriends. "I can think of a few reasons." But how did it relate to the bearer bonds and the news articles about Azarov?

Dani, what were you involved in? And with whom?

"Any idea what would've led Dani to go so far as to get involved with the Russian mob in the first place?" Summer asked. "Take such a dangerous chance?"

"Besides desperation?" Another shrug from Mike. "Maybe she was digging deeper into Alex Pope."

Summer straightened. "Alex Pope from the Einhorn security team? What about him would lead her to Russian mobsters?"

Alarm widened Mike's eyes. "You don't know? I told you they were shady. Why haven't you investigated them yet?"

An investigation was a process. Sometimes a marathon but never a sprint. "Just tell us what we're missing," Logan said.

"Alex Pope was born Alexei Popov. His family changed their names years ago. Maybe she found something that led her to that bar and grill."

Logan looked at Summer. "There's only one way to find out."

She nodded. "We need to ask Kirill Luzhin."

In the morning, they also had to fill in Declan Hart on everything they had learned.

"Don't go to Moscow," Mike said. "All I know for certain is that you don't want to mess around with the Russian mob. Not under any circumstances. Best to stay away from them. Please, listen to me. If Dani had, she might still be alive."

Chapter Eighteen

Summer lay in bed, staring up at the ceiling. Tomorrow, she was going to buy a giant whiteboard. Create a link chart showing everything that they knew so far about the case, persons of interest, along with the connections.

She created evidence boards when working on more complicated lawsuits. Looking at all the pieces visually tended to help. As a cop, Logan was probably accustomed to using them, too.

He might have ideas from a law enforcement angle about constructing one that she hadn't tried.

Rolling out of bed, she headed for the door as she considered creeping to his room next door and seeing if he was still awake.

Odds were high that he was. They could talk about everything, work through the details together.

In the middle of the night. With her in only a nightgown. And him in a pair of boxer briefs, hard chest bare, hair tousled.

Stopping with her hand on the doorknob, she reconsidered.

Bad idea. Unless she wanted to invite a different kind of trouble.

They were both struggling to keep their hands to themselves as it was. She didn't need to make it any harder.

But whenever she stared into his sky blue eyes, all she could think about was that kiss. His mouth pressed to hers. His hands on her body. His arms wrapped around her tight, holding her close. The tingles and ache for more. About what else he could make her feel.

About the here and now and how he had this way of making the word *long-term* disappear from her vocabulary, just with a look.

Think of the big picture, Summer.

Discussions about the evidence board could wait when the sun was up, and they were fully dressed. She climbed back into bed and grabbed the electronic tablet.

The alarm was set to *Away* mode. All was quiet.

She set the tablet on the pillow beside her and rolled over.

Closing her eyes, she tried to force her mind, and her libido, to settle down, so she could get a few hours of sleep.

DRIFTING BETWEEN A light sleep and drowsy wakefulness, Logan lay in bed.

His cell phone began buzzing beneath him, where he'd slid it between his back and the mattress. A bolt of adrenaline roared through him. Jackknifing upright in bed, he grabbed the phone and checked it.

Sure enough, it was a notification from the security cameras, indicating movement had been detected. He swore under his breath as he pulled up the live feed on the camera that had been activated.

It was the one he'd placed in the living room, covering the window in the kitchen and the others in the dining room.

A gloved hand reached through a perfectly round hole

in the window, likely made silently with a glass cutter, and unlatched the lock. The masked man shoved the window open, hoisted himself up on the sill and climbed inside the house wearing night vision googles.

NVGs?

Logan glanced at the clock on the dresser near the foot of the bed. It was dark.

The electricity must've been cut. Only reason the cameras were still working was because they had backup batteries.

Yanking on his jeans over his boxer briefs and stepping into his boots, Logan grabbed the shotgun on the bedside table. He snatched his holstered gun from the floor, hooked it on his waistband and crept softly across the room.

He slept with the door wide-open so he could monitor Summer's movements and hear any signs of danger.

Lifting the cell phone, he glanced back at the screen, keeping an eye on the professional killer. He was still in the kitchen, wiggling the stove out of place slowly, to mitigate any noise, but efficiently. The stove was connected to the propane tank outside.

Not good.

If he disconnected the hose from the line of propane, he could fill the kitchen with gas. Set something to ignite it. The explosion would cause the 500-gallon propane tank to blow as well, taking out most if not all of the house and them along with it.

His gut twisted as hot, prickling anger flooded him.

The only apparent positive of the situation was that the guy seemed committed to making their deaths look like accidents. Rather than stalk upstairs with a gun attached to a sound suppressor and put a bullet in their heads.

Logan stepped into the hall. Mapping out every floorboard that creaked in the house had been time-consuming, but it would pay off now. He treaded carefully in the hallway, avoiding any spots that would make a sound. Easing open the door to Summer's room, he wished he had lubricated the hinges with oil or bit of bearing grease.

A groan sounded. He stopped pushing the door, leaving it partially open. Glanced at the camera.

The guy in the kitchen held still. Listening. Waiting.

Just as Logan did.

Once the man seemed satisfied that no one was moving around upstairs, he went back to work on the stove.

Logan slipped into the bedroom. Summer was asleep on her side with her back to the door.

Shaking his head at her being in such a vulnerable position, he tiptoed toward her and knelt on the mattress. Eased closer. Reached over and put his hand on her mouth to keep her from screaming.

A FIRM HAND clamped down on Summer's mouth, snapping her spine straight and her eyes open.

Logan peered down at her. Then he pressed his lips to her ear. "The hit man is in the house," he whispered, and terror ran through her veins like ice water. "Don't talk. Do as I say. Understand?"

She blinked but nodded.

He glanced around like he was looking for something and sighed. "Here's my gun." He thrust the weapon in her hand. "I'll get you to the front door. Take Dani's truck. Mine could've been tampered with," he said, making her think of a severed brake line, a rattlesnake or black widow hidden inside the cab. "Do you have the keys?"

She looked over at her purse on the nightstand. The keys,

bearer bonds and Dani's cell phone were all inside. She met his gaze and nodded.

"Follow me closely." His voice was a whisper, his breath warm against her neck. "Step only where I do so we don't make any noise. When we get to the bottom of the stairs, run out the door and take the truck."

What about him?

She rolled over slightly, turning her face to his, bringing them nose to nose. "I won't leave you."

"Yes. You will."

Gripping his face with both hands, Summer shook her head. "Don't go after him. He'll kill you."

"I can't let him get away only to have another chance to try again."

She pressed her forehead to his, heart throbbing. "We have to go together."

"There's no time for this." Pulling away, he snatched her wrist, yanking her upright.

She lurched to her feet.

He grabbed her purse from the nightstand and shoved it toward her. "He's rigging the house to blow." His voice was a harsh whisper. "You have to get out."

Panic flared along with an icy jolt of fear. She shook her head again. How could he ask her to leave him behind?

Logan curled his hand in her hair, leaned in and dipped his head down. "Please," he said through gritted teeth. "Listen to me."

Then his mouth crushed against hers in a kiss that shocked the hell out of her.

The kiss was hard. Demanding. She raked her fingers in his hair, pressing closer to him. He was angry and afraid and desperate for her to do as he told her. She got that. But she wanted them both to be safe. Needed that even more.

He pulled his mouth from hers. Stared at her for a heartbeat. "I'm falling in love with you. I just wanted to say that in case...you know."

In case one of us doesn't make it.

In case he dies.

"Promise you'll leave," he whispered.

Her nerves fluttered at the dangerous gleam in his eyes. She didn't want him distracted, worrying about her, trying to protect her as well as himself. "I promise."

He held up the phone, checking the cameras, and she glanced at the screen.

The masked man, the assassin sent to kill them, was setting up candles on the kitchen table.

"Come on. Hurry." He led the way into the hall.

She trailed behind him closely, following where he walked, only stepping on the same spots on the floorboards that he used.

They crept to the staircase.

This would be trickier. Almost every stair tread creaked and groaned.

He skipped the first step entirely, landing on the corner of the second and then the middle of the third without making a sound. She'd watched him testing the stairs, pacing around the house over the past couple of days, but she'd thought he had some kind of obsessive-compulsive disorder and had dismissed it. The whole time he had been learning the house, memorizing the spots that made noise and where it was safe to step silently.

Logan truly was amazing.

Glancing back at her, he waited for her on the fifth step, where he was still concealed. Once they ventured beyond that point, anyone on the stairs could be seen from the kitchen. If the hit man looked up, he'd spot them.

Summer's hand trembled as she gripped the stair railing and snuck down behind him. Her entire body trembled. Her stomach churned so violently that she thought she'd be sick.

Logan glanced at the front door that was only a few feet away and turned back to her, searching her face.

Swallowing hard, she nodded that she was ready. Even though she wasn't. Still didn't know if she could leave him.

He skipped another step, angled so he faced the kitchen. The last two stairs he took sideways. With his hand outstretched, he beckoned to her as he stayed focused on the killer loose in the house.

Summer crept down, taking the same path Logan had. Faint amber light came from the kitchen, drawing her gaze. She hesitated.

Four candles were lit on the table.

The hit man raised his head, looking right at them.

"Go, Summer." Logan grabbed her wrist and shoved her toward the door. "Don't look back. Run!"

She bolted for the door. Unlocked it. Ripped the chain free from the guard. Flung the door open and flew down the porch steps. Dashed barefoot to Dani's truck. She snatched the keys from her purse, got the door open, jumped inside and started it. Throwing the gear in Reverse, she took out her cell phone instead of sparing a moment to even turn on the headlights. Slammed on the accelerator. Sped down the drive as she fumbled with her phone and called Declan.

LOGAN LOCKED AWAY his churning emotions and concentrated on the contract killer in the house. Shotgun raised, aimed at the hit man in the kitchen, Logan moved forward, drawing closer.

Head canted away from the candlelight that probably hurt

his eyes with the NVGs on, the guy didn't move. At first. Then he reached for the gun holstered on his hip but looked back at the stove like he was reconsidering.

A distinctive rotten egg odor suffused the space. Propane companies added a harmless chemical called mercaptan to give it the offensive smell. Otherwise, the propane would be odorless.

Gas permeated the kitchen. If either of them fired their weapons, the propane would ignite, killing them both in the explosion.

"Get down on your knees!" Logan said. "Hands behind your head!"

"Or what?" the man asked, so low it was barely audible.

Logan kept creeping forward through the living room, almost at the threshold of the kitchen. "I'll shoot." A total bluff. He hoped the guy didn't call him on it.

Tension built along with the cold silence and the amount of propane gas filling the house. With the lit candles, they had minutes. Not even. Seconds. Pressure welled in his chest behind his sternum.

"You won't shoot," the assassin said, his voice gruff. "You're not suicidal." Then he sprang onto the counter like a ninja, crossed his arms over his face and crashed through the full window.

Swearing, Logan bolted after him, leaped up into the sink and jumped outside into the darkness, landing beside the propane tank.

"Get to safety," Declan said over the phone. "I'll call 911 on my way over to the farmhouse."

"Okay." Summer finished backing down the drive and stopped in the road, preparing to turn and race toward town.

An explosion erupted, followed almost simultaneously by a second larger one that shook the ground. Most of the Granger house went up in a fireball, flames and debris shooting up into the dark sky.

Logan!

Her eyes burned and she swallowed the scream that rose in her throat. But even stronger was the rage that surged through her. "Oh my God."

"What is it?" Declan asked.

"The house! The house blew up. I have to check on Logan." She threw the gear in Drive and stomped down on the gas, speeding back up the driveway.

"No!" Declan warned. "Get out of there. Go to town."

But she couldn't. Wouldn't leave Logan behind.

What if he was hurt? What if he needed help? A hundred what-ifs spun in her head.

That professional hit man might kill him if the blast didn't. Pick him off while separated.

No one was watching his back. That was her job. They were a team. In this together.

"Come as fast as you can. I have to find Logan." Summer tossed the phone down and put both hands on the wheel as she raced toward the fire.

He was risking everything, and she wasn't going to let him do it alone.

THE BLAST HAD lifted Logan off his feet, propelling both him and the assassin through the air. Logan landed hard, the impact knocking the wind from his lungs and the shotgun from his hands. Fortunately, he'd gotten far enough away from the propane tank before it blew.

Dazed, he shook his head and got his bearings. He sucked

in air along with smoke and coughed. Intense heat from the blaze bore down on him. His pant leg had caught fire. He slapped out the flames.

The other man was scrambling up from the ground, headed for the darkness of the woods. Where he'd have the advantage cloaked in black and wearing night vision goggles.

One thing Logan had learned in his years in law enforcement was that violence wasn't what set people apart in a fight. It was the distance that a person was prepared to go.

Logan grabbed the shotgun and tore off after him. He couldn't let him get away. Not again.

This ended. Tonight. Because Logan was prepared to go the distance. All the way until that murderer was dead.

The hit man dashed into the trees and disappeared.

Reaching the edge of the woods, Logan stopped at the tree line and listened. There was no sound of pounding footfalls to follow. No movement. No shadows shifting in the breaks of moonlight filtering through the canopy of branches of leaves.

Where in the hell was he?

Hiding. Waiting. Baiting Logan into another trap.

The hairs on the back of his neck rose. Logan was being watched. Sensed it. Felt it deep in his gut. If he darted off into those trees, into the darkness, without knowing where that contract killer was lurking, Logan was a dead man.

A vehicle barreled up the slight hill around the back of the house. A truck with no headlights on.

Dani's truck!

Behind the wheel, Summer sped toward him. She laid on the horn, beeping. Sticking her head out the open window, she said, "The trees! He's up in the trees!"

Logan whirled on his heel back toward the woods as the truck's headlights popped on. The bright white light shining like a beacon in the night.

The assailant whipped his head away from the harsh glare, throwing his arm up to shield his face. Losing his footing on a branch, he fell, hitting the ground.

Behind him, Logan heard the truck skid to a stop and the door open, but he lifted the shotgun and pointed at the guy.

Ripping off the night vision goggles with one hand, the hit man drew his gun with the other hand.

Logan put his finger on the trigger and pulled it.

Thunk. The weapon didn't fire.

Jammed.

He'd only made certain that it was loaded and hadn't taken the time to properly test Dani's shotgun.

The other guy rose up on his knee, taking aim—dead center on Logan.

Three shots fired. *Bam! Bam! Bam!*

Logan's heart lurched as he froze. Expecting pain that didn't come. He glanced down at his chest. No blood. No wounds.

Then he realized the loud shots hadn't been fired from the sound suppressed gun. He looked back over his shoulder. Summer was standing not far behind him, Glock in her hands, still raised like she was prepared to fire again. At the sight of her, he lost another piece of his heart.

Logan spun back toward the threat in time to watch the masked man keel over onto the ground. He hurried to him and picked up the man's gun. Yanking off the black balaclava, Logan revealed an unfamiliar face. Checking for a pulse, he pressed two fingers on part of a spider's web that had been tattooed over the man's carotid artery, covering half his neck. The guy was part of Vory, connected to the Russian mob. Whoever he was, the stranger hadn't been the man in the photos on Dani's phone. The guy Logan suspected she'd been sleeping with didn't have any ink on his neck.

"He's dead!" Logan stood and headed toward Summer.

Lowering the gun, she ran to him and practically jumped into his arms. His heart was lighter than air. He wrapped her in a bear hug, lifting her from her feet, never happier to see or touch anyone in his life. Holding her close, he tightened his grip on her, determined to never let her go.

Chapter Nineteen

The EMTs had given Summer and Logan foil blankets to wrap around themselves after the medics insisted on examining them. Logan's lower leg had been treated for minor burns. Summer was astounded that he had refused painkillers, but his tolerance was clearly higher than hers.

Declan finished taking their statements as Logan held her hand. "Why didn't you let me know last night about this Kirill Luzhin in Moscow, Idaho?"

"I have the same question," Chance said, who'd brought Logan some clothes since he'd lost everything in the explosion.

Summer had only packed an overnight bag's worth of stuff and most of her things were still at the cabin.

Logan sighed. "I couldn't discuss an active investigation with you," he said to Chance. He looked at Declan. "I knew you had your hands full questioning the Einhorn team and Nielsens. I don't expect you to work around the clock. Figured I would let you know first thing in the morning."

Flattening his lips in a grim line, Declan shook his head. "Well, it's morning now," he said, gesturing to the lightening sky.

It was almost 5:00 a.m. and hard to believe that it was already Sunday. But she was grateful to see the sun rise after the night they'd had.

No arrests had been made, so she assumed Declan's interrogations yesterday hadn't produced much. "How did the interviews go with Einhorn and the Nielsens?"

Declan shook his head. "They all lawyered up. Barely answered any questions."

"Were you aware that Alex Pope was born Alexei Popov?" Logan asked.

"No, I wasn't. But I did find out that the homicides our guy here—" Declan hiked his thumb at the body bag "—is most likely responsible for are all loosely or closely related to the Russian mafia. There's a link to Einhorn or Nielsens. Maybe it's through Pope. Or should I say Popov. Whatever it is, if it exists, I'll find it. Kirill Luzhin might be the key."

Chance clasped Logan's shoulder. "I understand not telling me about the autopsy results, but you should've at least told me you were dealing with a Russian mafia hit man. I could've provided more support."

Logan shook his head. "You've done so much as it is. You and the IPS team are still doing a ton, going through the discovery."

"At least we know what we're looking for now," Chance said, "which should it make the process go faster."

Dani had made sure they had what was needed. "If those emails aren't there, we'll have to file a court order to have Einhorn disclose all corporate communications."

"Why wait?" Chance asked with a shrug. "I say we file tomorrow."

"We could request the court go through a third party," Summer said. "Have NovaTech legally turn over all of Einhorn's digital documentation to ensure nothing is excluded or deleted." Thanks to Dani connecting the dots that NovaTech was the key, that the data center housed all of Einhorn's secrets, and verifying it, they would have everything they needed for an airtight case.

"Stick to the lawsuit," Declan said. "I'm ordering both of you not to question anyone else regarding the deaths of Dani Granger, Jeff Arbuckle, and the attempts made on your lives."

Logan's jaw clenched. "But I wanted to go to Moscow. Talk to this Kirill Luzhin in person."

Declan raised his palm "Leave it to me. You two have been through enough. You're lucky to be alive."

"Listen to the man," Chance said.

"Luck has nothing to do with it. I'm alive because of Summer." Logan curled an arm around her shoulder. "Without her, I'd be dead."

She'd almost lost him. That hit man had had him in his sights. Ready to kill him. If she'd left him alone, he would be dead. Gone. Leaving a hole in her life and her heart.

All this time, she had been focused on long-term, and it was still important to her, but so was recognizing when she found someone special, when what they shared was not only meaningful but also profound and making the most of whatever time she had with him.

Resting her head on Logan's chest, she wrapped both arms around his waist. She might never feel this way about anyone ever again. The real regret would be walking away from him not knowing what might've been between them. Whether it lasted for a month, a week, or mere days.

However long they could be together, not holding back, she'd cherish it for the rest of her life. Deep in her heart, that was what she really wanted. To share her heart and her body with someone who felt the same about her as she did about him. Who truly cared. Who respected her.

Whom she could trust completely.

Everything that mattered she already had with Logan.

"Your stubbornness paid off." Declan eyed her. "This time." A sheriff's office vehicle pulled up and Declan turned around. "Don't push it. Both of you need to stand down. Get some rest and keep a low profile. This isn't over yet. We still need to figure out who hired the assassin. I'll contact the sheriff of Latah County, Idaho, and arrange backup to go with me to this Kremlin bar and grill. Today. I want to get to the bottom of who's behind all this."

Summer unzipped her purse, took out Dani's old cell phone, the news articles and the bearer bonds, and handed them to Declan. Then she gave him the passcode. "See if Kirill has tattoos on his body that match the ones in the photos."

"I'll do my best. As for this—" Declan gestured to the sheriff's vehicle "—and everything else, let me deal with it." He headed to the cruiser as Lester Tofteland stepped out. "Sheriff, this is a DCI crime scene. I'll be happy to give you a copy of my report once the case is closed. For now, your presence and your involvement are neither needed nor wanted."

"I think he's got that in hand," Chance said to Logan. "Do you guys need a lift or a place to stay?"

"We've got my truck. Just need to check it out and make sure it's safe first," Logan said.

"And I still have the cabin that I'm renting."

"The one-bedroom?" Chance asked, raising an eyebrow in a way that made her squirm.

"I'll take the sofa." Logan tightened his grip on her. "Or sleep on the floor."

"Sure you will." Chance pressed his palms together and rubbed them. "I'll help you check your truck and then you two can sort out your sleeping arrangements without my interference."

AFTER SHUFFLING INSIDE the cabin and locking the door, Logan took Summer's hand and sat down on the sofa with her.

"There's been tension between us since I kissed you. We could stay with Chance if you prefer. I love the guy, but he can be a lot."

"Yes, he can. No offense to your friend."

He smiled. "I just don't want to put you in an uncomfortable position by us staying here together."

She scooted closer, pressing her leg to his. "*You* don't make me uncomfortable, Logan. My feelings for you do."

"I understand."

"Remember how I told you that kissing you made me want more? A lot more?"

"Yeah."

"That was the problem."

"But why?" He wanted more every time he touched her, heck, looked at her. In his book, that wasn't a problem, it was a gift. Something rare that should be treasured.

"I've never been with a man," she said, spitting the statement out like it was a bad thing and hanging her head as though ashamed. "I'm a virgin."

He took in her words, letting them roll around in his head for a moment. "Okay." How that was a problem still eluded him. "Are you waiting for marriage? If you are, I'm fine with that."

Her head whipped up, and she stared at him as though he'd started speaking a foreign language. "Really?"

"Sure." He nodded. "I respect you, Summer, and your values." Nothing wrong with being old-fashioned.

She huffed a breath. "I'm not waiting for marriage."

This woman had his head spinning with confusion. "I don't understand. Then why haven't you been with anyone yet?"

"Because I want it to mean something. Not for it to be some empty physical act. I want it to be special, with someone I care about."

Sounded reasonable to him. "All right."

"Someone I'm in a relationship with. A relationship that has long-term potential. I get that not all potential is realized, but I don't want a fling. I want the person I'm going to be intimate with to want the same thing, to have the same intention. For the end goal to be a commitment. Or at least, I did, until you were nearly shot and I almost lost you."

Summer knew exactly what she wanted and shouldn't have to settle for anything less.

He admired that about her. "We care about each other. It's been fast, but I already know you're the type of woman who wants to take things slowly."

"I don't need slow. Not if it feels right. But I backed off the other night because I thought I needed long-term potential. And that's something we don't have."

"Why not?"

Her face twisted in confusion again. "Logan."

"Hear me out," he said. "After we met at the funeral for Dani's mom, I've thought about you. About the way you swept in and handled everything, so that Dani and her father didn't have to. About how you cleaned up late into the night without a single complaint."

"You did help me. Without complaint, too."

"I've thought about your smile. About your kindness. Your warmth." The smell of her, sensual and sophisticated. The sound of her laugh. "How I wanted to keep talking to you." Like they could talk forever and never run out of things to say to each other.

"But that was five years ago," she said, and he couldn't ignore the sadness in her eyes.

"Exactly." Interlacing his fingers with hers, he grinned. "I have to be honest about something else. I didn't only come here because I was needed. I came because I knew you'd be here. I didn't want to miss another chance at this."

Her eyes grew wide, and she tensed.

"Do you think less of me?" he asked.

She shook her head. "You saw a need and you filled it. You did it for Ric, you did it for Matt, and it's okay that you also did it for yourself. I think it's important for people like you, who give of themselves so easily, without asking for anything in return, to sometimes be a little selfish and take what they need."

Summer was exceptional. Singular.

"But I'm not sure what to do with all that," she said. "How does it erase the obstacle of distance when you go back home?"

Logan recognized Summer was a logical woman. One who strategized and planned. Details were important to her.

"I have a proposal," he said. "Let's explore what we feel. I want to kiss you again and hold you and not be afraid to do it. In exchange, I promise that we won't cross the line. We won't go to fourth base in the heat of the moment." Nothing wrong with second. Possibly even third. "We'll discuss it beforehand, without emotion clouding our judgment. As for a relationship, we're kind of sort of already in one. We just skipped the dinner and dancing parts."

"We are in something together. For however long we're here. Then we go our separate ways, I guess."

"A flight from where I live to Seattle is only three hours." Technically, he had to drive two hours to Denver for the flight, but he was fine with that. Not as though they were based on opposites coasts or had an ocean between them. This was doable. "Only logistics. Though if that's all too much of a headache for you, then I understand."

Somehow, he'd manage even though staying away from her would be like torture.

"It's not a headache," she said, surprising him. "It's a relief because I want more of all that with you, too." She smiled. "In my head, I was making it big and complicated. Insurmountable. But I like the way you see things. How you simplified it."

"We have to start somewhere, right?"

"According to you, we've already started. It was only a matter of how to proceed. Have you done this before, a long-distance relationship?"

"No."

"Have you ever been in love?"

"I thought I was when I was younger. With Amber Reyes, Chance's sister."

"Your sister-in-law?" Summer asked, deadpan, her eyes growing wide.

"It was years ago," So far in the past, he had been a different person. "We were just teenagers. But she only ever had eyes for my brother. Amber and I never dated. Never shared anything more than a few hugs. I had confused infatuation with something more. Truth be told, the only woman I've ever truly fallen for has been you."

She rocked back a little, still holding his hand. "Back at the house we were scared, and adrenaline was flowing. You don't have to say that now. It's not necessary."

"You're right, I don't. But it's true. I won't ever say something I don't mean. No secrets between us. No lies." He didn't want anything to get in the way of what he could have with Summer.

She slid her fingers into his hair and brought his face closer, but he was the one to kiss her. Cupping the back of her head, he licked into her mouth. The touch of her tongue sent a surge of heat pumping through him. Her arms came around his neck, and he pulled her closer, hauling her onto his lap. She tasted even better than last time. Hot and sweet. So good.

So perfect.

He'd wished he had called Dani a few months after her mother's funeral and got Summer's phone number. Even her address. Just showed up at her door and asked her out on a date.

Maybe that would've been too much, but he sensed she would've appreciated the grand gesture, especially if he had booked a hotel room for himself and made it clear he was only there to take her out, no strings attached.

The kiss deepened, growing more heated. She was clinging to him, moaning in his mouth. This thing between them felt completely right. Like every kiss before her had been a weak imitation of what it should be.

He eased back, and she blinked up at him with a dazed look.

"Wow," she said, breathless.

"Yeah." He wanted a lifetime of *wow* with her.

Chapter Twenty

A silver lining.

This thing she'd found with Logan, this relationship, was the one silver lining that had come from all the death and horror.

Summer and Logan had cleaned up and tried resting. Rest turned into making out and cuddling on the bed. They might have dozed off here and there in between kissing and touching and aching for more.

But he had made a promise and she liked ground rules. It was one of the reasons she loved practicing law.

They went out and purchased a giant whiteboard like she wanted. She already had a wireless printer and scanner. They discussed the details of everything they'd learned. Printed out pictures of the bearer bonds and the unknown tattooed man. Spent the rest of the day identifying the people of interest, mapping out all the facts, and listing their theories as to who hired the hit man. Their only consensus was that it was someone who didn't want to get their hands dirty. Who wanted distance from the murders.

"We need a break from this," Logan said. "Your stomach is starting to growl."

She hadn't even noticed, too preoccupied with the evidence board. "I guess you're right."

"Let's go to The Wolverine Lodge. Try to get a table overlooking the water and watch the sunset while we eat."

Dani's death had been proved a homicide. The hit man was dead. They had survived. Those were causes for celebration. "Give me a minute to change into something nicer."

"Why? You already look great."

She glanced down at her tank top and jeans and frowned. "This is our first official date. I want to change into something you'll remember." The comment made her think of Declan. Born with the boon and burden of remembering everything, and something about it made her sad for him. "I won't be long."

"When you say that, should I turn on the TV and prepare to wait for an hour?"

"Five minutes. Not a second longer." Not the sort to agonize over an outfit, she was always decisive and only purchased quality items that flattered her figure. Besides, it wasn't as if she had access to her entire wardrobe. She'd brought two large suitcases of clothes, not knowing exactly how long she was going to be there.

She hustled into the bedroom and opened her suitcases. One thing immediately stood out. A halter-strap fuchsia dress that hugged her torso and accentuated her cleavage, with an A-line skirt sprinkled with blue and yellow flowers along the bottom. She paired it with comfortable espadrille wedge sandals with straps that tied at the ankles and made her feel like she was walking on a cloud. Quickly, she brushed her hair, smoothing out the curls, and applied a little makeup to freshen up her face and hide the dark circles under her eyes. A spritz of the perfume Logan liked and she was ready in four minutes.

"Ta-da!" she announced, opening the door and strolling out of the bedroom.

Logan whistled. "You look so hot I would've waited an hour without complaint."

She suspected Logan would've waited without complaint regardless of what she wore. "Thank you," she said, doing a little twirl. "Mind if we walk? It's only a mile and it's a cooler day." The weather was beautiful. Mild. Sunny. Not too windy.

"Not at all. I didn't get to jog today. It'll be good to stretch my legs." He pocketed his keys, hooked his holstered gun on his waistband, put his cowboy hat on his head and they left.

They held hands as they strolled.

She loved the route to the restaurant. Once they crossed the creek, they could take the walking path adjacent to the lake. Logan could jog there while they stayed at the cabin.

At the crossing of Cutthroat Creek, they came to the quaint covered bridge that had a weeping willow on one end and a flowering purple tree on the other.

"I love this little bridge," she said. "It looks like something plucked out of a Thomas Kinkade painting."

Right before they entered, he pressed her up against the railing. His hands settling on her waist, stirring tingles in her thighs. "And you look like something plucked straight out of one my fantasies."

"Oh, really?"

Dipping his head closer to hers, he nodded. "I never say anything I don't mean."

She slid her arms around his neck and kissed him. He dug his fingers into her hair and pulled her against him.

His tongue tangled with hers, his wide shoulders under her hands, his body pressed against her.

The kiss was hot and hungry and the raw fierceness of it sent a shot of desire straight to her core.

One of his hands slid lower, cupping her butt, bringing her pelvis close against him. Awareness flooded her body as she felt the hard ridge of him through his jeans. Desire pumped through her hard and she arched her back, pressing her breasts to his chest. Combing her fingers up into his hair, she rocked her hips against him. He pulled her in even tighter, as though they couldn't get close enough.

She loved the way he kissed. How he tasted. She loved the way he smelled. Touched her like something precious and irreplaceable that he didn't want to lose.

His phone rang and he groaned. Slowly, he pulled away like it hurt to let her go and gazed down at her.

She saw desire burning right along with frustration in his deep blue eyes. Sliding her hands over his muscular shoulders, she rose up, giving him one more quick kiss on the lips. "Answer it."

"I want to shut the world out. Focus only on you and me for just one day."

She caressed his cheek. "We'll get the chance. Eventually."

LOGAN'S PHONE CONTINUED to ring.

Instead of answering it, he wanted to go back to kissing Summer. She was wearing a sexy dress. Smelled so good. Her face glowing, either from the walk or kissing. She looked relaxed, at peace, he dared think even happy.

"I'm a lucky man to have you in my life." That she wanted

him in the same way he wanted her. He'd never been so drawn to someone, like iron to a lodestone.

"No luck involved. You're the best man I know."

His phone stopped. "If it's important, they'll leave a message," he said, and they started walking under the bridge.

Summer's phone now rang.

The hairs on the back of Logan's neck rose and he got the sense they were being watched. Putting his arm around her, he glanced over his shoulder.

There was an old truck idling down the road. License plate obscured with a thick layer of mud. With the visor down and angle of the sun, he couldn't see the driver.

Dread tightened his gut.

"It's Declan," she said. She answered, "Hi. Logan is here with me and you're on speaker."

"I'm in Moscow." Declan's voice was strained. "Everything went to hell in a handbasket."

"What do you mean?" she asked.

Logan kept his gaze on the truck. Picking up their pace, he wanted to hurry to the other side of the bridge.

"There was a shoot-out. Two deputies are dead. Two more were wounded. We questioned a few thugs that we caught. Only one talked. I showed him the pictures of the tattoos. He translated the Russian word inked on the man's back. Means Azarov. The same name from the news articles. And get this. Kirill Luzhin doesn't exist. The name is a code word for trouble. If anyone came in there looking for a man by that name meant that person should be killed on sight, no questions asked. The Kremlin was a trap."

Mike Johnson.

"If Mike Johnson was your only source on this Moscow tip," Declan said, "then it's him."

They both heard the angry rumble of the truck at the same time. Engine revving behind them, the truck shot off down the road, tires spinning, rubber burning, barreling toward them.

Now that they were under the covered bridge, with two sides walled off, they were vulnerable.

Trapped.

"Run." Logan nudged her forward. Spinning around, he drew his gun. "Get off the bridge, Summer!"

The big truck sped under the covered bridge, bearing down on them.

Logan planted his feet in a wide stance, controlled his breathing, held his hands steady and took aim at the windshield. Driver's side. He pulled the trigger, firing four bullets.

The truck swerved back and forth, like the driver struggled to maintain control, but the vehicle kept coming straight at him.

He unloaded two more shots at the tires.

Veering sharply away—mere feet from Logan's position—the truck plowed into the side of the bridge. The tail end narrowly missed sideswiping him and the front crashed through the solid wood wall, but the vehicle was in no danger of tipping over the edge.

With his weapon trained on the driver's-side window, Logan hustled to the truck. He yanked open the door with his left hand, keeping the gun raised. Ready to shoot.

A single man sat behind the wheel. Deflated air bag in his lap.

Mike Johnson was slumped to one side. Baseball cap tucked low. Sunglasses covered half his face. Gunshot wounds in his chest. Blood soaking through his shirt. His shaking hand reached for a gun on the console.

Stepping up on the running board, Logan snatched the weapon from Mike's fingers and shoved it in his waistband, pressed against his spine. After making sure the guy didn't have any other weapons close at hand, Logan holstered his gun. He unclicked the seat belt, dragged Mike out of the truck and laid him on the ground.

Kneeling beside him, Logan looked over his injuries. Without immediate medical attention, Mike wasn't going to last long.

Summer ran back over, coming up alongside them. "I called the police. An ambulance is on the way."

"No ambulance." Mike shook his head. "Better to let me die here than the hell they'll put me through in prison."

"Who?" Logan asked.

"My family. I'm supposed to be dead already. If they find out that I'm still alive, my punishment will be worse than death."

Summer crouched near Mike's head. "You're Nikolai Azarov."

Mike, Nikolai, nodded.

"But why?" she asked. "Why did you kill Dani?"

"She knew I was in love with her. Used it against me. Slept with me. Made me think that she felt the same. Only to ask me to search Einhorn Industries records. To get her incriminating evidence."

"And you told her no," Logan said.

A man in hiding from the mafia, with everything to lose, wouldn't want to risk exposure in something like a lawsuit.

Mike nodded. "Dani wouldn't let it go, but I didn't realize that until she showed me what she'd found. What she'd pieced together about me."

"She searched your house," Summer said. "Found the bearer bonds."

"I stole them from my family. To start over. Faked my death for a clean slate."

"Dani took the pictures of your tattoos and must've had the word on your back translated." Summer's eyes welled with tears. "Dug into the name Azarov and figured out who you really were."

Swallowing hard, Mike nodded again. "She blackmailed me into giving her the Einhorn information. Promised she'd destroy the evidence about my identity. Give back the bearer bonds. That we could be in a real relationship." He took a wheezing breath, and Logan could tell that his lungs were filling up with blood. "But then Jeff Arbuckle wanted to depose me. Dani tried to convince Jeff that the information was leaked from a data breach of NovaTech, but Jeff insisted that I had to be deposed. No way around it. I couldn't risk that, and Dani refused to get rid of the files I'd given her. Told me that everything had gone too far. That she needed them. For the lawsuit. She left me no choice. I had to make it all go away."

"There's always a choice," Logan said. "You just made the wrong one."

Sirens wailed in the distance, drawing close.

"Dani cared for you." Summer clenched her hand into a fist. "And you killed her."

"I loved her. Trusted her." Mike coughed up blood. "Let her see my body. My life in ink. Let her have free rein of my home. And she betrayed me. Because she didn't care about me. Not enough. She was going to ruin my life. The only thing that mattered to her was the lawsuit."

"I don't think she ever wanted to expose you," Summer said. "When she took those pictures of you, she tried to protect you by not showing your face. She never told me about you or the bearer bonds, or the NovaTech files. She must've thought that she could come up with a workaround with Jeff to keep you out of it."

"She failed," Mike said. "I tried to have my mess cleaned up. But you two just wouldn't die. A couple of more accidents and I would've been free. Would have been safe."

If he survived, he was going to answer for all his crimes.

Mike clutched Summer's forearm. "I'm sorry." Another wheeze. "Dani suffered." He shook his head, his face wrenched in pain. "Wanted it to be quick. Told him…the man I hired to make it…look like an accident. Quick."

A sheriff's cruiser pulled up along with an ambulance.

Mike's hand slipped from Summer's arm and fell to the pavement. His head lolled to the side. Eyes open but seeing nothing. He was dead.

Logan took her hand and stood, pulling her up beside him. He moved her away from the body and held her. "Everything is going to be okay."

It was over. The men who'd tried to kill them were gone.

Summer was safe.

A battle still had to be fought with Einhorn Industries in court, but the worst of it was behind them.

Now they could focus on the future.

A future together.

Chapter Twenty-One

Three weeks later

"Congratulations," Logan said, seated across from Summer at an outside table overlooking the lake at The Wolverine Lodge. He raised a glass of wine the waiter had poured moments ago. "Here's to making Einhorn Industries pay."

Once they got the emails, legally, from NovaTech, and showed the opposing counsel their smoking gun, Einhorn had settled out of court. For billions that would be paid out to the plaintiffs, the other farmers and the people on the reservation who had joined the lawsuit.

Smiling at him, she was unable to tamp down the elation rising in her chest. With Logan in her corner, covering her back, she felt as though she could take on the world. "Thank you. But it was a group effort. I couldn't have done it without Chance and the other guys at IPS. *And you.*"

"With Einhorn shutting down and forced to clean up Snowberry Creek and the Bigfork River, people won't have to worry anymore."

Someone approached their table.

Hattie. The woman with auburn hair who had been at the AA meeting and worked at the restaurant. She set a breadbasket down in front of them. "I read in the *Beacon* what you two did. Catching Mike Johnson and exposing the dirty truth about Einhorn's fertilizer." She pursed her lips. "I tried to warn you two about Mike."

"Warn us?" Logan asked. "When?"

"The night you came in and picked up a to-go order. I was trying to tell you that there was something fishy about the way Mike had been acting. I've known that man for twenty years since he moved here. Not once had I ever seen him pose for a photograph. The man avoided cameras like a vampire avoids sunlight, worried they'll be incinerated into ash. Know what I'm saying?" She narrowed her eyes. "Then out of the blue, at Dani's five-year sober celebration, he whips out his phone and insists someone takes pictures of the two them. They both smiled like nothing was wrong, even though I'd seen them arguing days before. Mike could be a little scary at times. Next thing I knew, Dani turned up dead, I started thinking how convenient it was that Mike had a picture of the two them as bosom buddies. Grinning. As though he wanted proof there was no ill will between them. A distraction from the truth."

Mike was good at distractions. Alex Pope's family had changed their names from Popov, but not for nefarious reasons. He'd only mentioned it to keep them looking in the wrong direction. Then there was the *hacker*, who was really him, and the setup at the Kremlin, using the fictitious Kirill Luzhin, whose name was a code word to have them killed. Mike Johnson had been full of deadly secrets.

"Did you ever mention Mike's odd behavior to the sheriff?" Logan asked.

"No. I didn't have any proof," Hattie said. "Only a hunch. But I did tell Sheriff Tofteland that Dani was five years sober and didn't seem as if she was on the verge of a bender. He dismissed me like I had a screw loose in my head. So, I went to Mike and asked him if he did the same. You know, tell the sheriff the truth. Mike told me it wasn't his business. Didn't want to get involved. Warned others in AA to stay out of Einhorn's way. That didn't sound like a bosom buddy to me."

Summer touched Hattie's arm. "Thank you for telling us now. For caring about Dani."

"I'm just glad you got justice for her. For her and Jeff Arbuckle. And all those people poisoned by Einhorn." Hattie shook her head. "An evil thing they did, fooling us into believing the fertilizer was safe. But even braver of you to take them on. I spoke to the manager and your meal is going to be comped. Enjoy dinner on us tonight. Everyone thanks you."

Emotion clogged her throat at Hattie's words. All Summer could do was nod before the woman walked away.

Logan reached across the table and took her hand. "Are you okay?"

"When I came here and people realized I was the lawyer leading the war against Einhorn, they hated me. Now..." She shrugged.

"Now they see you for who you really are. Not someone here to ruin but to rescue. Dani would be proud of you."

Summer liked to think her best friend was looking down on everything and smiling.

"Instead of folks treating you with disdain," Logan said, "you'll get the admiration you deserve."

"It will be nice to be greeted with a smile rather than a scowl since I'm going to be here indefinitely." She was already looking for a house to buy.

With the big win, her firm would get its cut and then she wanted to move on. Someone had to monitor the health of people who still might eventually get sick from the chemicals in Snowberry Creek and Bigfork River. Someone had to put pressure on Einhorn to ensure that everything was properly cleaned up. Payouts would take time, and someone had to manage that as well.

She figured there was nobody better suited to be that someone than her.

"Speaking of indefinitely," Logan said, "I've been thinking about staying here, too."

"Staying?" The idea was a shock and a thrill rolled into one. So far, he was using up his vacation days, which they both knew would run out sooner or later. She'd chosen not to stress out about it and simply enjoy whatever time they had together. "But what about your job and your family. You're talking about a life-altering decision."

"Summer, you've already altered my life. In all the best ways. Sure, we could do this long-distance, but I don't want to, and I don't think you do either."

She didn't. Going to bed every night with Logan, making love to him, waking up in his arms, holding him, kissing him, talking about everything face-to-face. That was what she wanted most. To deepen their close connection.

"Why should we put ourselves through that torture, when there's no need," he said. "I can do law enforcement anywhere. Chance even told me if I ever wanted a job with IPS, then I'd have one. I've been ready for a major change for a while. My place isn't on the Shooting Star-Longhorn Ranch. My home is here, with you."

Her heart was doing somersaults. But she didn't want

him to regret such a big choice. "Are you sure? There's no rush to decide."

He smiled, the flash of his dimples tempting her to lean across the table and kiss him. "Now you sound like me after you told me you were ready to make love."

She remembered the conversation, outside, in the bright light of day, holding hands. Not in the heat of the moment. He'd been such a gentleman, wanting to ensure she didn't have any regrets.

But she had been certain.

Logan had lit candles, taken his time, drawing out her pleasure. The experience had been tender and passionate and better than any fantasy.

How could she ever regret making love to such an incredible man who made her feel desired and so special?

"Summer, we have something good. Great. This feels right. You and me. I've got a good chunk of money saved. I was thinking we could buy a house together. Make it ours."

Stunned, she gaped at him. "That's serious."

"I'm serious. About you. About a future together. I want to put down roots with you. Not in Cutthroat Creek. I was thinking Bitterroot Falls," he said, drawing a smile to her face. "I want to take the next step. But we don't have to if you want to take things slow. I can rent my own place. Everything has been fast and furious for us. I don't want you to be overwhelmed. That's why I've been waiting to bring it up."

The warm, intense look in his eyes made her chest fill with joy and nerves, all at once. "It has been fast, but I love you, Logan."

He reached over and stroked her cheek. "I love you, too."

Leaning across the table, he cupped the back of her head and kissed her. "Does that mean—"

She cut him off with another kiss. "It means I'm ready. For us to take the next step." They were already living together. Quite happily. Effortlessly even in tight quarters. "I don't need slow when it feels right and it does to me, too."

"I want everything with you, Summer Stratton."

Smiling, she felt the same. Loving and supporting each other, building a life together, she was certain their future would be nothing short of amazing.

* * * * *

COMING SOON!

We really hope you enjoyed reading this book.
If you're looking for more romance
be sure to head to the shops when
new books are available on

Thursday 22nd May

To see which titles are coming soon, please visit
millsandboon.co.uk/nextmonth

MILLS & BOON

OUT NOW!

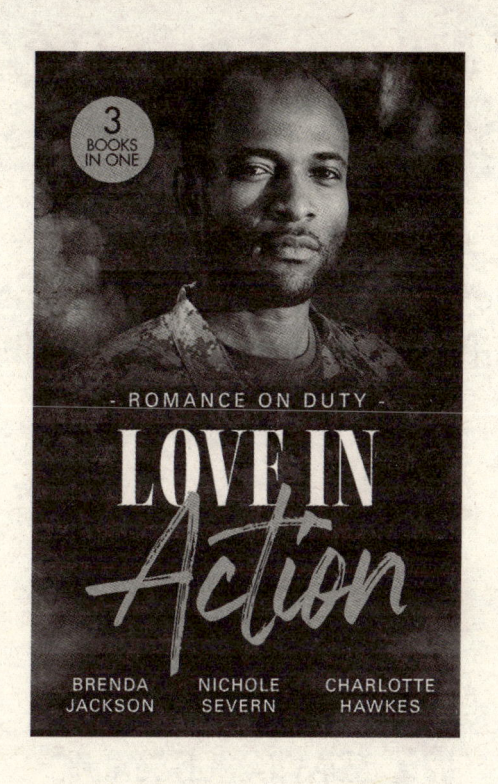

ROMANCE ON DUTY

LOVE IN *Action*

3 BOOKS IN ONE

BRENDA JACKSON · NICHOLE SEVERN · CHARLOTTE HAWKES

Available at
millsandboon.co.uk

MILLS & BOON

LET'S TALK
Romance

For exclusive extracts, competitions and special offers, find us online:

- **f** MillsandBoon
- **X** @MillsandBoon
- **◉** @MillsandBoonUK
- **♪** @MillsandBoonUK

Get in touch on 01413 063 232

For all the latest titles coming soon, visit
millsandboon.co.uk/nextmonth